WANTING MORE

"I've written down the phone number where I'll be staying," Brett murmured silkily. "If you have any problems, call me."

Jo snatched the paper out of his hand, her gaze skimming the list swiftly. "I think I can handle it," she assured him.

"Do you think so?" His tone sent a chill rippling down her spine. "Do you really think so?" Slowly, his eyes holding hers, he lowered his head.

Jo did not have to fight to keep from stepping back; quite the contrary, she had to fight a sudden need to step into him. Holding herself tautly still, she watched his descending face, positive he'd turn away at the final moment. She was wrong. When his lips brushed hers, her eyes widened in astonishment, then her long lashes fluttered and lowered. That whisper touch brushed her lips a second, then a third time. A ripple of pure delicious sensation shivered through her. Why, why was he teasing her with these almost kisses? And why didn't he touch her, embrace her, crush her to him?

Books by Joan Hohl

Published by Zebra Books

SIMPLY WONDERFUL

Joan Hohl

ZEBRA BOOKS
Kensington Publishing Corp.
http://www.kensingtonbooks.com

Dear Reader:

I have always believed that love stories—tales of the trials and tribulations of men and women finding each other and the true loves of their lives—were favorites, told perhaps by roving troubadours and, who knows, possibly even around fire pits in prehistoric caves, long before the advent of the printed word of romantic fiction.

I love reading those stories; I love writing them.

I wrote the two stories presented in this volume, *Breeze off the Ocean* and *While the Fire Rages,* early in my writing career in the 1980s, under the pseudonym Amii Lorin—a name I created by combining the names of my two beautiful daughters, Amy and Lori, who were, and are, and will always be the enduring lights of my life and my proudest productions.

These stories focus on two independent women and the strong men they fall in love with. You will note, I'm sure, that the stories were written in a certain style, as dictated by the marketplace at the time. I could have made changes—but why, when, in essence, these stories are vintage, timeless stories of love and romance?

I sincerely hope you will enjoy them as much as I enjoyed writing them.

Happy reading,
Joan Hohl

CONTENTS

BREEZE OFF THE OCEAN

ONE

Micki's foot eased off the gas pedal as she drew alongside the toll booth of the Delaware Memorial Bridge.
After tossing her coins into the exact-change catchall, she
pressed down on the pedal to begin the climb over the
high-girdered twin span. Even though she had actually
just begun her journey, as soon as she'd left the bridge
and had driven onto Route 40 she had the feeling of
coming home.

In her mind she checked off the names of the towns
she'd drive through. Woodstown, Elmer, Malaga, Buena,
Mays Landing.

"Mays Landing."

The softly murmured name brought a curl of excitement simply because from there it was a relatively short
hop on Atlantic Route 559 to Somers Point, then home.
At the thought of the Point a small smile tugged at her
soft, full lips. She had had fun at the Point, she and the
group of kids she'd palled around with all those years ago.

One particular memory wiggled into her mind and
her smile deepened. They had been playing a game of
tag, she and seven other kids, when one of the boys—
Benny Trent—had let out a loud yelp of pain and begun
hopping around on one foot. They had all laughed and
jeered at him until they saw his great toe become scar-
let with blood. As they crowded around him, Benny had
dropped onto the sand, twisting his foot to get a closer

look at the wound. A deep gash, inflicted by a jagged, half-buried clam shell, ran diagonally across the pad of his toe, bleeding profusely.

One of the other boys, a college student a few years older than the rest, had taken a Red Cross first aid course and, after examining the gash, declared that it would definitely need stitches.

Off to the hospital they went, en masse, laughing and joking to keep the pale Benny's spirits up.

"Boy, Benny," Cindy Langdon, Micki's best friend, had jeered. "How dumb can you get? Didn't your mother ever tell you you can get hurt if you go jumping up and down on a stupid clam shell?"

At the hospital Benny was led away to have the wound cleaned and stitched, and the rest of the children had camped, noisily, in the waiting room, much to the obvious exasperation of the hospital personnel.

When Benny returned, his toe almost twice its size from bandaging, the taunts and jokes began again.

Micki shook her head ruefully at how callous they'd all been, then brought her attention sharply alert as she drove through Woodstown's early afternoon traffic. After she left the town behind, the traffic was sparse and Micki allowed memory to have its way again.

She and the other kids hadn't been altogether heart-less, she thought with amusement. For two weeks they had slavishly waited on Benny hand and foot and that bonehead, as Cindy called him, loved every minute of it.

That memory triggered off others and Micki laughed aloud on realizing Benny had usually been the target of their banter. In the case of Cindy, well, her gibes had been downright insulting. If, at that time, anyone would have told them that eventually Cindy would be married to Benny, they would all, Cindy included, have become hysterical. But, two years ago, that was exactly what had happened.

Micki had not been able to attend the wedding, as she'd been on the West Coast on a buying trip, but she had sent a lavish wedding gift, along with her surprised congratulations.

It would be good to see Cindy and Benny again, Micki mused, as she headed the little silver car straight as its namesake—Arrow—toward the coast. How many, Micki wondered, besides Cindy and Benny, had made their home there? Except for Cindy, Micki had completely lost touch with the rest of her gang.

There had been eight of them that traveled around together regularly. At intervals their number swelled, for beach parties and dances and the like, but the eight had remained constant from grade through high school. They were all of the same age, with one exception, Tony Menella, who had been two years their senior. It had been Tony who had advised Benny to have his toe stitched. Where was Tony now? Micki sighed. She simply didn't know. A small smile curved her lips at the thought that she'd probably find out where they all were before too long. Cindy would know not only where they were but what they were doing, as Cindy had always kept tabs on all of them.

Memories, one after the other, kept Micki company as she made her way steadily toward the coast. Growing-up memories, many happy, a few sad, invaded her mind. Only one did she push away, refuse to recognize. That one particular memory she had not looked at for a long time; she had no intention of doing so now.

The miles sped by, even more quickly after she'd turned onto Atlantic Route 559, and as she drove through Somers Point she switched off the car's air-conditioner and opened the window beside her. Excitement mounting, Micki passed the sign reading WELCOME TO OCEAN CITY and at that instant a breeze off the ocean told her she was home.

Just getting across the Ninth Street Bridge was a project. In mid-July the influx of tourists added to the going-home-from-work crowd to make traffic a late afternoon nightmare. Undaunted, Micki inched along serenely. She loved the sound, the smells, everything about her hometown, and the traffic, compared to the suppertime crush around Wilmington, didn't bother her a bit.

Drinking in the sights avidly, Micki observed the number of people, mostly families, on the sidewalks, obviously coming from the beach, lugging beach chairs, umbrellas, and other beach paraphernalia, and shepherding youngsters. Micki knew that most were headed to apartments or motels, some to prepare dinner, others to bathe and dress before going out again to dine at one of the city's many fine restaurants or fast-food shops.

There were changes, of course, as there always were in a resort city, and Micki noted them automatically. At one place several well-remembered buildings had disappeared and at another a very classy new restaurant now presided. The changes did not fill her with dismay. On the contrary, she had grown up with changes and through it all the city basically remained the same. It was still a clean city. A city full of churches. A family-oriented resort city that was lovely to vacation in and equally lovely to grow up in. To Micki it would always be the same. Except for one brief visit, she had been away for six years, and yet it was the same. Home.

She turned off Ninth onto Wesley and after several blocks the traffic thinned out considerably. Two more turns and there was hardly any traffic at all. And then there was the house she was brought to four days after her birth.

How achingly familiar it was, with the lacy-leafed mimosa in the middle of the front lawn and the profuse banks of fuchsia and white azalea bushes on either side of the front steps. Although she could see that the awnings were new, they were of exactly the same pattern as those that had always shaded the windows and large front porch.

With an emotional lump closing her throat, Micki turned the car onto the short driveway that ran along the side of the house and parked the car in front of the one-car garage at the end of the drive a short distance behind the house.

The soft whooshing sound of the kitchen screen door being pushed open came as she pulled the key from the ignition.

"Micki!" Micki's father, Bruce Durrant, called as he strode along the flagstone path that led from the house to the garage. "Welcome home."

"Oh, Dad!" Micki flung the car door open and slid out into her father's arms. "It's so good to see you."

"Let me get a look at you." Grasping her arms, he leaned back, his eyes roving lovingly over her face. "You look more like your mother every time I see you," he murmured. "You've grown into a beautiful young woman, Micki."

"You wouldn't be just a tiny bit prejudiced, would you?" Micki laughed tremulously, blinking against the sudden hot sting in her eyes.

"Not in the least," Bruce denied firmly. "Your mother was an exceptionally lovely woman and you do look like her, maybe you're even more lovely."

Micki's eyes had been busy also and she noted the gray that now sprinkled her father's dark hair, the lines that radiated from his eyes, and the grooves from his nose to the corners of his mouth. Rather than distracting from his good looks, the signs of full maturity added character to his face and the silver among the dark strands of his hair lent a touch of distinction. Pleased with her perusal of him, Micki felt her smile widen.

"You look pretty good yourself, Mr. Durrant." Somehow the smile stayed in place. "How are you feeling?"

The hands grasping her shoulders gave her a little shake. "What a little worrywart you are." He chided softly. "I'm fine. Dr. Bassi assures me the ulcer is completely healed. I swear I haven't had a twinge of pain in months."

Micki's startlingly bright blue eyes gazed deeply into her father's dark brown ones. A sigh of relief escaped her lips at the happiness and contentment she found there. Happily Micki banished the memory of the panic and fear she'd experienced the night Regina had called her. God! What a horrible night that had been. Regina's voice, tight with fear, waking her with the news of her father's collapse with a perforated ulcer. Fighting the terror of the unknown, Micki had driven through the silent pre-dawn hours with a strangely icy composure. Thankfully, for Regina had been on the verge of falling apart, Micki's composure had lasted through the following nerve-racking two days, but after Dr. Bassi had told them that her father was out of danger, Micki had gone to her old room and relieved her anxiety by sobbing into her pillow.

Now, satisfied with the obvious signs of his glowing good looks and well-being, Micki gave him another quick hug. With her absorption in the most important man in her life, Micki didn't hear the repeated whoosh of the kitchen screen door.

"Are you two going to stand here in the driveway the whole two weeks of Micki's vacation?" Micki's stepmother, Regina, teased.

Micki's entire body tensed at the sound of Regina's velvety, throaty voice, then she made herself relax. What was past was past, she admonished herself sharply, and best forgotten. With unstudied grace, she swung her small slim frame out of her father's embrace, one hand reaching out to take the pale one Regina had extended.

"Hello, Regina." Micki was slightly amazed at the even

tenor of her voice. "No need to ask how you are; you look great, as ever."

It was true. At thirty-nine Regina was as exotically beautiful as she had been when she had married Bruce Durrant at twenty-five, the exact same age that Micki was now. Her glossy black hair, worn smoothed back off her face in an intricately curved twist, was completely free of silver. Her pale-complexioned, unbelievably beautiful face was completely free of any sign of encroaching age. And her tall frame was still willowy, completely free of any unsightly bulges. And that voice! Oh, the hours a very young, twelve-year-old Micki had spent trying, unsuccessfully, to emulate that voice. Even today, as then, Micki had no idea of how pleasing to the ear her own soft, somewhat husky, voice was.

"You do not look the same," Regina returned easily. Then, to Micki's surprise, she echoed her husband's words of a few minutes ago. "You grow more like your mother every time I see you, and everyone knows how lovely she was."

Micki managed to hide her startled reaction to Regina's compliment in the general confusion of collecting her suitcases and getting them into the house.

Regina trailed behind Micki and her father as they lugged the cases to her bedroom and lingered after Bruce left the room with a promise of a pre-dinner drink for Micki as soon as she'd settled in.

"Micki?"

Micki's hand stilled in the act of unlocking her largest suitcase at the hesitant, uncertain note in her stepmother's voice. Features composed, Micki turned to gaze at Regina.

"Yes?"

"Do you suppose we could possibly be friends now?"

Regina's tone had smoothed out, but an anxious expression still clouded her beautiful black eyes.

"Do you?"

As soon as they were out of her mouth Micki wished the words unspoken. Why, she chided herself, hadn't she simply said yes and let the whole sorry business remain buried?

"I would like to try," Regina answered quietly. "I have always liked you." At Micki's slightly raised eyebrows, Regina stated firmly, "Yes, I have. And there is no reason now why we shouldn't be friends. I think you'll find I'm not quite the same person since your father's near brush with death. It's sad, but I nearly had to lose him to realize—well—just exactly how foolishly I was behaving."

"Regina, you do not have to—" Micki began, but Regina seemed determined to have her say.

"You were very patient with and kind to me while your father was so very ill, even though you were nearly out of your mind with worry yourself. I have not forgotten that and I never will." Regina paused, as if uncertain how to continue, and then, with a light shrug of her elegant shoulders, she plunged on forcefully. "I love your father very much, I always have. Yes, really," she vowed as Micki's brows rose again. "The only explanation, or excuse, I have for my previous behavior is his neglect of me—due solely to business pressures, I admit—after our marriage and my selfish reaction to that neglect."

"Regina, please—"

"No, Micki, let me finish," Regina insisted. "When we married, your father was a very handsome and charming man, as indeed he still is, and I wanted to be the only important thing in his life, even to the exclusion of an eleven-year-old child."

"I remember," Micki inserted, then felt petty at Regina's wince. And yet, she defended herself silently, she *did* remember, painfully.

"Yes, of course you remember," Regina went on doggedly. "That's why I must say all this, clear the air between us." Again she paused, wet her lips nervously. "From the time I was fourteen I was aware of my attraction to the opposite sex and I used that attraction to punish your father. It was foolish and immature, I know, but I realize now that at the time I *was* foolish and immature. I—I had to almost lose Bruce before I woke up to my own stupidity." She closed her eyes briefly and when she opened them again her lashes glistened with teardrops.

For several long moments the two women stared at each other. Micki's eyes, carefully veiled, revealed nothing of what she was feeling. Regina's eyes held mute appeal. Slowly, as if gathering strength, Regina drew a deep breath.

"And now, about that incident six years ago," Regina said softly.

No! No! a voice screamed inside Micki's head. What came out of her parched lips was a strangled whisper.

"No, Regina. I do not want to talk about that."

Regina's eyes flickered with alarm and her tone dropped to a murmur of self-reproachment.

"Oh, God, it still hurts you." One pale hand was extended, as if in supplication. "Oh, my dear, I had no idea the pain went so deep. How can you ever forgive me?"

Micki was saved from answering by the sound of her father's strong, impatient call from the bottom of the stairway.

"What in the world are you two women doing up there?" His tone took on a mock petulant edge. "I'm getting very lonely down here all by myself."

Regina's head snapped around to the bedroom's open doorway, then swung back to Micki.

"I'm sorry," she whispered. "Please believe that. I—I—" She shook her head and cleared her throat. "We better go down. Leave the unpacking, I'll help you with it later."

Forcing her stiff facial muscles into relaxation, Micki left the room, and Regina's line of conversation, gratefully, silently determined that that particular subject would not be brought up again during her visit.

Surprisingly, or maybe not too surprisingly, with the air between the two women somewhat cleared, the evening passed pleasantly.

During dinner Micki brought her father and Regina up to date on her activities, saving the most important detail for last. They had carried their coffee into the living room and as Micki sipped at her creamy brew with a contented sigh, the only indication she gave as to the import of her news was an added sparkle in her usually bright blue eyes.

"Oh, by the way," Micki drawled diffidently. "Just before I left the shop for this vacation I was informed I was being promoted to head buyer."

A short silence followed her casually tossed statement, a silence that revealed to Micki exactly how aware her father and Regina were of the importance of her announcement.

After leaving the small college, where she had been studying business merchandising, so precipitously only six weeks into her second year, Micki had considered herself fortunate in acquiring the job of salesclerk in a very exclusive ladies' boutique, which was located in the lobby of one of the largest, most prestigious hotels in Wilmington. It was not the job of salesclerk that excited Micki, but the knowledge that the boutique was just one of a large chain of similar shops that ranged along the entire East Coast. When she had been interviewed for the job by the shop's manager, a tall, slim woman in her mid-forties, Micki had been informed that due to the size of the independently owned chain, the chance for advancement was excellent for anyone who did not object to relocating. Micki had been quick to assure the somewhat aristocratic woman that she had no objections at all to relocating, as Wilmington was not her hometown.

It had taken time and much hard work on Micki's part, but eventually the promotions did come and for the last eighteen months she had been assistant buyer for the Wilmington shop. And now—could it have been only yesterday?—this latest promotion.

"Micki, that's wonderful!" her father exclaimed, jumping out of his chair to come across the room and bestow a huge hug on her. "Congratulations."

"And you haven't heard the best part yet," Micki gasped laughingly when he'd released his crushing hold. "The position is for the Atlantic City store."

"Atlantic City?" Bruce repeated softly, then he nearly shouted. "Honey, that means you can move home."

Still laughing, Micki nodded her head. Totally absorbed in each other, both Micki and her father had completely forgotten Regina. In the old days Regina would have made her presence known forcefully, now the voice that penetrated their euphoria was soft, hesitant.

"May I add my congratulations to your father's, Micki?"

"Oh, Regina, I'm sorry," Micki murmured contritely. "Of course you may."

"Yes, darling," Bruce inserted, one arm encircling his wife's waist to draw her close. "Of course you may. We're a family." He paused an instant before adding, "Aren't we?"

A quick glance of understanding and truce passed between the two women.

"Yes, Dad," Micki agreed firmly. "We are a family."

Regina's black eyes spoke eloquently of her relief and thanks and Micki was amazed at the feeling of peace that washed over her. For the most part the fourteen years of her father's second marriage had been turbulent and Micki greeted the cessation of hostilities with a silent prayer of thanks. Still, she didn't want to strain the ties of this newfound accord, so she tacked on with equal firmness, "But I'll be looking for my own apartment."

"In Atlantic City?"

Bruce and Regina spoke in astonished unison and Micki fully understood the reason for their astonishment. It was a well-known fact that living accommodations in Atlantic City were almost as hard to find as brontosaurus teeth since the influx of the big hotels with their gambling casinos. The added fact that the shop Micki would be working in was located in one of those hotels lent a sprinkling of spice to her excitement. Now she hastened to correct their impression.

"No, not in Atlantic City, here in Ocean City. Atlantic City's such a short run up the coast I doubt it will take me any longer to get to work from here than it did in the early morning crush in Wilmington."

"The way I understand it," Bruce said quietly, "there are already quite a few people that are employed by the hotels making their home here." He hesitated, his eyes mirroring his sadness. "But why do you want to look for an apartment? Why can't you stay here at home?"

"Oh, Dad." Micki smiled weakly. "I've been on my own for almost six years now. I'm used to having my own place. I've got an apartment full of furniture and things I've acquired over those six years." Her smile deepened, became impish. "But I have made arrangements to have my stuff packed and sent here in the interim—if you don't mind?"

"Mind?" Bruce echoed. "Of course we don't mind."

"Not at all." Regina seconded her husband's words.

"Oh, sure." Micki's laughter rippled through the comfortable room. "But wait until you have all my stuff dumped onto your doorstep. You may wish you'd given a very firm no."

Regina made fresh coffee and the three of them settled around the kitchen table to make plans and discuss the pros and cons of various areas in which Micki might be interested in apartment hunting. During the course of the discussion the section of the city in which Cindy and Benny lived came up and at the mention of the young couple's name the topic of the conversation veered to them.

"I haven't seen either of them since they made final settlement on the house," Bruce told Micki. "But Cindy did call me at the office after they'd moved in, to again thank me for finding the property for them and inform me that they were absolutely thrilled with it." He grinned broadly. "Those last words are an exact quote from Cindy."

"Sounds so much like her I can almost hear her voice," Micki grinned back. Her father owned a flourishing real estate business and it pleased her to know Cindy had gone to him when she was ready to buy a home. "It will be wonderful to see Cindy and Benny again."

"Did they know you were coming home?" Regina asked. "And that you'll be staying?"

Micki was shaking her head before Regina had finished speaking. "No, I wanted to surprise them," Micki answered. Then her eyes shifted to rest lovingly on her father. "Besides which, I wanted my first evening at home to be free of interruptions."

The answering look of love in her father's eyes and the understanding smile on Regina's lips deepened the feeling of well-being inside Micki. Stifling a yawn behind her hand, she pushed her chair away from the table and stood up.

"I'm going to have a shower then go to bed." Another yawn was unsuccessfully hidden. When Regina moved to get up, Micki shook her head at her. "You don't have to come up, Regina. I can finish my unpacking in the morning." After kissing her father lightly on the cheek, she wished them both a good night and swung out of the room.

Alone in her bedroom Micki stood still just inside the door and let her eyes roam slowly over familiar things. Everything was the same as she'd left it. Even the paint on the walls, though fresh, was the same bright daffodil yellow as it had always been. When her eyes touched the double, leather-bound picture frame sitting on the nightstand by the bed, they stopped. Her gaze unwavering, Micki walked across the room and picked up the frame.

The picture on one side was an enlargement of a snapshot that had been taken on the front lawn. Three figures stood under a mimosa tree. Micki's mother was turned slightly from the camera as she smiled up at her husband, and between them Micki, at age six, her favorite doll clutched in her arms, grinned impishly at the camera. The picture had been snapped by a close friend of her mother's the summer before her mother's death in a fiery highway accident.

Micki blinked over hot tears before shifting her gaze to the other side of the frame. It had been years since she'd really looked at the studio portrait of her mother and now, remembering her father's words when she arrived, she studied the color shot carefully before lifting her eyes to her own reflection in the dressing-table mirror opposite the bed. Yes, the well-defined features were very similar: a slim, straight nose; high, though not prominent, cheekbones; softly rounded chin, although Micki's did have a more determined cast. If the color in the photo was true, they shared the same bright blue eyes and fair skin tone. But her mother's hair, worn long and smooth at the time, was a gleaming auburn with deep red highlights, whereas Micki's, which she wore short in an attempt to control her loose, unruly curls, was a dark chestnut. Yes, there were similarities, but her mother had been beautiful, and in Micki's own opinion, she was not.

With a brief, what-does-it-matter shrug, Micki replaced the frame, then stood eyeing her suitcases dispassionately. Sighing softly, she flicked the clasps of the largest case and opened the valise. Do it now, she told herself firmly, or everything will be crushed beyond wearing.

Micki kicked off her sandals and moved silently over the plush carpeting as she placed her clothes in the closet and drawers. When the bags were empty, Micki placed them against the wall beside the bedroom door for storage in the large hall closet in the morning, then turned back to the room, a tiny smile of satisfaction tugging at her lips. Everything about the room satisfied her.

Her father had given her carte blanche in decorating it when she was sixteen, and now, nine years later, everything about the room still pleased her. Micki's eyes sparkled as they skimmed the white wicker headboard, chair, low table, and clothes hamper. A stroke of genius that, she thought smugly. Who would have thought, nine years ago, that wicker would become so popular, not to mention expensive.

Humming softly she slipped out of her white denim slacks and pulled her blue-and-white striped shirt over her head. Her lacy bra and filmy bikini briefs followed her slacks and shirt into the hamper. She put on a terry robe, pulled the belt tight, scooped up a short, sheer nightie, and made for the bathroom for a quick shower.

Micki was patting her five-foot-two frame dry when she heard her father and Regina come up the stairs and go into their room. Gritting her teeth, she mentally clamped a lid on the flash of remembered pain and resentment the sound of their bedroom door closing sent through her. Always that sound, by the very intimate connotations it conjured, had had the power to hurt her, make her feel cut off from her father, bereft. Now she pushed those feelings away. You're a full-grown woman, she told herself sternly, with a full, rich life of your own. Go to bed, go to sleep, what's done is done and can't be changed. Forget it.

Minutes after she'd returned to her room, there was a soft tap on her door. Thinking it was her father coming to wish her a second good night, Micki called, "Come in," without hesitation, then wished she hadn't when she saw it was Regina. Fearing a repeat of their earlier conversation, Micki tried to forestall the older woman.

"Whatever it is, Regina"—Micki faked a huge yawn—"could it wait until morning? I can hardly keep my eyes open."

Regina bit her bottom lip nervously, hesitated, then drew a deep, courage-gathering breath.

"Micki, I don't want to upset you, please believe that, but"—she drew another, shorter breath before rushing on—"we must talk about Wolf."

"No!"

The one word escaped through Micki's lips like a muffled explosion and she flinched as if the other woman had actually struck her.

"But you don't understand." Regina's tone held a pleading note. "We must discuss this, he's—"

"Regina." Micki's voice was low, intense with warning. "This is still my room. I'm asking you to please leave it so I can go to bed."

"But Wolf—"

"Regina." Micki's teeth were clenched in an effort to control her voice. "You asked me earlier if we can be friends. Well, I'm willing to try, but there is one condition. I cannot, *will* not, discuss that person. Not now, not ever."

"Oh, Micki," Regina sighed. "You don't understand."

"And I don't want to," Micki snapped. "Do you want me to leave this house in the morning? Find a motel room until I can get an apartment?"

"No!" Regina exclaimed in alarm. "Of course not. Your father would—"

"Well, then." Micki didn't wait to hear what her father would do. "The subject will remain closed and forgotten.

As long as Dad looks as well and happy as he does now, I'm content to meet you halfway toward friendship. I fully expect you to do the same. Do you get my meaning?"

Regina's eyes closed briefly in defeat and she nodded. Before staring directly into Micki's eyes, she murmured, "But please don't say I didn't try."

Micki wondered over those parting words several minutes after Regina left the room. What in the world could she have meant? With a shrug of her shoulders she turned toward the bed, then stopped and became very still, the echo of that name searing through her mind.

Wolf.

Wolf—a predatory animal's name that suited perfectly the predatory human male. A mental picture formed and, her face twisted with pain, Micki pushed it from her mind.

Damn, damn, damn Regina, for saying that name out loud.

Memories crowded in threatening to overwhelm her. Shaking herself like a wet dog, Micki moved jerkily to the bed. No, she would not allow the memories to gather, collect in her mind. Forcing herself to stand very still beside the bed, she breathed deeply. In. Out. In. Out.

"I must call Cindy."

In. Out. In. Out.

"I must go apartment hunting."

In. Out. In. Out.

"I must run up to Atlantic City and check out the shop, introduce myself."

In. Out. In. Out.

"I've controlled these emotions before, I will tonight."

Doing the breathing exercise, speaking softly, Micki felt the pain recede, the trembling leave her body. After what seemed a very long time she slipped between the bedsheets, closed her eyes, and cried as if her heart were broken.

TWO

The next morning Micki woke early, refreshed and ready to face a new day. Surprisingly, after her violent crying bout, she had slept deeply. The realization that she had once again won the battle against her memories added to the feeling of well-being her uninterrupted rest had instilled.

Glancing at the bedside clock, she sat up quickly and slipped off the bed; if she hurried she could have breakfast with her father. She thrust her arms into her robe and left her room at a near run, dashed into the bathroom to splash cold water on her face and brush her teeth, then hurried back along the hall and down the stairs.

"Morning." Micki breezed into the kitchen and planted a kiss on her father's smooth, freshly shaven cheek before seating herself at the old-fashioned wooden table.

"Morning, princess."

Micki's perfect white teeth flashed in a grin of delight at her father's use of the pet name. It had been years since he'd called her that, and she loved the sound of it.

"I thought you'd sleep in this morning." Bruce grinned back before adding, "What got you awake so early? Regina and I didn't wake you, did we?"

"No." Micki shook her head emphatically. "I must have been slept out." She smiled her thanks as Regina placed a glass of juice in front of her. "I'm used to getting up early, you know."

"All the more reason to sleep in when you get the chance," Bruce replied placidly. "Regina's scrambling eggs—would you like some?"

"No, thank you." Micki's mild grimace drew a chuckle from her dad.

"Kids!" The soft exclamation took the sting from his word. "Who can figure them out? You always loved eggs for breakfast until that last year you were in college."

Micki's stomach seemed to turn over and for a moment she felt trapped while she raked her mind for a reply. Thankfully neither her father nor Regina noticed the way her face had paled, as their attention was occupied by Regina serving the eggs.

"I guess I just got tired of them," Micki finally managed weakly, eyeing the creamy yellow mound on the plates.

"Just like that." Bruce snapped his fingers. "It doesn't make sense."

"Stop teasing, Bruce." Unknowingly, Regina saved Micki from the effort of finding a more plausible excuse. "As youngsters mature, their tastes change." As she sat down at the table, Regina offered Micki a tentative smile. "Don't mind your father, Micki. He's in a very good but devilish mood this morning, due, I'm sure, to your being home again."

The grin her father flashed at her confirmed Regina's words. A slow, silent sigh fluttered through Micki's lips as she returned Regina's smile.

"I can see"—Micki deliberately lowered her voice conspiratorially—"you and I are going to have to stick together to keep this feisty man in line."

Bruce's head snapped up from his plate, his glance sharp between the two women. The spark of hope that had entered his eyes seemed to grow into wonderment as he studied first his daughter's then his wife's friendly expressions.

Micki fully understood the almost breathless stillness

that seemed to grip him. The two women had been opponents, at first silent and then very vocal, since the day Bruce married Regina. He had coaxed, cajoled, and even ordered Micki to make more of an effort at getting along with her stepmother. The only thing he'd achieved was to fill Micki with a deeper sense of resentment. She had made an attempt at friendship with Regina. At the very vulnerable age of eleven she had welcomed the idea of a mother. Regina, a younger, beautiful Regina, had quickly disabused her of that idea. Without actually saying the words, Regina had left little doubt in Micki's young mind of exactly where she stood. If Micki wanted her father's attention, she would have to fight for it. Micki had fought silently but bitterly, and until last night, she had thought it was a battle she could never win.

Now the gentle smile Micki gave her father erased the doubt lingering around the edges of his expression. She saw him swallow with difficulty and the action brought a corresponding lump to her throat. Shifting her eyes, she caught the quick flutter of Regina's lashes and the lump grew in size.

"Princess," Bruce murmured solemnly, "I wonder if you realize how happy I am to have you home." The slight emphasis he placed on the word *home* told the full story.

"And you can have no idea how happy it makes me to be home." Micki let her own emphasis reflect his before she laughed a little shakily. "And if you don't eat your breakfast, you are going to be late for work."

"Oh, but you see"—Bruce followed her lead in lightening the mood—"that's the fun part of being the boss. I can breeze in and out of the office whenever I please." He paused, a mock frown creasing his forehead. "The only thing is, as I have a very important client coming this morning, I damned well better please to get moving."

After her father had left for the office and Regina had

refused her offer to help with the dishes, Micki went to the phone in the living room to call Cindy.

"Hello." Cindy's bubbly voice sang across the wire after the fourth ring.

"Hi, Cindy, how are you?"

"Micki!" The exclamation was like a small explosion. "Where are you? Are you here in Ocean City? How are you? When did you get home? Are you home?" The questions followed each other in such rapid succession Micki laughingly shouted to get a word in.

"Cindy, if you will take time to breathe, I'll explain the wheres and whys." The small silence that followed these words allowed Micki to continue briefly. "I am home, yes, and—"

"Then don't bother to go any further," Cindy broke in. "Jump in your car and come to the house, I'm dying to see you." She hesitated, then asked apologetically, "Or did you have other plans for this morning?"

"As a matter of fact," Micki laughed, "my only plans for today were to come and see you, if you had no other plans. Does that make any sense at all?"

"Perfect sense," Cindy declared happily. "So why are you still on the phone? Get truckin'." She hung up before Micki could even tell her she would.

Still smiling, Micki went to the kitchen to tell Regina where she was going, adding she had no idea when she'd be back.

"Oh, that will work out perfectly." Regina's smile was still somewhat tentative. "I have a lunch date with Betty Grant and we'd planned to do some shopping after lunch. How is Cindy feeling now?"

The question startled Micki, wiped the smile off her face.

"She sounded fine," she answered slowly, then asked anxiously, "Why? Has she been ill?"

"No, no," Regina soothed. "Not ill, but she did have a

few bad moments at the beginning of her pregnancy, you know."

Everything inside Micki seemed to freeze with an emotion she couldn't begin to put a name to. Cindy pregnant? Why hadn't she told her?

Regina glanced up from the dish she was drying; her face grew puzzled at Micki's stillness. "Is something wrong?" she asked with concern.

"No." Micki shook her head and forced the smile back to her stiff lips. "I—I didn't know Cindy was pregnant."

"Didn't know?" For a second Regina's eyes were totally blank, then they widened with dismay. "Oh, damn," she groaned. "Cindy must have wanted to surprise you and now I've ruined it for her."

"You couldn't know, and I'll play dumb when she tells me." Micki wet her parched lips as she turned toward the doorway. "Cindy will have her surprise." Moving swiftly through the doorway, she added, "I'll see you when I see you."

Inside her room Micki leaned back against the door and closed her eyes, a soft moan catching at her throat. Hugging her midriff tightly as if to contain the pain inside, she dug her teeth into her lower lip. For a few moments the remembered torment was so real she wanted to cry out against it. Oh, God, she thought sickly, would the hurt never go away? Breathing deeply, exactly as she had the night before, she forced herself to a measure of calmness. She had to get dressed, go see Cindy, and act surprised and happy about her pregnancy. She was happy for Cindy.

By the time Micki backed her car out of the driveway, she had her emotions under control. Driving slowly through the mid-morning traffic, she glanced around quickly. The tourist season was in full swing. People of all ages, shapes, and sizes were on their way to the beach. Cyclists pedaled their way toward their destination. The

streets were crowded with cars; people coming into the
city, people going out of the city, and some just driving
around pursuing their business, and over all, the gulls
soared and dipped and sang their raucous songs. Micki
loved it. She always had and as she drove through it she
felt the stiffness ease out of her body.

It was not a very long drive, as the house Cindy and
Benny had bought was located just south of where the
long boardwalk ended. From Cindy's letters Micki knew
it was a double unit building fronting the beach and
ocean. The reason the young couple decided to buy a
double unit was the obvious one: the increasing cost of
real estate. The summer rental on the apartment made
up half of the yearly mortgage payments. The cost of the
building had been exorbitant but, Cindy had written, for
a place of their own, it had been worth it.

Cindy was waiting at the door, and as soon as Micki
drove onto the crushed-stone driveway, she pushed the
car door open and ran to meet her.

After incoherent greetings and fierce hugs were exchanged, the two women stood back to examine each
other, identical smiles of pleasure on their faces. Extending a slim hand, Micki placed it gently on the bulge
that was Cindy's belly.

"I'm so happy for you," she said softly. "But, why didn't
you tell me?"

"I wanted to surprise you." Cindy laughed. "If you remember, you wrote that you were thinking of spending
your vacation at home this year and, well, I just wanted
to see your face when you saw me."

"You nit." Micki shook her head in mock reproach.
"Was my expression worth keeping the secret all this
time?"

"Well worth it," Cindy affirmed, taking her arm and
leading her to the house. "You looked absolutely stunned."

A mental picture of how she'd reacted to the news a

short time ago allowed Micki to answer with complete honesty. "I assure you I was. When is the big event slated to happen?"

"Around Christmastime," Cindy replied happily. "Oh, Micki, don't you think that's exciting? I mean, a baby for Christmas."

"Very exciting," Micki murmured. She stepped over the threshold directly into a large, airy living room, resplendent with plants of all kinds, a half dozen of which hung from the ceiling.

The apartment was larger than Micki would have expected. In addition to the living room there was a tiny dining room, a roomy kitchen, one and a half baths, and three bedrooms, one of which was in the process of redecoration.

"The baby's room," Cindy explained needlessly.

"I love it," Micki enthused honestly. "All of it. And the fact that it's practically right on the beach makes it worth whatever you paid for it."

"That's what we thought," Cindy nodded. "Of course we don't know what it will be like in the winter, but we're delighted with it just the same."

They wandered back into the kitchen and from there onto the wide, awning-covered deck.

"I thought since it's so hot already this morning, we'd have lunch out here."

"Wonderful." Micki stared entranced at the view of the beach and sun-sparkled ocean the deck afforded. "Oh, Cindy," she breathed softly, "this place was worth almost any amount of money, just for the view."

"I know—it's super." Cindy laughed. "Benny and I have breakfast out here every nice morning."

"How is Benny?" Micki asked belatedly. "And how does he feel about becoming a father?"

"He's fine." Cindy smiled softly. "And he's so excited about the baby he can hardly wait." The smile grew into a grin. "We were shopping last week and would you believe I had to drag him out of the sports department? He wanted to buy the baby a football, for heaven's sake."

"Knowing Benny, I can believe it." Micki grinned back. "Do you think most men get a little soft in the head about their first child?"

Micki didn't even hear Cindy's answer, for suddenly she felt like a large hand was squeezing all the air from her chest. Dear God, why did the most innocent remarks still have the power to hurt her like this?

Cindy laughed and pulling herself together, Micki managed to laugh with her. The sudden explosion of air eased the constriction of her lungs, and as the conversation switched to the more immediate subject of lunch, Micki felt her emotional gear shift back into normal.

By the time they had finished their melon and gone on to small salads and cold chicken sandwiches Micki was glad she'd decided on a spaghetti-strapped sundress that morning. The July sun was brassy in a cloud-free blue sky. Even with the sea breeze wafting under the awning, by one o'clock the heat drove them indoors.

By the time Cindy had filled Micki in on the comings and goings of their friends and Micki had imparted her own news about her job and her plans to make her home permanently in Ocean City, most of the afternoon was gone.

After agreeing to have dinner with Cindy and Benny one evening, Micki left, cautioning Cindy to get plenty of rest to combat the enervating effects of the heat.

Driving through the shimmery heat waves that rose from the street, Micki reflected on what Cindy had told her about their mutual friends. They had really scattered—one as far away as Alaska. But Tony Menella was back. After finishing college, he had gone to work for a large advertising firm in Trenton, but a little over a year ago he'd packed it in and come home. He was working in Atlantic City, but he was living in Ocean City, much the same as Micki herself would now be doing.

Into her own thoughts, she stopped at an intersection when a car cut in front of her and, glancing up, let her gaze skim over the area. Idly she studied a new motel on the opposite corner. Very classy, she was thinking when she was startled alert by the opening of her passenger side door.

"What in the—!" Micki began, head swinging around. The words shriveled on her lips as she saw a long, lean frame settle into the seat next to her and felt the impact of the odd, silver-gray eyes of Wolf Renninger.

"It's safe to drive on now."

The soft, taunting words broke through the shock gripping her mind and by reflex Micki started the car.

Her mental process was set into motion at the same time. Anger searing her mind, she glanced around sharply for a parking space. She wasn't hauling his carcass anywhere.

"Pull into this lot here." The taunting edge to his tone was more pronounced, as if he'd read her thoughts and was amused by them.

Gritting her teeth, Micki glanced in the direction he'd indicated and saw it was the parking lot belonging to the motel she'd been looking at.

"But I can't park on that lot it's—"

"It's all right," Wolf interrupted, "I work there."

Angrily Micki spun the wheel and drove the car onto the lot, following his terse directions to a section marked EMPLOYEES PARKING—PRIVATE. The moment the car was stationary Micki turned to face him, blue eyes shooting bright sparks of anger.

"Now just what do you think you're doing?"

"Hello, Micki." Wolf's soft voice laughed at her. "It's been a long time."

"Not nearly long enough," Micki snapped acidly. "Why did you get into the car? What do you want?"

The smile that curved his sometimes hard, always sensuous lips sent a shiver racing along Micki's spine and she gripped the steering wheel to keep her hands from trembling.

"I want to talk to you," Wolf replied smoothly. "And look at you."

"You've had your look," she said sharply. It was true. From the minute he'd entered the car his eyes had clung to her face like a beauty mask and it was making her very edgy. "So talk."

"Not here, it's too hot and I'd hate to see you melt all over the upholstery." That unnerving smile touched his mouth briefly. "Come with me, I have an apartment in the complex." The taunting laugh came back into his tone. "Or are you afraid?"

"Afraid of you?" Micki knew it was foolish to accept his challenge, but she also knew she had to prove something to him—and herself. Swinging open her car door with a flourish, she quipped, "Lead the way to your lair, Wolf. Or is it den?"

His soft laughter did strange things to her equilibrium, and for that reason only she allowed him the liberty of taking her arm.

He led her through a side entrance into the motel lobby, which was lavishly decorated in a south-seas motif, past the curious stares of the two men behind the reception desk, and up the curving stairway. As she mounted the last step, Micki barely had time to register the fact that the stairs opened onto what appeared to be a short crosswalk that connected two sections of the motel for, without pausing, Wolf turned right along the short crosswalk to where it connected with a long hallway. At the junction he turned left and strode along the hallway to the very end. The only difference between the door he unlocked and all the others that faced each other along the hall was the absence of a number.

The door opened into a fair-sized living room, but what caught Micki's attention, and her breath, was a large picture window on the far wall. From that height the window gave a panoramic view of beachfront and ocean. Without a word Micki entered the deliciously cool room and crossed the plush bronze carpeting to stare out the window. Micki was not unlike numerous other people as to the hypnotic effect the movement of the ocean had on the emotions. But Wolf's quiet voice jerked her out of her mesmeric state.

"Would you like a drink?"

The arched look she threw him drew his soft mocking laughter.

"A soft drink?" he chided. "Iced tea? Perrier?"

"Do you have lime?"

"Yes."

"Perrier with lime then, please."

Micki watched him as he went around the waist-high wooden bookshelves that divided the living room from the kitchen. While he went about the business of getting the drinks, she made a quick inventory of him. He had changed, matured, as she had herself and the change was heart stopping. He had been good-looking at thirty. Now, at thirty-six, life had left its stamp on him.

The square, determined jawline now proclaimed iron control. His golden tan skin stretched shiny and smooth over his long straight nose, his high cheekbones, and the angular planes of his face. The silver-gray eyes, arched over by thick, dark brows, now held a calculating sharpness. He wore his dark brown hair short in back, but its wavy thickness was completely intact. And his six-foot-plus frame, never thick, had pared down to the lean, sinewy look of the predator whose name he bore. One would not call him merely good-looking now. There were any number of adjectives one might apply, ranging from devastating to dangerous. One might even add slightly cruel-looking, but never merely good-looking.

Micki caught herself following his every move, a breathless sort of excitement clutching her throat at the sheer masculine look of him. *Don't be an idiot,* she told herself harshly. *Play it cool. Play it safe. He's trouble, pure unadulterated trouble, and no one knows it better than you.*

Casting her eyes away in search of something more worthy of her appraisal, she fastened on the living room. Masculine to the point of Spartan, Micki was surprised to find she really liked the effect the warm earth tones of bronze, brown, and gold, with a splash of green here and there lent the room. He probably didn't have a thing to do with the decor, she decided disparagingly. *I'll bet every room in the motel is decorated in the same way.*

"Like it?"

His quiet voice, startlingly close to her ear, made her jump. His next words brought a tinge of pink to her cheeks. "I decorated it myself." He cocked his head to one side as his eyes roamed the room. "Personally, I think I did a damned good job."

"Oh, I'm sure it's perfectly suitable"—Micki waved her hand carelessly—"for a man."

"You've grown up." The simple statement was issued as he handed her her drink. "Grown more beautiful too." The rider was accompanied by that disquieting, sensuous smile. He lifted his glass to her in a mock salute and Micki's brows arched at the amber-colored liquid it contained.

"A little too hot for the hard stuff in the middle of the day, isn't it?" she asked bitingly.

"I've yet to be flattened by a single glass of bourbon and water." His silvery eyes roamed insolently over her face and body. "It takes something a little more heady to put me flat."

She was perfectly well aware of what that something was. A warm female body, any warm female body. She lifted her chin and stared him straight in the eye. "You said you wanted to talk to me," she enunciated clearly. "What about?"

"About how you are." Wolf's voice had dropped an octave. He moved closer to her and she didn't like having to tilt her head back to look up into his face. His voice went lower.

"About what you've been doing."

"I'm fine." Micki's throat felt parched and she took a swallow of her drink before adding, "I've been working."

Long, hard-looking fingers began teasing the bow on her dress straps and a remembered chill of pleasure feathered her arms. Micki opened her mouth to tell Wolf to stop as she lifted her head. The words and her breath dried up in her mouth. He had lowered his head and his face was so close she could smell the pungent aroma of bourbon. Now his voice was so low she wasn't sure for a moment that she heard him correctly.

"About who you're sleeping with."

For a full five seconds she stood stunned, then indignation kicked fury through her veins and retaliation from her mouth.

"That's none of your business!" She spun away from him, setting her drink down on a glass-topped table as she headed for the door. Hand on the knob, she turned back to him, eyes glittering with anger.

"But of one thing you may be sure—he's not already tied, legally, to another."

Micki turned the knob and pulled the door open. The palm of Wolf's hand hit the solid wood forcefully, slamming it shut again. Micki stood perfectly still, almost afraid to breathe. The quietness of his tone unnerved rather than calmed her.

"What, exactly, is that last dig supposed to mean?"

While he spoke he turned her around and forced her face up to look at him. Micki flattened herself against the door, hating the havoc the look of him and the scent of him created within her. His hard, taunting mouth was too close. Alarm vied with a sudden, urgent need to feel the touch of that mouth. Alarm won, sending her tone to sub-zero.

"I'm not a fool, Wolf." With effort she managed to not only meet but hold his intent gaze. "I never was the complete fool you thought I was."

"I never thought you were a fool," Wolf denied sternly. He loomed over her, his head lowering until his mouth was no more than a sigh away. "Baby, baby," he murmured hoarsely. "Why did you run from me?"

"Why?" Somehow she pushed a dry laugh from her throat. "Because this fool suddenly smartened up and realized what she didn't want."

His lips caught, played with hers. "Tell me now you didn't want this." His hands came up to grasp her hips, arch her close to him. Moving slowly, caressingly, they reached over her waist, settled possessively over her breasts. "Or this," he groaned into her mouth. When he felt her shudder, his hands moved again, long fingers encircling her throat while his thumbs stroked her collarbones. His breathing ragged, he rasped, "Or this," as his mouth crushed hers.

For one blinding instant everything inside Micki urged her to surrender. Then reason, plus a dash of self-preservation, took over and she went as cold and unresponsive as a stone.

Wolf didn't force the issue. Within seconds of her withdrawal he lifted his head and stepped back.

"I haven't the vaguest idea what you've been talking about." His silvery eyes had a dangerous, calculating gleam. "But I intend to find out."

"Don't waste your time," Micki choked out. She wet

her lips and felt her heart thump when his eyes dropped
to her mouth. Pushing her words a little, she went on.
"When something's dead, it's dead. And what happened
between us died a long time ago."

"Prove it."

He rapped the words at her so fast she blinked in
confusion.

"Prove it?" she repeated indignantly. "It doesn't have
to be proven. It's evident."

"Not to me." His tone was hard and unyielding. "You
have to prove it to me, if you dare."

"How?"

Micki eyed him warily, somehow certain she was walking into a trap, yet unable to resist flinging his challenge
back at him.

"In no way that's frightening, so stop looking like a startled doe ready to bolt for the bushes." His soft, reasoning
tone made her more wary still. She didn't trust him and it
showed in her expression. His sigh was elaborately exaggerated. "Simply agree to see me occasionally, talk to me."

"And that's all?" In no way could she keep the blatant
surprise from her face. His soft laughter skipped along
her nerve endings.

"That's all."

It was too simple. Micki knew it was too simple, yet she
had accepted his dare. Momentarily she had a very uneasy feeling she'd been had. Well, so be it, she shrugged
mentally. If things got sticky she could always find an excuse for not seeing him. And maybe, just maybe, she
could finally banish the pain, consign the memories to
oblivion forever. Self-confidence won.

"All right." If she was so sure of herself, why was her
voice so whispery? "I must go now," she lied. "I'm expected
for dinner."

"Not so fast." His hand came up to catch her chin, lifting
her face so he could see her eyes. "When can I see you?"

"I—I don't know." Her tongue stumbled over her words. "I have a lot to do and—"

"Friday," he cut in. "For dinner. I'll pick you up at seven thirty."

"All right, Friday." Micki tried to ignore her sudden leap of anticipation. "I'll be ready."

"Good." His hand dropped to her arm and he moved back, away from the door, drawing her with him. Ignoring her insistence that he needn't walk her to her car, he ushered her through the doorway and along the hall.

The heat hit her like a physical blow when they stepped out of the building. And like some blow to the head it seemed to knock her thinking back onto dead center. Was she out of her mind agreeing to have dinner with him? It sounded innocent enough, but Micki had the sinking sensation that Wolf hadn't had an innocent urge since puberty. She waited until he had opened the car door for her and she had slid onto the seat before glancing up with a hesitant, "Wolf, about Friday."

"What about it?" They were the first words he'd uttered since leaving the apartment and Micki feared the hard sound of his tone.

"Where are we going?" she sighed in defeat. "How should I dress?"

The sardonic curve of his mouth left her in little doubt that he'd been perfectly aware that she'd been about to make a stab at getting out of the date.

"Nothing fancy." Wolf's grin was pure animal. Wolf animal. "We'll take a run down the coast to Wildwood. The restaurant's quiet and the food's good. I hope you like Greek food."

"I do."

Micki turned the key and the motor sprang to life. Wolf closed the door gently but firmly. Knowing there was no possible way out of it now, Micki backed the car around and drove off the lot.

* * *

By the time Micki parked her car in the driveway of her father's house she had a nervous stomach and a sick headache. Moving listlessly, she followed the flagstone path to the back door. Before entering, she straightened her spine and composed her features. The scene that met her eyes was so homey and domestic that for a brief moment she felt like an interloper. Regina stood at the kitchen counter grating cheese to top the salad Bruce was tossing in a large wooden bowl.

"Hi, princess, you're just in time for dinner." Her father's warm tone sent the alien feeling packing. "How's Cindy?"

"Blossoming." Micki grinned. Stealing a slim wedge of tomato from the bowl, she added, "I love the house."

"Did she have the fun of surprising you?" Regina turned from the cheese, an uncertain smile on her lips.

"Mmm," Micki nodded, finishing the tomato. "I was properly stunned."

"I'm glad." Regina transferred the grated cheese to the table. "Run into anyone else you know?"

Micki felt her face go stiff. Had her seemingly accidental meeting with Wolf been planned? Could his desire to see her, talk to her, be part of Regina's campaign to cement a friendship between herself and Micki? Micki stared at Regina's mildly inquiring expression as her mind went over those few fantastic minutes she spent in Wolf's apartment. No, she decided firmly. If the meeting had been part of a let's-be-friends play, Wolf would not have made his own play. Her father rescued her from the need to answer Regina's question.

"What's all this about a surprise from Cindy?"

"I didn't know she was pregnant," Micki answered quickly.

"And I inadvertently let the cat out of the bag before Micki left this morning," Regina supplied contritely.

"But all went well." Micki finished the tale dramatically. "Boy, was I surprised."

During the dinner Bruce glanced at Micki and asked, "Are you going with us tonight, honey?"

"Oh, dear, I forgot," Regina moaned, her face stricken. "I was so busy telling Micki something I wasn't supposed to, I failed to tell her what I was supposed to."

Totally confused, Micki begged, "Do you think you could untangle that for me, Dad? I'm afraid I must have missed something."

"Nothing very earth-shattering," Bruce chuckled. "We've been invited to watch the Night in Venice from the Gallagers' deck. When Dolly and Mike heard you'd be home, they asked me to tell you to come along, as they'd love to see you."

"The Night in Venice," Micki replied faintly. "I—I don't know—I—"

"You don't have other plans, do you?" Her father's face wore a confused question mark.

"No, but," Micki hedged, then offered lamely, "but I don't want to intrude."

"Intrude!" Now his face reflected sheer disbelief. "Dolly and Mike were at your christening. How could you possibly intrude?"

"All right." For the second time in less than two hours, Micki sighed in defeat. "I'd like to come."

It was a bare-faced lie. The last thing Micki wanted was to sit on that particular deck. It was on that deck she had been introduced to one Wolfgang Karl Renninger.

THREE

As soon as the dishes were rinsed and stacked in the dishwasher, Micki escaped to her room with a murmured, "I'll be ready," when her father said they would be leaving around eight.

After stripping off her clothes, she headed for the shower. She felt half sick to her stomach and there was a throbbing in her temples that grew stronger with each passing minute. Standing under the tepid spray, water cascading over her head and down her body, Micki decided her acceptance of Wolf's taunting challenge had not been too bright. She knew what he wanted. What he'd always wanted from any woman hapless enough to wander into his orbit. And he thought she'd under persuasion be willing to answer his wants.

About who you're sleeping with.

His words echoed in her mind so clearly she jerked her head around to see if he hadn't somehow slipped into the shower with her. Knowing she was being silly, yet unable to control her reaction, she turned the water off and stepped out of the stall. Raking her memory, she tried to recall his exact tone as well as his words. Once again his words, complete with his shading, came sharp and clear.

Had he sounded derisive? Mocking? Angry? Micki shook her head, she couldn't pinpoint it. The word jealousy leaped into her mind, but with a snort she rejected it. Wolf jealous? Never.

Another thought slithered into her mind and she felt herself go hot then cold. That he'd asked the question in the first place must mean he'd taken for granted that she was sleeping with someone. The vaguely sick feeling in her stomach deepened. She had not denied it. Quite the opposite. The reply she'd flung at him could easily be taken as confirmation.

Her thoughts tormented her as she dressed. Damn him. Whenever she considered herself, her life-style, at all, it was along the lines of independent, self-sufficient, and confident. In less than one hour Wolf had managed to undermine her self-image. Suddenly she felt vulnerable, confused, and much younger than her twenty-five years. Damn him. Her last thoughts before leaving her room were *He's going to give me trouble, I know it, and I don't know what to do about it.*

They walked to the bay, enjoying the sweetness of the early evening ocean breeze. The Gallager house was full of people, as it always was the evening of Night in Venice. As it was still early, most of the people were milling about, laughing, talking, helping themselves to the large array of snacks Dolly had set out.

Micki had always enjoyed the Gallagers' company. About her father's age, they were a warm, friendly couple who liked having people around. When she was a little girl, Micki had loved visiting them.

After exchanging greetings and hugs and a few moments of small talk, Micki wandered out onto the nearly empty deck. She knew that before too long both the deck she was on and the one above her would be crowded with people, but for now, for just a few minutes, she could savor the near solitude.

As she crossed the deck toward the railing, Micki glanced around. As far as she could see on either side, on the docks at street endings, on the porches and wide decks of apartment houses and private homes, people were gathered for the once-a-year show.

Making her way to a chair placed in a corner of the deck, Micki gazed out over the bay, affected, as she'd always been, by the molten gold sheen cast on the water by the fiery ball of westering sun.

She sat down and looked around idly, then froze in the chair, her hands gripping the armrests. Closing her eyes, she stifled a groan against the memory that would no longer stay locked away.

She had been sitting very near this spot when she'd first seen him. He had had one broad shoulder propped against a support beam and was half sitting on the rail when she'd felt his eyes on her and glanced up. She'd frozen then too, held fast to the chair by the bold stare from his silvery eyes. Micki experienced again the breathlessness she'd felt that night, the sensation that although six feet of deck separated them he was actually touching her. The shortness of breath had lasted until Mike had strolled up to talk to him and drew his eyes away from her.

Micki had studied his profile covertly while the two men talked. In his late twenties or early thirties, she'd judged, and was, without question, the most sexy, exciting-looking male she'd ever seen.

She'd been positive her heart had stopped when at Mike's quick, smiling nod, he'd lazily pushed himself away from the rail and followed Mike over the deck to her.

She had been amused at his name when Mike made the introductions and she'd made no attempt to hide it when she raised her eyes to his.

"Wolfgang?" she'd repeated in a laughing tone.

"Pitiful, isn't it?" he'd drawled. "It's a traditional name in my family. I, unfortunately, got tagged with it, being the firstborn male child." His eyes seemed to absorb her as he added, "Call me Wolf."

"And *are* you?" Micki had been amazed at the insolent sound of her voice. "A wolf, I mean."

"Of course," he'd returned smoothly, a wicked grin flashing on his tan face. "Isn't everyone who is single and unattached on the prowl?" He'd cocked his head to one side and those bold, silver eyes roamed over her, from head to foot to head again. "If you weren't so young, I may have decided to stalk you." His eyes laughed at the sudden pinkness in her face. His voice dropped to a low caress. "I still might."

Struck speechless, Micki had stared at him, praying for some bright, crushing words to pop into her head. None did, and then it didn't matter, for someone—that throaty voice could only have belonged to Regina—inside called to him and he turned away from her. He took one step, then glanced back at her, the wicked grin flashing again.

"A pleasure meeting you"—he paused—"young Micki."

Micki had gone all hot and flushed, first with embarrassment, then with anger. *He spoke to me as if I was a little girl,* she'd thought furiously, *and I'm not. I'm nineteen, for heaven's sake and I hope I never see that bigheaded, overbearing Wolf again.*

Even so, her anger and hope notwithstanding, his image filled her mind the rest of the night and she saw very little of the evening's entertainment.

"Well, honey, I see you've found a good seat for the show."

Micki blinked away the past and glanced up at her father, a shaky smile on her lips.

"Yes," she answered vaguely, noticing, for the first time, that it was nearly dark. "Shouldn't it be getting under way soon?"

"How far away were you?" Bruce laughed. "If you'll

merely look to your right, you'll see it's nearly on top of us."

Micki's eyes followed the direction of his casually waved hand. Then she whispered a surprised, "Oh!" Sure enough, the procession of gaily decorated, brightly lighted boats of all sizes was indeed nearly on top of them.

For several minutes Micki watched the parade of boats, enjoying the reflection of the lights on the water, laughing at the clowning antics of the men in the smaller boats, and waving at the people of all ages aboard the cleverly festooned crafts.

But her eyes soon drifted to that one spot at the rail, clouding over with the rush of memories.

She had not seen him again for almost a week. Then, when she was finally beginning to get his image out of her mind, she felt the touch of his silvery eyes again. At the time she'd thought it was very strange. She'd been walking near the far end of the boardwalk with Cindy and two other girls, all of them laughing as they munched on slices of pizza, when she felt an eerie shiver skip down her spine. What had made her lift her head, glance around, she didn't know, but she'd just felt compelled to look. This time he was propped against the boardwalk's pipelike railing, his eyes fastened on her. He didn't call to her or even wave, but the grin flashed white and wicked and his eyes seemed to speak of things beyond her wildest imaginings. She had caught herself just in time from choking on her pizza and had hurried on, but after a dozen steps she'd glanced back to find his eyes still on her.

Early in August she'd seen him again. That time she'd been leaving the theater after the early evening showing of a controversial R-rated movie. She had been with her gang and the comments, both pro and con on the film, were flying hot and heavy. Wolf, with a beautiful, high-fashion-type redhead clinging to his arm, was going in to the late evening showing. Micki nearly bumped into him. There was no grin this time, but as he passed her one eyelid came down in a slow, suggestive wink.

And then, in late August, there was a cookout at a friend's beachfront house and all the unbelievable events that followed it.

There must have been twenty of them, not counting her friend's parents and the people they'd invited. After they'd eaten, they'd split up into two-man teams for a sand-sculpting contest, which, the adults vowed, they'd judge impartially. Micki had been teamed with Tony Menella, and even with all the horseplay and general craziness, their sculpture of a reclining nude had won hands down.

As twilight settled gently on the beach, Cindy had suggested they go hunting in the sand. They'd started out as a group, but their ranks thinned as some quit to go back to the house and others roamed farther along the beach.

Toting a brown bag to hold her dubious treasures, Micki found herself alone with a boy she'd met that night for the first time. Searching her mind, she came up with the name David Bender. She crossed her fingers in hope it was the right one.

"What happened to all the other kids?" Micki's fingers twined behind her back. "David?"

"Beats me." He glanced around scanning the beach. "'I guess most of them got bored." His still boyishly slim shoulders lifted in a shrug. "Did you find anything worth keeping?"

"No." Micki laughed.

"Me either." David laughed with her. "Want to sit and rest awhile before heading back?" He shot her a shy look. "We've come down the beach pretty far."

"Okay," Micki answered flippantly, plopping down at the base of a low sand dune. "You're from up near Margate, aren't you?" she asked after he'd dropped onto the sand less than a foot away from her.

"Yeah," David nodded, not looking at her, his eyes fixed on the darkening ocean.

Sighing softly, Micki leaned back against the gentle slope of the dune, her eyes studying him with mild interest. About her own age, she thought, maybe even a little younger. He still had the look of the high-school boy, she mused from the exalted distance of one completed year of college. Unbidden, a picture of Wolfgang Renninger rose in her mind. Micki had to compress her lips to keep from laughing out loud at the comparison. Unfair, she chided herself sternly. Wolf's a mature man, while David's still in the throes of adolescence. She should have remembered how hot the blood can flow in teenaged boys.

"You're a very pretty girl." David's voice came softly close to her ear. During her perusal of him, he'd settled back into the dune, turned onto his side to face her. "Are you dating anyone?"

Startled out of her contemplation, Micki turned her head to find his face close to hers. Surprised, she smiled nervously. "No. I'm too busy with college and—David, what—?"

His soft, moist lips silenced her. With an inward sigh, Micki lay perfectly still, his inexperienced kiss drawing no response from her. It was a mistake. Her lack of interest seemed to spur a determination in him to make her feel something. The pressure on her lips increased painfully. Suddenly his hands pushed her beach wrap open, tore at the skimpy top of her bikini as his body rolled on top of her.

Her first reaction was sharp anger. Who did this jerk think he was, pawing at her? Bringing her hands up, she pushed at his shoulders, fully expecting him to move off her at once and apologize sheepishly. Fear began when she couldn't dislodge him. He was a lot stronger than he looked. With all her twisting and turning she could not escape his lips. She couldn't breathe and she felt sure that if he didn't lift his head soon she'd faint from lack of air. Panic shot through her when his fingers dug into her now-exposed breasts and one bony knee attempted to pry her legs apart. This couldn't be happening. Not to her.

Blackness was stealing into her mind when his lips slid from hers, moved to fasten, hurtfully, on the soft skin on the side of her neck.

"David, stop," Micki gasped between huge gulps of consciousness-saving breaths. Fear lent inspiration as, struggling frantically, she lied. "I've got to get back, my father will be coming to pick me up."

"You don't have to go anywhere," David panted, his fingers digging viciously into her breasts. "I heard you tell Cindy you'd be alone all weekend because your folks are out of town."

His lips moved in a sucking action, drawing a cry of pain from her. Nausea filled her throat when his knee succeeded in pushing her legs apart and his slender frame pressed her deeper into the gritty sand.

"David, please stop." She was crying openly, her sobs catching at her throat when she felt his hand move down her body, tug at her bikini bottom. "No!" Her voice rose in a muffled scream of pure desperation.

"Hey!" David yelped loudly, then suddenly his weight was removed, yanked away from her violently.

"You stupid jerk." The enraged, unfamiliar growl was followed by the stinging sound of a hard, open-handed blow and a loud cry of pain from David. "Get the hell out of here or I'll break you in half."

Still crying, blinking against the tears that blurred her vision, Micki cringed back when big hands grasped her shoulders, lifted her from the sand.

"It's all right, he's gone." The soft tone that had replaced the enraged growl was recognizable now as belonging to Wolf Renninger.

"He—he—he tried to—"

"I know," Wolf snapped, preventing her from saying
the word *rape*. "But it's over now," he went on in a softer
tone. He pulled her impersonally, protectively against
his broad, hard chest, brushed the sand from her back
with his big hand. "I'll see that you get home safely."

"Oh, no," Micki moaned, rubbing her forehead back
and forth over the smooth material of his shirt.

"No?" Wolf repeated impatiently. "What do you mean,
no?"

"You don't understand," she wailed. "Dad and Regina
are away for the weekend. I'll be alone in the house and
David knows it. What if he—?" Micki paused to swallow
a fresh lump of fear. "I don't want to go home."

He cursed softly, then was very still for long seconds before, moving away from her, he said decisively, "Okay, you
can come with me for a while, then I'm taking you home."

The harshness of his voice confused and frightened
her. Meekly, after hurriedly tugging her suit top into
place and fastening her beach wrap at the neck, she followed in his wake as he walked around the sand dune
and strode toward the road where a low-slung car was
parked.

"Come on," Wolf gritted irritably at her slow progress
through the tall grass.

As she slid onto the seat of the sports car, Micki
slanted a quick look at him through her long lashes,
wondering what she'd said, or done, to make him so
angry. Surely he didn't think she had encouraged David
in any way? She jumped when the door slammed beside
her, and again when his own slammed, after he'd folded
his long frame onto the seat behind the wheel. Opening
her mouth to ask him what was wrong, Micki glanced at
him and closed her lips quickly at the hard, rigid set of
his face. Wolf started the car and made a U-turn on
Ocean Drive, heading away from the city.

"Where are we going?" Micki asked hesitantly.

"I've got my boat docked not far from here," he replied tersely. "I have to move it."

They drove a short distance beyond the city limits, then Wolf turned off the drive toward the bay where he parked the car on a small lot in front of a rather run-down building with a red neon sign that read BAR & GRILL.

"Where were you?"

The question was punctuated by his hard tug on the hand brake. For a second Micki blinked at him in confusion, then his meaning registered.

"At a cookout beach party, at a friend's home."

"Did you go dressed like that?" he snapped.

"No, of course not," Micki snapped back, beginning to feel a little steadier as the shock from her experience receded. "My clothes are at the house."

"What's this friend's name and phone number?"

"You're not going to call her?" Micki cried.

"Yes, I am," Wolf sighed in exasperation. "When you don't come back they're liable to call the police. If they haven't already."

Micki hadn't thought of the furor her absence might cause. Chastised, she murmured the name and number.

"Okay, I've got it." He opened the car door and stepped out. "Stay here, I'll be back in a minute."

The door swung closed with a loud bang. Biting her lip, Micki wondered again why he was so angry. As the minute stretched into five and then ten, Micki's temper flared. What was he doing all this time? Probably having a drink with the boys, while she sat alone in a dark parking lot. And who did he think he was anyway? He had no right to snap and snarl at her. By the time he returned, she had talked herself into a fury.

"What were you doing all this time?" she demanded the minute he'd opened the door beside her.

"Don't take that tone with me." Wolf's soft voice held a definite warning. "What I do, who I make time with, is no concern of yours. If you've got any sense at all, you'll guard that nasty little tongue. You couldn't even handle Joe College back there. I'd crush you like an annoying little gnat. Now get out of the car, I'm taking you home."

"But—" she began.

"Out," he cut in harshly.

Micki bit her lip, feeling very young, and very inexperienced, and very, very stupid. He was right, of course, she had no right to question him. If it hadn't been for him . . . She shuddered. Belatedly she remembered she hadn't even thanked him. No wonder he was angry. Knowing what she had to do, she drew a deep breath, slid off the seat, and stood before him, her head bent.

"I'm—I'm sorry, Mr. Renninger," she whispered contritely. "I know you must think I'm an ingrate." Wetting her dry lips, Micki lifted her head to look at him, her eyes made even brighter by the shimmer of tears. "I—I haven't even thanked you for helping me. But I am grateful, truly, and—and—" She had to pause to swallow against the tightness in her throat. "I wanted you to know I didn't invite that attack."

"I didn't think you had." Wolf's much gentler tone brought a fresh rush of tears to her eyes. "Don't cry, Micki." His hand came up to cradle her face, one long finger brushed at her tears. "I know it was a bad experience, but you're unhurt and—" He broke off and leaned toward her. "He didn't hurt you, did he?"

"No, not really." Micki shook her head, drawing a deep breath to combat the increase in heartbeat his nearness caused. "The only thing hurt is my dignity."

"It will heal," he murmured, lowering his head closer to hers. His fingers shook as if he'd had a sudden chill, then he snatched his hand away as though her skin had burned him. "Come on, kid, I've got to get you home."

The gentleness had gone, replaced by an edgy roughness Micki didn't understand, as she didn't understand
the hard emphasis he'd placed on the word *kid*.

"But what about your car?"

"It isn't mine. It belongs to the guy that owns this place."

Grasping her arm, he hurried her around the building and onto a rickety pier. Secured to the pier, bathed
dimly in the glow from the building's side windows, was
a cabin cruiser that brought a small gasp from Micki.

"Is that beautiful thing yours?" she asked in an awed
tone.

"Yes," Wolf replied shortly. "Go aboard, I want to cast
off."

"Please." Micki's hand caught his arm as he turned
away. "Could I have a quick tour of her before we go?"

The muscles in his arm tensed under her fingers and
Micki was sure he was about to refuse. Then with a soft
sigh of resignation, he said crisply, "All right, a very quick
tour."

He helped her to board the shadowy craft, then, one
hand at her waist to guide her, he led her across the deck
and down a short flight of stairs with a murmured,
"Careful." There was the sound of a switch being flicked
and Micki blinked against the sudden light that filled the
small salon she was standing in. Glancing around at the
sparse, masculine furnishings, she breathed, "How many
does she sleep?"

"Ten," Wolf replied curtly, indicating a narrow portal
across the room. Micki stepped through the portal into
an equally narrow passageway, which had two doors on
each side. When she hesitated at the first door on her
left, Wolf grated, "Get on with it."

Biting back the retort that sprang to her lips, Micki
pushed the door open. The cabin contained a small fitted
dresser and four fitted bunks. The cabin next to it was exactly the same. As she withdrew from the second cabin,

Wolf opened the door directly across the passage, with a terse, "The head."

The small, but adequate-sized bathroom was equipped with a stainless steel toilet, shower stall, and fitted wash-bowl. Wolf was standing at the open door of the last cabin when she emerged from the head. He made a half bow as she approached him. "The captain's quarters," he drawled mockingly.

Feeling herself grow warm under his mocking glance, Micki unfastened her beach wrap and preceded him into the cabin. It was larger than the other two cabins. Instead of fitted bunks it contained a built-in bed, not quite as wide as a regular double bed.

At sight of the bed, Micki's body was suddenly suffused with warmth. Feeling constricted, she pulled her wrap open. Casting about in her mind for something to say to the silent man standing just inside the cabin, she turned slowly.

"Is—is this where you sle—" The words died on her lips at the sudden, fierce look on his face. Her breathing stopped as he walked to her, his silvery eyes gleaming dangerously behind narrowed lids.

"What's wrong?" she gasped, terrified by the look of him.

"That creep bastard marked you," he snarled softly, bending over her to examine her throat and the smooth skin below her shoulders.

"Oh, no," she groaned, her hand flying to her neck. "Is it very bad?"

"Bad enough," he clipped, straightening. "Sit down, I'll get some antiseptic to put on it."

Disregarding his order, she walked to the small mirror above the dresser and leaned toward it to peer closely at the red marks.

"I told you to sit." The hard sound of his voice set her teeth on edge.

"I'm not a dog," Micki flared, close to tears.

"You're telling me," he drawled, holding his hand out to her. "Come on, let me dab this stuff on you."

Ignoring his hand, Micki walked by him stiffly. Sitting down gingerly on the very edge of the bed, she lifted her head to expose her neck, and closed her eyes. When the antiseptic touched the abrasion, she drew her breath in sharply and shut her eyes more tightly to stem the corresponding sting in her eyes.

"Sorry," he muttered softly. He was so close, his warm breath feathered her skin, setting off a clamoring inside her that ended in a visible shiver. "I could whup him for doing this to you." The soft intensity of his tone increased her shivering. Keeping her eyes tightly closed, holding her breath, Micki sat immobile. Something strange was happening to her. Something strange, and a little scary, and almost unbearably exciting.

The feather light touch of his lips on her skin felt like a touch from an exposed electrical wire. Trembling, Micki moaned deep in her throat. She heard his raspy, indrawn breath an instant before he sighed softly, groaned, "Dear God, Micki."

His mouth touched hers gently, experimentally. When she didn't flinch away, the pressure increased and his hands grasped her upper arms. Her heart beating wildly, Micki returned the kiss. She gasped against his mouth when the hard tip of his tongue moved slowly across her lips, but she obeyed the silent command to part them. His mouth still gentle, exploring, he straightened, drawing her to her feet in front of him.

Micki didn't know what was happening to her. She had been kissed before, many times, but never had she felt this sweet joy zinging through her veins, this light-headed, intoxicating sensation. When she swayed toward him, touched his body with her own, he lifted his head, held her away from him.

"I've got to take you home," he rasped unevenly.

"Why?" Micki asked huskily.

"Don't you know?" Wolf groaned. "Have you really no idea of the effect you're having on me?"

Elation shot through her, gave her the courage to lean toward him, slide the tip of her tongue across his mouth. He went stone still, then gritted. "Where the hell did you learn that trick?"

Micki's eyes went wide at his rough tone. "From you, just now. I've never—never—"

"Why did you do it?" His growl had lost its bite.

"Because"—Micki wet her lips, felt a curl of excitement when his eyes dropped to her mouth—"because I was afraid you weren't going to kiss me again—and I wanted you to."

"You're too young to know what you want." Micki's head was shaking a denial before he'd finished speaking, but he didn't give her time to voice it. "If I kissed you, I mean really kissed you, you'd be fighting me in a cold panic within seconds, exactly like you were fighting that teenage Don Juan back at the beach."

"No, I wouldn't," Micki denied softly. "I didn't want him to kiss me. I do want you to."

His silvery eyes stared hard into hers, then dropped to her mouth, then lifted to her eyes again. "I must be out of my mind," he muttered. "I never should have brought you here after the jealousy I felt of that punk."

"You felt jealous of David!" Micki exclaimed. "But why?"

"Because"—Wolf's voice was very low as he drew her slowly against his long frame—"I wanted to be in exactly the same position he was in, you beautiful fool."

This time there was very little gentleness. His lips crushed hers, forcing them apart roughly. His tongue probed hungrily. Flaring lights actually seemed to explode behind her eyes. Raising her arms, she curled them around his neck, needing suddenly to be closer to him. He half groaned, half growled into her mouth, then his hands moved across her shoulders, down her back, molding her to his hard body. Responding to the demands of her body, Micki arched her hips against him. At once lips pulled away from hers, moved in a fiery path over her cheek to her ear.

"Micki, stop me while you still can." His voice held half plea, half command.

"I don't want you to stop." The moment the words were out she knew she spoke the truth. She had never behaved like this before in her life, yet she knew she wanted to, had to, belong to this man.

Although his hands still held her tightly to him, he lifted his head, gave her another of those hard stares. "You've been with a man before?"

Micki hesitated, knowing somehow that if she told him the truth he'd put her from him, take her home. Praying that in the dim light her flush would look like guilt, she lowered her lashes, whispered, "Yes."

A flash of something—pain, disgust—twisted his face. He gave an almost imperceptible shake of his head, then lowered his mouth to within a whisper of hers. Again she heard that half groan, half growl.

"I don't care." His hands spread over her hips, pulling her tightly against him. "Oh, God, baby, I want you."

Her wrap and her bikini were removed gently but swiftly. For the first time in her life Micki stood naked before a man, amazed that she felt no shame or fear. As he undressed, his eyes, gleaming like liquid silver, moved slowly over her body, the burning, naked hunger in them igniting an eagerness in her to be in his arms, be part of him.

Slowly, expertly, his mouth and hands an exquisite torture, he fanned the flame inside her to a roaring blaze. Gasping, moaning softly deep in her throat, her lips leaving tiny, urgent kisses on his neck, his shoulders, she welcomed him when, finally, his body covered hers. Moments later he cursed her.

"Damn you!" Wolf's tone held anger, but an odd note of satisfaction as well. "You lied to me."

"Yes," she admitted into the curve of his shoulder, her arms tightening around his waist, refusing to let go.

"Oh, baby, baby." He kissed her mouth tenderly. "I'm sorry."

"I'm not," Micki replied honestly. "I wanted this as badly as you did, Wolf."

"Sweet Lord, I've found myself a sexy teenage vixen," Wolf muttered huskily, his body moving excitingly.

"You'd better enjoy it while you can," Micki laughed teasingly. "I'll only be a teenager two more months."

"A vixen and a tease," Wolf moaned between short, quick breaths, then, "Oh, God, Micki, kiss me."

Micki's initiation into the world of serious lovemaking lasted until three o'clock the following morning. Wolf was a master tutor, and under his ardent guidance she caught a glimpse of the wondrous things his eyes had seemed to speak of that time on the boardwalk. Exhausted, she curled still closer to him, heard him laugh softly as his arms tightened around her.

"That was just the first chapter of the text," he teased. "Do you think you'll graduate?"

"Cum laude," she murmured sleepily and was rewarded by a light kiss on the corner of her mouth.

"Go to sleep, sweetheart," Wolf whispered into her ear.

FOUR

"Wake up, sweetheart."

Micki jumped at the sound of her father's quiet voice, the gentle touch of his hand on her arm.

"Is it over?"

Sitting up straight, she winced at the twinge of pain at the base of her spine and brought her hand up to massage the stiffness in her neck caused by the hard rim of the aluminum chair. Glancing around, she saw the deck was empty of all the other people. What time was it?

"Over an hour ago." Bruce laughed softly. "The party's breaking up. It's time to go home."

"I'm ready."

Moving carefully, Micki lifted her cramped body out of the chair, one hand going to her mouth to cover a wide yawn. In a young-girl, sleepy voice, she apologized, thanked, and said good night to her indulgently smiling host and hostess, then followed her father and Regina out to the hushed sidewalk.

Trailing a few steps behind the couple, she watched as her father's arm slid around his wife's waist, heard his low voice murmur something close to her ear. Regina apparently disagreed with what her father had said, for her head moved slowly in a negative shake. The argument, if that's what it was, was obviously not over anything very serious. With a sigh of relief, Micki heard Regina laugh softly.

Dropping a few steps farther behind in order to give

them complete privacy, Micki's fingers curled tightly into the palm of her hand. Well, she'd missed it again. It had been six years since she'd gone to watch the Night in Venice and she'd seen practically none of it. And for exactly the same reason—thoughts of Wolf had absorbed her attention, her senses.

Angrily rejecting the image of him that rose in her mind, Micki centered her thoughts on the couple a few feet ahead of her, wondering if she could be the bone of contention between them. She hoped not, but had the sinking sensation that she was. For all Regina's declared wish that they be friends, Micki was still very unsure of her. Their past relationship had been fraught with so much jealousy, so much resentment, that Micki was unconvinced of the permanency of their truce.

The minute Micki entered the house, Bruce ended her conjecturing.

"There is only one way to find out," he stated in a tone of amused exasperation. "And that's ask her."

"Bruce, please," Regina pleaded softly. "Not tonight, she's tired and—"

"She's wide awake now," Bruce insisted, studying his daughter closely. "Princess, I'm going to ask you something and I want you to answer honestly. Will you?"

"Yes, of course." Micki's gaze flew from her father's laughing eyes to Regina's worried ones. What was this all about? Her father answered her silent question.

"I want to take Regina on a second honeymoon," he said quietly, his suddenly serious, love-filled eyes resting on his wife's face.

"And?" Micki prompted, confused as to what a proposed second honeymoon had to do with her.

"Regina insists that it would be selfish of us to go away at this time."

"Selfish?" Micki repeated blankly. "I don't understand. In what way would it be selfish?"

A satisfied grin spread over her father's face. "You see?" he asked Regina before turning back to Micki. "Regina is afraid you'll feel, well, deserted, if we went away so soon after your return home."

"But that's ridiculous!" Micki cried. "When were you thinking of going?"

"Not till the end of the month." Bruce's eyes filled with pride and tenderness as he studied Micki's face. "It will take me until then to tie up some loose ends at the office."

Micki looked directly at Regina. "By the end of the month I expect the majority of my time will be spent in learning my new job." Her eyes swung back to her father. "I think a second honeymoon is a lovely idea, especially as I don't remember your ever having a first."

"It was impossible for me to leave the office at that time," Bruce defended himself. "And since then the time just didn't seem right." Bruce paused, then went on softly. "With one thing and another."

"Well, then," Micki spoke quickly, knowing too well that she was the one thing and Regina's behavior the other. "If you feel the time is now right, then go, and don't worry about me. I'm quite used to taking care of myself." At the contrite expression that crossed her father's face at her last words, Micki willed a sparkle into her eyes and shaded her voice with teasing excitement. "Where were you thinking of going, or is that a secret?"

"No secret." Micki felt relief rush through her at the way her father's face lit up. "I had thought San Francisco, I've always wanted to see it." His voice grew eager. "We could rent a car, drive through the Redwoods, along the coast, Carmel, Big Sur."

Watching Regina's face, Micki could see her father's eagerness reflected there. Although she had been arguing against the trip, it was obvious Regina wanted to go.

"Sounds super." Micki spoke directly to Regina. "So do

it. Make your arrangements and take off. I promise you I will be fine."

Grabbing Regina up in a bear hug, Bruce spun her around, laughing. "What did I tell you, darling? Is my girl something special or not?"

"Very special." Regina spoke for the first time. When he turned back to Micki, Regina mouthed a silent thank you at her.

Wide awake now, Micki murmured, "I think I'll sit on the porch a few minutes," when her father and Regina moved toward the stairs. "You two go on up, I'll lock up." Micki stepped out onto the porch, then turned back to get a sweater from the hall closet. A mist rolling in off the ocean had turned the air cool and clammy. Settling back on the porch lounger, she watched the mist swirl and thicken, turn the light from the street lamp into an eerie orangish glow.

The mist had been like this that morning.

Shifting irritably on the thickly padded cushion, Micki tried to push the thought away. She didn't want to think about it. Didn't want to remember. Her shifting, her silent protests, were in vain. The floodgate of memory, which had sprung a leak earlier, now burst completely, swamping her, carrying her helplessly back through time.

Micki stirred when the warmth of Wolf's body was removed from hers. Through eyelids heavy with sleep, she watched him, his form barely discernible in the gray, predawn half light. Moving noiselessly, he stepped into his jeans, fastened them, then pulled a battered sweat shirt over his head. Fear shot through her as he moved across the floor to the door.

"Wolf?" Micki's voice betrayed her fear. "Where are you going?"

At the sound of his name Wolf turned, the fear in her tone brought him back to the bed in a few long strides. Bending, he dropped a soft kiss on her lips.

"I have to move the boat," he explained quietly, one long finger outlining her mouth. "Go back to sleep. As soon as I have her docked at the marina I'll come back to bed." His lips touched hers again, lingered, then he was moving across the cabin, out the door.

Micki closed her eyes tightly, but it was no good; she couldn't sleep with him gone. Slipping out of the bed, and a moment later out of the cabin, she hurried into the tiny bathroom. She was stepping under the shower spray when she heard the boat's engine flare into life. Bracing herself with one hand, she washed her body with the other while Wolf backed the boat away from the pier and swung it around. When the craft was relatively steady, she stepped out of the shower stall, grabbed for the towel, probably Wolf's, that hung on a small fitted bar, and rubbed herself down briskly.

Back in the cabin, she stretched languorously. The tautening of her breasts brought the remembered feel of Wolf's hands, and her nipples set into diamond-hard points. *Oh, Wolf.* Just to think his name sent her blood racing through her veins, set her pulses hammering out of control. She couldn't wait until he'd docked the boat, she had to see him now.

Glancing around, she grimaced as her eyes settled on her bikini and beach wrap, lying in an untidy heap where Wolf had tossed them. Shaking her head in rejection of the beachwear, she went to the cabin's one small closet and rummaged through shirts and jackets—obviously too short to cover the bare necessities—until her hand clutched and withdrew a bright yellow rain slicker. Pulling it on hastily, uncaring how incongruous she looked, she left the cabin, fastening the buckle closings as she went.

Not once did she pause to ask herself why she was where she was, with a man she knew practically nothing about. Not once did she wonder about how suddenly it had happened. She was there. It had happened. Never before had she felt so tinglingly alive, so totally happy. But she didn't even pause to think of that. The only thought that filled her mind was that she had to be near him, see him. The whys and how of it would torment her later.

When she stepped onto the deck she came to an abrupt halt, her hand groping for something solid to steady herself with. An off-white mist lay over everything, muffling sound, obscuring visibility. The deck was beaded and slick with moisture. Placing her bare feet carefully, Micki moved cautiously toward the canopied section that housed the wheel, and the man who stood at that wheel, alert tenseness in every line of his tall, muscular frame.

She thought her progress was silent, yet the moment she stepped under the canopy, his left arm was extended backward.

"Come stand by me." Wolf's hushed tone blended with the cotton blanket that surrounded the boat.

Without a word Micki moved to his side, sighed with contentment when his arm closed around her, drew her close to his hard strength.

"Why didn't you go back to sleep?" Still the same hushed tone, not scolding, a simple question. He did not look at her, and her eyes following the direction of his intent gaze, she answered as simply.

"I wanted to be with you."

She saw his hand tighten on the wheel at the same instant the muscles in his arm tautened. He slanted her a quick glance and an amused smile curved his firmly etched mouth.

"I see you've made free with my shower and bath soap." The smile deepened. "Bedecked yourself with the latest yachting creations from Paris also."

"But of course," Micki teased back. "This particular number was labeled MORNING SUNLIGHT THROUGH HEAVY GAUZE CURTAINS. Does my lord approve?"

Wolf's soft laughter was an exciting, provocative attack on her senses.

"But of course," he mimicked her seriously. "Still, I think I prefer the, er, more basic ensemble you were wearing earlier."

Flushed with pleasure, Micki rubbed her warm cheek against his cool, mist-dampened sweat shirt. Misunderstanding her action and the pink glow on her face, he chided her softly.

"You're a beautiful woman, babe." Wolf's soft tone brooked no argument. "Every soft, satiny inch of you. There's no reason for embarrassment." He paused, then slanted another, harder look at her. "Do you feel shame?"

"No!" Micki's denial was fast, emphatic. "Or embarrassment either." Rising on tiptoe, she placed her lips on the strong column of his throat. "I'm—I'm pleased that you find me attractive."

"Attractive?" Micki could feel the tension ease out of him. "I don't think that adjective quite makes it." Leaning forward, he peered, narrow-eyed, through the moisture-beaded window. "If I ever get this damned boat docked I'll try to come up with the right one. Now be still and let me get on with it."

Barely breathing, Micki watched as he inched the craft along through the mist-shrouded water, and sighed with relief when he murmured, "There's the marina." When he removed his arm, she stepped back ready to follow any order he might issue.

"Have you ever driven a boat?" Wolf asked tersely as he backed the vessel into the slip.

"Yes," Micki answered quietly, then qualified, "But never one this large."

"Good enough." Their voyage through the mist completed safely, all his intent tenseness fled. His silvery eyes glittered teasingly. "You hold her down and I'll tie her up."

Suiting action to words, he drew her to the wheel, gave

a few brief instructions, and then he was gone, swallowed up in the gray-white mist. A moment later she heard the dull thud as the securing line landed on the pier, and then another as he followed it.

When the craft was secured, its engine silent, Wolf slid his arms around the bulky slicker at her waist and held her loosely.

"You hungry, baby?" His low tone, the way his eyes caressed her face, drove all thoughts but one from her mind. "Do you want some breakfast?"

Micki was shaking her head before he finished speaking. Not even trying to mask her feelings, she gazed up at him, her eyes honest and direct.

"I want to go back to bed."

"Good Lord," he breathed huskily, his arms drawing her closer. "What did I ever do to earn you as a reward?"

Pleasure radiated through her entire body at the warmth of his tone, the emotion-darkened gray of his eyes. Her arms, made clumsy by the too-large raincoat, encircled his neck to draw his head closer to hers. A shiver of anticipation skipped down her spine as his hands slid slowly over the smooth, stiff material of the garment.

"Are you wearing anything at all under that slicker?" His face was so near, his cool breath fanned her lips.

Mesmerized by the shiny, tautened skin of his mist-dampened cheeks and the motion of his mouth, Micki whispered a bemused, "No."

His parted lips touched hers in a brief kiss before she felt her lower lip caught inside his mouth, felt his teeth nibble gently on the tender, sensitive skin. Moaning softly, she flicked his teeth with her tongue. Instantly his arms tightened, crushing her against his hard body, and his lips pushed hers apart to receive his hungry, demanding mouth.

Awareness of him sang through every particle of her being. Squirming inside the stiff, confining coat, she strained her body to his, thrilled to the feeling of his body straining to hers.

"Wolf, Wolf." The words filled her mind, whispered past her lips to fill his mouth.

Lifting his head, he stared deeply into her eyes, his own eyes now nearly black with desire. His gaze dropped to her mouth.

"Why are we standing here?" His murmured groan held near pain. One arm clasped firmly around her waist, he led her along the slippery deck, down the steps, and into his cabin. Releasing her, his hands moved to the buckles on the coat.

"I swear, if I don't soon feel the silkiness of you against my skin, I think I'll burst into flames."

And in a sense he did, engulfing her in the conflagration.

They didn't leave the boat all that day or night. In fact they hardly set foot out of his cabin, except when hunger drove them to the tiny galley for sustenance.

At those times they worked together, mostly getting in each other's way. Micki, clad in her mid-thigh-length beach wrap, juggled a frying pan around Wolf's large frame as she endeavored to prepare a cheese omelet on the small two-burner cooking unit. Wolf, wearing a belted, knee-length terry cloth robe, stretched long arms around and in front of her in his effort to make a pot of coffee and open a jar of olives.

When Micki opined that had they followed the simple method of flipping a coin to determine who would get the meal the job would have been completed a lot faster, Wolf retorted that it would also have been one hell of a lot less fun.

They went through the same bumping into and laughing procedure while preparing a canned soup and canned corned beef sandwich supper, washed down with canned beer.

And both times, after appeasing the hunger of their stomachs, they went back to the appeasement of their seemingly insatiable hunger for each other.

They slept for short periods when exhaustion could no longer be held at bay, waking every time to come eagerly together, resentful of the hours of separation the need for sleep had imposed.

At one of those times, late in the night, Micki woke first and lay quietly, unmoving beside Wolf's sleeping form. Touching him with her eyes only, she studied him minutely, imprinting his likeness on her mind, in her soul.

Although by now she knew him fully in a physical sense, he was still a stranger. A stranger she was deeply, unconditionally in love with. It was a sobering thought. Sobering and somewhat frightening, for although he had murmured countless, impassioned, exciting love words to her, none had been words of love for her. But then, she had not spoken of her love for him either. Maybe it was all too new, too sudden for both of them. And maybe, she thought with a sageness beyond her years, the avowals of love now would ring false, take on the shadings of an excuse for their wild coming together. Micki shrugged mentally. It didn't matter. She'd face the reality of it all tomorrow. For right now, she knew she loved him, would probably always love him.

Micki's eyes misted over as she stared at his face. He had made her so unbelievably, joyously happy. She loved her father dearly, yet she knew that should Wolf ask her, she would go with him anywhere in the world with never a backward glance. She had had no promises of undying love, had had no solemn words spoken over her, still she felt like a bride on her honeymoon. And no girl's honeymoon, she was certain, had ever been more idyllic, more perfect than this one.

"Why are you crying?" Wolf's tone, though soft, held hard concern.

Blinking against the moisture, Micki snuggled close to him.

"Because I'm happy," she whispered, her lips brushing his taut jaw. "Haven't you ever heard that women cry when they're happy?"

"Yes, I had heard that." The movement of his lips at her temple sent tiny shivers down the back of her neck. "In fact there have been several occasions when I have been the recipient of those happy tears." The admission was made tonelessly, without conceit. "But never for so little."

"Little?" Tilting her head back, Micki looked up at him, her eyes reflecting her confusion. "I don't understand. What do you mean—for so little?"

Lifting his head, he studied her expression, as if trying to determine if her confusion was authentic. Obviously deciding it was, he shook his head in wonder. "Always before, the tears were in response to a gift from me." Wolf's eyes held hers steadily, gauging her reaction. "Jewelry, flowers, things like that," he shrugged, "but always a tangible, usually expensive, object."

Micki gazed back at him, trying, but failing, to keep the hurt from her eyes.

"And you think," she asked softly, "your gift of this weekend, being an intangible gift, has no value?"

"Honey, I didn't—" Wolf began.

"You're right." His eyes widened slightly at the firm words that cut across his protest. Blinking against the hot moisture that clouded her eyes, Micki placed the tip of her finger over his mouth, silencing whatever he was about to say. "There can be no price tag attached to the gift you've given me, simply because, to me, this weekend has been priceless." Despite her efforts, two tears escaped, rolled slowly down her face. "I never dreamed this kind of happiness, this perfect contentment. was possible to achieve."

Her voice faltered and she lowered her eyes. Hesitant but determined, she went on softly. "This is the gift you've given me, Wolf, and that's why I was crying."

A stunned silence followed her small speech and Micki began to tremble, certain she'd shattered the harmony they'd shared till now.

"Good God, can this woman be real?" Wolf's hushed tone held a hint of genuine awe. Glancing up at him, Micki saw he was no longer looking at her, but was staring at the night-blackened porthole. As if unaware of her, he went on, in the same hushed tone. "She offers me her innocence, her youth, her trust, then absolves me with her tears for my greedy use of them."

In the shadowy light Micki thought she saw his eyelashes flutter suspiciously, then all thought stopped as she was hauled, almost roughly, into his arms.

"You can have no idea what your words mean to me," Wolf whispered raggedly, "because I have no idea where to begin to express my feelings. But what I said was true. I am greedy and I don't want to waste one minute of our time together."

They left the boat in a once-again mist-shrouded predawn. Like the morning before, Micki woke to find Wolf getting dressed.

"Wolf?" The one softly murmured word held both a question and a plea for him to come back to bed.

"I was just going to wake you." Wolf's eyes devoured her. "It's time to go, baby."

"But, I don't—" Micki's protest died as his features settled into lines of hard determination. Trying a different tactic, she asked innocently, "Aren't you going to kiss me good morning?"

Although a smile curved his lips, he shook his head emphatically. "No way, honey. If I come over there, it'll be noon before we get off this tub. I want to get you home while there's at least a chance no one will see you. If anyone even suspects we've spent the weekend together, your reputation will be shot to hell."

"I don't care about that—" Micki began earnestly.

"I care." Wolf's tone was suddenly harsh. "And you should too." The fingers of his right hand raked through his hair and rubbed absently at the back of his neck. Wolf sighed and went on less harshly. "I'm eleven years older than you. Can you imagine your father's reaction if he found out about this?"

Micki could, only too well. The thought alone sent a shudder rippling through her slender frame. She groaned softly.

"Exactly," Wolf said flatly. "At any other time I wouldn't give one goddamn what your father, or anyone else for that matter, thought about me. But right now I can't afford that unconcern. So don't argue, babe. I'm going to go make some coffee. By the time it's ready I want to see you in the galley fully"—his eyes shifted to her discarded bikini and his tone went dry—"dressed."

They stepped off the boat into a pearl-white cloud. Halfway along the narrow pier Micki paused to look back at the apparition-like outline of the craft, bobbing gently in the ruffling bay waters. When she turned back to Wolf, her face was wistful, her eyes sad. One strong arm encircled her waist, drew her close. Bending over her, he murmured, "We'll come back, honey."

Micki's eyes lit up. "When? Can we come back tonight?" The light dimmed as he slowly shook his head and she walked beside him to the car park.

"Although I'm crazy about the way you look in a bikini, I want you to get all dressed up to go out for dinner tonight."

"Can't we have dinner on the boat?" The light was

back and for a moment he didn't answer, seemingly bemused by the sparkling blue of her eyes.

"You'd rather have dinner on the boat than go out somewhere?" Wolf laughed.

"Yes," Micki answered gently. "Can we? Please?"

"You're absolutely something else." Wolf's tone shivered over her skin like a caress. He stopped walking and turned to her, his arm tautening as he crushed her to him. In complete opposition to his crushing hold, his kiss was a tender blessing that robbed her lungs of air, her legs of strength.

"All right, we'll have dinner on the boat." He started moving again, his arm possessive around her waist. "But I still want you to get dressed up. I'll come for you about eight. I have an appointment in Cape May this afternoon." He stopped beside a late-model Lexus, unlocked the door, and held it open for her. Seated in the car, Micki watched him, loving the long, lean look of him, as he strode around the front of the car and slid into the seat beside her. Frowning, he turned to her. "If I can shorten the meeting, which I doubt, I'll call you. But I can't make any promises."

His tone held such finality Micki didn't have the courage to argue.

When he pulled up in front of her home, Wolf reached across her body to open her door, gave her a quick, hard kiss, and growled, "Get out of here, babe. I've got to get home and grab some rest or I'll be useless at the meeting this afternoon." The soulful eyes Micki lifted to his turned the growl into a groan. "Oh, God, baby, will you get out of the car?" His hands came up to cradle her face, his mouth was a hungrily searing brand. Then he moved back behind the wheel with an ordered, "Go."

Micki went, on the run, not stopping until she was inside her own bedroom. After stripping off the very wilted beachwear, she dove, stark naked, between the sheets.

Laughing and crying at the same time, she hugged herself fiercely. Oh, Lord, she was so crazily, wildly in love with that man, it was almost scary.

She woke late in the afternoon, automatically reaching for the solid bulk of Wolf's body. When her hand found nothing but emptiness, she opened her eyes and sighed on finding herself in her own bed. Stifling a yawn, she stretched contentedly. The sensuous movement of her body between the smooth sheets evoked the sensuous thoughts of Wolf's expertly arousing hands and she gasped softly at the sudden, sharp ache that invaded the lower part of her body, the small hard points that thrust against the sheet covering her breasts. God, she was well and truly caught, she thought fearfully, if the mere thought of him could have this kind of effect.

Rolling her head on the pillow, she stared at the fake-gem-encrusted tiny alarm clock on her small nightstand. Two fifty-eight. Micki groaned aloud. Five hours until she'd see him. Kicking off the sheet, she jumped out of bed. She had to do something to fill those hours. Pulling on a light cotton robe, she left the room and went to the kitchen.

Forty-five minutes later, Micki stood at the sink, a small smile curving her lips, washing the dishes. She hadn't realized she was so hungry! It had required a large glass of orange juice, two poached eggs, three slices of toast, and three cups of coffee to appease her suddenly ravenous appetite.

Leaving the kitchen spotless, she went back to her room, made her bed, then headed for the bathroom for a shampoo and a shower. Humming softly as she stood under the warm shower spray, Micki didn't hear her father and Regina enter the house. She was standing before the medicine cabinet mirror, blow drying her hair, when her father tapped on the door and called, "Hi, honey, will you be very long? I'd like a shower."

Shutting the dryer off, Micki disconnected the plug and opened the door. "Hi, Dad," she said as she leaned toward him and kissed his whisker-rough cheek. "Welcome home, have a good trip?"

"Gruesome," Bruce grimaced. "You know what New York is like in August. Why the hell these realtors had to have their conference there is beyond me." He sighed wearily. "I was tied up in meetings most of the time, which didn't do a thing for Regina's patience. She should have listened to me and stayed at home."

Fleetingly, and for the first time since her father's marriage, Micki thanked the powers-that-be for Regina's stubbornness. "Well, you're home now and the bathroom's all yours. You can have your shower. And, Dad"—one slim hand caressed his cheek—"have a shave too."

"Brat." A larger hand made contact with her bottom. Smiling happily, Micki went to her room. She was plugging the blow dryer into the wall socket by her dressing table when the phone rang. Wolf! The dryer dropped onto the table's mirror-bright surface with a clatter as Micki ran across the room. Flinging the door wide, she dashed along the hall and started down the stairs.

"Hello."

Micki was halfway down the stairs when she heard Regina answer the phone. She took one more step down then froze, her hand gripping the railing at Regina's velvety, incredibly sexy-sounding words.

"Wolf, darling, couldn't you wait? We haven't been in the house a half hour. I know how impatient you are and I was about to call you."

Eyes widening in disbelief, Micki waited breathlessly through the small silence while Regina listened to whatever Wolf was saying. When she spoke again, her words sent a shaft of pure hatred through Micki.

"The trip was exactly as you warned me it would be—

dreadful. I could have kicked myself for not staying here to go with you as you wanted me to." There was another short pause, then, "Bruce? No, he's having a shower, how could he know? I told you we just got in. Yes, of course, darling, I want that as badly as you do."

Feeling she couldn't bear to hear any more, Micki, moving like a zombie, started back up the stairs. The sound of her name stopped her.

"Micki? No, she's not here. But then, she rarely ever is." Regina paused to listen again, then replied with a sigh, "I don't know, possibly with Tony Menella, she's been seeing a lot of him lately. She does not confide in me, but I'm sure she doesn't know."

Ordering her numbed body to move, Micki retraced her steps to her bedroom. Standing in the middle of the room, she stared sightlessly at the wall. Wolf and Regina? The words became a tortured scream in her mind.

Wolf and Regina? Oh, dear God, could Regina be one of the women who had cried on receiving a gift, usually expensive, from Wolf? Shaking all over, Micki blinked her eyes and when she did, her gaze touched the bed. Hot color flared into her cheeks on the thought that Wolf had robbed her father like an outlaw. First his wife, now his daughter.

Choking back the bitter gall that rose in her throat, Micki silently berated herself. *You fool, you young, stupid, virginal fool. Correction,* she thought, fighting against a growing hysteria, *ex-virginal fool.*

"Micki?"

The sound of Regina's soft voice, followed by a gentle tap on her door, turned the budding hysteria into cold fury. Before she could answer, the door was opened and Regina entered the room, closing the door behind her.

"I thought you were out. Have you been in your room all this—"

"What do you want?" The voice that slashed across Regina's words held cold contempt and a new maturity.

"Micki." Regina hesitated, then asked bluntly, "Were you out with Wolf Renninger while your father and I were away?"

"That's none of your business." Striding across the room, Micki brushed by Regina on her way to the door. At the contact, her robe parted at her throat, revealing the abrasions David's plundering mouth had left on her skin.

"Did Wolf do that?" Regina gasped, pointing at the dull red mark.

"That's also none of your business," Micki snapped, one hand covering the spot. "I want you to leave my room." Her other hand grasped the doorknob to yank the door open but released it again at Regina's sharp words.

"You are a fool."

Spinning to face her, Micki looked her straight in the eye and spat, "Aren't we all?"

"Micki, you don't know this man." Regina's tone held an oddly pleading note. "Believe me, he lives up to his name. The women buzz around him like bees at a honey pot. I must make this my business if you're to be kept from being hurt."

"I can take care of myself." Micki actually had to fight the urge to laugh in Regina's face. Hurt? Regina didn't know the meaning of the word.

"With a man like Wolf?" Regina asked, then answered her own question. "I hardly think so. He told me he was picking you up at eight." At Micki's nod a strange, almost crafty look entered her eyes. Very softly she said, "Don't be surprised if he's—well—somewhat tired. Or were you aware of the fact that he's spent the afternoon with a woman in Cape May? He was calling from her home actually."

Micki didn't want to believe her, but how could Regina know he was in Cape May unless he'd told her? Sickness churning in her stomach, Micki fought to maintain a cool facade. Wanting to get Regina out of the room before she humiliated herself by throwing up in front of her, Micki waved her hand airily, forced herself to laugh lightly.

"I had no intention of going out with him," she lied. "I told him I would to get rid of him." Drawing a deep breath, she rushed on. "Do me a favor, Regina. When Wolf comes, tell him I'm out," she paused, then added, "with Tony."

FIVE

A chill rippled through Micki's body, partly from the dampness, partly from her thoughts. Tugging the edges of her sweater together, she stood up and went into the house. After locking the doors and hanging the sweater in the closet, she went up the stairs slowly, her face blank of expression, her eyes dull.

Six years! For six long years she'd suppressed all thoughts of him. And now, after being home only one day, he filled her mind to the exclusion of everything else. Why? Why had he been on the street at the exact time she stopped for that car? If she hadn't seen him, spoken to him. But she had seen him, had spoken to him. More stupid still, she had snapped at his tauntingly tossed bait.

Closing her bedroom door quietly, she walked across the darkened room, sank wearily into the fanned-back peacock chair, clasped her hands tightly in her lap. She was trembling all over and she felt sick to her stomach, as sick as she'd felt that night.

She had not gone with him that night, had not seen him. But she had heard him. From her bedroom doorway, she'd heard her father, innocently, for he really thought what he said was the truth. *Tell Wolf that she'd gone out with Tony Menella.* And she'd heard Wolf reply, "But we had a date for dinner," his voice rough with anger and confusion.

A shudder shook Micki's slender body. Closing her

eyes, she rested her head back against the smooth wicker. He had called every day during that following week, and each time either Regina or her father told him the same thing. She was with Tony. She hadn't been, of course. She'd been hiding in her bedroom like a fugitive. And like a fugitive on the run, she stole away the next week without seeing him or talking to him again. Her father never knew the real reason she insisted on going back to school early.

But running away had not ended it. Oh, he had not tried to see her at school or contact her in any way, but he was with her in more ways than one. Although remembering the hurt caused actual pain, she had been unable to stop thinking about him. The feel of him, the scent of him, the taste of him, was in her blood and no amount of self-determination had succeeded in repelling him. And then, four weeks after she'd returned to school, she knew the life of him was inside her too.

Strangely, the realization that his child was growing inside her body banished the pain, replaced the hurt with deep contentment. She'd decided that even if she could not have the man, she could, and would, cherish his seed. There would be problems, not the least of which was her father, but thoughts of the baby had eased the ache in her heart and she grew daily more determined to have it.

Her euphoria had lasted two weeks. A euphoria only slightly dampened by her sudden aversion to eggs in the morning. Then horrible cramping pain in the middle of one night and a sticky, wet, red-stained sheet had burst her bubble of happiness. When she wakened in a hospital near the campus, one look at the faces of the doctor and nurse who were beside her bed told the story. She was one again, her body had repelled Wolf's issue. It was while she lay in that sterile room alone, once again hurting unbearably, that her mind repelled Wolf's image.

No one except the hospital personnel knew of the miscarriage and three weeks after her twentieth birthday she left school. Luckily she had found a job and a room within a week of her arrival in Wilmington. She had not gone back until her father's illness two years ago. At that time she had not seen Wolf, nor had his name been mentioned. She had assumed he was no longer there, had moved on to greener pastures.

Over the years she had dated at least a dozen different men. And, in fact, was seeing one man exclusively before she came home. His name was Darrel and he'd asked her to marry him. She had been completely honest with him, without mentioning a name or circumstances. He knew he would not be the first, yet he'd asked her to marry him. Darrel was handsome, and Darrel was rich, and Darrel was successful. The perfect answer to any young woman's romantic dreams. But Micki was not any young woman. She had left him in Wilmington, two nights before, with her promise to think about his proposal.

Micki moved her head restlessly back and forth against the wicker, not even attempting to wipe away the tears that ran freely down her face. She knew what her answer to Darrel would be. She liked him, she respected him, but she did not love him. She loved Wolf. It was crazy. It was stupid. It was also an irrevocable fact. Nothing that had happened over the last six years had changed that. Within two nights and one day he had wrapped himself immovably around her heart. She had suspected even then that she would always love him. Now there was no doubt in her mind at all, and she could not go to Darrel loving Wolf.

Sighing softly, Micki stood up and began to undress. She would have to contact Darrel soon, give him her answer, and that answer would have to be no.

In sudden anger Micki tossed her clothes into the hamper, tugged a silky nightdress over her head, and flung herself across her bed. Burying her face in her pillow, she wept quietly, damning the night she'd laid eyes on Wolf Renninger, damning the love for him that consumed her, and damning her own stupidity in accepting his challenge. She had been all right as long as she could not see him, be near him. But she knew that if she went with him Friday night it would just be a matter of time before she found herself in his arms, and in his bed, again. The urge to surrender that had swept through her that fateful afternoon had been all the proof she needed. She loved him and in loving him she wanted him desperately.

Rolling onto her back, Micki brushed impatiently at the tears on her cheeks. For six years she had repressed all her normal physical wants and needs. She had been called frigid. Some had even suggested therapy was called for. Micki had laughed at some and ignored them all. She knew exactly how normal her response could be. She had felt the hunger fire her blood. That hunger was for one man only. She had found the kisses, the light caresses, of several men pleasing. But only one man's mouth and hands could set her whole being alight. And now that one man, that Wolf, was stalking her again.

"No!"

The firm exclamation sounded loud in the dark room. Sitting up in the middle of the bed, Micki clenched her hands into fists. She could not go through that pain again. She would not expose herself to it. This time when Wolf came to pick her up she really would not be home. The decision made, Micki lay down again and went to sleep.

On Thursday Micki called the shop in Atlantic City to ask if it would be convenient for her to stop in sometime Friday afternoon. The enthusiastic reception her request was met with left her with a feeling of deep satisfaction.

Friday afternoon she bathed and dressed with extra care, then went looking for Regina to tell her she would not be home for dinner.

"If Cindy or anyone calls," she tossed casually over her shoulder, as she headed for the door, "tell them I expect to be late getting home and I'll return their call tomorrow."

Not wanting to field any questions Regina might throw, she hurried out the door and into her car. During the drive up the coast she determinedly pushed all thoughts of Wolf and his possible reaction to her action out of her mind.

It was a beautiful, hot day, the sun a bold yellow disc in a cloudless, blatantly blue sky. A day, Micki thought reminiscently, for healthy young things to laugh and romp on the scorching hot sand.

After parking the car near the hotel in which the shop was located, Micki walked along slowly, craning her neck like a tourist at the many changes that had taken place in the years since she'd last been in the city. So many of the old familiar buildings along the long boardwalk were gone, replaced by the large, elaborate hotels. The air literally reverberated with the sounds of construction.

Inside the hotel the air hummed a different tune. The place was crowded with people, all, it seemed, with one objective in mind—to get into the casino as quickly as possible.

Weaving in and out of the throng, Micki made her way to the reception desk. The cool, unruffled young man behind the desk gave her directions to the boutique politely, while running a practiced eye over her face and figure. When she thanked him, equally politely, he gave her an engaging grin and asked if she was free that evening.

"No, sorry," Micki grinned back. "I have an appointment."

"Why is it always some other guy that has all the luck?" He smiled sadly, then turned to the very impatient lady standing next to Micki.

The short exchange amused her, and with a jaunty step Micki walked through the lobby to the escalator the young man had indicated. As the steps moved up, her eyes roamed over the interior of the casino. The room was huge yet, incredibly, every square inch appeared to be occupied by humanity.

At the top of the escalator Micki paused to get her bearings. Directly across from her was the small cocktail lounge the desk clerk had mentioned, so the boutique should be a little farther down this wide expanse of hall. She found the shop exactly where he'd said she would.

With a knowledgeable eye Micki studied the displays inside the small windows on either side of the entrance to the shop. The one window proclaimed sun and fun with slightly reduced summer togs. The other window was a forecast of coming fall with soft plaid skirts and cashmere blazers. Very nice, Micki mused, very, very nice.

The manager of the shop turned out to be the woman Micki had spoken to the day before, and she was turned out very well indeed. A few years older than Micki, the woman, though not really beautiful, gave a good impression of being so. Her hair was a natural flaming red. Her skin a sun-kissed ivory. She was taller than Micki and her very slender body was beautifully clothed in an exquisite raw silk sheath that had Micki murmuring a silent prayer of thanks for the urge that had made her dress with such care.

While Micki had been studying the woman, the redhead had been making her own evaluation and they seemed to reach the same conclusions at exactly the same time. For just as Micki was giving thanks, the redhead smiled and extended a slim, long-nailed hand.

"Jennell Clark," she offered in a soft drawl. "And you must be Micki Durrant."

"I am." The hand Micki stretched out was just as slim, the rounded nails every bit as long. "How do you do?"

"Very well, actually." Jennell's soft laugh was a delight to the ears. "Glad to have you with us." Her eyes ran over Micki again. "If you buy for the shop as well as you buy for yourself I have a feeling I'll be doing even better."

"Thank you," Micki laughed with her. "I'll do my best." Then unable to exactly place the soft drawl in Jennell's tone, she asked, "Are you from the South?"

"Yes," Jennell again favored her with a laugh. "But not too far south, Richmond, Virginia. Where are you from?"

"Only a little south of here," Micki grinned. "Ocean City, New Jersey."

Jennell introduced her to the shop's other two employees, a petite, pretty young woman named Lucy and a strikingly beautiful black woman named Georgine. The three of them filled Micki in on the running of the store in no time.

The rest of the afternoon flew by so quickly, Micki was surprised when Jennell said it was time to close the shop. She was on the point of saying good-bye when Jennell asked, "Do you have plans for dinner? I mean do you have a date or are you expected home or anything?"

Micki thought fleetingly of Wolf, then shook her head. "No, no date or plans or anyone expecting me."

"Then come have dinner with us," Jennell coaxed. "Lucy's guy is out of town. Georgine's between guys and I"—an impish smile curved her red lips—"I'm punishing my man at the moment."

"Punishing?" Micki laughed.

"Well, just a little," the redhead drawled. "He was getting much too possessive and I'm letting him know I won't be owned. Will you come?"

As both Lucy and Georgine added their pleas to Jennell's, Micki agreed and the four of them left the shop, all talking at the same time.

They had dinner in a small restaurant where the decor was unexceptional and the food out of this world. While they ate, Micki learned that all three women came from other shops in the chain. Jennell from one in Washington, D.C., Lucy from one in Baltimore, and Georgine from one in New York City.

"I've been here for over a year," Jennell volunteered. "Georgine came a few months after I did and Lucy joined us three months ago. Your predecessor came from Philadelphia at the same time as I did." She fluttered her lashes dramatically, drawled oversweetly. "She's been transferred to Miami." Jennell smiled derisively. "She went too far with the boss."

"You didn't like her?" Micki's question was greeted by rolled eyes and snorts of laughter.

"Honey," Jennell drawled softly, "I could sooner like a rattlesnake."

"She really wasn't very pleasant to work with." This from the small, somewhat shy, Lucy.

"She was a first-rate bitch," Georgine, every inch as worldly as she was beautiful, stated flatly.

"Yes," Jennell concurred. "Our buyer decided to play footsie with the owner. He shipped her out when she became demanding. I mean"—the drawl was laid on thick—"one just does not fool around with that man. Let alone demand marriage."

Micki frowned. When Jennell had said the boss, Micki assumed she'd been referring to their regional manager, Hank Carlton. But she'd just now said the owner and Micki had never met the owner, had not, in fact, ever heard his name mentioned. She was about to ask Jennell who the owner was when Lucy said something about finding a new man for Georgine and the thought went out of her head.

Their suggestions to Georgine ran from the ridiculous from Lucy:

"You could take an ad in the personal column like: Wanted: good-looking man between the ages of twenty-five and forty, must be fantastic dancer." To Micki she confided, "Georgine would rather dance than eat."

To the outrageous from Jennell:

"You could always station yourself on the boardwalk and smile sweetly at all the better-looking men. Of course," she drawled heavily, "you'd have no idea which ones could dance. But then, look at all the fun you could have teaching them."

"The way my luck's been running," Georgine grinned, "if I took a newspaper ad I'd only get replies from the uglies and the crazies." The grin grew wider and her eyes sparkled impishly. "And if I stationed myself on the board-walk, I'd probably wind up with my fanny in the canny."

A smile teased Micki's lips as she drove home that evening. She had enjoyed the dinner and the company very much. They had lingered, laughing, over their coffee until the arch look of the proprietor sent them, still laughing, out of the restaurant.

The three women had insisted on escorting Micki to her car, where they stood talking for an additional twenty minutes. By the time Micki drove her car off the parking lot she felt as if she'd known them all her life.

She'd had a good time, she told herself as she drove the car up the driveway of her father's house, a very good time. She had hardly thought about Wolf all evening, she realized as her fingers turned the key, shutting off the engine. Well, she mentally qualified, she hadn't thought about him too often, she admitted as she pulled on the hand brake. So, okay, he'd been in her thoughts constantly, she finally confessed disgustedly as she swung out of the car and headed for the kitchen door. But she had enjoyed her day and her evening.

"That you, princess?" her father called as she closed the door.

"No," Micki called back. "I'm a burglar, I've come for the silver."

"Good luck," he laughed. "We are strictly a stainless steel family."

"Well, in that case, I guess I'll go back to being the princess." Micki smiled, entering the living room. "At least I'll have a title, even if there is no silver to inherit."

"Hi, honey." Although her father smiled, one brow went up in question. "Did you forget you had a date this evening?"

"A date?"

Even with the sudden acceleration of her pulse, Micki had somehow managed to keep her tone innocent.

"With Wolf Renninger," Bruce prompted gently, then he winced. "I wouldn't say he was exactly happy when I told him you weren't here." He paused, his eyes narrowing in thought. "I had the oddest feeling that I'd gone through the same thing before." A frown leveled his brows. "What are you up to, young lady?"

"I—I'm not up to anything," Micki murmured nervously. She hated deceiving her father, yet she couldn't bring herself to confide in him. "I got caught up in the business of the shop and when the shop manager asked me to join her and the two women who work in the store, I accepted. I simply forgot I'd made the date with Wolf."

Micki wet her dry lips, trying not to see the sharp-eyed glance Regina gave her. Her father's memory might be a little cloudy, but Regina's certainly wasn't.

"Wolf has called twice in the last hour," Regina supplied quietly. "He seemed to be becoming angrier every time I had to tell him you hadn't come home yet."

"I think if the phone rings you had better answer it," Bruce advised. "You forgot the date and you can apologize your way out of it."

The words were no sooner out of his mouth when the doorbell rang. Micki's body jerked as though someone had touched a live wire to her.

"Go to it, girl." Her father flipped his hand in the direction of the front door. "I think there's little doubt who that is." He stood up, his hand reaching for Regina's. "We'll be discreet and give you some privacy."

The bell sounded again and Micki started for the door, her steps betraying her trepidation. Her father's soft laugh sounded from the stairs.

"You're not going to the gallows, honey," he chided. "Just give him your sweetest smile and he'll forget why he's angry."

I'll bet, Micki thought grimly, her hand shaking as she reached for the doorknob. She swung the door open bravely, then bit her lip fearfully. Wolf, looking hard-jawed and cold-eyed and madder than hell, stood, hands thrust into his pants pockets, staring balefully at her. Stepping out onto the porch, Micki closed the door softly behind her, her mind searching for something to say. Wolf brought her search to an end.

"I don't believe it." His cool tone, so opposed to the hot anger in his eyes, sent a tremor bouncing down her spine. "I really don't believe it."

"What?" Micki was almost afraid to ask.

"You did it again." A touch of wonder colored the cool tone. "Do you get your kinky little kicks out of standing up many of your dates, or do I alone hold that honor?"

"Wolf." Micki had to fight to keep her voice even. "I'm sorry."

"Yeah." Wolf smiled crookedly. "I'll bet you are."

"All right, I'm not," Micki snapped. "If you'll recall, I didn't want to go out with you in the first place."

Angry herself now, she moved away from him, down the porch steps, and along the front walk to the pavement without the slightest idea of where she was going.

"But you did agree to have dinner with me." His long strides brought him alongside her before she'd taken six steps on the pavement. "Didn't you?"

"Yes," she admitted, turning south when she reached the corner.

Matching his stride to hers, Wolf walked beside her silently. *At least he didn't ask me where I'm going,* she thought wryly.

"Where the hell are you going?"

His impatient words followed on the heels of her thought and Micki couldn't repress the smile that tugged at her lips.

"I said something funny?" His tone was not amused.

"No," Micki sighed. "It's just that I don't know where I'm going."

"That's pretty damned obvious," Wolf drawled sardonically, leaving little doubt in her mind he meant the direction of her life, not her impromptu walk.

"I just felt like walking," Micki shrugged in annoyance.

"I see," Wolf drawled softly.

"You didn't have to come along," she snapped irritably.

"True," he agreed, with a maddening calmness.

Their quick stride ate up the blocks during their exchange and when they had to stop at a corner to wait for traffic Micki realized with surprise that they were near the city's shopping district. Grasping her arm, Wolf began walking east.

"Where the hell are *you* going?" Micki flung his words back at him.

"To the boardwalk," he answered imperturbably.

"Whatever for?" she demanded.

"Why does anyone stroll the boards?" He shrugged, elegantly. "To gaze at the ocean, to feel the sea breeze against the skin, to wander in and out of the shops." He slanted a barbed look at her. "To have something to eat. At least those who have been stood up and didn't eat any dinner do."

His hand placed firmly at the back of her waist propelled her up the ramp and onto the boardwalk still crowded with people at ten o'clock at night.

"Come on, babe, I'll buy you a slice of pizza at Mack and Manco's." His eyes raked her face. "Not exactly what I'd planned but," he shrugged, "I like the pie and it will fill up the hole in my stomach."

Unsure if he was telling the truth or not about not having eaten, Micki allowed him to lead her to the pizza stand. The stand's outside counter was three deep with people and, grasping her hand, Wolf edged around the bodies and drew her inside the shop. While they waited for two seats to become vacant Micki watched, as fascinated as she'd been as a young girl, the swift, dexterous movements of the young men behind the counter as they assembled the pizzas and slid them into and out of the ovens. And the aroma! Even though she'd had dinner, Micki ran her tongue over her lips in anticipation.

Once seated, they were served quickly and Micki was soon convinced Wolf had not been lying about not eating. He consumed four slices of pizza to her one and as soon as they were out of the shop said, "Let's walk awhile, then we'll hunt up some dessert."

"On top of all that pizza!" Micki exclaimed.

"Look at me, Micki," Wolf urged chidingly. "Tom Thumb I'm not. I've got a big body and it's got to be filled occasionally. It is now"—he glanced at his watch—"ten thirty-five. That pizza was the first solid food I've had since somewhere around noon." His tone went bland. "Yes, I am going to sink some dessert on top of all that pizza."

"Solid food?" Micki jabbed at him, as if that's all she'd heard of his statement.

"Did I ask you if you'd been drinking?" Wolf jabbed back harder.

Fuming, Micki walked beside him, uncomfortably aware he was laughing, if silently, at her. After several quiet minutes, curiosity and a concern she didn't want to feel got the better of her.

"Were you drinking, Wolf," she asked softly, "on an empty stomach?"

"I had a couple of beers in a bar over at the Point," Wolf replied equally softly. "To pass the time while I waited for my date to put in an appearance."

Feeling her face flush, Micki looked away from him and glanced into the faces of the people moving around them. Up until that point her mind had been so full of Wolf she'd been only surfacely aware of the hum of voices, the sound of laughter around her. Tugging her hand free of his grasp, she walked to the rail and stared out at the dark, white-capped water.

"Why didn't you keep our date?"

Wolf bent his long frame beside her, rested his forearms on the top rail, propped one foot on the bottom rail. He had removed his suit jacket and it dangled in the air over the beach, held in the fingers of one hand.

Micki's eyes clung to the gentle movement of the jacket, held so carelessly in those strong fingers. Not unlike the way he handles women, Micki thought suddenly, a shiver feathering her back. The idea of being held in those strong hands, even carelessly, made her feel sick with longing.

"I asked you a question." Wolf's edged tone jolted her back to reality.

"I went up to Atlantic City this afternoon to introduce myself to the manager of the shop I've been transferred to," Micki explained nervously. "We got talking shop talk and the time slipped away. By the time the shop closed, I'd forgotten about our date and when she asked me if I'd like to have dinner with her and the other two women who work there, I said yes."

"You are a very bad liar, babe," Wolf grated, not looking at her. "Now would you like to tell me the real reason?"

"Honestly, Wolf, you are—" Micki began angrily.

"Honestly?" He cut her off. "I don't think so, sweetie. I honestly think you've been lying through your teeth. Why the hell won't you level with me? Did you go out with another guy?" He was on the attack now and Micki felt cornered by his stinging tone. "Someone you ran into after you agreed to go with me? If so, why the hell didn't you call me and break the date?"

Micki turned to face him, her eyes bright with anger. "Would you have let me break the date?"

Wolf's silvery eyes turned the color of cold steel as he stared into hers. "Probably not," he finally snapped, after a few long, nerve-racking seconds.

"That's what I thought." Micki wrenched her eyes from his, stared sightlessly out over the ocean. "So I simply decided not to keep it."

"*Were* you with another man?" Wolf's tone held a strange, breathless quality Micki couldn't define. For a brief moment she considered telling him she had been out with another man, then she sighed and murmured, "No."

She heard her sigh echo beside her before his voice, close to her ear, sent tiny little chills skimming over her body.

"What are you afraid of, honey?"

"Wh-what do you mean?" she stammered. "Afraid of?"

"Are you afraid, if you go with me, I'll get you alone and want to touch you?" His breath fluttered the hair near her ear; his words started a fluttering in her midsection. "Afraid I'll want to hold you in my arms and kiss you?" His voice went low. "Afraid I'll want to make love to you?"

Micki's hands gripped the rail. She couldn't answer, she couldn't move. In fact, she could hardly breathe.

"You'd be right." Wolf's voice was very low now, low and urgent. "I do want to do all those things."

Motionless, unseeing, Micki stood as if fused to the boards beneath her feet, the need to have him do all those things draining all the color from her face. Oh, God, how she ached to be in his arms, and yes, in his bed. Her own thoughts frightened her into action. Pushing herself away from the rail, she dashed across the boardwalk, dodging in and out, around the startled faces of people. Wolf caught up to her as she came off the ramp.

"Running away again?" His tone was now sharp with exasperation.

"I simply want to go home." Micki shrugged his hand from her arm. He slid it around her waist, held on tightly.

"What are you running from, do you know?" Wolf asked tiredly. "Did you know six years ago?"

"Shut up," Micki cried, then lowered her voice at the sharp glance a man passing them threw at her. "I don't want to talk about six years ago. I don't even want to think about it."

"Why?" Wolf rapped softly. "Why don't you want to talk about it?" Micki was almost running in her urgent need to get home. Wolf tightened his hand at her waist even more, forcing her to slow down. "Why don't you want to think about it?"

"I told you why in your apartment the other day." Micki lied frantically. "It's dead and there's nothing as dead as a dead love affair."

Wolf came to an abrupt halt and grasped her shoulder to turn her toward him.

"So that's what it was," he rasped, "a love affair." His soft laughter had the sound of rusty metal being scraped. Micki felt fear clog her throat. "I'll give you a hundred dollars against a Mexican peso I can breathe life into it again." His fingers dug into her soft flesh to draw her closer. "What kind of gambler are you?"

His mouth touched hers and at that moment a car full

of teenage boys drove by. Laughing and hooting, the boys called encouraging suggestions to Wolf and though he released her, he threw them a wicked grin.

Micki used his momentary inattention to move away from him. Wolf was right behind her.

"For God's sake, kid, slow down." His big hand swallowed hers, held fast. "I wasn't going to hurt you."

The mere thought of you hurts me, Micki's mind cried silently. Shaking her head to dislodge the thought, she said bitingly, "I know that, but I hate being put into a position to receive that kind of taunting catcall." She tried to tug her hand free, shot him a sour look when his fingers tightened. "And I'm not a kid."

"Then stop acting like one," he bit back. "Those boys didn't mean any harm." Micki withdrew into a stony silence. Walking steadily, her eyes straight ahead, she sighed with relief when they turned the corner onto her street. She couldn't wait to get into the house for the simple reason she wanted to be with him so badly.

Wolf stopped, pulling her up short, several yards from the house. With a casual wave of his hand he indicated a flame-red Ferrari parked at the curb.

"Come have a drink with me," he coaxed. "I haven't had my dessert yet."

"I don't want a drink," Micki said flatly, swinging away from him again. "I'm not thirsty, I'm tired."

Hurrying up the front walk, she prayed her father had not come back downstairs and locked the door. She had to get away from Wolf. She knew it. She had been tempted to go with him, had wanted to go with him. And she knew that given even the few minutes it would take her father to come down and open the door for her, Wolf would be able to persuade her into going with him.

"Why are you so tired?" Wolf's hand on her arm made her pause in front of the door. "It's only eleven fifteen."

"I'm not physically tired, Wolf." Micki had not turned

her head, and her words seemed to bounce off the door, back into her face.

Wolf's hand left her arm to circle her waist and she felt her throat go dry when he stepped closer to her. With trembling fingers she clutched the doorknob as if grasping for a lifeline.

"Micki, baby." Wolf's soft voice, only inches from her ear, was a nerve-shattering temptation. "If you're not really tired, come with me."

"But I am really tired," Micki insisted in a dry, crackling voice. Her hand turned the knob and pushed, relief washing over her when the door gave under pressure. "I'm tired of this conversation. I'm tired of defending myself." Turning her head, she forced herself to meet his gaze levelly. "I'm tired of your company, Wolf."

Wolf stepped back as if she'd actually struck him. His face drained of all expression and quite a bit of color. His lips thinned. His eyes narrowed.

"Okay, baby." His lips barely seemed to move around the muttered words. "I guess you can't make it any clearer than that." He turned away, started down the porch steps, then turned back swiftly. "But if you change your mind, you'll have to call me. I won't be calling you." His lips twisted, almost as if he were in pain. His voice rasped against her ears. "I've had about all I can take of your brand of rejection."

Micki gasped audibly. Stung by what she considered was the unfairness of his taunting words, she retaliated without thinking.

"Don't hold your breath."

"Very classy," Wolf drawled stingingly. "And you say you're not a kid. You've said very little to prove otherwise tonight."

His silvery eyes, sharp with scorn, moved dismissively over her body, then, with a shrug, he turned away again.

Hurt unbearably by his sarcastic words and the scorn in his eyes, Micki was goaded into trying to hurt back.

"If you hurry, Wolf," she called softly, as he started down the walk, "you can drink a gallon of dessert before the bar closes."

"Grow up, kid," Wolf tossed back disparagingly, not even bothering to look back.

SIX

Wolf's parting shot nagged at Micki's mind for most of the following week. She just could not decide what exactly he'd meant by it. Not "Grow up, kid." She understood that well enough. But the prior one, the one about his having had enough of her brand of rejection, that bothered her. She was sure the gibe could not be taken at face value, for that would indicate his being hurt, and that concept she could not accept.

During that week, the last of her vacation, Micki kept very busy and away from Regina's questioning eyes. She spent hours on the beach, soaking up sun, acquiring a deep tan that made her eyes look an even brighter blue. She saw, or spoke on the phone to every one of her friends still at home, including Tony, who called and asked her to have dinner with him on Saturday night. She accepted eagerly for two reasons. One, she would be truly delighted to see Tony again and two, she was ready to jump at any excuse to get out of the house.

Determined to keep her mind occupied every waking minute, she lived that week on the run. From house to beach, back to the house to shower, then out again to have lunch or shop with Cindy, or visit her old haunts. For several hours on Tuesday afternoon she lost herself in the nineteenth century by way of the Historical Museum. All other thoughts were sent packing as her imagination was caught, then consumed, by the lifelike reality of the priceless antique furniture and household articles used in the display areas set up as living room, dining room, bedroom, kitchen, and nursery.

A small smile tugged at her bemused expression as she imagined herself and her friends dressed in the apparel worn at the turn of the century, carefully preserved and kept in glass cases, in the Fashion Room.

As she moved slowly through the Sindia Room, she could almost feel the anxiety of the crew of the four-masted bark when it was driven onto the beach in a gale on December 15, 1901.

The contemplative state induced by her visit into yesteryear stayed with her through the remainder of the day and evening and left her with the surety that an individual life was indeed too short to be wasted.

On Thursday evening she agreed to go with her father and Regina to the Music Pier for the concert given nightly by the Ocean City Pops. Her father and Regina went inside the large building on the pier while Micki sat on a bench outside as she had years before, watching the ocean's constant movement while she listened to the music.

The strains of Rodgers and Hammerstein music, blending with the muted roar of the sea, evoked memories of her girlhood. In the years she'd been away, she hadn't consciously realized how much she'd missed it all. And now, the atmosphere, the ambience, seemed to seep through her skin into her heart. Irrevocably her wandering thoughts led to Wolf.

Moving restlessly on the slatted wood bench, she fought in vain against the image that would no longer be pushed away. Silvery eyes mocked her struggle. Sighing softly, Micki closed her eyes while the essence of him took control of her senses, her emotions. Where was he tonight? What was he doing? Most importantly, who was he doing it with? Her own thoughts bedeviled and hurt her, yet she could no longer keep them at bay. She was resentful, hurt, jealous of his activities, his companions, even though she knew she had no right to be. She loved him distractedly, passionately, and that love had the effect of slashing her to ribbons inside.

She needed him in every way, and the growing intensity of that need sparked near panic. With a sickening feeling of humiliation clogging her throat, Micki faced the realization that unless she found a way to dislodge his occupation of her mind she would be reduced to calling him, as he had suggested she should.

With determination spawned by desperation, she made plans for the rest of the summer, pushing aside the nagging reminder that the best laid plans . . . She had to overcome her emotional obsession with him. She had to—somehow. For one tiny moment she allowed herself the remembered breathlessness aroused by his arms, his mouth, then, with a quick, sad shake of her head she wished him to Siberia, or some other, much hotter, place.

The sound of the sea and the music lulling her into a somewhat dreamlike state of wishful thinking, Micki convinced herself of her eventual success. She would throw herself vigorously into her new job and fill her non-working hours by finding and settling into a new apartment. Even though she had made arrangements to have her things packed and trucked to her father's house when her lease ran out at the end of August, she could take a run up to Wilmington to oversee the removal. Born of desperation, ideas popped into her mind. There were any number of things she could do to stay busy and, she vowed fervently, she would do them, all of them, to escape the hold Wolf had on her.

Riding the crest of optimism as bravely as a surfer skimming a wave, Micki walked home from the concert with a jaunty stride, humming snatches of the music she'd heard.

"I get the distinct impression you enjoyed the concert," her father teased.

"Very much," Micki affirmed, flashing him a smile. "I always have. The tenor soloist was pretty good, at least what I could hear out at the rail sounded good."

"I liked the aria the soprano sang," Regina inserted quietly. "Even though I can't remember the name of it and your father knows absolutely nothing about opera. Do you know it, Micki?"

Know it? Micki hadn't even heard it. Shaking her head, she frowned.

"No, I'm sorry, Regina, I'm afraid I don't know any more about opera than Dad does."

"It doesn't matter really," Regina smiled. "It's just been tantalizing the edge of my memory, if you know what I mean?"

Did she ever, Micki groaned silently. When it came to a subject tantalizing the memory, she was an expert. Veering sharply from the thought, she launched into another song, singing where she knew the words, humming where she didn't.

"Do you have plans for the weekend, honey?" Bruce's soft voice cut into her slightly off-key version of "A Cockeyed Optimist."

"Yes," Micki nodded. "I've been invited to Cindy and Benny's for dinner tomorrow and I have a date with Tony Saturday."

Micki didn't miss the sharp-eyed glance Regina shot her at the mention of Tony's name. In an effort to block any questions from her stepmother, she rushed on. "Why? Was there something you wanted me to do?"

"No, no," Bruce assured her. "We were invited to a cookout Saturday evening and you were included, if you were free."

"A cookout? Where?" Micki asked curiously.

"At Betty and Jim Grant's," Regina answered for her

husband. "Betty wanted to meet you and thought this might be a good time and way."

"And I would like to finally meet her," Micki assured her. For Micki, Regina's friend Betty had been a warm voice on the phone. They had become friends while Micki was away. Although she had not intruded at the time of Bruce's illness, her voice had been a bracing encouragement at the other end of the line during those nerve-racking days. "Ask her if I may have a raincheck."

"Not necessary," Bruce put in smoothly. "I would like you to keep two weeks from Saturday open, honey. There's a celebration party being planned for that night and, as the Grants will be there, you will meet Betty then."

"A celebration party?" Micki's brows went up. "For what?"

"A big-time developer and several realtors, myself included, are on the verge of closing a very big deal. It's been in the works for some time, and we decided a celebration was in order. We'd like you with us for two reasons. First, simply to have you join us in celebrating the successful conclusion to some very long, hard negotiations. And secondly, because it will be the last evening we'll spend together for a while as"—he paused to glance at his wife—"Regina and I will be flying to the West Coast the following afternoon."

"You're actually going?" Micki cried happily. "Terrific. How long will you be gone? Where are you going? I mean, are you going to stay in Frisco the whole time or are you planning to take in other places—Vegas, Mexico?"

"I believe you are nearly as excited as we are," Bruce laughed when Micki finally ran down. They were almost home and as they turned onto the front walk he dropped an arm around her shoulders. "The minute we get into the house we'll show you our itinerary."

He removed his arm to unlock the door. "We plan to be gone the last two weeks of August." With a wide courtly sweep of his arm he ushered them inside. "So will you go to the party with us?"

"Yes, of course, if you want me to go," Micki answered quickly. "Now, lead me to your itinerary."

They sat around the kitchen table, tall, moisture-beaded glasses of iced tea in front of them, until after midnight, Regina and Bruce talking at the same time, cutting in on each other as they outlined their plans for Micki.

For Micki, Friday evening was an unqualified success. Cindy had gone all out in her preparations for dinner and the dining-room table gleamed with her best china and crystal (Micki's wedding gift to them). The menu complemented the entree of fried chicken. The consomme was delicious, the small parslied potatoes cooked to just the right peak, and the tiny creamed peas and pearl onions tender. For dessert Cindy served a rich homemade cheesecake Micki was sure she could not possibly manage, but she did.

"Is this the same girl who could not boil an egg seven years ago?" Micki asked Benny with not altogether mock surprise.

"Can you believe it?" Benny laughed. "You should see the pile of cookbooks this woman has collected." His eyes caressed Cindy's face. "She has been a very busy lady since you left, Micki. She's learned to sew so well she now makes most of her own clothes and now she is knitting." His tone was so full of pride, his eyes so full of tenderness as he gazed at his wife, Micki felt the hot sting of tears behind her lids. "I swear," he murmured, "she began knitting tiny things the day after she conceived."

"You big oaf, will you stop?" Cindy's glowing face proclaimed her love as she chided Benny. "You're embarrassing me."

"Why?" Benny's hand caught and held Cindy's tightly. "Because I love you and I don't care who knows it?" He lifted her hand to his lips, bestowed a light kiss before adding, "Besides which, Micki's our friend, our best friend, why would you be embarrassed in front of her?"

"Oh, Benny."

Cindy's half sigh, half whisper brought a lump to Micki's throat and in an attempt to dislodge it she drawled dryly, "I can do a fantastic disappearing act if you two want to be alone."

"Would you?" Benny teased.

"Don't you dare," Cindy gasped.

The banter flew back and forth all evening. The closest they came to a serious subject was while they considered the best location for Micki to begin her apartment hunting.

Micki was in a mellow mood when she left and as she drove along the almost deserted streets a gentle smile curved her lips. Cindy and Benny were so perfectly suited and so obviously in love it was a joy just being in their company. Who would have believed it, back when Cindy was tossing insults at Benny every five minutes? Had, Micki wondered, Cindy been attracted to him even then? Very likely, Micki decided. The insults and taunts were probably the adolescent Cindy's way of venting that attraction. And Benny? Micki's smile grew tender remembering how good-naturedly he had taken Cindy's constant ribbing. What a delight they were to be with, Micki mused. If only Wolf were . . . Micki put a brake on her thoughts abruptly. Scathingly she told herself *if only* must surely be the most overworked words in the English language. You can *if only* from now until the first day of forever, she scolded herself mentally, and it will change nothing. So forget it. Forget him.

Her date with Tony the following evening was a mixture of fun and sadness. The fun began the minute she opened the door to him, for she was caught in his arms and twirled around in the air.

"Micki." Tony laughed down at her when she stood once more firmly on the floor. "You look as gorgeous as ever, only more so. God, what a sight you are for these weary old eyes."

"Weary old eyes, my Aunt Sara," Micki laughed back. "It's good to see you too, Tony. What are you up to these days?"

"Oh, about five-eleven," Tony drawled. "Maybe six feet."

"I'd have been disappointed if you hadn't said that."

Although Micki's tone was teasing, there was an underlying note of seriousness to it. It was silly, she knew, yet she would have been disappointed. His predictable rejoinder had reaffirmed their friendship, their closeness.

She had been around twelve the first time he'd quipped the reply to her. It had been summer then, too, and on that afternoon Micki had felt deserted and alone as all her girl friends were otherwise occupied. Without much hope of finding a companion, she had scuffed her way forlornly to the playground. She had found the fourteen-year-old Tony, looking every bit as dejected and forlorn, leaning against the playground fence. He had been watching, with lofty teenage amusement, the antics of a group of toddlers and had not seen Micki approach.

"None of the kids are around today," Micki had grumbled as she leaned against the fence beside him. "What are you up to, Tony?"

Maybe it was the sound of abject self-pity in her voice. Micki never knew, but when Tony turned to look at her, all signs of his own dejection had vanished. His expression was one of consideration and when he answered his tone was serious.

"Oh, about five-three, maybe four."

"Huh?"

She was wrapped up in her own misery, so his quip had gone completely over her head. She had gazed up at him blankly for several seconds before the dancing gleam in his sky-blue eyes and the betraying shake of his skinny shoulders turned the light on in her head. Her reaction was way out of proportion to the humor in his remark. The young, very naive Micki became convulsed with laughter.

"You goof!" she had gasped when her giggles had subsided somewhat. Balling her hand into a small, tight fist, she swung it at his arm. Tony caught her by the wrist before her fist made contact and shook it gently.

"Come on, you silly ass." Tony's grin had held amusement, and a dash of superiority. "Since we're both alone, we may as well be alone together."

They had kept each other company for the rest of the day and until nine thirty that night. After they had plumbed all the diversions offered by the playground, they moved onto the beach and from there to the bay to watch the fishing boats return. From the bay they went to Tony's home where Micki had promptly been invited to supper. After a quick phone call to her father obtaining permission for her to stay, Micki and Tony earned their supper by pulling weeds out of his mother's flower bed. And from the time they left the supper table until Tony's dad ran her home at nine thirty, they had engaged in a hotly contested game of Monopoly—which Tony won.

From that day until Micki left to go back to college six years ago, their greeting to each other had been the nonsensical, "What are you up to?" the only variance being the inches in Tony's reply.

Now, they stood, one twenty-five, the other twenty-seven, laughing into each other's face exactly as they had all those years ago.

"Tony, you are still a goof." Micki shook her head sharply, fighting the tears of affection that suddenly threatened. Sliding her arms around his waist, she gave him a quick, hard hug. "Do you think we'll ever grow up?"

"God, I hope not," Tony murmured fervently into her hair, returning her hug fiercely. When he released her, he glanced around curiously. "Where's your dad and Regina?"

"At a cookout." Micki's laughter, finally under control, threatened to break out again at the crafty expression that stole over Tony's face.

"We're all alone here?" he whispered slyly.

"Yes," Micki whispered back. "Why?"

"You want to stay here?" he leered exaggeratedly. "Fool around a little." His voice went very low. "We could play doctor."

"No!" Micki exploded into gales of laughter all over again. Grasping his arm, she urged him toward the front door. "Come on, you nut, you asked me out to dinner, so let's go dine."

They drove to an Italian restaurant in Wildwood, where Micki declared the food almost as good as Tony's mother's. Tony did most of the talking while they ate, telling about his job in Trenton, why he had decided to make the move home, and all about his present job and apartment.

A soft light in her eyes, Micki watched him while he talked, noting the changes in his face. He was, she decided, one fine-looking young man. His swarthy skin tone and wavy dark hair were set off, given an appealing look by his light-blue eyes and perfect white teeth. A small pale scar, earned in a high school football game, which broke the line of his left eyebrow, added a rakish touch to his visage. Yes, indeed, a very fine-looking young man.

After dinner Tony took Micki to a bar that catered to the dance crowd. The minute the waitress had taken their order and turned away from their minuscule table, Tony stood up and tugged at her arm.

"Come on, Micki, let's show them how it's done."

Tony had always been a good dancer and Micki quickly discovered he'd improved with age. Lithe, agile, he moved around the floor, and her, in a sensuously serpentine way.

From that afternoon in the playground Micki had never felt awkward with Tony, and after only a momentary hesitation, she gave herself fully to the music and the beat.

"Yeah, do it, girl," Tony encouraged, undulating smoothly in front of her. "Crank it up."

By the time they left the bar some four hours later, Micki's head was slightly fuzzy from a combination of the loud music and the drinks she'd consumed. Her body was damp with perspiration and she felt as if her legs might fall off at any moment.

As they drove back to Ocean City, Micki leaned her head back against the seat with a contented sigh. The breeze rushing in through the car's windows cooled her overheated skin and Micki inhaled deeply, savoring the scent of the sea.

"Do you want to come to my place and see my etchings?" Tony's quiet voice nudged her out of a half doze.

"Do you have some?" Micki asked innocently with deliberately widened eyes.

"No," he admitted ruefully, then added brightly, "but I make pretty good coffee. Would that do instead?"

"That would do perfectly," Micki laughed, unsuccessfully trying to smother a yawn.

Tony's apartment was on the third floor of a large, old building, kept in excellent repair. Mumbling, "Why didn't you warn me about the stairs?" Micki groaned as they trudged upward. The apartment comprised the whole of the third floor and consisted of a fair-sized bedroom, a large kitchen-living room combination, and a

small bathroom. The furniture was sparse, but what
there was was comfortable and well chosen.

"Make yourself at home," Tony tossed casually, walking to the kitchen area. "Coffee will be ready in a few
minutes, I have one of those almost instant things."

Micki sank onto the overstuffed sofa and sighed sleepily as the soft cushions seemed to envelop and cradle her
tired body. Half asleep, the sound of Tony's quiet movement touched the fringes of her mind. There was the
rattle of a tray being placed on the coffee table and a CD
sliding into the player, then, as the cushion beside her
depressed from Tony's weight, the voice of Bruce Spring-
steen came to her softly from the stereo.

"Are you asleep?" Tony's voice was low and soft and
very, very close.

"Almost."

Lifting her heavy lids, Micki smiled into the light-blue
eyes only inches away from her face. One arm resting on
the back of the sofa, he leaned over her, his expression
serious, somewhat sad.

"I'm going to kiss you, Micki," he murmured. The
scent of alcohol came to her as his warm breath whispered over her face. Micki knew her own breath held the
same tinge.

"I know."

His lips touched hers gently and then, with a low groan,
his arm slid around her waist, his chest crushed hers, pushing her body deeper into the cushions, and his mouth
became a driving force that searched hers with an urgency
that held near desperation. At first, startled into stillness
by the very intensity of his action, Micki lay unresponsive
in his embrace. Then, her own feelings of desperation
swamping her, she curled her arms around his neck, returned his kiss with equal fervor. Stretching his frame
beside her, his hand moved down her back to the base of
her spine, urging her body to meet his. Hope flaring that

maybe this time she'd feel something, if only a tiny quickening of desire, Micki arched her body to his, her arms tightening around his neck.

Other than the mild, pleasant sensation she usually felt when being kissed, there was nothing. No spark of excitement danced along her limbs, no fire rushed inside her veins, no longing to give herself up to sensual pleasure clouded her senses. She yearned for those sensations, longed to feel them, yet, even when Tony's hand moved over her rib cage to stroke her breasts, there was nothing. She could have wept in frustration and disappointment. Attuned as she was to those emotions, she felt them reciprocated from Tony when, with a strangled moan, he released her and flopped back against the sofa.

"It's no good, is it, Micki'?" It was posed as a question, yet it wasn't one. She answered anyway.

"No, it's no good, I'm sorry."

"It's not your fault." The sigh he emitted seemed to come from the depths of his being. "It's mine."

Leaning forward, he poured coffee into the two cups on the tray, lifted one, tasted it, then stood up abruptly.

"Better drink your coffee while it's still hot," he advised softly, walking to the window on the other side of the room.

Shifting to the edge of the sofa, Micki added milk to her coffee and sat staring at it, her eyes sad and misty.

"Goddamn!"

Tony's sharply expelled curse startled her upright, her eyelashes fluttering in bewilderment.

"Tony?"

Her soft entreaty brought his body around to face her, a small, apologetic smile on his lips.

"I'm sorry, Micki." Tony's lips twisted. "But I was hoping, no praying, that something would ignite between us. It would have been perfect, we're so compatible. We can laugh and talk so easily together without strain that I thought—maybe—we could make love together as easily."

Micki frowned, and knowing she misinterpreted his words, he added hastily, "Not just sex, but love—you know." His lips twisted more harshly. "The real thing, stars and music, the whole shootin' match."

"Yes, I do know." Micki's frown deepened. "It would seem that we're suffering from the same malady. You've been hurt badly, haven't you?"

"God, yes!" Tony's softly groaned exclamation tugged at her heart. Then, as the full content of her words sank in, his eyes sharpened on her face. "You too?" At her nod he probed. "Do I know him?"

Unblinking, Micki stared at him steadily until, turning palms out, he lifted his shoulders and pleaded, "Forget I said that. Bad, was it?"

"Yes."

"I know the feeling." He laughed humorlessly. "I've been there. Hell, I'm still there."

"She didn't"—Micki paused to choose her words carefully—"care for you?"

"That's the stinger." Tony's smile hurt her. "She loved me."

"But then, why?" Micki's face wore a puzzled expression. "Tony, I don't understand."

"Neither did I." He laughed harshly, puzzling her even more. Reading her expression, he lifted his shoulders again in a weary, defeated way. "I threw it away, honey," he stated flatly. "I had it all in my hands and I threw it away."

"Tony!" Micki cried in exasperation. "You are not making any sense."

"Nothing new about that," Tony sighed. "I haven't made much sense for some time now." Tilting his head, he asked quizzically, "Was I always stupid, Micki?"

"Tony!" Micki begged. "Will you stop wallowing in self-pity and explain?"

"Am I doing that?" he asked, startled, then he smiled. "Yes, I guess I am. Sorry, hon. Are you sure you want to hear it?"

Micki nodded emphatically. "Of course. We're friends, aren't we?"

"Yes, friends." Tony's smile softened. "Okay, friend, you asked for it." Drawing a deep breath, he began. "I met her in Atlantic City. She's a supper-club singer." At the slight rise of Micki's eyebrows, his hand sliced through the air dismissively. "Oh, she had no great ambitions, no burning drive to be a star or anything. But she has an appealingly soft voice, perfect for the supper clubs, and it was a way for her to earn a good living. She comes from upstate New York and she arrived in Atlantic City via New York City." He paused and his smile turned whimsical. "We met— introduced ourselves—at a blackjack table."

"She's a gambler?" Micki exclaimed.

"Lord, no!" Tony laughed, then sobered. "Even though she gambled, and lost, on me."

"But how?" Micki cried. "Tony, *will* you explain?"

"All she wanted was marriage, children, and believe it or not, she wanted me for their father."

"You didn't want to get married?" The idea didn't surprise Micki. Many guys shied away from that total commitment.

"Hell, yes," he disabused her at once. "I wanted that more than anything in the world. But, Micki, she was so lovely and I had so damned little to offer her."

"Ah, Tony—" Micki began, but Tony's self-derisive chuckle cut her off.

"That's exactly what she said. In exactly that tone of voice. But, you see, I wanted to have everything perfect for her. I wanted to wait until I could give her a home and all the nice things that go in it." He smiled ruefully. "She didn't want to wait, told me she'd enjoy working with me to get the things we'd need." He drew a deep breath, went on slowly, painfully. "I wouldn't listen, wouldn't even consider it."

"But, Tony, most young couples work together to set themselves up." Micki's face revealed her astonished reaction to his words.

"I know, I know, but—" He paused to wet his lips. "Micki, you know me, I'm great in the light moments, like earlier this evening, but when it comes to the heavy stuff, well, I freeze up. And with her it was even worse. I wanted her so much, yet I was almost afraid to touch her. I didn't merely love her, I put her on a pedestal, literally adored her. I—"

He turned away from her, his shoulders slumping, and Micki's heart ached for him all over again. When he turned back to her, his face was pale.

"She wrote me a letter." His soft tone betrayed the strain he was feeling. "Told me a friend she used to date had come down to A.C. to see the casinos and had looked her up. He asked her to marry him." Tony grimaced, but continued. "She said she couldn't wait anymore, so she was going back home with him, was going to accept his proposal." Suddenly his eyes shot blue sparks and his fingers raked his hair roughly. "I should have dragged her off the pedestal and into my bed. That's what I meant when I said I threw it away."

Micki sat staring at him long moments before, rising quickly, she walked around the sofa, her mind working at what it was about his narration that bothered her.

"Did she love you, Tony?" she finally asked.

"Yes," he answered at once. "I'd bet everything I own on that, Micki."

"Oh, Tony!" she exclaimed impatiently. "Did she take your brain with her when she left?"

"What do you mean?" he bristled.

She ignored his question to ask one of her own. "How long ago did she leave?"

"Two months, one week, and four days ago. Why?"

"Oh, for heaven's sake," she groaned. "Tony, you don't need a friend, you need a keeper. Didn't it ever occur to you she might be trying to get you off dead center?"

"In what way?" he snapped.

"Probably the second oldest way there is," she snapped back. "You made sure she couldn't use the first. She took a powder, took off, leaving a letter designed to make you jealous. You, dumbhead, were supposed to go after her."

"Do you really think so?" he asked hopefully.

"Is she married?" Again Micki brushed off his question to pose one of her own.

"I don't know."

"Why don't you?"

"For God's sake, Micki, you sound like a trial lawyer," Tony growled. "How would I know?"

"Men!" Micki's eyes lifted as if beseeching help from above. "Do you know what town she comes from? Her parents' name?"

"Well, of course." He sounded almost angry. "But what has th—"

"Call them, ask them," Micki cut in sarcastically. "They very likely know if their daughter has gotten married."

"Just like that?" Tony snapped his fingers. "Just call and ask? Come on, Micki, I can't do that."

"Why not?" Micki nearly shouted in her exasperation with him. "What's so unusual about a friend calling to find out if a proposed marriage came off? A friend might want to be sure before sending a wedding gift."

Tony's eyes grew bright, then dimmed again. "What do I do if she answers the phone?"

"Ask her, you idiot," Micki chided. "And if the answer is no, then coax, plead, beg her to come back to you. Promise her anything, but—" she paused, her eyes twinkling. "Give her yourself, your love."

In a few long strides, Tony crossed the room, caught

her to him and hugged her fiercely before releasing her to gaze fondly into her eyes.

"You're wonderful," he said clearly. "I'll do it. Oh, baby, the guy that let you get away had to be completely crazy."

Micki winced, as much from the name *baby* as the rest of his words. Tony was instantly contrite.

"Oh, Micki, I'm sorry. What happened? Don't tell me he acted as stupid as I did?"

"No," Micki shook her head, her gentle tone robbing the denial of its sting. "He didn't put me on a pedestal." Her tone went rough. "In fact he treated me like a silly fool, called me a youngster, a juvenile." Feeling her cheeks flush, she dropped her eyes. ."And he didn't have to drag me into his bed, I practically jumped into it."

"I know what it cost you to say that." Tony's hand caressed her hot face. "But what happened? What went wrong?"

"I found out, after it was too late, that he was using me." Biting her lip, she lifted overbright eyes to his. "I was a very willing, convenient plaything for a weekend."

"He told you that?" Tony demanded, outraged.

"No, of course not," Micki sighed. "But the way I found out, well, it left no doubt at all as to his intentions. Oh, I'm sure he would have been willing to fit me into his schedule every now and then, as long as I didn't become difficult—or boring."

"Micki, stop." Tony's eyes were anxious, his tone concerned.

"Don't worry, Tony," Micki shook her head at him. "It all happened a long time ago. I'm fine now, really."

"Oh, sure." His tone called her a liar. "That's why you tried so hard to work up a response to me a while ago. The experience shattered you so badly you're still trying to put the pieces together." His eyes grew soft. "I can see why it would. If you know me, I know you as well. I was around, I saw how fiercely you guarded your innocence.

For you to give it up so willingly, you would have to be very much in love. And it still hurts, doesn't it?"

"Yes," Micki whispered.

He gazed at her silently several seconds, then his eyes narrowed in thought.

"You said it all happened a long time ago." He hesitated before probing. "Was it that time six years ago, right before you went back to college, when you called me and begged me to say yes if anyone asked if we were seeing each other regularly?"

"Yes," Micki admitted with an apologetic smile. "I'm sorry, Tony, but I'm afraid I used your name a lot at that time. I literally hid behind it."

"Sorry? Now who's being an idiot?" he scolded. "You may hide behind my name, or me, anytime the need arises. Now come on, it's late, I'd better get you home."

When he stopped the car in front of her house, he kissed her gently on the mouth and whispered, "If things go right, I'll send you an invitation. Okay?"

"You'd better," Micki warned.

"A promise," he vowed. "And, Micki, toss off that load of guilt and shame you've been toting."

"Yes, Tony," Micki promised meekly.

SEVEN

As she slipped into bed, Micki prayed her hunch about Tony's girlfriend had been right. She was almost sure it was, as it was exactly the sort of thing she might do in the same situation. Anxious for him, wanting to see him happy, she hoped it would not be long before, keeping his promise, he sent her an invitation to his wedding.

As to her promise to him, there was no need to worry about that, simply because she never had felt guilty or ashamed. At first, sure she should have them, she'd wondered about her lack of those feelings. The searing pain, the disappointment, the anger she'd had, hadn't had the power to change what had been a joyous experience into anything else. She'd discovered sheer delight, an exquisite Eden in Wolf's arms, and nothing that happened after that had been able to erase it from her mind.

What disturbed her was her inability to find that Eden in any other man's embrace. It was not a man's mouth that ignited the spark, but Wolf's mouth. It was not a man's hands that fanned the flame, but Wolf's hands. And it was not a man's body that could consume her in the blaze, but Wolf's body. With sad defeat, Micki faced the possibility that no other man but Wolf held the key that could unlock her emotions.

What do I do in that case? Micki wondered sleepily. Marry another man, any other man—Darrel—and act out a part the rest of my life? The thought sent a shudder down her spine and her last coherent thought was *I must call Darrel.*

It was mid-morning before Micki woke. Fuzzy minded, heavy lidded, she stumbled down the stairs and into the kitchen. Her father paused in the act of pouring a cup of coffee to give her a grin devoid of any sign of sympathy.

"Hangover?" he chirped brightly.

"No," Micki denied honestly. "But I do feel like a washout. I think I'll just loaf around the house today if I want to be in decent shape to start my job tomorrow."

"Sound thinking," Bruce intoned. "By the way, you had two phone calls last night, Wolf Renninger and a Darrel Baxter."

"Wolf?" Micki pounced on the name. "What did he want?"

Bruce shot her a sharp glance before lifting his shoulders in an I-don't-know shrug. "You'll have to ask Regina, she took the calls." Heading for the doorway Micki had just come through, he added, "If anyone wants me, I'll be on the front porch reading the paper."

Micki itched with the desire to go in search of Regina but deciding to be prudent, she poured herself a small glass of juice and a cup of coffee, dropped a slice of bread into the toaster, and sat down to wait for Regina to find her. She didn't have long to wait. Regina came into the kitchen as Micki was finishing her toast and starting on her second cup of coffee.

"Good morning, Micki," Regina greeted quietly. "Did you have a good time last night?"

"Yes, thank you," Micki answered warily, studying her stepmother's face for maliciousness. Finding none, she blurted, "I hear I had some calls last night."

"Yes," Regina nodded. "A guy named Darrel Baxter called soon after you left, and a short time later Wolf called."

"What did they want?" Micki asked quickly.

"To speak to you, of course," Regina replied smoothly.

"What did you tell them?" Micki demanded sharply.

"Really, Micki." Regina's eyes flew wide at Micki's tone. "What could I tell them? I informed them both that you were out for the evening with Tony Menella. You were, weren't you?"

"Yes, yes, of course," Micki sighed contritely. "I'm sorry, Regina. I got in very late and I'm irritable this morning."

"I've experienced the feeling," Regina smiled. "Oh, yes, Mr. Baxter said he'd call sometime today."

"And Wolf?" Micki was almost afraid to ask. What, she wondered, was he up to? Why had he called when he had assured her he would not?

"Wolf said thank you very coldly and hung up," Regina replied from the counter, where she was getting herself a cup of coffee. Turning to Micki with the pot held aloft, she asked, "Can I heat yours up?"

"Yes, please."

Micki brought the cup to her lips, gulped most of the lukewarm brew down her suddenly parched throat, then handed the cup to Regina. After refilling the cup, she carried both cups to the table and sat down on the chair opposite Micki.

"Micki." Regina's tone held confusion. "What's going on?"

"Nothing's going on," Micki returned quickly. "I don't know what you mean by going on."

"You know perfectly well what I mean," Regina sighed. "The day you came home you absolutely refused to discuss Wolf Renninger. In fact you would not allow me to speak that person's name. Since then he has called here several times and you have seen him at least once that I know of. Last night Wolf's tone was not only cold, it was"—Regina hesitated, as if searching for the exact word—"proprietorial." Having found the word, she placed hard emphasis on it before going on. "I don't like feeling in the middle, while still in the dark."

When she paused for breath, Micki seized the opportunity to declare flatly, "He has no right to sound proprietorial."

"Right or not, he did," Regina retorted. "Which leads me to suspect he will be calling again. Now don't you think it's time we talked frankly about what happened six years ago and clear up that mess once and for all?"

"No!"

The chair scraped the floor and nearly toppled over as Micki jumped up. She was at the doorway when Regina's voice, sounding both tired and impatient, stopped her.

"Micki, you don't understand," Regina argued. "There are things you must know. Things about Wolf and—"

"I don't want to hear it," Micki cried, rushing through the doorway. "And I won't listen."

"For heaven's sake, Micki," Regina called after her. "This is ridiculous."

"So, okay," Micki shot back as she swung around the banister and started up the stairs, unaware of her father standing in the front doorway holding the screen door open. "I'm ridiculous."

"What in the— Micki?" Bruce's voice was sharp with concern. "What's all the shouting about? I doubt any of the neighbors missed a word."

"I'm sorry, Dad, but I can't—I won't—" Micki paused at the growing look of confusion and alarm on his face. "Oh, hell," she sighed, running up the stairs.

"Micki!" Bruce called after her, then called sharply, "Regina!"

Micki didn't wait to hear any more. She ran inside her room, slammed the door, and leaned against it, breathing heavily and fighting tears. Oh, why did Regina persist in tormenting her? If she really wanted a smoother relationship between them, why didn't she let the subject drop?

Still tired from her physical and emotional exertions of the night before, Micki's thoughts tumbled, none too rationally. Were Regina and Wolf still seeing each other behind her father's back? But if they were, why had Wolf insisted she go out with him? Wasn't one woman at a time enough for him? *Damn Regina,* Micki silently cursed her, *if she hurts Dad again I'll* . . . Not knowing exactly what she'd do, Micki's fury turned to Wolf. Why was he doing this? And why, after stating so flatly that he would not call her again, had he called last night? Were Regina and Wolf working together to drive her away? That thought brought her up short.

"Please, no."

Moving her head back and forth against the smoothly finished door, Micki wasn't even aware that she'd whispered the words aloud. The very possibility of her reasoning being correct tightened a band of pain around her head. If it was true, if their affair was still going on, she, simply by being her father's daughter, and being in the house, was a definite threat to them.

Her breathing suddenly constricted, Micki stumbled across the room and dropped onto the bed. Six years ago she had thought the intensity of the pain she suffered at the image of Wolf and Regina entwined together, exactly as she and Wolf had been, could not possibly be deepened. She had been wrong. The anguish she felt now far superceded what had been before.

"Goddamn you, Wolf Renninger."

The muted curse held more the sound of an animal's snarl than the lucid words from a reasoning mind. And like an animal's claws, her elegantly long, painted nails dug viciously into the rumpled bedcovers on the unmade bed.

Harsh, rasping breaths were drawn in roughly around the unreleased sobs gripping her throat. And eyelids were anchored firmly against hot tears she refused to let run free. Curled up tightly into the fetal position, Micki's slim ball of a body caused the mattress to tremble with the force of the shudders that shook through her.

Dear God, the silent plea was wrenched from the depths of her being, *I take it back, don't damn him. Just, please, please, make him go away and leave me alone before I give in to my need for him and damn my own soul in the giving. You see,* the chaotic thoughts ran on, *I love him so terribly, and if he manages to get me alone, I don't know how long I can hold out against the urge to lose myself, my very identity inside his arms. If you have any mercy, help me. And, if you have any justice,* she added irreverently, bitterly, *you'll give a small slap to Regina's conscience.*

By the time she finished her somewhat unorthodox prayer, Micki's sobs filled the room and her tears soaked a patch of the sheet under her face. The sound of her sobs blocked out the quiet tap on her door and a second later the click the latch made as the door was opened. Nor did she see the alarm that filled her father's eyes as they encountered her shaking form. The anxious sound of his voice told her she was no longer alone.

"Princess, what is wrong?" Bruce probed gently, bending over the bed to stretch his hand out and smooth her hair from her damp face. "What has happened to make you cry like this? Was it something Regina said or did?"

Yes, it was both those things. Micki had to bite back the words as, rolling onto her back, she shook her head and lied. "No, of course not." Swallowing down her sobs with the air she drew into her lungs, she hiccuped, then rushed on. "I'm tired. Tony and I danced for hours last night and despite what I said, I'm afraid I drank too much. After that I went to Tony's apartment with him and—"

"You did what?" Bruce's voice, sharp with sudden anger, cut across her babbling explanation. "That's why you're crying, isn't it? What did he do to you?"

"Do?" Micki asked blankly. "What do you me—?" She

stopped, stunned, as her mind caught up with his train of thought. Before she could deny his impression, he was speaking again.

"Answer me!"

Never before had Micki heard quite that harsh a tone from her father, seen such fury in his eyes. Struck momentarily speechless, Micki stared at him in wonder.

"Well, if you won't answer me"—he swung away from the bed—"maybe he will."

"What do you mean?" Micki squeaked. "What are you going to do?"

"I'm going to call him," Bruce snapped, moving toward the door. "Better still, I think I'll go see him."

"Dad, stop!" The sobs, the tears, were forgotten as Micki scrambled off the bed to run after him, clutch at his arm. "It's not what you're thinking. I swear nothing happened."

"He didn't try to make love to you?" Bruce rapped.

"Well, not really—he—" Micki floundered.

"That's what I thought." Bruce shook her arm off, continued toward the door.

"Dad, please, nothing happened."

At the frantic, pleading note in her voice, Bruce turned to look at her, his angry eyes raking her face.

"Suppose you tell me exactly what did happen."

"Tony did kiss me," Micki admitted. "But he didn't really want me." His body stiffened and again she caught his arm, explained. "Dad, Tony is crazily in love with a girl he met in Atlantic City. What he really wanted was someone to pour his heart out to."

"And that's all?"

Watching the anger drain out of his face, Micki expelled a long sigh of relief. Her father's fury was an altogether new experience for her, never having been exposed to it before. If she hadn't seen it with her own eyes, she would not have believed it. For a few seconds there, that furious man had been a stranger, not the gentle father she thought she knew. Subdued by this new facet of her father's personality, she avowed, softly, "That is absolutely all."

"All right." Although the anger had left his expression, it still edged his tone. "But what the hell possessed you to go to his apartment in the first place?"

"But why shouldn't I have gone with him?" Micki asked, genuinely puzzled.

"Why?" Bruce exclaimed. "You know full well why. You're not that naive."

"No, I'm not," Micki returned with force. "And I'm no longer a little girl. And Tony's is not the first guy's apartment I've been in. Good grief, Dad, I'm twenty-five years old, not sixteen."

"And everyone knows twenty-five-year-old women never get attacked." Bruce's voice dripped sarcasm. "Or hurt. That only happens to sixteen-year-old girls."

"Oh, Dad," Micki sighed. "I'm fully aware of what goes on out there in the big bad world, but I can't hide myself behind locked doors, or wrap myself in cotton."

"No, you can't," he agreed, then qualified, "but you don't have to invite trouble or go looking for it either."

Knowing there was no way she could win, but unwilling to give in, Micki insisted, "I don't go looking—"

"Micki," Regina's call ended the argument. "You're wanted on the phone."

Casting a rueful glance at her father, Micki left the room. Who, she wondered in amazement, would have believed he'd react like that. And what in the world would he have done had he ever found out about the weekend she'd spent with Wolf? A shudder rippling through her, she started down the stairs only to stop suddenly, her breath catching in her throat. Could that be Wolf on the phone now? Slowly, her steps lagging, Micki descended the stairs, went into the living room, and picked up the receiver.

"Hello?"

"Micki?"

The well-modulated sound of Darrel's voice left Micki weak with relief and, contrarily, a bit disappointed.

"Yes, Darrel. How are you? I was planning to call you this afternoon."

"Where?"

His query stopped her for a moment. What did he mean, where?

"At your apartment, of course," she finally answered. "Where else would I call?"

"Since yesterday afternoon"—Darrel's voice held a smile—"my mother's summer place in Cape May."

"You're calling from Cape May now?"

"Isn't that what I just said?" He laughed indulgently. "I'm glad I finally found you at home." No laughter or even a tinge of a smile now. "Did you have a good time last night?"

Something—was it censure—about his tone annoyed her, so she answered oversweetly. "Yes, I had a wonderful time." Well, she had, for the most part anyway. Her answer met a short silence. When he spoke again, his tone conveyed a worried mixture of anger and hesitation.

"How—nice." Again there was a tiny silence. "Micki, mother's having a small dinner party this evening and she expressly asked me to bring you. Will you come?"

Expressly? I'll bet. Micki's mouth curved wryly. She was very well aware that his mother did not consider her nearly good enough for her precious son. Should she go? Why not? she asked herself. Mrs. Baxter would know before too long that Micki posed no threat to her plans for Darrel's future.

"I'd love to," she lied blandly. "What time should I come?"

"I was hoping you'd agree to my coming up there now," he said quickly. "Then we could have some time alone together before returning here for dinner. Also it would afford me the opportunity to meet your father and stepmother."

Don't bother, pal, you're on your way out. The outrageous thought skittered into Micki's mind, only to be swept quickly out again. Whatever was the matter with her? Why was she feeling so bitchy? It's all Wolf's fault, him and his damn phone call after telling her he wouldn't call. The fact that there was no sense at all to her reasoning didn't bother her in the least.

"Micki? Are you there?"

"Yes, yes, Darrel," Micki assured him. "I was just trying to remember if I'd made any commitments for the day." Liar. "As I can't remember any, yes, you can come up. Say, in an hour?"

"Good, I'll be there."

"How should I dress?"

"Oh, casually I'd say. See you in an hour."

After she had replaced the receiver, Micki stood staring at the instrument, the wry smile back on her lips. Oh, casually, the man said. Oh, sure. As casually as labels that read Prada or Versace and that ilk. In other words, girl, she told herself as she left the room, you had better dress casually—to the teeth.

Micki spent the entire hour on her appearance, choosing carefully everything she put on down to the shade of polish she brushed on her nails. On opening the door for Darrel, she counted the time well spent by the expression on his face.

"You're so lovely," he said softly. He took one step, his arms reaching for her, then, realizing where he was, he stopped, placed his hands lightly on her waist and bent to kiss her cheek. "I've missed you, sweetheart."

"And I've missed you," Micki replied, trying in vain to infuse conviction into her tone.

After making the introductions, Micki stood aside watching Darrel charm her father and Regina. No one she had ever met could be quite as charming as Darrel. Intelligent, handsome, urbane, his athletically slim body encased in perfectly tailored clothes, he was every parent's dream of a good catch. By both her father's and Regina's reaction, they were not any exception.

After a two-week separation, her own reaction to him surprised her. Watching him, listening to him, she heaved a silent sigh of relief that she had decided not to marry him. He was almost too perfect. Too good-looking, too well turned out, too charming. How, she wondered, could she have ever lived up to that, or with it, twenty-four hours a day? A picture of her own jean-clad, barefoot, tousle-headed form, as she usually was when around the house, rose in her mind, and she had to fight the grin that tugged at her lips. While working, Micki always looked like she'd stepped off the cover of a high-fashion magazine. But when she was at home, well, that was a different story. To her own way of thinking she was more real when she was at home.

After they had left the house and were in his car—a custom-made black Cadillac—driving south, Micki continued with her train of thought. Studying him and the situation objectively, she was convinced that had she married him she would have lost her real self, the essence that was Micki Durrant.

With a small jolt of surprise Micki suddenly realized that Darrel had seen her only in her workday facade. What, she mused, would he think of the tomboyish Micki who could still scamper up a tree with the best of them? Or, the curves revealed by a bikini not withstanding, become joyfully covered with gritty particles as she erected a sand castle of enormous proportions? She did not have to witness his reaction to know it. Again an impish grin tugged at her lips, more successfully this time.

"What amuses you?" Darrel's tone held just a touch of the petulant child left out of a secret. Yes, indeed, she decided, Darrel would be very hard, if not impossible, for her to live with.

"Life," Micki answered, her bright-blue eyes dancing. "And its funny little twists and turns."

"I find very little amusement in twists and turns," Darrel intoned. "I like my life well planned and ordered. After we're married"—he seemed unaware of Micki's small gasp—"you'll have no more twists and turns, and I'm sure you will find life less unnerving."

Not to mention a lot less exciting, Micki thought scathingly. How was it possible, she asked herself, for a man to be so charming one minute and so pompously dull the next? She didn't even try to work out the answer to that one, as having already rejected him in her mind, she proceeded to do so in fact.

"But we're not going to be married." Although her tone was gentle, it was also flat with finality.

"Not going to be—!" The big car swerved slightly before Darrel's white-knuckled hands gripped the wheel and straightened it. "But I thought it was settled."

"I don't know why you should have thought that," Micki said quietly. "The only promise I made to you before I left Wilmington was to think about your proposal. I have, and I've reached the conclusion that it simply would not work."

"But of course it would work," he insisted. "Why wouldn't it?"

"In the first place," Micki replied calmly, "your mother does not approve of me. And—"

"You're wrong," Darrel interrupted sharply. "At least she no longer objects to the union. She has reconciled herself to the—"

"And in the second place," she cut him off forcefully, "I'm not in love with you."

"But you would learn to love me." He was actually pleading! "I could make you love me."

"No, Darrel, you could not," she assured him gently, but firmly. "Of that I am very sure."

"There is someone else?" His eyes had left the road for a moment as he asked the question. Micki's momentarily unguarded expression was all the answer he needed. "Yes," he sighed, glancing back at the road. "I can see there is."

"I'm sorry." The words sounded inadequate, even to her own ears, yet they were all she had to offer.

"Sorry? Sorry?" His tone held an anger she'd never heard from him before. "What good is sorry? Why didn't you tell me at once? When I first asked you to marry me?" His voice died away, then came back more strongly. "Why the hell did you let me hang like that when you knew the answer was no all along?"

"But I didn't—" Micki began, then stopped, aghast at what she was admitting to him.

"You didn't know?" he finished for her. "You mean it's some man you've met within the last two weeks?"

"Yes—no!" Micki cried.

"What do you mean, yes—no?" Darrel demanded. "For God's sake, Micki, make up your mind. It's either one or the other."

Having arrived at their destination, Cape May's charmingly quaint shopping mall, Micki was allowed a few minutes to form her answer while Darrel searched out a parking space.

The second the car was motionless, he turned to face her, his expression grim.

"Well?"

"Well," Micki began slowly, "both yes and no are correct." At his look of disbelief, she hurried on. "Yes, really, Darrel." Micki hesitated, wet her lips, then admitted, "I met, and fell in love with, him some years ago. I was very young." Again she moistened her dry lips, looked in every direction but his. "I had hoped, was sure, that it was all over." She paused to draw breath and he took the opportunity to question her.

"That's why you really came home, wasn't it?" His voice was heavy with accusation. "To see him."

"No, it was not," Micki denied. "I never expected to see him again. When I ran into him, purely by accident, I—I realized nothing had changed for me."

"For you?" Listening carefully, Darrel had caught the inflection in her last two words. "He doesn't love you anymore?"

"He never did." It wasn't easy but she managed to lift her head and meet his penetrating glance. "All he ever wanted was an affair. He still does."

"And you've agreed to this?" he exclaimed, astonished. No man knew better than Darrel exactly how cool and unresponsive Micki could be.

"Of course not," Micki snapped icily.

"Well then," he argued, "if there is no future for you with him, why not—" That was as far as he got before Micki trod on his words.

"I'll tell you why not. Very simply, I can't marry or sleep with one man while loving another." She smiled sadly. "I'm sorry, Darrel, but that's not my style."

"Yes, I know." Darrel's smile matched hers for sadness for several minutes before he shrugged. "I suppose, under the circumstances, dinner at mother's would not be a good idea. She was halfway expecting an announcement of our engagement." His shoulders moved again. "I'll call her and tell her we can't make it, and face the questions tomorrow." The sadness left his smile, replaced by all the charm he was capable of. "You will have dinner with me, won't you?"

"No pressure?" Micki asked warily.

"No pressure," he vowed. "I may not know you all that long, but I know you well enough to be sure no amount of pressure would change your mind."

Micki had a sudden urge to cry. The words *no amount of pressure* brought home to her more than anything else how very vulnerable she was. It would, she knew, take very little pressure from Wolf to turn her into a pliant, shivering love slave. *How very little we know each other,* she thought sadly. She was considered very strong-willed and near frigid by most, if not all, of her friends. What would Darrel's reaction be, she wondered, if he were exposed to a tenth of the passion that had consumed her while on Wolf's boat? A conjured picture of Darrel's shocked visage exchanged the hovering tears for a fleeting smile.

"What are you thinking?" he probed. "You're so quiet, and for a second there I wasn't sure if you were going to laugh or cry."

"For a second there, I wasn't sure either," Micki laughed softly. "I wanted to cry for what might have been. Darrel, would you do something for me?"

"Of course," he answered at once. "Anything. What is it?"

"Would you buy me a sandwich?" Her eyes bright with the recent moisture teased impishly. "I just realized I haven't eaten for hours and I'm starving."

Up until then the car's engine, which he'd left on to run the air-conditioner, had purred softly. As he turned to shut off the engine, he shook his head ruefully.

"You're unbelievable, Micki." As if against his will, he smiled. "To use a very trite phrase, how can you think of food at a time like this?" His smile deepened and grew into a grin. "But now that you mention it, I could eat a sandwich myself."

They left the cool confines of the car to brave the fierce assault from the sun and the waves of heat rising from the sidewalk. Strolling along the perimeter of the shopping mall, they came upon a restaurant with a low-walled patio. On the patio were a half dozen umbrella-shaded tables surrounded by wooden deck chairs. Only two of the tables

were occupied, and the waitress, looking somewhat forlorn, cast them a hopeful look.

"What do you think?" Darrel laughed softly. "The
patio? Or would you prefer the air-conditioned dining
room?"

"Oh, the patio," Micki grinned. "I don't think I have
the courage to bypass that waitress."

Chatting pleasantly, the waitress took their orders of
grilled cheese and bacon sandwiches and iced tea before
reluctantly disappearing through a door at the far end
of the patio.

"Well," Darrel sighed, pushing back his chair. "I may
as well find a phone, face the music, and get it over with.
I'll be back in a minute, if I'm lucky."

"Take your time, I'll be fine." Micki waved him away.
"Please convey my regrets to your mother." A low grunt
was the only reply she received.

A mild breeze ruffling her hair, Micki leaned back in
the chair and let her gaze roam over the surrounding
area. Moving lazily, her eyes passed a glare of red, then,
a soft gasp escaping her parted lips, her eyes honed in
on the flame-colored car.

With something akin to panic, Micki watched as the
sports car was maneuvered into a small parking space.
Even without a good view of the man behind the wheel,
Micki knew who was driving that brazenly painted, rich
man's toy. She very seriously doubted there were two
cars like that on the whole of the south Jersey coast.

A growing ache gripping her throat, Micki watched as
Wolf stepped out of the car, walked around to the other
side to assist his passenger in alighting. Hating herself,
yet unable to tear her eyes away, Micki studied the
woman as she stepped onto the street and straightened
up. At that distance Micki could only get an impression
of the woman. That impression was tall, willowy, her platinum hair gleaming in the sunlight, her face partially

concealed by overlarge sunglasses, her teeth flashing whitely in a crimson mouth.

"Here's your tea." The waitress's lilting voice drew Micki's attention. "Your sandwiches will be along in a moment."

"Thank you, I need that," Micki croaked. "I'm parched."

Sipping gratefully at the cold drink, Micki kept her eyes firmly on the glass, determined not to look at him again. An instant later, unable to stop herself, she lifted her head and froze, the ache in her throat culling forth a corresponding one in her chest. Fighting a desire to jump up and run, she watched as the couple walked in a direct line toward her. Aware that as yet, due to the obviously deep conversation they were engaged in, Wolf had not spotted her, Micki had to force herself to stay in her chair.

Let him pass by without seeing me, please, Micki begged silently. Apparently it was not to be, for at that moment Wolf turned from the woman and saw Micki. His step quickened and his eyes widened, then, looking beyond her, narrowed.

"God!" Darrel's harassed voice reached her an instant before he slipped into the chair beside her. "My mother should have gone into law, she would have made a fantastic D.A."

Tearing her gaze from the silvery eyes fastened on her, Micki stammered, "Bad, was it?"

"Rock bottom," he groaned. "She had more questions than a prosecutor." Raising his glass, Darrel took a long swallow. "Oh, that's good, even though I'm sorry now I didn't order something stronger."

Micki barely heard him. An odd, eerie feeling cloaking her, she knew without looking that Wolf and the tall woman had entered the patio. She didn't even blink when his low voice drew her head around.

"Hello, Micki."

Blue eyes locked with silver and for one mad second

Micki was tempted to ignore him. The sure knowledge that in no way would Wolf allow her to get away with it chased temptation out of her mind.

"Hello, Wolf," Micki replied with amazing coolness. "Cape May seems to be a very popular place today."

"Yes, doesn't it." Until that minute his eyes had refused to release hers, now they swung pointedly to Darrel, who had risen at Wolf's greeting.

"Darrel Baxter," Micki smiled painfully. "Wolf Renninger and—" The breath died in her throat as, shifting her gaze, Micki got a good look at the woman by Wolf's side. Her hair was not platinum, but a beautiful true silver and, although she was still strikingly lovely, she appeared to be somewhere in her middle sixties.

"Bianca Perriot," Wolf finished for her. "Bianca— Micki Durrant and Darrel Baxter."

Returning the woman's enchanting smile, Micki extended her hand, felt her fingers grasped in a firm handshake at the same time the two men performed the same act.

"Micki." Bianca's voice was every bit as enchanting as her smile. "What a delightful name. Is it a given name or a nickname?"

"Given," Micki answered softly. "In honor of my Irish grandfather, who by all accounts, was a real Mick."

Bianca's laughter tinkled on the air like the sound of tiny bells before, turning to Darrel, she placed her hand in his and queried, "Baxter? Are you by any chance related to Martha Baxter?"

"My mother." Darrel's tone betrayed his surprise. "You're acquainted with her?"

"I know her very well. I knew your father also." Once again that enchanting smile came to her lips. "My late husband was as avid a golfer as your father was. They played together quite often, leaving your mother and me to amuse ourselves at the clubhouse."

During this exchange, though Micki determinedly kept her attention centered on Bianca Perriot's animated face, she was uncomfortably aware of Wolf's eyes devouring her. When Darrel spoke again, his words went through her like a blast of arctic air.

"Were you and Wolf planning to have something to eat here?" At her assenting nod, Darrel asked, "Then won't you join us? We'd love the company, wouldn't we, Micki?"

What could she possibly say? Her eyes wide with shock, she swung her gaze to Wolf. The glittery spark that blended with the silver told her she'd get no assistance from him. He was enjoying her discomfort. Biting back a moan, she curved her lips in a parody of a smile and lied.

"Yes, of course, we'd love to have you join us."

EIGHT

Uncomfortable and uneasy, Micki stole another glance at Wolf as he seated Bianca. At the same moment his glance shifted to her, his eyes glittering wickedly.

"All set to start the new job tomorrow, Micki?"

The lazily drawled question turned her unease into dismay. With those few words Wolf had managed to convey a familiarity between them to Darrel and Bianca. Pretending she didn't notice Darrel's startled reaction, Micki glared daggers at Wolf, her lips straining to keep her smile in place.

"Yes," she answered softly. "I've enjoyed my vacation, but I'm ready to go back to work."

"Micki is a buyer for Something Different boutiques," Wolf informed Bianca, adding to the familiarity. "She has just been transferred to the Atlantic City store."

"Oh! But—" Bianca began, her face mirroring confusion.

"Promoted."

The sharp word Darrel flung at Wolf cut across Bianca's quiet voice. For several seconds his eyes blazed a challenge at Wolf, then, as if suddenly realizing his rudeness, he smiled at Bianca and murmured, "I'm sorry I interrupted. Micki was promoted." His eyes flashed to Wolf. "Not transferred."

"Yes, of course." Wolf's cold as steel eyes contradicted his smooth tone. "I knew that."

Feeling caught in their crossfire and growing angry at the childish way they were squaring off at each other, Micki snapped, "Transferred, promoted, what difference does it make?"

Without waiting for a reply from either of them, Micki continued, "Either way, I begin tomorrow and I'm eager to start. Now," she finished strongly, "can we drop the subject?"

Bianca's puzzled expression slowly changed to one of amusement as her eyes shifted from one to the other of them. Her lips twitching, she soothed, "Micki's right, it is unimportant and—oh, good, here's our waitress."

The tension around the table eased with the arrival of the waitress, even though Micki felt the angry stiffness in Darrel when his arm brushed hers as he drew his chair closer to the table.

The waitress placed the delicious-looking, open-face sandwiches in front of Micki and Darrel, whipped two menus out from under her arm, and offering them to Bianca and Wolf, chirped, "Can I get you folks something to drink?"

"I don't need that." Wolf waved the menu away. "I'll have a Reuben and a beer."

"And," Bianca smiled, "as those sandwiches look good enough to eat, I'll have one of those and a glass of Chardonnay."

"You can bring me a beer too," Darrel inserted as the waitress moved to turn away. "Micki?"

"Another iced tea." Micki smiled faintly at the woman before, in a chiding way that left little doubt she was reminding Darrel of his manners, she emphasized, "Please."

At any other time Micki would have enjoyed being in Bianca's company, even though the exact relationship between the attractive woman and Wolf tormented her more than she cared to admit to herself. Being a permanent year-round resident of Cape May, Bianca was a fount of information on the town's history. Had it not been for her enlightening conversation, the atmosphere around the table would have been much more uncomfortable.

Even so Micki could hardly wait until the food had been consumed and the check was presented. Sighing with relief, Micki smiled brightly at the waitress when she placed the check on the table. The smile turned to a silent groan as hostilities were resumed between Wolf and Darrel.

"I'll take care of that."

Moving swiftly, Wolf's hand grabbed the check out from under Darrel's.

"But I invited you to join us." Darrel's angry glance clashed with glinting silver.

"But we intruded on your, er, privacy." Hard finality laced Wolf's tone as, turning away check in hand, he strode toward the building's entrance.

Finally they were back in the car heading for Ocean City.

"He's the man, isn't he?" Darrel shot the question at her savagely after some fifteen minutes of total silence. The suddenness of his attack startled Micki out of the blue funk she'd drifted into.

"W-what man?" she hedged.

"You know damned well what man," he growled frustratedly. "The bastard who's willing to fit you into his schedule now and then."

"Darrel, please."

"Please, hell," he snorted. "Do you have any idea how it makes me feel, knowing you turned me down for a man like that? Oh, I grant you," he sneered, "he's got the kind of looks that attract women. Of all ages apparently. As lovely and charming as Bianca Perriot is, the fact remains she is old enough to be his mother."

"Darrel." Micki's tone was sharp with admonishment. "Don't jump to conclusions. You don't know—"

"Don't kid yourself," Darrel interrupted jeeringly. "A man like Wolf—how apt, that name—doesn't waste his time on any woman unless she's putting out."

"Darrel!" Micki's shocked exclamation revealed the depth of pain his words had inflicted.

"Darrel what?" Unrepentant, he continued to fling words at her like blows. "Face the facts, Micki, he's a user and age means nothing. What does he do for a living?"

"I . . ." Micki paused, wet her lips, then admitted, "I don't know."

"I thought not." He shot a pitying glance at her and went on mercilessly. "I'll tell you what I think he does. I think the polite term is paid escort but, to call a spade a spade, I think he's a stud for hire."

"Be quiet!" Micki shouted angrily. "Don't you dare say another word. Even if what you say is true, it is none of your business." Her voice dwindling to a soft sigh, she added, "Or mine either."

They covered the remaining miles to her home in uneasy silence. The minute he stopped the car in front of the house, Micki flung the door open and ran out.

"Micki, wait," Darrel pleaded. "I'm sorry, I—"

"I don't want to talk about it," Micki snapped coldly.

"May I call you later in the week?" he called after her.

"No," Micki flung over her shoulder. "Or ever again."

"Micki!"

Walking quickly, she went into the house and closed the door on the sound of his voice. Her breath coming in gasps, Micki ran up the stairs and into her room. Taking short, agitated steps, she paced her room, around the bed to the window, then, turning sharply, back to the door again.

It wasn't true, she assured herself. What Darrel said wasn't true, it couldn't be, could it? No, of course it couldn't be. But what did he do for a living? What kind of job was it that paid enough to afford him the expensive clothes he wore, that boat and—she winced—that fantastic car. How much did a car like that cost anyway? More bucks than an ordinary job paid, of that she was sure. And the pants and shirt he was wearing today! Micki's trained eyes had told her they were hand tailored and had very probably cost him more than she earned in a month. And Bianca Perriot's simple little summer frock had practically screamed the words *created in Paris*. Was she very wealthy? Very, very likely, Micki decided. And the suspicious little thought crept into her mind: Had Bianca's still-smooth, diamond-bedecked slim hand written the check that had paid for Wolf's clothes?

Aghast at herself, Micki tore out of her room and along the hail to the stairs, running from her thoughts. It didn't work; her thoughts followed her. A note on the kitchen table informed her that her father and Regina had gone out for dinner. Alone, the quiet of the house pressing in on her, she curled up in a corner of the sofa, paperback in hand, in a vain attempt to lose herself.

She was reading a paragraph for the third time when the phone rang. Silently apologizing to the author, she put the book down and lifted the receiver.

"Hello?"

"Micki?" Tony's exuberant voice attacked her eardrum. "I couldn't wait to send you an invitation, I had to call you."

"You called her?" Micki exclaimed. "You talked to her?"

"I'm with her now," Tony laughed. "I didn't sleep at all last night. I kept thinking about what you said, asking myself should I, shouldn't I? Anyway, I called her first thing this morning and damned if you weren't right. Not only is she not married, or getting married—except to me— there was no ex-boyfriend at all." His laughter this time held a rueful note, and Micki could imagine him shaking his head. "I'll tell you, friend, it's a good thing I spilled my guts out to you last night; she was about ready to give up on me."

"After waiting this long?" Micki chided. "I somehow doubt that."

"Yes, well, she's not waiting any longer," Tony said determinedly. "And neither am I. We're getting married next Saturday and we want you to come. Can you make it, Micki?"

The anxious note that had crept into Tony's voice brought a rush of tears to Micki's eyes. "Can birds fly?" she shot back at him with a shaky laugh. "Just tell me what time, where, and give me directions and I'll be there with wedding bells on."

"If you'd want to, you could fly into Albany and I could meet the plane," he suggested. "Save you all that driving."

"You're on," Micki agreed. "I'll check into flight schedules tomorrow. Suppose you call me sometime midweek and I'll let you know what time."

"Will do. And Micki?" Tony's voice went rough with emotion. "We both thank you."

"You're both welcome," she whispered. Then she added, "Tony, does she have a name?"

"Shirley," Tony laughed. "Don't you love it?"

After she'd replaced the receiver, Micki went back to the sofa, a small smile curving her lips. Tony Menella getting married! Unbelievable. Memories rushed over her, and caught up in the flow, the tormenting suspicions about Wolf were pushed to the back of her mind.

The first thing that greeted Micki when she walked into the shop Monday morning was an announcement. Georgine, her large, dark eyes bright with excitement, was fairly twitching with news.

"I've been transferred."

"Transferred?" Micki cried. "Where? When?"

"The boss was in the day after you were here," Georgine laughed. "Told me they were opening a new store, asked me if I'd like to manage it."

"Manage? Georgine, that's wonderful," Micki enthused.

"That's what I thought," she drawled. "Then, when he told me where the store is he asked if I still wanted it." Her dark eyes rolled expressively. "I asked him if he'd like my eye teeth." Her beautiful face was drawn into a sober cast and her voice rasped deeply. "'No, thank you,' the man said, 'I've got a good set of fangs of my own.'"

The word *fangs* sent a picture of Wolf flashing into Micki's mind, and shaking her head impatiently, she pleaded, "Georgine, will you tell me where the store is?"

Georgine mentioned a large hotel chain, then said casually, "The one in Honolulu."

"Honolulu?" Micki repeated in an awed tone, then, much louder, "Honolulu?"

Jennell's soft laughter drifted to her from across the width of the shop, where both she and Lucy had stood watching Micki's reaction to the news. Then she drawled huskily, "Isn't it a shame? I mean, some poor girls have no luck at all. First Georgine can't find a man, now she gets shipped almost to the end of the earth—poor thing."

Georgine's excitement infected them all and Micki's first week at the store flew by without a hitch. Even her plans for attending Tony and Shirley's wedding went smoothly. Plans were also made by Micki, Jennell, and Lucy to take Georgine for dinner on Friday night, as she was leaving for Honolulu on Monday.

When she learned Micki was flying to Albany Saturday morning, Jennell suggested she pack a valise, bring it with her to the shop Friday, and spend the weekend at her apartment.

"I'll drive you to the airport Saturday morning and pick you up again Saturday night," Jennell said. "That way you won't have to leave your car at the airport."

All Micki's arguments about not wanting to put Jennell out ended up against a stone wall. Jennell was determined and Micki finally, laughingly, gave in.

Friday night was pure fun. After a wildly expensive dinner they went bar hopping, having decided there was safety in numbers, flirting madly and dancing until Micki thought she'd drop.

Saturday morning, still half asleep, Micki waved goodbye to an equally sleepy Jennell, boarded the plane, and promptly fell asleep, dead to the world until the plane touched down in Albany. A grinning Tony woke her completely with a bear hug and resounding kiss on the mouth.

"What are you up to?" Micki grinned back at him when he released her.

"I wanted to bring Shirl with me to meet you, but I'm not allowed to see the bride before the ceremony." His grin flashed again. "So come on, friend. You and I are going to have some lunch and you can hold my hand between now and then. Maybe you can even prevent the nervous fit I feel coming on."

Micki's first glimpse of Shirley was just before the ceremony and with that quick look she knew why Tony had put the young woman on a pedestal and had hesitated about making love to her. Small, fragile Shirley had the face of a cover model. Her own breath catching in her throat, Micki could well imagine the impact Shirley had on a supper-club crowd.

Although the ceremony was brief, it was beautiful and moving, and as Micki left the small church, she had to dab quickly at her eyes to blot the tears.

At the champagne supper given by the bride's parents, Micki discovered the girl behind the breathtaking face was not only very nice, but intelligent and quick-witted as well. When they saw her off at the airport, Micki kissed Shirl on the cheek and whispered, "I know you'll be very happy." Then loud enough for Tony to hear, "Keep this clown in line, won't you?"

"This clown wants a kiss too," Tony retorted, repeating his bear hug performance of that morning.

Tears in her eyes, Micki kissed him, warned him he'd better take damned good care of her new friend, then walked away from them with the advice they get on with the honeymoon and let her sniffle in peace.

Jennell was waiting as promised and had to hear all the wedding details on the way back to her apartment. Micki had all day Sunday to rest in the apartment by herself, as Jennell decided to do her boyfriend a favor and spend the day—and night—with him.

The nighttime part Micki found out about when Jennell telephoned the apartment around nine.

"Would you be all right on your own tonight, honey?" Jennell drawled the question hesitantly.

"Of course," Micki said at once. "Why?"

"Well, this deliciously bad man wants me to stay with him tonight, but I told him I'd have to confer with you first."

"Would you like to stay?" Micki asked devilishly.

"Is the ocean salty?" Jennell laid the drawl on thickly.

"Then stay," Micki laughed. "And Jennell—"

"Yes?"

"Be good."

"Are you crazy?" Jennell purred. "I'll be terrific."

Laughing softly, Micki replaced the receiver, then went still as a strange thought struck her. Why was it, she wondered, that she was so liberal-minded about her friends' sleeping arrangements and so rigid about her own? She knew, because Jennell had been open and frank, that this "deliciously bad" man was not the first

Jennell had slept with, yet she in no way thought of Jennell as promiscuous.

In fact, now that she gave it some thought, Micki could not come up with one name out of all her female friends who had not unashamedly admitted to sleeping with their current man. Why did she have to be odd woman out? Were her moral guidelines too narrow? Micki had never thought so, but, damn, she was the one alone tonight, every night.

The questions, all with the same theme, chased each other around in her mind as she prepared for bed. As she slid between the sheets the answer, which had been demanding exposure, finally broke through her self-imposed mental barrier. Very simply, she had felt no desire or even the slightest urge to be with any man other than one Wolf Renninger. And that one man scared the hell out of her. What had Darrel called him? A user of women? From her own experience Micki was very much afraid Darrel's judgment was correct. And what scared her was the almost certain feeling that should he get his hands on her again she would revel in his using, lose herself completely, and when his use of her was over, be lost forever.

Micki's second week in the shop sped by as quickly as the first. Georgine's absence was felt in more ways than one. Not only did they miss her droll sense of humor but her help in the shop as well. A sudden spurt of business kept them all on the run, and by the end of the week had nearly wiped out their stock of marked-down merchandise.

Saturday morning, half asleep and yawning, Micki walked into the kitchen to find her father and Regina talking over their after-breakfast coffee.

"Good morning, princess," Bruce smiled gently, studying her sleepy-eyed face. "You look tired, rough week?"

Returning the greeting, Micki nodded in answer. She had seen little of them all week, as staying late after the store closed to help Jennell straighten and restock the shop, she had shared a quick meal with her before driving home. She had found the house empty every night but Monday and had been asleep before they had returned.

Now Micki smiled her thanks as Regina placed a glass of juice and a cup of coffee on the table in front of her and murmured, "How was your week?"

"Oh, not bad," Bruce replied casually, too casually. That and the bright sheen of excitement in his eyes alerted her. "As a matter of fact we concluded that deal I was telling you about a couple of weeks ago. Do you remember?"

"Yes, I remember," Micki emphasized with a nod. "It's a very big deal?"

"Involving millions eventually," Bruce grinned. "And it's all signed and sealed and tonight we celebrate."

"I remember that also," Micki laughed before jumping up. Then she went over to her father and hugged him. "Congratulations. You've been working on this some time, haven't you?"

"A good long time," Bruce sighed, shaking his head. "With all the maneuvering and negotiating and people involved—several gears." He exhaled harshly. "For a while there, when I was hospitalized, I was afraid I was out of it. But this one," he nodded at Regina, "was fantastic. She became my legs, did all the running around for me, eased the pressure. And she shares equally in the rewards. So you may extend your congratulations in her direction as well."

Stunned, Micki stared at Regina for a moment. Regina's expression, a mixture of hesitancy and hope, loosened her tongue.

"Congratulations, fantastic lady." Micki's tone, though light, held real sincerity.

"Thank you."

The two simply spoken words conveyed an equally simple message to Micki. The hostilities between them were over. Micki nodded her head sharply once, sniffed, cleared her throat, then asked overbrightly, "What time does the celebration begin and where?"

"It began right here a moment ago," Bruce answered huskily. "It will continue at another realtor's place with a cold buffet lunch between one and two thirty and a clambake supper at seven. We'd like to leave here around twelve thirty, as the place is some miles inland. Can you be ready by then?"

"Yes, of course." Micki smiled, swallowing around the tightness in her throat caused by the suspicious brightness in his eyes. "How many people will be there?"

"Thirty or forty I expect." He grinned at the look of dismay that crossed her face. "Don't worry, honey, you'll know quite a few of them."

On arrival at the large country house Micki judged her father's estimate to be short by at least ten. But he had been right about one thing, she did know quite a few of the people.

Micki stayed with her father and Regina until after they had finished lunch, then she wandered off on her own to explore the extensive and beautiful grounds.

The place looked like a picture out of a magazine, and content with her own company, Micki strolled across the putting green, around the tennis courts, and onto the fringes of the pool area. Shading her eyes against the fierce glare of the sun's rays striking off the water, Micki watched a group of teenagers playing Follow the Leader off the diving board.

Continuing on, she completed her wide circling of the grounds, ending up on the other side of the house. It was another hot, humid day in a long summer that had grown monotonous with hot, humid days. As she threaded her way through the cars parked in front of the three-car garage, Micki brushed her hand over her perspiration-slick face, shivering as sweat trickled between her breasts and down her back.

Walking around the front of the house, she headed for the patio from where she'd begun her exploration. There were few people there, as most of the younger ones were either in the pool or engaged in other outdoor games and the older ones had retreated into the air-conditioned house where several bridge games were in session. After unwisely gulping down two gin and tonics at the small bar that had been set up at the end of the patio, she found a lounge chair in the shade, sank onto it, and was asleep within ten minutes.

As the sun trekked its way west, it inched up Micki's body, waking her when it touched her face. Bathed in sweat, her clothes plastered to her, feeling headachy and half sick, she went to the ground floor powder room. The cool interior of the house was a shock to her overheated body, and after rinsing her face and neck, she stood long minutes resting her forehead on the cool tiles. The rattle of the doorknob jerked her upright, and leaving the room she smiled wanly at the woman waiting to enter.

"They're about ready to serve the clambake," the woman informed her as she stepped into the powder room.

The thought of food made Micki's stomach lurch. She made her way slowly back to the patio and was about to step outside when she stopped cold, her breath suddenly constricted in her chest.

Wolf, looking cool and relaxed in chinos and a pale blue shirt, stood at the bar talking to two men. About to retreat and find another way to the area where the tables had been set up for supper, Micki heard the one man say, "Since you're alone today, Wolf, what do you say we do a disappearing act after supper and hunt up some action?"

"No, thanks." Wolf's soft laughter sent a shiver through

Micki. "When this Wolf goes on the prowl, he prowls alone."

The sickness increasing inside, Micki turned away sharply. His own words seemed to confirm Darrel's opinion of him. How could she be in love with a man like that? And what was he doing here anyway?

She was halfway across the room when her steps faltered, then stopped, her hand reaching out for something to hang on to. The room seemed to be moving around her and she felt funny, almost floaty. Then her fingers were caught by a hard male hand and a sharp voice demanded, "Micki, what's wrong? Are you sick?"

"I—I feel funny." Was that watery voice hers?

"Sit down." As he spoke, Wolf guided her into a chair, lowered her head gently to her knees, muttering, "Damn, no one's around, they're all at supper."

The light-headedness passed and Micki urged, "I'm all right now. Please go back to your friends."

"Don't be ridiculous," Wolf snapped. "I'm taking you home."

"But—"

That's as far as she got, for scooping her into his arms, Wolf ordered, "Be quiet," and carried her out of the house. He deposited her in his car and had turned to walk around to the driver's side when she exclaimed, "Dad and Regina! They'll wonder what happened to me."

"Relax," Wolf soothed. "I'll tell them."

Within minutes he was back sliding behind the wheel. Her head resting against the seat, eyes closed, Micki heard the engine roar to life, felt the car move slowly as he drove onto the road, then with a sudden surge, the Ferrari seemed to literally fly along the highway. Afraid to open her eyes, Micki listened for the siren's wail from a patrol car all the way home.

When Wolf brought the car to a stop in front of her

home, Micki stirred lethargically and murmured, "Thank you."

He didn't bother answering. He picked up her handbag and dug through it until he found her keys. Holding them up, he asked, "Which one?"

Ignoring her protests that it wasn't necessary, he helped her from the car and into the house. Once again the air-conditioned coolness went through her like a shock, and dropping into the first chair she came to, Micki closed her eyes against the renewed dizziness. She heard Wolf moving away and had to bite back a plea for him to stay.

Tears were slipping out from under her tightly closed lids when she felt something cool and wet touch her face. Wiping gently, Wolf bathed her face and neck.

"That's good," Micki sighed. Nearly unconscious, unaware that she spoke aloud, she murmured, "I haven't felt this bad since the abortion."

The damp cloth stopped moving and stirring restlessly she pleaded, "Don't stop."

"What abortion?" There was an odd, breathless quality to Wolf's husky tone that confused her already fuzzy mind. "When?"

She'd forgotten the question, and moving her head from side to side, she frowned and murmured, "What?"

"Your abortion, Micki," Wolf urged, his voice sounding strange. "When did you have it?"

The mistiness was clearing now, and opening her eyes, Micki stared in confusion into Wolf's pale face. He looked strained, with white shadowy lines around his mouth.

"When, Micki?" The tone of his voice flicked at her like a lash.

"While I was still in college," she answered honestly, actually afraid to lie to him. "Six years ago."

NINE

"Six years ago?"

The question emerged softly through lips that barely moved. Wolf was absolutely still for long, frightening moments then, his hands grasping her arms painfully, he pulled her to her feet to face him.

"You got rid of my baby?" he whispered hoarsely. When she didn't answer at once, he began to shake her hard. Fear closed her throat, making it almost impossible for her to answer. Feeling the faintness closing in on her again, she forced two words past the fear.

"Wolf, please."

He didn't even hear her. His face a terrifying mask of rage, he shook her harder and shouted, "You killed my baby?"

With a low moan Micki welcomed the blackness that covered her mind, blanking out the harsh sound of Wolf's voice.

When she opened her eyes again, she was lying on her bed. Wolf was sitting on its edge bending over her, his silvery eyes cold and blank. The expression of contempt on his face sent a shudder rippling through her and she began to shake. When he moved, her heart thumped wildly, and when his hands again grasped her arms, she brought her palms up against his chest, pleaded, "Wolf, please."

Before he could speak or even move, there was a loud exclamation from the doorway.

"Micki, Wolf!" Bruce said sharply. "What in the hell's going on here?"

Micki froze, her mind, her whole body seemingly turned to stone. His face becoming amazingly calm, Wolf released her and stood up with an easiness that was contradicted by the tenseness she could feel in him.

"Not what you apparently think," he replied smoothly. "Micki fainted."

Bruce obviously didn't believe Wolf, for he snapped, "You have no right in Micki's room."

"Not yet," Wolf returned. "But I will have very soon. Micki and I are going to be married."

"No!"

"Married!"

Micki's choked whisper went unheard, covered as it was by her father's loud exclamation.

"Yes." Wolf's flat tone held a ring of finality and the icy silver glance he threw at her told her he'd listen to nothing from her.

Panic-stricken, Micki moved to get up to run to her father for protection, but the look of delight on his face stopped her.

"Wolf, that's great news." Smiling broadly, hand extended, Bruce walked to Wolf and clasped his hand warmly. "I couldn't be more pleased." Losing its brightness, his smile turned rueful. "I must admit that, for a minute there, I thought you—"

"We *have* been lovers, Bruce." Wolf's cool tone sliced across Bruce's words.

In shocked disbelief Micki's eyes darted from Wolf to her father, who looked, for a moment, like a time bomb ready to go off. A muscle in his jaw twitched from the pressure of his clenched teeth. Was Wolf crazy? What had possessed him to say such a thing? Trying to ward off the fight she felt sure was coming, Micki rushed into speech.

"Dad, let me explain." Micki scrambled off the bed and ran to her father, placing a detaining hand on the bunched-up muscle in his arm. "It happened—" That was as far as she got.

"It happened," Wolf repeated her words with cold finality, "because we both wanted it to happen." Ignoring her gasp, he stared coolly into Bruce's furious eyes. "Cool off, Bruce. So, okay, we didn't wait for the words, the ring, the document." He paused, then underlined, "Did you?"

The question caught Micki by surprise and in unwilling curiosity she glanced at her father's face.

"No."

Even though the light of battle had gone out of Bruce's eyes and Micki could feel the tension easing in his arm, Bruce had not given the answer. The softly spoken word had come from Regina who stood, until now unnoticed, in the doorway. Bruce turned his head to gaze for several seconds into his wife's composed face then, turning back to Wolf, Bruce echoed honestly, "No, we didn't wait."

"I *am* going to marry her, Bruce."

Wolf's statement, delivered with what Micki thought was overbearing confidence, vanquished what was left of her father's anger while at the same time igniting her own. Before she could voice her protest however, her father again clasped Wolf's hand.

"You've made your point, Wolf. I'm sorry if I came on a little heavily as the outraged father, but Micki's my only child and very important to me."

"I understand." Wolf accepted his surrender gracefully. "I'll take very good care of her, Bruce."

Feeling invisible, anger seethed inside Micki. Wasn't she going to be allowed to speak at all? Apparently not, for before she could open her mouth, Regina suggested from the doorway, "We still have that bottle of champagne we were saving for a special occasion, Bruce. Don't you think this is the time to open it?"

"The perfect time," Bruce agreed, grinning broadly. "What are we standing here for? Let's go crack it open." He turned, began walking to the doorway, then, as if in afterthought, glanced back at Micki. "You feel all right now, honey?"

She wasn't even allowed to hand out her own health reports, for Wolf answered for her.

"She's fine now. I think the excitement got to her."

Excitement! You fatuous jerk, Micki thought furiously, *I'll excitement you!* Frustrated anger searing her throat, Micki watched her father drape his arm around Regina's shoulders as he left the room. The moment they were out of hearing she turned on Wolf.

"Have you gone mad?" Incensed, she spat the words at him. "I wouldn't marry you if I was ugly as sin and desperate. And, as you got yourself into this, you can damned well get yourself out of it. I'm going down there and stop them before they open that stupid bottle."

She spun away from him only to be spun right back again forcefully. Wolf's hand grasping her upper arm held her still. His voice, cold as ice, sent a chill skipping down her spine.

"No, you're not." His eyes bored into hers like steel drill bits. "You are going down there with me and accept their toast, and, as soon as they are back from the coast, you are going to marry me. You owe me."

"I owe you!" In her astonishment at his charge Micki missed the menace in his tone. "I owe you nothing."

"You owe me," he repeated coldly. "One child. When you produce that child, you may have your freedom."

Eyes widening in disbelief, Micki stared at him. He isn't mad, she thought wildly, he's a raving maniac. Fighting to control the renewed panic in her voice, she sneered, "You have got to be kidding. There is no way I'd share a child with you."

"I didn't say share it," Wolf sneered back. "I said produce it. You got rid of my baby," he added crudely, "and you're going to damn well replace it."

"But that was six years ago!" Micki cried, not even attempting to correct him about how the child was lost.

"I don't give a damn if it was a hundred and six years ago. You're going to give me my child, my legitimate child. So stop arguing and let's go down and join the celebration." He started toward the door, dragging her with him. Before stepping through the doorway he paused, cocking one eyebrow at her. "Unless, of course, you want me to give your father—in minute detail—a blow-by-blow description of the weekend we spent together?" Again he paused before adding silkily, "And exactly how old you were at the time? You have"—he glanced at his watch unconcernedly—"fifteen seconds to decide."

A picture of her father's outraged expression of a few minutes ago followed by the fury he'd displayed about her being in Tony's apartment flashed through Micki's mind. Decide? What was to decide? She knew positively that should Wolf tell her father about that weekend their relationship would be irreparably damaged. Oh, he would not stop loving her, but he would never trust her again. The taste of defeat burning bitterly in her throat, she lashed out at him unthinkingly, "You rotten son-of-a—"

"Watch it." Wolf's warning, though soft, silenced her. Releasing her, he strode out of the room and along the hall. For one rebellious second Micki hesitated, then, hating herself, she hurried after him.

Wolf stayed long after the last drops of wine had been drained from the bottle. Stretched out lazily on a chair in the living room as if he belonged there, he smilingly lied through his teeth to her father and Regina.

Yes, he had been seeing Micki for some time, he assured

them. And yes, they were both sure they did not want a large wedding. And no, unfortunately, they would not be able to get away on a honeymoon trip at this time, as, he was sure, Bruce and Regina could fully understand.

That part puzzled her. Why could her father and Regina fully understand that of all things? That question was answered for her after Wolf finally left, making a big production of drawing her out onto the porch with him, ostensibly to bestow a good-night kiss, in reality to warn: "Don't say anything stupid."

Flaming mad, Micki went back into the house prepared to take her chances and tell her father the truth. Her father's first words to her rang the death knell on that idea.

"You've made me very proud and happy, honey," he praised her seriously.

Her guns effectively spiked, Micki pondered his words in confusion. Somewhere along the road she had definitely missed something. Her father spoke as if he not only knew Wolf, but knew him well. And it was more than apparent that his opinion of Wolf differed vastly from Darrel's. Choosing her words carefully, Micki tried to close her intelligence gap.

"I'm relieved that you're pleased," she said slowly. "I was a little apprehensive about your reaction."

"Apprehensive?" Bruce's eyebrows shot up. "But why?"

"Well." Micki stole a glance at Regina. "He does have something of a reputation with women, doesn't he?"

"Micki," Regina inserted urgently before her father could answer. "Please let me explain."

"What's to explain?" Bruce waved his hand expressively. "So over the years he's been seen with a lot of different women. He chose you. Good Lord, did you think I wouldn't realize what a compliment that is? The man is a millionaire several times over and a damned attractive one in the bargain. I'd have to be out of my mind to object to him as a son-in-law."

Micki's attention to her father's small speech ended with the words *millionaire several times over.* Wolf, a millionaire? Micki shuddered. Forcing herself to concentrate, she caught her father's last words.

"—and I have enormous respect for him. You just put your mind at rest about the other women, honey. At thirty-six he's obviously been waiting for the right woman. I'm delighted that woman is you."

What could she possibly say? There was no way she could look into his happy face and say, *Look, Dad, I hate to burst your bubble, but the threat of a firing squad wouldn't make me marry Wolf Renninger. Why? Because you see, Dad, he only wants me for the length of time it will take to produce one child. A child he mistakenly thinks I owe him. He may be wealthy and he may be attractive, but he is also vindictive and he wants what he believes is his due. And, Dad, I'm afraid that in the process he is going to tear me into tiny little pieces.* No, she very definitely could not say that.

What to do then? Micki shuddered. There was nothing she could say to him. Fatalistically Micki determined to give Wolf his due then run for what was left of her life. Hell, she shrugged mentally, everyone got divorced today anyway. Her mind made up, Micki pushed aside the small voice that cried, *That attitude may work for other people but not for you, it will destroy you.*

Presently the conversation switched from that of Micki's future wedding to the more immediate topic of Bruce and Regina's vacation trip. After receiving her father's repeated instructions on what to do if . . . with a gentle smile, Micki excused herself and went to her room. Convinced she wouldn't sleep, yet deciding she may as well be comfortable while awake, she had a tepid shower, slipped a nightie over her head, and slid between the sheets, where the exhausting events of the day caught up with her and she fell promptly asleep.

* * *

The morning was half gone before Micki woke. Feeling dull and still tired, she lay staring at the ceiling trying to come to grips with the unbelievable happenings of the night before. That Wolf was a millionaire was in itself plenty to think about, especially as she had begun to suspect Darrel was right in his assessment of him. But that her father obviously knew him much better than she did herself, and liked him as well, was almost too much to assimilate. How had they originally met? And not only how, but why had they become so well acquainted? Wolf had called her father Bruce. Not Mr. Durrant, but Bruce, and to Micki that indicated a friendship, at least of sorts. Frowning, Micki got out of bed. She would simply have to ask someone.

She found that someone sitting at the kitchen table drinking coffee.

"Good morning, Micki." Pushing his chair back, Wolf rose to his feet, his eyes cautioning her to watch her reaction to his presence.

"Good morning," she managed huskily. "What are—I didn't expect to see you this morning."

"Wolf's going to drive us to the airport," Bruce said placidly. "He's got the motel station wagon."

"How nice," Micki cooed, looking away from the silvery eyes that sparked with fire at her tone. "And at exactly what time does the exodus begin?"

Unaccustomed to sarcasm from her, Bruce and Regina turned surprised eyes to her.

"Are you all right, princess?" Bruce asked, a frown creasing his forehead.

"Yes, of course, I'm sorry." Micki was instantly contrite. For heaven's sake, she chided herself, a sarcastic mouth won't solve anything. Lowering her eyes, she murmured,

"I think I'm missing you already, and you haven't even left yet."

"I knew it," Regina wailed in dismay. "I knew it was too soon after her homecoming to go away."

"No, Regina, really," Micki rushed to assure her. "I don't mind. I guess I'm still a little washed out from yesterday."

Bruce's eyes flicked from his wife to his daughter, an indecisive expression on his face. While Wolf sat silently, his eyes narrowing on Micki.

"Bruce," Regina said softly, "maybe with the wedding coming up this isn't the best time—"

"This is the perfect time," Wolf interrupted quietly. "If anyone has earned a vacation, you two have." His glance, cold and hard, sliced back to Micki. "You leave the 'princess' to me."

"We-ell, if you're positive," Bruce asked hopefully.

"I'm positive," Wolf replied in a hard tone. Then, his tone lighter, he grinned. "By the time you get back, all the arrangements will have been made and you can sit back and enjoy watching me hang myself."

Bruce and Regina returned his grin and the bad moment was past, except for Micki, who wanted very badly to slap Wolf's face.

The jet made its charge down the runway and then it was airborne, its nose lifting regally toward the sky. Biting her lip, Micki watched the plane until it was swallowed up into the sun-splashed expanse of blue.

"Come on, Micki," Wolf chided dryly. "I'll take you home and let you cry on my shoulder."

Micki flinched away from his voice and the hand he placed at the back of her waist. Ignoring the hard thump her heart gave at the forbidding lines his face set into, Micki moved away from him quickly. At the car she again shook off his helping hand and slid onto the seat without looking at him. The way he palmed the gear lever as he shot out of the parking area told her clearly how angry she'd made him.

The silence was broken only one time on the drive back to her home. That was when he asked, "Would you like to stop for dinner?" And she answered, "No, thank you."

When he stopped the car in front of the house and reached for his door release, she said sharply, "Please, don't bother to get out. I'm tired, I have to work tomorrow and I'm going to bed."

She could feel his icy eyes boring into her back until she closed the front door and heard the car roar away from the curb.

The week that followed was nerve-racking for Micki. Business was slow at a time she very badly needed to keep busy. Wolf did not come to the house or call all week, and by Sunday night she had to mentally chide herself to stop pacing.

What was he trying to do? She had heard him tell her father that all the arrangements would be made when he and Regina got back and they would be home in one more week. Was he trying to upset her? Make her nervous? The questions tormented her as she paced from room to room, tired but too uptight to sit still.

Monday afternoon, busy at last checking over the arrival of a shipment of clothes purchased for the holiday season, Micki went into the shop to question Jennell on an item, not bothering to look up when the door opened.

"On your toes," Jennell drawled softly. "The boss just walked in with a very enticing piece on his arm."

Glancing up, Micki felt her stomach flip and heard her breath hiss through her dry lips. Cool, relaxed Wolf walked toward her, his head bent slightly to one side as he listened to what the woman beside him said. A small smile playing at his lips, he nodded, then lifted his head to stare coolly into Micki's eyes.

"Hello, Jennell." Wolf's smile deepened. "This is Brenda Rider, Micki's replacement."

During the short, shocked silence that followed Wolf's announcement, Micki felt her hands go cold while her temper flared red hot.

"Micki's re—?" Jennell stopped short, her eyes flying to Micki's. "You're leaving?"

"Yes," Wolf answered for her. "To get married." A wicked light sprang into his eyes as he tacked on casually. "To me."

"Married!"

"Married!"

Jennell's outcry was echoed by Lucy, who at that moment came out of the stockroom to see what was keeping Micki.

"But she never said a word," Jennell moaned. Turning reproachful eyes on Micki, she asked, "Why didn't you tell us?"

"I think I can answer that." Wolf again answered for her. "Micki wanted an easy, comfortable working relationship with you girls and she was afraid if she told you that would not be possible."

"Yes, I see," Jennell murmured, then, her eyes widening in alarm, she gasped. "Oh, Micki, that first day, I told you about—"

"It doesn't matter," Micki, fully aware that Jennell was referring to the previous buyer, cut in hastily. "It's of no importance really." Ignoring the questioning look Wolf leveled at her, she turned to the woman with him. "How do you do, Brenda. I'm, as you heard, Micki and this is Jennell and Lucy." A small devil taking sudden possession of her, Micki lifted her hand, waved it in a shooing motion at Wolf and ordered, "Go away, Wolf, we'll take care of Brenda."

Another small silence followed Jennell's and Lucy's barely concealed gasps. Smiling sardonically, Wolf walked up to Micki, bent his head, and kissed her soundly on the mouth. When he lifted his head he grinned wickedly before, strolling to the door, he drawled, "You're the boss, baby—for now."

When she left the shop he was waiting for her, as she knew he would be. Falling into step beside her, he said, "We're having dinner together. I think it's time we talked."

He took her to a small, elegant, dimly lit dining room in another casino hotel. As it was still fairly early, only two of the room's tables were occupied, and given their choice of empty tables, Wolf indicated his preference for a secluded corner on the far side of the room. As they waited for their pre-dinner drinks, Micki's eyes scanned the room, the other diners, the black-jacketed waiter, everywhere but Wolf's face. When the drinks were served, Micki smiled vaguely at the waiter and studied his slender, retreating form, wondering irrelevantly if he had to lay flat on his back to close his skintight pants.

"Now that you've done a complete inventory of the place and its occupants," Wolf inquired dryly, "do you think you could force your attention in this direction?"

Micki turned her head slowly, a disdainful expression on her face. Her icy glance didn't quite come off, however, as the flush that tinged her cheeks robbed it of its effect. Wolf, sipping at his martini, watched Micki intently, which deepened the heat in her face even more. Unable to maintain his narrow-eyed survey, Micki lowered her eyes to the glass of Merlot in front of her. His soft, weary-sounding sigh drew her eyes back to his.

"How did it go with Brenda this afternoon?" His even tone warned her he was just about at the end of his patience.

"Very well," she answered tightly, not even trying to hide her resentment. "As I'm very well aware you knew it would."

"Cool it, Micki," he advised softly. "We're not going to get anywhere if you keep this attitude."

"What gives you the idea I want to get anywhere?" she asked coldly.

"Calm down, babe." Wolf cautioned. "Okay, you're steamed, but damn it, Micki, I want you to stop working."

"I will not be ordered—" She broke off as the waiter approached their table to take their dinner orders. The minute he'd walked away again, Micki snapped angrily, "I will not be ordered around."

"And I told you I don't want my wife working," Wolf snapped back.

"I'm not your wife yet." Micki had to speak very softly to keep from shouting. "And I don't want—"

"I don't particularly care what you want," Wolf cut across her soft voice coldly. "It's done, you've been replaced, face it. Face this as well, there is no way you're getting out of this marriage, I want what's mine, and I usually get what I want."

"Spoken like a dyed-in-the-wool spoiled brat," Micki sneered. "It must be wonderful to be rich."

"It sure as hell beats being poor," Wolf taunted, his lips twitching with amusement. "I'll give you six months, then ask you if you agree." Then his face sobered and the near-smile disappeared. "You may have anything your tiny little heart desires as my wife, Micki."

For some reason the hard emphasis he'd placed on the word *tiny* caused a sharp pain in the area mentioned. Hating the idea that he could hurt her so effortlessly, Micki taunted nastily, "In exchange for one child?"

"Precisely," Wolf answered coldly.

Once again they fell silent as the waiter served their meal. Staring at the food disinterestedly, Micki felt her eyes burning suddenly with a rush of memories. How totally different this was compared to the makeshift meals they had laughingly prepared and shared that long-ago weekend.

Automatically Micki put food in her mouth, chewed without tasting, desperately loving the Wolf she'd known then, desperately trying to hate the Wolf who sat opposite her now. When he spoke, his tone had thawed, but the taunting note remained.

"Would you care to hear my family's history?"

"If I must." Glancing up sharply, Micki leveled an accusing look at him. "I've been working for you right along, haven't I?"

"I honestly didn't know it, Micki." Wolf's tone held the clear tone of truth. "I seldom bother with the shops in any way. Not, that is, until the last few months."

"The previous buyer?" Micki asked oversweetly.

"The previous buyer," he agreed calmly. "She was no babe-in-the-woods; she knew the score. I suspect her vision was clouded by dollar signs. When she became possessive, I shipped her out." He paused, one brow raised as if asking if there were any questions. When there were none, he continued. "As I had done the shipping, I was given the job of replacing. I asked for a list of qualified possibles; your name was on it."

"You chose me deliberately?" she asked tightly, hating the thought of the previous buyer, yet refusing to let him know.

"Yes," Wolf answered bluntly.

"As a replacement in the store?" Micki asked smoothly. "Or—other places?"

"Don't push it, Micki," he warned softly.

"Okay." Micki backed off hastily. "Commence with the history."

"It's a long story," Wolf began. "But I'll cut it to the bone. It started with my great-grandfather who, as a young man, bought an inn with rooms for overnight guests along the Lancaster Pike near Lancaster, Pennsylvania. He prospered and as he did, he bought more inns and several small hotels in the southeastern part of the state. He was a rich man by the time he declared he was ready to retire. Leaving the running of his business in the capable hands of his only child, my grandfather, he grabbed his long-patient wife and took off for Florida."

Here his story was interrupted as the waiter came to clear the table and take their order for coffee. When that service had been completed, Wolf continued his narrative.

"Like most men who survive on work, he couldn't rest until he'd explored the possibilities in Florida. Before he died he'd acquired six hotels along the southeast coast. When he died he was a millionaire. My grandfather followed bravely in his footsteps. Deciding to take a chance, he invested heavily in a new type of travelers' accommodations: the motels. Payday, bonanza, and the whole bit. It was a smashingly successful venture.

"My grandfather's marriage had produced two sons. My father," he grinned, "Wolfgang the third, and my uncle Eric, who was ten years his junior. Eric was killed in the last days of Vietnam. His death triggered a heart attack that killed my grandfather a few months later. As Eric was childless, the growing monster, as we called the family business, went to my father. Here's where my mother enters the picture. Working beside him, she learned the business inside out. My father had one passion besides my mother. He loved to sail. He was drowned, blown overboard, during a yacht race off the coast of South America. That left my mother and the rest of us to manage the business."

"The rest of you?" Micki probed.

"My father had better luck than his father and grandfather," Wolf supplied. "I have two brothers and a sister. My sister's the baby." Taking a test sip of his coffee, he glanced around the now-crowded room. "Family history to be continued," he said quietly. "Drink your coffee, Micki, and let's get out of here."

TEN

They were quiet as they left the hotel, the silence broken only when Wolf asked if Micki would like to gamble for a while before going home. Her only answer was a sharp shake of her head, which he accepted without comment.

"Go on with your story," Micki urged as soon as they'd left the heaviest traffic behind. "Or should I say your saga?"

"Got you interested against your will," Wolf taunted gently. "Didn't I?"

His soft, teasing tone did strange things to her breathing and for a flashing instant she ached all over for the feel of his arms around her. The mere thought of his mouth against hers drew a low moan from her throat that she somehow managed to turn into a whispered, "Yes."

"Where was I?" he asked himself. "Oh, yes, my brothers and sister. Eric is thirty-four, dark, unbelievably handsome and married to a rather plain, incredibly lovely woman we all adore. They have two fair-haired, beautiful little girls. Eric takes care of the southeast, and now Honolulu, operations."

"Where does he live?" Micki asked when he stopped to draw a deep breath.

"Near Miami," Wolf replied. "Brett is thirty-one, taller than I, very slim, fair like our mother, not quite as handsome as Eric, and married one year to a vivacious redheaded ex-flight attendant. They have no children—too busy having fun. They live in Atlanta. Brett handles things in the mid-Atlantic coastal area. While I, as you've probably figured out by now, take care of the northeast coastal area business."

"Is your mother retired?" Micki interjected.

"My mother?" Wolf laughed. "Hardly. At sixty-one, she is still beautiful, energetic, and she holds the reins on the rest of us with iron control. She saw the potential in condominiums a long time ago. It was through her that the company branched out to include them. Now"—he shot her a smile that made her heart skip—"I've covered everyone but Diane. As I stated, Di is the baby of the outfit. She just turned thirty. She's blond, a beautiful reflection of our mother, and every bit as headstrong. When she finished college, she told mother she wanted to do something different." He threw her a what-can-I-tell-you look. "Mother listened to her ideas, thought about it all of ten minutes, then, presto, we're in the boutique business. Di worked like hell in the shops until going into semi-retirement when her first child was born five years ago, she has two boys. Di and her husband also live near Miami, as does our mother. Her husband took on the mantle of manager."

"Hank Carlton," Micki inserted his name.

"Yes." They had been parked in front of her home for several minutes. Now, stepping out of the car, Wolf finished. "And there you have it. Any questions?"

"Yes," Micki answered, sliding off the seat. "Several."

"How about posing them over a cold drink?" he chided softly when she'd stopped short at the door. "All that talking has dried me out."

Micki stared at him for some moments before, giving in with a short nod, she unlocked the door and went in. Heading for the kitchen, she waved at the living room and murmured, "Make yourself comfortable. What would you like to drink?"

"Plain water," he called after her. "Two ice cubes."

When she went into the living room, his drink in one hand, a glass of iced tea for herself in the other, he was sitting on the sofa, long legs stretched out in front of him, his head back, eyes closed. He had removed his jacket and tie and had opened the first three buttons of his shirt and the sheer, masculine sight of him sent a shaft of longing through her that was so intense her hands trembled. His eyes opened at the tinkling sound made by the ice tapping the insides of the glasses. Straightening, he took the glass she extended, patted the cushion beside him, and said, "Light and fire away."

Micki sat in the very center of the cushion, then stared into her glass to avoid looking into Wolf's amusement-filled eyes.

"How and when did you meet my father?" she blurted suddenly.

"I met him a few months before I met you." Although Wolf's tone was serious, it held a fine thread of laughter. "He handled the real estate transaction on the property where the motel now stands. He has been involved in every one of our property transactions in this area since then."

Micki turned wide, astonished eyes to him. "The big deal they were celebrating Saturday a week ago, that was yours?"

"The company's," he corrected gently. "Yes. And the big deal concerned not only another motel in the area, but a condominium in Cape May as well. Your father, several other realtors, and I had our work cut out for us talking Bianca Perriot out of the land the condo's going up on. Over six years of work, as a matter of fact."

"Bianca Perriot?" Micki repeated faintly, a sick feeling invading her stomach.

"You remember, you met her a few weeks ago," Wolf prompted.

"Yes, of course, a lovely woman." Micki hesitated, but she had to ask, had to know. "You said over six years ago?"

Nodding, Wolf smiled ruefully. "The property had been in her husband's family for years. She wasn't sure if she should let it go." His tone took on a bitter edge. "She's the person I had an appointment with the day I brought you home from the boat. She batted all of us back and forth like tennis balls until a few weeks ago. It was motels and condos that brought me into this area in the first place."

Feeling foolish and stupid for the suspicions she'd harbored about Bianca, Micki was only too glad to change the subject.

"Brought you from where?"

"I was fairly well established in a New York office when I received orders from H.Q. to scout out the possibilities along the south Jersey coast," Wolf enlightened her. "At first I sent my assistant, whose reports were not very promising. I relayed the reports to H.Q. and received in reply just eight words. They were *If you want a job done right, move.* I moved."

Unable to believe anyone would dare issue an order like that to him, let alone that he'd meekly obey it, Micki stared at him in wide-eyed wonder.

At the look of shocked incredulity on her face, Wolf threw his head back and roared.

"Oh, honey," he finally managed between gasps for breath. "I assure you I did—post-haste. When that chairlady of the board gives an order, people better jump, most especially her sons. Since she took over, she has nearly tripled the company's combined income. No one argues with her."

"I see," Micki said softly, then a trifle fearfully, "and will I be expected to meet this business wizard?"

"Most certainly," he grinned. "She's looking forward to it. But don't let the thought throw you, it's only her sons she cracks the whip at. Away from the office she's the most charming woman you could meet and a very understanding mother-in-law to my brothers' wives."

"You said," Micki rushed in as soon as he'd finished, "she's looking forward to meeting me. She knows about me?"

"Of course," Wolf answered easily. "I told her I was getting married when I flew to Miami to fill her in on the latest developments here." He paused before adding sardonically, "I was gone all last week—in case you hadn't noticed."

Micki felt her cheeks grow warm at the piercing look he gave her, and trying to hide her nervousness, she jumped up and asked, "Can I get you another drink?"

"No, thank you." Wolf's tone had changed. All business now, he went on briskly. "Sit down, Micki, we have plans to make."

"What plans?" Micki asked sharply, sitting down on the exact same spot she'd just vacated.

"You know damned well what plans," Wolf sighed tiredly. "I told your father that everything would be taken care of by the time he and Regina got home and I intend to see that everything is." His tone went brisk again. "Now we can do this the easy way, or we can do it the hard way, but, either way, it will be done. So, if you have any preferences, let's hear them."

"Like what, for instance?"

"Damn it, Micki." Wolf stood up abruptly, as if having to get away from her, and strode across the room. Turning suddenly, he raked his long-fingered hand through his hair and barked, "You know like what. Like do you want a church wedding with all the attendant hoopla, or would you prefer something more simple? If you want a big splash, we have got to get it together. As I understand it, a large wedding takes several months to arrange. Personally I'd just as soon get it over with. The sooner the better."

Subdued by his outburst, Micki sat silent so long Wolf growled, "For chrissake, Micki, talk to me or I'll go ahead on my own and make all the arrangements."

"You seem to forget," Micki shouted at him. "I don't want to get married at all."

Striding back across the room, Wolf bent over her and said harshly, "I haven't forgotten a thing. Not one single thing. Do you understand?"

Cringing back into the sofa, Micki whispered, "Yes, damn you." Closing her eyes against the hard glitter in his, she added, "Make any plans you like. It means nothing to me."

She felt him move closer to her, felt his warm breath whisper over her skin an instant before his mouth covered hers. Steeling herself against an onslaught, she was completely undone by the gentleness of his kiss. His lips explored hers tenderly, coaxing them apart as he sat down beside her and drew her gently into his arms. Determined to remain cold in his arms, Micki groaned with dismay when her mouth, then her body, responded hungrily to his. Bringing her hands up to his chest to push him away, her fingers, as if with a mind of their own, sought his warm skin at the opening of his shirt. She was trembling on the brink of surrender when he lifted his head and whispered, "I think I'll very much enjoy making you eat your words. But don't worry about it, I'll sweeten them for you."

Shocked into cold reality by his taunt, Micki pushed at his chest. Breathing harshly, she growled, "Get out of here. I don't want you to touch me or even look at me. You sicken me."

Anger flared in his eyes before his narrowed lids concealed it. Rising to his feet in a quick, fluid movement, he picked up his jacket and headed for the door tossing over his shoulder, "I'll call you when the arrangements are completed."

"Drop dead," Micki called after him, feeling very childish when she heard his mocking laughter.

Micki heard nothing from him until Friday morning. During the interval she received three post cards from her father and Regina, alternately extolling the beauties of the West Coast and their growing excitement about her marriage.

Wolf's first words to Micki when she answered the phone Friday morning were, "I'll pick you up in half an hour. We're going for the license."

Three hours later they were back at the house, everything taken care of. They would be married, Wolf had informed her coldly, late Tuesday afternoon. It would be a civil ceremony, no fuss, no bother. Even the witnesses would be impersonal county employees.

Wanting to weep and forcing herself not to, Micki held her head high and snapped, "That's fine with me," and walked into the house, forcing herself not to run.

Panic built steadily during the rest of that day and all day Saturday. Sunday brought relief in the form of her father and Regina's return, and chagrin in the form of Wolf's arrival at the house soon afterward.

For several hours Micki managed to avoid speaking directly to Wolf. Intent on keeping her father and Regina talking, she coaxed an almost hour-by-hour description of their activities from them. Finally, unable to pull one more question from her mind, Micki grew silent and tense.

"Now that my inquisitive offspring has apparently run down," Bruce laughed teasingly, "perhaps one of you will answer a few questions for me."

Leaving Wolf to the answering, Micki went to the sink to make a pot of fresh coffee, and as it was already past dinnertime, to prepare a light supper of salad and sandwiches.

Both Bruce and Regina voiced protest at the meager wedding plans. Wolf listened to all their arguments patiently but remained adamant in his resolve to go through with them as stated. The shuffling around as Micki served the hastily put together meal ended the argument. By the time Wolf left, Bruce and Regina had resigned themselves to the inevitable.

Monday morning, Labor Day, Micki stared out her bedroom window at the bright, hot day, and wished she'd accepted Cindy's invitation to join them for a barbecue. Sighing at the memory of Cindy's excitement on hearing that Micki was getting married, she turned listlessly when Regina entered the room.

"We have really got to talk now, Micki," Regina said nervously, "about Wolf, and what happened six years ago."

"I don't see what good—"

"Maybe none," Regina interrupted, closing the door. "I'm afraid I made a bad error in judgment that day."

"Error in judgment?" Micki repeated blankly. "In what way?"

"In the depth of your feelings for Wolf. I thought you an immature teenager infatuated with an older, exciting man. And it wasn't like that, was it? You were very much in love." Without waiting for Micki to comment she went on. "You still are."

"Am I?" Micki asked carelessly.

"Your cool facade doesn't fool me, Micki," Regina chided. "I've watched you ever since you came home. As much as you try to hide it, you light up at the mere mention of his name."

"Why are you doing this, Regina?" Micki whispered.

"Because I must," she answered tightly. "Because I can't let you marry him thinking there had been something between us. There wasn't."

Micki went cold. Then she got hot, blazingly hot.

"Then why did you infer that there was?" Micki asked bitingly. "What was the purpose?"

"I thought I was protecting you," Regina explained. At the look of disgusted disbelief that crossed Micki's face, Regina insisted. "I truly was, Micki. Wolf had been involved with several women that I knew of. But they were mature women able to take care of themselves. You were only nineteen, and when I saw that mark on your neck—" Regina shrugged. "I just felt I had to do something to keep you from getting hurt."

"But I heard you talking to him on the phone," Micki argued.

"On the phone?" Regina looked blank, then confused. "But as far as I can remember, all we talked about was real estate. I had gone to New York with your father against Wolf's advice, and he as much as said I told you so. He had stayed to talk to Bi—"

"I know," Micki cut in weakly.

Later, after Regina left, Micki paced her room like a caged tiger. Six years! The words hammered in her brain. She had run away for nothing! What a fool she'd been! What a child! All this time she could have been with him. That thought brought her to a standstill. But could she? Wolf had had, did have, a reputation with women. How long would she have lasted before he shipped her out of his life? But she had been carrying his child. That he would have wanted. That he still wanted. And that, she thought sadly, was all he wanted.

Even so, she faced Tuesday morning with hope. Wolf had said she could have her freedom after she'd produced a child, but maybe, just maybe, she could make him change his mind. She loved him. She had to try and make him love her too.

Pale-faced and trembling in her off-white shantung sheath, Micki stood beside an Arman-clad Wolf and repeated the traditional vows.

The one concession her father had won from Wolf was that he and Regina would take Micki and Wolf for dinner after the ceremony. He chose a well-known restaurant in Wildwood where, over bright red lobsters, he solemnly lifted his glass of champagne and wished them happiness. Wolf was pleasant and amusing and Micki was trembling with nervousness.

The dinner seemed unending but finally it was over. Her stomach churning, Micki added very little to the banter that flew back and forth between Wolf and her father and Regina as they drove back up the coast.

They were met at the motel by the manager, who wished them smiling congratulations, and a grinning good night. Wolf was quiet as they walked up the stairs and along the hall, so quiet Micki felt all her nerves tighten. The minute he closed the door, she made for the window like a homing pigeon.

"Would you like something to drink?" Wolf's voice came to her from the direction of the kitchen.

She had eaten very little all day, had barely touched her dinner, and had had three glasses of champagne but she said, "Whatever you're having," hoping it would calm her nervousness. She turned as he strolled into the room, a glass in each hand.

"That's a fantastic view," she murmured breathlessly, taking the glass he extended.

"There's one exactly like it in the bedroom," Wolf drawled softly, his eyes lingering on her lips.

Suddenly parched, Micki lifted her glass and drank thirstily, then, her throat on fire, her eyes smarting, she gasped, "What is that?"

"Scotch and water," Wolf laughed softly. "You did say whatever I was drinking."

"Yes," she exhaled deeply. "But if you don't mind, I don't think I can finish this." She handed the now-half-empty glass back to him and turning, added jerkily, "I—I think I'll have a shower."

Forty-five minutes later, clothed only in the filmy nightgown and matching robe that had been a bridal gift from her father and Regina, Micki stood in her bare feet, staring out the huge square bedroom window that looked out over the beach and ocean. The bedroom was decorated in the same earth tones as the living room, the furniture modern with straight, clean lines.

Hearing the shower shut off, she shivered and curled her toes into the soft fiber of the carpet. Wolf had come into the room while she was brushing her hair and, with hardly a glance at her, had gone directly into the bathroom. When the bathroom door opened, she closed her eyes. The thick carpet muffled Wolf's light tread and when his finger touched her shoulders she jumped, startled.

"Relax, honey." Wolf's warm breath ruffled the hair at her temple. "This isn't going to hurt a bit."

His hands moving slowly, he slid the robe over her shoulders and down her arms to her hands, where the garment dropped soundlessly to the floor. She shivered as his fingers trailed back up her arms to the ribbon bows on her shoulders that kept the gown in place. His lips teasing the sensitive skin behind her ear, his fingers tugged open the bows and the sheer gown slithered sensuously down her body.

For tormenting moments his hands caressed her shoulders, her throat, before he turned her slowly to face him. Raw desire shimmered darkly in his silvery eyes. As he bent his head to hers, Micki, torn between apprehension and anticipation, breathed.

"Oh, Wolf."

Expecting the searing brand of his mouth, Micki closed her eyes. His lips barely touched hers. Light as down he brushed her mouth with his, again and again, slowly building in her a need for his kiss. Adding to the tantalizing touch of his lips, his fingertips drew maddeningly fine lines down the side of her neck. When the tip of his tongue danced along her lower lip, she moaned with the urgency only this man could arouse in her.

With a small sob she coiled her arms around his neck and at that moment his mouth crushed hers, while his arms, encircling her body, drew her close to him. His kiss was hard, demanding and giving at the same time, and Micki gave herself up to the sheer joy of it.

Without breaking the kiss, Wolf straightened. His arms, holding her tightly, drew her up with him, then, her toes dangling inches above the floor, he carried her to the side of the bed. Sliding her body against his, he set her back on her feet. Wordlessly he lowered her to the bed and stretched his long length beside her.

All thought ceased for Micki. All she wanted was the feel of his mouth, his hands, his body. It had been so very, very long, and she loved him so very, very much.

Wolf's mouth played with hers, teasing her, delighting her. His tongue pierced and explored while his hands caressed and grew bold, exciting her to the edge of endurance. When his lips left hers she threw back her head to give him access to her throat. Making a moist path, his lips moved down the arched column to the hollow at its base where he paused to explore with his tongue, then, moving on, his lips climbed the soft mound of her breast to its summit, closed around its hard peak.

Micki was unaware of the soft moaning sounds she was making deep in her throat until Wolf, returning to kiss and tongue-tease her neck near her ear, whispered, "That's right, honey, purr for me. Purr like the amoral little cat you—"

It took ten full seconds for his words to sink in and when they did Micki froze.

"What did you say?" Her voice sounded loud after the murmurings of lovemaking.

"I think you heard me." Lifting his head, Wolf looked at her coolly.

"You think I'm immoral?"

"Not immoral, honey, amoral," he corrected. "Like a cat that doesn't know any better."

"Let me go," Micki whispered around the pain in her throat. "I said let me go," she snapped when he made no move to obey. "I don't want you."

"Oh, but you do, and I know it," Wolf whispered. "I'm a male and that's all that's required, isn't it?"

Micki didn't think; she reacted. Curling her hand into a small fist she lifted her arm and punched him right in the mouth. Wolf's head jerked back and then he laughed.

"I really am going to enjoy making you eat your words and anything else that comes to mind."

Moving swiftly he caught her mouth with his, kissing her sensually, erotically until she was breathless and had stopped struggling against him. Then with slow deliberation, using all the expertise he possessed—and that was considerable—he set a blaze burning inside her that only one thing would quench. His own breathing ragged, he growled, "I'll make you forget Tony, and Baxter and God knows how many others. By the time I'm through with you, no other man will ever satisfy you. You may hate me everywhere else, but you'll beg for me in bed."

"No." Micki's head moved from side to side. What did he mean Tony and Baxter and the many others? Surely he didn't think . . .

"Wolf, no, I—"

"Yes," Wolf rasped against her mouth, silencing her.

It was past noon when Micki woke up. She was alone in the bed, and, if the still quiet was any indication, in the apartment. Turning her head wearily on the pillow, she gazed out the huge window at yet another blatantly blue sky. Now, in early September, after a long summer filled with blatantly blue skies, Micki wished for chill, cloudy days to match her mood.

Stirring restlessly, she closed her eyes. Where the hell were all the cold, rainy days people were always singing about? Spreading her fingers, she smoothed her palm over the sheet where Wolf had lain, humiliating heat warming her body. He had made good his threat—several times over. She had not only welcomed him she had urged him to join with her; she had literally begged.

With a groan she rolled over, her body replacing her hand on the now-cool sheet, her face burrowing into the indentation Wolf's head had made in the pillow.

Curling into a tight ball, she wept the tears of the damned. He had stripped her of all pride, all pretense. Inside her head she could hear the echo of her own damnation.

"Wolf, please—please," she had pleaded.

"You'll have to do better than that," Wolf had taunted.

"What do you want of me?" she'd wept.

"Everything," he'd growled harshly. "Your body, your soul, your mind. I'd ask for your heart, but I know you don't possess one."

That, more than anything that followed, had hurt her the most. He thought her amoral. A hedonistic little alley cat incapable of deep affection or love. A hard shudder shook her body. She had made one attempt to tell him how she felt. Nearly incoherent, sobbing into his shoulder, she'd pleaded, "Wolf, please, don't do this to me. I love you."

Wolf had become still for a moment, and then his harsh laughter struck her with more force than if he'd used his fist on her.

"Oh, sure," he'd taunted coldly. "Me and Tony and Baxter and probably every other male you've ever met in between. Save your love song for the naive ones. I don't need or want it. But I do want everything else. So coax me, honey. Change your love song to a lust song and I just might hear you."

And all the time he'd been inflicting those hurtful words on her he'd also been inflicting an exquisite brand of torture. With his hands, with his mouth, with his entire body, he had pushed her up one side of the mountain called desire and chased her down the other side.

Mindless, lost, and groping in the world of the senses he'd created around her, she had clutched at him, pleading, sobbing, begging him to find her, save her.

And when, finally, he had, not once, but over and over again, she had completed her own damnation by humbly thanking him.

Now, alone, eaten alive by love, Micki wept into the pillow that still held his spicy, masculine scent.

By the time Wolf returned to the apartment, most of the day was gone—as were all traces of the tears she'd shed.

Barefoot, dressed in jeans and a cotton sweater, Micki sat curled up in a chair, an unlooked-at magazine on her lap.

Coming to a stop three feet in front of her chair, Wolf, looking drawn and bone tired in an obviously hand-tailored business suit, studied her makeup-free face brooding.

"How young you look," he said softly. "Young and innocent and untouched."

"Wolf."

Her anguished cry seemed to snap something inside of him. Flinging himself into the chair opposite hers, he closed his eyes and massaged his forehead with his fingertips. As his hand moved, he raked his fingers through his hair and looked up at her.

"I'm sorry, baby." His voice was raw and soft. "I've had one hell of a day reliving all I said to you, did to you last night. And the damning thing is I meant to do it. Planned to do it."

"Why, Wolf?" Micki whispered brokenly.

"Because I couldn't stand the thought of all those other men," he replied harshly. "Or that you had rejected my child." His eyes, glinting with resentment and anger, pierced hers. "You didn't have to get rid of it, Micki. All you had to do was call me." His voice went raw with emotion. "I'd have taken care of you. I wanted to take care of you."

"But, Wolf, I—"

"You had no right, damn you." Wolf's stinging words cut across hers as if he hadn't heard her. "You had no right to have it scraped from your body like a detested growth."

"Wolf, stop," Micki commanded in sudden anger. "I—oh!" With a gasp she cringed back against the chair, for Wolf had jumped to his feet, crossed the space between them, and stood looming over her.

"Stop, hell," he snarled. "Let's have it out in the open. It's been festering in my guts long enough. I'd have kept it, Micki. I thought that weekend was beautiful and to have a child from it would have made it perfect."

Really afraid of him now, yet unwilling to admit it even to herself, Micki glared up at Wolf and challenged him. "Are you going to beat me, Wolf?"

"Beat you?" Wolf frowned, then followed her eyes as they dropped to his tightly clenched fists. Sighing deeply, he backed up, his fingers slowly uncurling. "No, Micki." He smiled ruefully as he lowered his body wearily into the chair. "I did enough damage to you last night without taking my fists to you." His eyes flashed briefly. "But I felt I had to obliterate in my mind as well as yours the memory of all those other men."

Hot, swift anger seared through Micki's mind. He had said those words one too many times.

"Goddamn you, Wolf, there were no other men!" Micki cried. "There has never been any other man." With a sudden violence that startled him, she flung the magazine across the room and said bitterly, "And I didn't kill or get rid of or chase your baby." The spurt of fire died as quickly as it had flared, leaving her pale face with a haunted look. "I wanted your baby, Wolf." Her voice was husky with remembered pain. "I wanted it desperately. I lost it."

"But you said abortion." Wolf's tone revealed his mental torment. "Your exact words were, 'I haven't felt this bad since the abortion,' don't lie to me, Micki, not now."

"Yes, I said abortion, because that is the correct term." Wolf winced and she added strongly, "That is the correct medical term, Wolf. I did not reject your baby, my body did."

The eyes that stared into hers lost their silver clarity and grew uncertain with doubt. Her eyes filled with tears.

"I don't have to lie to you, Wolf. Go to the hospital. Check the records," she urged. "If the doctor that took care of me is still there, I'll give my permission for you to talk to him." Her voice caught on a sob, and brushing the tears from her cheek, she whispered, "I held the thought of your baby very closely, Wolf. Losing it was like losing part of myself."

Wolf was quiet a long time and Micki watched, her bottom lip caught between her teeth, as the clouds of doubt left his eyes.

"Oh my God!"

The whispered words were more a plea than a curse. Dropping his head back onto the chair, he stared through the window at the sky. When his eyes came back to hers, the silver had changed to a bleak gray.

"Why did you run away from me six years ago, Micki?" he asked wearily. "Was I too old for you? Had I frightened you?"

"No!" Micki exclaimed.

"Then why?" he demanded. "For six years I've asked

myself that question. Why, after that fantastic weekend, had you run? When I came for you that night I wanted to give you"—his hand waved in an encompassing circle—"everything. Damn it, Micki, I was prepared to do anything to keep you with me. I wanted to marry you." His tone went ragged. "Why did you run?"

Tears stinging her eyes, Micki swallowed against the tightness in her throat and whispered, "I thought you were having an affair with Regina."

"WHAT!"

The word seemed to bounce off the walls.

"I know, now, that it wasn't true," Micki said quickly. "But for six years I thought it was. And I couldn't stay with you thinking you and she had—" Micki shuddered.

"God," Wolf groaned, then, "Tony?" Before she could reply he added harshly, "How I hated that name. It seemed every time I called you all I heard was that name. Tony. Tony. Tony. Even when I mentioned your name in the shop I heard, 'She's in Albany with Tony.' Were you?"

"I went to Albany to attend Tony's wedding," Micki said quietly. "He's a friend. A very good friend. Nothing more."

"And Baxter?"

"Darrel asked me to marry him," she explained. "I said no. And as for any others over the years, casual dates, all of them."

"Come here to me, babe," Wolf coaxed, holding out his arms to her. "You can do whatever you like when you get here. Kiss me, punch me in the mouth again, anything. But come let me hold you."

Jumping out of her chair, Micki ran to him, snuggled into his arms.

"We make a pair," he murmured into her hair. "Me, going out of my mind thinking you're jumping in and out of bed with every guy you meet. And you, eating your heart out because you believed I was sleeping with your stepmother, and God knows how many others. Oh, yes, we make a fine pair. We deserve each other."

"Don't we though?" She laughed up at him.

There is something incongruous about grocery bags sticking out of an open Ferrari, thought Micki suddenly while she lifted the bags off the seat. A small smile curving her lips, she closed the car door with a quick sideways thrust of her hip.

Wolf, waiting at the open kitchen door of the large beachfront rancher, relieved her of her burden with a terse, "Where the hell have you been all this time? Your father and Regina and my mother and the rest of the clan will be here in less than two hours."

"I know, I'm sorry," Micki apologized, dropping her glasses, keys, and purse onto a chair. "The store was packed," she explained, beginning to empty the bags he'd placed on the table. "And the checkout lines didn't seem to move." She sighed. "And then I ran into Mrs. Jenkins and she talked and talked and—"

"Somewhat like you're doing right now?" Wolf asked dryly.

"Oh, Wolf—" Micki began, then broke off, alarm-filled eyes flying to his at a loud wail from the interior of the house. "Is something wrong with Cub?" she asked anxiously.

"No, of cour—" Another wail reached them.

Dropping the box of snack crackers she was holding, Micki started for the doorway, only to be brought up short by Wolf's hand grasping her wrist.

"Cub is fine," he said firmly. "Tammy is giving him his bath." He grinned. "And you know how much he loves that."

Micki sighed with relief, then gave a gasped "oh" when Wolf, with a quick tug at her wrist, pulled her against him.

Holding her loosely in his arms, he complained, "Cub is fine, but I'm feeling neglected." Bending his head, he caught her lips in a light kiss that very quickly turned into a hungry demand.

Bemused, lost in the scorching wonder of Wolf's mouth, Micki was raising her arms to circle his neck when another irritated wail brought her to her senses. Sliding her mouth from his, she scolded, "Wolf, stop it. What if your mother should walk in right now?"

"She'd understand perfectly," Wolf replied blandly. "And say I was a true Renninger," he teased. "Mother's been over that mountain."

Feeling her cheeks go pink, Micki made a move to break free of his arms. All she accomplished was to find herself held more tightly against him.

"You look tired," he murmured. "I think you should go lie down for a half hour or so. If you like, I'll come with you, rub your back." His eyes gleamed wickedly. "And your front."

While he was speaking, his right hand was moving. Under her sweater, up her side and, on his last word, over her breasts. Even through the lacy material of her bra the hardening tip his fingers found, caressed, proclaimed the effect he was having on her.

Stepping away from her suddenly, he clasped her hand and strode through the room, taking her with him.

"Wolf, the groceries!" Micki yelped, practically running to keep up with him.

Without breaking stride, he growled softly, "That's what I pay a housekeeper for."

When he reached the master bedroom with its wide, sliding glass doors facing the ocean, he swung her inside, slammed the door, and said softly, "We have two hours before the horde descends on us for the birthday party for the Wolf's cub." His eyes caressed her, inflaming her senses. Without conscious thought her fingers went to the zipper on her skirt. Silvery eyes followed her hands and his voice went husky. "I've been waiting for you all afternoon, planning a party of our own."

Watching him yank his navy polo over his head, desire flared inside Micki, sweeping all thoughts from her mind but one.

Within seconds the floor was littered with their clothing and they were on the large bed, mouth to mouth, flesh to flesh, together.

Her soft throaty moans inflaming him, Wolf husked, "Oh, God, I love you, baby. I love you."

Later, wrapped in Wolf's arms and the afterglow of their lovemaking, Micki sighed in contentment.

"After the way you celebrated your cub's birthday," she teased softly, her hand stroking over his hip. "I can hardly wait to see what you have planned for our anniversary."

Fleetingly the memory of their wedding night invaded her mind and her hand paused in its caressing movement.

Wolf's soft laughter dissolved the memory. His hand covered hers, urging it onward on its journey down his long, taut thigh.

"Maybe I should put you in charge of planning that party," he murmured against her hair.

Tilting her head back, she looked up into his wickedly gleaming eyes.

"You're getting pretty inventive in that department." Dipping his head, he covered her invitingly parted lips with his own, his hand leaving hers to spread possessively, protectively over her still flat belly. When he lifted his head, his eyes traveled down her body to his hand.

"When are you going to make your announcement?"

"Oh, not until after Wolfgang has been duly honored," she grinned. "Do you think I should tell them I'm already positive this one's a girl? Wolf, what?"

Sitting up suddenly, Wolf had replaced his hand with his lips.

"I love you, my daughter," his warm breath fluttered across her skin, exciting her, warming her. "And I love your mama."

Micki felt tears sting her eyes even as her body moved sensuously under his mouth as he trailed his lips up to her throat.

"And I love her daddy," she whispered huskily, some long moments later.

WHILE THE
FIRE RAGES

For Vivian Stephens,
who started it all for me,
with deep respect, appreciation, and gratitude.

ONE

Brett Renninger stood at the wide window staring at the wind-tossed, grayish-green sea. The Atlantic flung its waves with uncaring force against the shoreline bordering Ocean City, New Jersey. The wide window covered most of the wall in what was now an office but had been the living room of Brett's brother Wolf's apartment. The personal quarters he kept in one of many Renninger hotels.

Wolf.

Brett sighed, deeply, soundlessly. It was over three weeks now, three long, tension-filled weeks. He had been the logical choice to take over, but even had he not been, he'd have volunteered. Of course, he had not had to volunteer—he'd been summarily drafted.

Had anyone asked him if he could metaphorically fill Wolf's shoes one week, one day, ten minutes before the call came, Brett would have answered promptly, emphatically: No way!

That phone call. Brett's lips twisted. The memory of it was vividly clear and fresh. Perhaps it always would be.

As his hands had been employed with a bottle and a corkscrew when the phone rang in his Atlanta apartment, he had nodded his assent when the lovely young woman sitting close to him on the long, leather couch asked sweetly, "Would you like me to answer that, Brett, honey?"

Brett could even remember the assessing glance he'd swept over the curvacious blonde as she rose languidly, experience again the curl of desire he'd felt watching her glide across the plush carpeting to where the phone rested on his desk. He'd returned his attention to the business in hand as the blonde murmured a husky hello, only to slice a frowning glance at the slim gold watch on his wrist when she said softly, "Brett, honey, it's a Mrs. Renninger. Your mother?"

He had returned to Atlanta late that afternoon, after a three-week-long trip to New Mexico to iron out the final details concerning the company's plans for the erection of a tri-complex condominium unit. In the seconds required to set aside the bottle and walk to his desk, he'd chided himself for ever entertaining the belief that his mother would wait until he was in his office the following morning for her regulation briefing on his trip. Not on the outcome, of course, for that was—at least in his mother's mind—a foregone conclusion. Thus he'd deliberately laced his tone with rueful amusement and dispensed with the usual greeting.

"Yes, sir?" he'd drawled insolently, fully expecting to hear his mother's appreciative chuckle ripple along the line from Miami. The tightly controlled tone of his mother's voice washed the amusement from his face.

"Wolf has been injured in an accident, Brett. He's in a hospital in Boston."

Brett could still feel the shock of his mother's opening statement, could hear the echo of his own exclaimed, "What?"

"Micki called me less than ten minutes ago," she'd supplied tensely. "I have no details, as she was practically incoherent but"—the choking pause that followed instilled cold fear in Brett—"I—she—Brett, she said the doctors aren't sure if they can save him."

Standing at the window, staring sightlessly at the roiling sea, Brett shivered with the memory of the never-before-heard stark terror in his mother's voice. In truth, the emotion that had momentarily gripped him had come damned close to something like terror.

His big brother, Wolf?

Thankfully, the need for action had sent the destructive emotion into retreat almost immediately.

"I'll leave at once, Mother," he'd begun with forced calm.

"I'm going with you, I've called Eric," she said, referring to her third son. "He's having the Lear readied. We'll be in Atlanta within two hours."

"I'll be waiting."

Never would he forget that early-morning flight north: his mother's colorless face—for the very first time revealing every one of its sixty-five years; Eric's handsomeness, strangely enhanced by his rigidly controlled expression; his own thoughts of Wolf. Wolf—the hero of his boyhood, the—

The rustle of papers from behind him scattered the memory. Turning slowly, Brett ran a contemplative gaze over the gleaming dark head bent over Wolf's large, rectangular desk.

The super-efficient assistant. Brett's assessment was not complimentary. Lids narrowing over eyes chilled to a steely gray by his thoughts, he inventoried the woman's exterior.

Even seated, her height was obvious. Somewhere between five feet nine and ten, he estimated—correctly. Slender—almost too slender, her fine bone structure lending an appearance of fragility.

Brett had to suppress a snort of disdain. A confection spun of pure steel, he condemned scathingly, his glance raking her delicate facial features, the pink-tinged ivory skin that covered them, the beautifully sculpted lips that hid perfect white teeth.

Thick, long hair in a rich, dark brown adorned her classically shaped head. Brett knew that when, eventually, she raised her eyes from her work, she would gaze at him from gold-flecked hazel eyes surrounded by lashes as dark and full as her hair, and so long as to appear artificial.

Brett had committed the vitals to memory: JoAnne Lawrence; age twenty-eight; unmarried; degree in business management, a certificate in hotel management. She had gone to work for the Renninger Corporation on completion of training, first as an assistant manager, then manager of a Renninger hotel in Pittsburg, Pennsylvania. Three years earlier she had been hired as the assistant to the assistant to the East Coast manager of Renninger Corporation—Madam President's firstborn, Wolfgang. She had secured the coveted position of first assistant fifteen months before when Wolf's righthand man, wanting a change, asked for and was granted a transfer to the newly open Hawaii region.

His face free of expression, Brett stared at the shining crown of her head. Oh, yes, he knew quite a bit about Ms. JoAnne Lawrence—usually referred to as Jo. He had made it his business to know. Neither idle curiosity nor personal interest had motivated his research. His interest in her had been aroused in a hotel lounge in Boston late one night nearly three weeks ago by the stricken face and anguished voice of his sister-in-law, Wolf's wife, Micki.

"He was with a woman, Brett," Micki had blurted suddenly. "Probably his assistant, Jo."

At first, Brett had given little credence to her outburst.

The waiting, nerve-shattering days following Wolf's accident had left them all on edge. Micki was distraught and very close to exhaustion. Hurting for her, feeling protective, he had tried to soothe what he thought were her irrational fears.

"Honey, if this Jo whoever is his assistant, his being with her would be the normal order of business."

"Not if he was trying to conceal it, and from all indications, he was."

"What indications?" Brett had deliberately injected a chiding note into his tone.

"I know how you feel about Wolf, Brett, but please, don't patronize me." Micki had blinked furiously against the tears shimmering in her eyes.

Brett was very fond of Micki. In fact, he rather envied Wolf. His brothers, at least, had been extremely lucky in their chosen life mates. Seeing Micki so near the breaking point alarmed him.

"I'm sorry." Reaching across the dimly lighted table, he'd clasped her hand with his. "Okay. Tell me what these indications are."

"I had a commiserating call from a friend at home today," she'd begun haltingly. "She'd read of Wolf's accident in the paper. I was thanking her for her concern when she interrupted with 'and to think I saw you only hours before it happened. I called to you but you were already in the car. But, of course, Wolf told you he saw me'—I was stunned."

"And that's it?" he'd asked incredulously.

"No." Micki shook her head impatiently. "I was confused. I told my friend Wolf hadn't mentioned seeing her. Then I asked her where she'd seen him. She said right in front of the hotel, *this* hotel. She added that Wolf seemed distracted and in a hurry, and that he hadn't even acknowledged her greeting."

"But, honey, I fail to see any indication of a clandestine

meeting in that!" Brett, fully aware of Micki's utter weariness, had tried to reason with her. "It sounds to me like the work of a malicious woman whose nose had been put out of joint because a man, an *important* man, did not give her the recognition she probably thinks she deserves."

Micki had been shaking her head in denial before he'd finished his rationalization. "No, Brett, not this woman. She is one of our best friends. In fact, I'm sure you know her. Cindy Grant? She and her husband, Benny, are the cub's godparents."

Now, as he had three weeks ago, Brett smiled gently at the reference to Wolf's son, dubbed "the cub." Now the smile was as fleeting as it had been that night.

"Okay, there was no malicious intent on Cindy's part." He'd sighed. "But I still cannot believe you think this sketchy information enough evidence to bear out a conviction. *If* the woman in the car was his assistant, she had every right to be there."

"Oh, it was her." Micki's bitter tone had been a shock simply because Brett had never heard the like of it from her before. "I checked. She was registered." Her lips twisted. "Her room was on the floor above his."

Considering what she'd been through the preceding days, Brett had stifled his growing impatience. "Honey, she's his assistant. There's nothing at all unusual ab—"

"No. Not as a rule," she'd interrupted harshly. "She travels with him quite often. And, like a fool, I'd believed quite innocently."

Brett had felt heartsick at the pain in her voice, the anguish in her usually so-bright blue eyes. He knew only too well what she was going through. Perhaps that was why she'd confided in him and not Eric. She'd sought a fellow sufferer. Still, unconvinced, he'd objected.

"Micki, there is no proof."

"Wolf told me, before he left, that she would not be going with him." Micki's response had had the measured sound of a death knell. "He offered the information. I had not asked. I think I have a very good case, Brett," she'd gone on in a whisper, her voice reedy with weariness. "By the way, her name is Jo Lawrence. She's beautiful."

Beautiful?
Hardly.
At that moment it seemed the vibrations from Brett's intense stare penetrated the concentration Jo Lawrence was applying to her work. Lifting her head, she met his stare with thought-clouded hazel eyes, one perfectly shaped, dark brow arching questioningly.

"Is something wrong, Mr. Renninger?"
Everything's wrong, Ms. Lawrence.
"No." The tiny frown that briefly marred her smooth brow told him his attempted smile had been cynical. "I was just thinking."
"I see."
Her eyes drifted to the window to gaze out at the wind-ruffled, white-capped waves. Sitting up straight, she raised a slim hand to massage the back of her neck.
Beautiful?
In sudden decision, Brett strode to the door, taking his jacket from the back of a chair as he passed it.
"I'm going to run out to the house," he said, referring to the home Wolf and Micki owned a short distance away. He tossed the toneless statement over his shoulder without looking at her again. "If you need me for anything, call me—or put it on hold till I get back." He was very careful not to slam the door behind him.

The silver Porsche gleamed dully in the watery, late-afternoon sunlight. As Brett pushed through the wide, double-glass entrance doors, his eyes caressed the sleek lines of the powerful machine, parked in the no-parking section in the motel forecourt. He'd made sure the car was driven up from Atlanta for him as soon as possible and was happy now that it was at his disposal. It didn't really matter where he parked the car since, as the motel was closed for the season, the large lot was empty.

Standing beside the car, the wind sweeping back his gold-streaked, ash-blond hair, Brett breathed in deeply, filling his lungs with the crisp, sea-scented air. A raucous, mournful cry drew his attention, and, tilting his head back, he followed the gliding flight pattern of a lone sea gull. The bird's solitary passage struck a responsive chord in him.

For what seemed a very long time now, he'd known a like, if earthbound, solitude. Even when in the company of others—others, in his case, being female—his soul had emitted a silent, lonely cry.

"Damn all women."

Even as he muttered the oath Brett knew he didn't mean it. There were women and then there were women. Most assuredly he would never damn Micki or his brother Eric's lovely wife. But there were others, like his former playmate—in no way had she ever been a real *wife* to him—and the woman whose presence he'd escaped moments ago.

What in blazing hell were you thinking of?

The admonition was not self-directed. In his mind he flung the question at possibly the one and only man he'd hesitate in verbalizing it to: his brother, the formidable Wolfgang.

Damn you, Wolf, you had it all! Brett, folding his long length behind the wheel, mentally chastized the idol who had suddenly developed feet of clay. You had Micki, and two beautiful children, and the good life, and you risked it all—and for what?

Brett shook his head in wonder as he inserted the key into the ignition. With his inner eye he envisioned the object of his censure whole, that slashing grin softening the chiseled planes of his face, his eyes glittering silver, the formally lone Wolf.

Do you love her, big brother? Or were you merely playing king stud?

Twisting the key with unnecessary force, Brett growled, "Get it in gear!" He was not referring to the car, which had quickly purred to life without a complaint.

Driving along the nearly deserted streets instilled in Brett a vaguely eerie sensation. It was as if the warning had gone out to evacuate and everybody had heard it but him.

Brett smiled at the whimsical thought. Actually, he rather liked the desolate look of the summer resort town in mid-October. He did not like the oddly abandoned look of his brother's large white-brick ranch house.

Separating the proper key from the others on his gold ring, Brett loped along the flagstone walk to the wide door. Before he had a chance to put the key to use the door was opened by Wolf's housekeeper.

"Well, hello, Mrs. Jorgeson." Brett's smile was easy; he liked *this* woman. "I didn't expect to see you here today."

"Good afternoon, Mr. Renninger." Gertrude Jorgeson's return smile revealed a mutual regard. "I'm putting up the last of the tomatoes."

"In what way?" Brett's frown conveyed his ignorance of the hows and whys of putting up anything.

"Into sauce and stewed tomatoes." Gertrude smiled through eyes grown wise from sixty-one years of observing life. "Your brother and your sister-in-law love stewed tomatoes."

"I see." Brett's tone was noncommittal. He personally hated stewed tomatoes. "Well, I won't get in your way. I'll be in Wolf's study."

"All right." Gertrude smiled again. "Would you like a cup of coffee?"

"No. Thank you." Brett grinned. "I think I'll help myself to the Scotch."

"As you like." The small, well-rounded woman turned back toward the kitchen. "Call me if there is anything I can help you with."

In the study, Brett went directly to the liquor cabinet set into one wall between well-stocked bookshelves. After measuring a good two inches of the expensive whisky into a short, squat glass, he splashed in a token amount of seltzer water, then, sipping at the liquid appreciatively, he glanced around the comfortable room.

The earth-tone colors, the functional yet luxurious furnishings, the oversized desk, stamped the room as Wolf's domain. However, there were small signs indicating the domain had been invaded.

A smile softened Brett's finely molded lips as his eyes paused on a large, brazenly red fire engine parked neatly in one corner. He had witnessed his nephew tearing through the house on the riding toy with the same panache Wolf displayed behind the wheel of his equally brazen red Ferrari.

His thought banished the soft smile. The Ferrari was gone, totally demolished in the accident. It was several seconds before a twinge of pain in his jaw brought Brett out of his reverie to the realization of his tightly clenched teeth.

Damn, it was only a car! A car can be replaced. He would gladly write out his own personal check for a half dozen Ferraris if only Wolf . . .

Literally shaking himself out of his introspection, Brett moved purposefully to the desk. It had grown completely dark beyond the window behind him before he pushed the padded leather covered chair back and stood up.

The plot sickens.

Raking long, bony fingers through thick strands of slightly wavy hair, he grimaced sourly at the innocent-looking envelope on the desktop. The tightness in his stomach bore out his appraisal of the play unfolding in his mind.

Raising eyes gone steely gray with anger, Brett ran his gaze slowly around the room, seeing everything, seeing nothing, the document neatly folded inside the long, buff-colored envelope imprinted on his inner vision.

Does she love him?

Damn it! Whether or not Jo Lawrence was in love with Wolf should not be his uppermost consideration! Micki was the one who would suffer from this. *If* she found out.

Lids narrowing over eyes now icy with calculation, he sliced his gaze back to the desk. He had discovered the damned thing inside the locked top drawer of the desk, which, as he was in possession of Wolf s keyring, he'd opened without the slightest compunction.

As expected, he'd found everything pertaining to the company in perfect order. It was that one long envelope that had shaken him.

It was his job to make sure Micki did not find out.

"Damn!"

His very long, deceptively lean looking frame taut with frustration and anger, Brett snatched the empty whisky glass and walked out of the room with his habitual long stride.

He rinsed the glass under steaming hot water and placed it in the draining rack beside the sink, his mind examining the ways in which to handle this new, unsavory development.

He strode back into his brother's study, his eyes, cold as the North Atlantic, fastening on the cause of his anger.

Crossing to the desk, he extended a hand to pluck the envelope up, then, turning abruptly, he walked out of the room. After activating the computerized alarm system to secure the house for the night, he left the house and loped to the low sports car shimmering like liquid silver in the moonlight.

The weightless document lay heavy in Brett's breast pocket as he backed the vehicle out of the driveway. Instead of making the turn that would take him back to the center of town, he spun the leather-covered wheel and headed toward the bay.

Now, in early evening, the streets were even more deserted than they'd been when he left the motel. The uncanny sensation of being the only living being in a dark, abandoned ghost town was even more pronounced.

Parking at the base of a street that dead-ended at the bay, Brett uncoiled his considerable length from behind the wheel and strolled to stand on the wide, oily-looking wood pilings.

The moonlight struck a glittering path across the ever-shifting water, dancing in time to the muted swish as wavelets wound themselves around the spindly legs supporting long, narrow docking piers. Empty now, the berthing slips had a forsaken look that would vanish with the return of spring and the water craft of all sizes, both motorized and those with the tall masts.

To the lone man, standing with hands thrust deep into the pockets of hand-tailored pants, the scene was more conducive to contemplation than depression.

Because of the frantic mental state his sister-in-law had been in, Brett had found it relatively easy to convince Micki of Wolf's fidelity.

Without shame or misgiving, he had lied through his teeth.

The memory was strong, fanning the anger seething in him to a full, outraged blaze.

"I must know," Micki had whispered brokenly. "Brett, please, you must find out if it's true."

Suspicion aroused is not guilt proven. Brett would have preferred living with the doubt.

"To what purpose now, honey?" he'd soothed, attempting to dissuade her, knowing too well the hell in facing the truth. "You've been through so much, and you've got to get through a lot more. Why put yourself through the agony of—"

"You don't understand," she'd interrupted fiercely, grasping his hand tightly. "I don't want to know for myself." Her lids dropped over eyes sparkling like blue jewels from their glaze of tears, and she swallowed with obvious difficulty. "I'd just as soon *not* know, but you have got to go to New York and find out if it's true."

"You're right, I don't understand," Brett exploded, if softly. "If you would rather not know, then why . . . ?"

"For *him!*" Again she'd not let him finish. "I think—I thought I knew him, and the man I thought I knew would not enter lightly into infidelity. He must love her very much."

Brett had actually felt the pain that had scored her face. In that instant the rage had been born deep inside him.

"Go to New York, Brett." Micki's eyes pleaded as effectively as her quivering voice. "And, if you find it's true, bring her back with you."

"What!" Mindful of the other patrons scattered around the dimly lighted lounge, Brett had managed to keep his tone low, but it was all the more intense for the incredulity lacing it.

"If"—a spasm fleetingly distorted her lovely features and she bit her lips before correcting herself harshly—"*when* he comes around, he will need the strength of the woman he loves."

Her slender hand grasping his tightened, oval nails digging into his palm. Brett felt the pain, not in his hand but in his heart. The rage spread fiery fingers into his mind with her next impassioned words.

"I hate it, Brett. I hate the very thought of it." Two tears escaped their blinking bounds to slide slowly down her cheeks. "But I want him to live. Oh, dear God, I want him to live, and I will use anyone, suffer *anything*, if it will help him." Staring directly into his eyes, she'd begged, "Don't think of me, Brett, think of him. Go to New York."

Of course he'd given in to her. How could he not? The affection and respect he'd felt for her from the beginning blossomed into pure filial love. He would do anything, perform any task she charged him with.

After escorting her to her room, he had gone to his own long enough to pick up a few things. One of those things was the phone, over which he informed his mother of his intentions—but not his motives. Another of those things was Wolf's briefcase, which he'd taken possession of on arrival but not as yet opened.

During the short flight from Boston to New York, he'd perused the contents of Wolf's case. Most of the papers inside were directly related to the reason Wolf had gone to Boston in the first place—that of the feasibility of renovating a rather run-down, old hotel into modern condominiums and the company's acquisition of same if the resultant figures proved out that feasibility.

One slim folder stood out glaringly in its difference.

The data confined between the covers of the cream-colored folder had come from the personnel manager directly to Wolf. One quick glance over the four sheets of pristine white paper and Brett had a crawling suspicion he was closer to knowing the answer to Micki's question.

During the cab ride from Kennedy to Wolf's spacious apartment with its panoramic view of Central Park, Brett came very close to hating the formerly adored one.

It had been a long day. In truth, it had been three very long days, each one riddled with fear as Brett, his mother, Eric, and Micki, so brave, so vulnerable, waited, waited, waited.

Brett had been tired, and disillusioned, and bitter, yet, before dropping onto Wolf's over-oversized bed, he had more thoroughly studied the four sheets of paper. Each paper contained a detailed account of the professional performance of four company employees—three men and one woman.

The information had been gathered, at Wolf's request, for the purpose of choosing a replacement for a retiring senior executive of the East Coast branch of Renninger Corporation.

The lone female under consideration for the coveted position was JoAnne Lawrence.

The following morning, feeling charged with restless energy after days spent in the confines of hospital waiting rooms and corridors, Brett politely declined the apartment doorman's respectful offer of a cab.

Had he wanted to ride, there would have been no need to do it in the back of a world-famous—infamous?—New York City cab. All that would have been required were a few words spoken into a telephone and a limousine, plush, comfortable, fitted out to the nines, would have been waiting at the curb for him. When the occasion warranted, Brett was not averse to using his name, position, power, or wealth. This particular morning, Mr. Renninger chose to walk.

His brother's briefcase firmly in hand, he strode off, appearing, at least to the casual glance, much like hundreds of other young executives en route to the city's amalgam of offices. The more discerning eye would have noted the supple leather of handmade shoes, the fine material of perfectly tailored charcoal gray suit, the real silk of pearl gray shirt. The discerning female eye would appreciate the long, toned torso, the thick crop of sun-streaked, loose waves caressing a beautifully sculpted head, features so sharply etched as to appear austere in their masculine beauty, lips that promised heaven in their pleasure, hell in their disfavor. At the moment the tightness of those lips proclaimed extreme disfavor with someone.

Brett's strides ate up the sidewalk. Seeming so self-absorbed as to be aware of nothing around him, he was, in fact, fully conscious of everything within the radius of his near-perfect vision. Eyes dull steel, flat in contemplation of what may lay at destination's end, he strode on, his mind alive with his sister-in-law's charge:

"Go to New York, Brett, and, if you find it's true, bring her back with you."

Now, as he approached the tall glass-and-steel building that housed the offices of East Coast Region—Renninger Corporation, his mind repeated the same silent reply as the night before.

No way in hell!

Stepping out of the elevator at the twenty-third floor, Brett walked briskly down the carpeted hall to the office of the personnel manager. When he walked out of the office, fifteen minutes later, the retiring senior executive's replacement had been chosen. The choice was not a female.

From personnel, Brett took the elevator up three more floors. His body taut with purpose, he strode to a solid, un-marked door, twisted the handle, and, eyes narrowing with intent, stepped inside.

"May I help you?"

The query was directed at him from a frowning woman seated behind an open laptop. Her confused expression made a demand: Who the hell are you? And how did you get up here unannounced?

A sardonic smile teased Brett's tightly compressed

mouth. It *had* been a long time since his last foray into New York.

"Is Ms. Lawrence in?" Brett asked quietly, the smile tugging harder at his lips as he observed the confusion deepen in the woman's eyes. Her expressive face telegraphed her mental self-questioning: Should I know this man? Is he someone important?

"Yes." The woman nodded. "But she is very busy. She asked not to be disturbed."

"She'll see me." His cool, deliberately arrogant tone brought out the backbone in the woman who, at any other time, Brett would have found more than passably attractive.

"Really?" she replied with matching coolness. "I doubt it. She *is* very busy."

"Use your intercom," he instructed patiently, "and inform your boss that *her* boss is waiting."

"Her boss?" The woman's brows drew together. "I don't understand."

Brett sighed. Of course she didn't understand. How could she? Hanging on to his patience, he smiled benignly.

"Tell Ms. Lawrence Brett Renninger wants to see her."

Suddenly, a door three feet to their right was thrust open and a melodious but impatient voice demanded:

"Reni! Who are you socializing with? I need that report you're working on."

"Ms. Lawrence, I . . . I . . . he . . ."

The attempted explanation died on her lips as JoAnne Lawrence followed her voice into the room.

At first sight of her something that had died inside Brett made its first faint stirrings toward resurrection.

Beautiful?

Brett was hard put not to laugh aloud. As a descriptive adjective, beautiful, in regard to the tall woman glaring at him, seemed woefully inadequate.

"Who are you? And what are you doing in here?"

Brett had been thankful for her imperious tone; it reminded him of exactly who this woman was.

"Oh, Ms. Lawrence," Reni began, "he's . . . he's . . ."

"Reni! Will you please finish that report!" JoAnne's eyes sliced a quelling glance to Reni, then shot back to him. "Answer me!"

"With pleasure." Brett felt a curl of satisfaction when her impossibly long lashes flickered at his too-smooth, too-soft tone. Experiencing a sensation quite like joy, he let her have it with both barrels.

"Brett Renninger," he introduced himself silkily, feeling the curl of satisfaction spreading at the stillness that gripped her. "And I am here in the capacity of your employer for the duration."

In retrospect, Brett had to admit her aplomb was magnificient. There was a split second of appalled hesitation, then she stepped toward him gracefully, slim right hand extended.

"I'm sorry, Brett," she apologized in a soft, clear voice. "Come right in."

A cool breeze skipped across the water, ruffling its inky-dark surface. Brett shivered inside the insufficient protection of his barn jacket. Chilled out of his reverie, he moved his shoulders in a tension-relieving shrug, a vague hollowness inside bringing awareness of how long it had been since he'd eaten.

At least he attributed the empty feeling to hunger.

Turning abruptly, he frowned as his ear caught the faint crackle of the envelope nestled inside his breast pocket. The hole in his middle grew to a mini chasm.

Cold all over, Brett strode to the low-slung car, repressing a shudder as he slid behind the wheel. Punishing the ignition once again for his own conflicting emotions, he slammed his palm against the gear stick and backed the car the length of the street.

It had been so ridiculously easy to reassure Micki of Wolf's fidelity.

Cruising along the deserted street, a grimace broke the tight line of Brett's lips. He had simply relayed almost verbatim JoAnne's—rehearsed?—response to his interrogation in her office that morning.

Yes, she had been with Wolf in Boston.

No, the original arrangements had not been for her to accompany him.

Wolf had called her late in the afternoon the day after his arrival in Boston.

"I don't like the setup." JoAnne had quoted Wolf. "I think they believe they're dealing with a lightweight here. They should know better. But then, so should I. I failed to run a routine check. Get research on it now. I want a full report by tomorrow noon, hand delivered, by you."

Yes, she had delivered the report to him the following afternoon. They had gone over it together during dinner.

Yes, he had booked a room for her at the hotel but, as she had scheduled a meeting with his staff for the following morning, he drove her to the airport sometime around eleven that night. She had flown back to New York on the same company plane that had carried her to Boston.

Yes, he must have been on the way back to the hotel when the accident occurred.

Micki had gratefully, tearfully swallowed it whole; hook, line, and sinker.

Brett was a different type of fish. Keeping his own council, he had decided to search out the true depth of JoAnne's seemingly still waters.

Depth indeed!

Brett's entire body felt icy except for that one rectangular spot on his chest. The envelope crackled again as he mounted the steps in the silent motel.

Unlocking the apartment door, he strode angrily inside and stopped dead. Assuming she'd have gone to her own room by now, he had not expected to find her waiting for him. Brett voiced the first thought that came to his mind.

"Trouble?"

"No." Her sleek, dark hair moved sharply in the negative. "I just now decided to call it a day." An odd, sad smile brushed her soft, moist lips. "Possibly because I also just realized I haven't eaten since breakfast. Let's grab some dinner."

TWO

Absently unaware of the sensuousness of her actions, Jo toyed with her tulip-shaped wineglass, the fingers of her left hand caressing the stem with long, evocative strokes, the tip of her right forefinger slowly circling the rim.

Oblivious to the gray gaze following her finger play, she sighed with the unwilling realization that for the last several hours her thought pattern had mirrored the movement of her fingertips—round and round.

Why does he dislike me so?

After three weeks of regular repetition, the question was a familiar, if painful, refrain. She had repeatedly scoured her mind for reasons for his antipathy, and she came up blank time after time. Other than that first regretful morning in her office, she had scrupulously shown him all due respect. Surely the man had more intelligence than to carry a grudge for so slight an infraction! He had barged unannounced into her office! Her reaction to his sudden appearance had been completely normal.

Yet, since that first morning, uncomfortable waves of tension simmered between them whenever they were in the same room together, regardless of the number of feet that measured the distance between them.

It was more than unnerving; it was disheartening, because her initial reaction to him had been very positive, deeply favorable. In effect, Jo didn't even have to *be* in

the same room with him to reexperience her initial reaction; all she had to do was *think* of him and tiny little
physical devils began a game of touch and run with her
libido. It was enough to make a fully mature, intelligent,
reasonably level-headed woman weep with longing!

Though Jo was unconscious of the yearning sigh that
whispered through her lips, Brett, very obviously, was not.

"Tired?"

Blinking herself out of the fruitless introspection, Jo
donned a mask of nonchalance before raising her eyes
to his.

"Yes." Her reply was blunt for two reasons; first, it was
nothing but the plain truth; second, his taunting tone
had instilled a chill. Was it her imagination, or did he
continually use that exact tone with her for some reason
she was too dim to decipher? Keeping a rigid harness on
her own tongue—which did itch to lash a bit—she
added tonelessly, "It's been a long three weeks."

For some obscure reason her statement seemed to
anger him. Jo's carefully constructed mask slipped to
reveal bafflement when Brett stiffened abruptly.

"I imagine it has been," he drawled icily. "Time has a
tendency to drag when you're missing someone."

Jo's bafflement retreated at the advance of sheer incredulity. What the hell was he talking about? Missing
someone? Whoever could he . . . good grief, he
couldn't possibly be referring to Gary? How had he
even heard of that ill-fated involvement? Though she
wasn't aware of any gossip about her breakup with Gary
Devlin, there was always the chance he had heard
through the company grapevine. This man would
surely demand to know all there was to know about an
assistant he had no voice in choosing. All there was to
know officially, and unofficially. But why would he
think she was missing Gary? It was almost a year and a
half since . . .

"If you're ready to leave?"

Brett's cold query put an end to her conjecturing. Employing fierce determination to keep her eyebrows from joining in a frown, Jo let a cool nod suffice for an answer. Inside, she seethed to tell him to go take a flying leap into the bay. Who the hell was he to think he could speak so condescendingly to her!

Inside the sports car, Jo sat rigidly erect, staring out the windshield all the way back to the motel.

Did he *have* to smell so damned good? Jo blessed the darkness that concealed the rush of heat to her face at the unexpected thought.

Slowly, very carefully, she inhaled, drawing the mingled scent of pure male and expensive aftershave into her senses.

I wonder what he tastes like. The heat in her cheeks intensified at the reflection. Jo shifted against the supple leather covering the bucket seat, becoming more uncomfortable from the heat uncoiling inside than the warmth singeing her outermost layer of skin.

Eyes forced ruthlessly forward, she forbade her sight the pleasure of examining his breath-robbing, austerely handsome face, the contemplation of the possible ecstasy his beautiful mouth could wreak on hers.

What does he look like stripped to the buff? That consideration cut her breath off in her throat.

I am going totally mad!

Thankfully, at that moment Brett drove the car onto the motel parking lot and her musings were shifted to the edge of consciousness. The ensuing opening and closing of car doors were the only sounds that broke the silence from the time they left the car until they came to an awkward halt at the door to her room.

For one pulse-shattering, brief instant, Jo fancifully imagined she saw a flame leap in the remote grayness of the eyes studying her face. Then, with a brusquely muttered good night, he spun and strode to the door of Wolf's former lair.

Stepping quickly into the pitch-black room, Jo closed and locked the door, then sagged back against its solid support. After gulping in numerous deep, calming breaths, she pushed her limp body erect, her hand groping for the wall switch.

For one infinitesimal moment there she had actually thought he might kiss her. What would she have done if he had? Jo frowned as she mentally listed her possible responses. Would she have chastized him in a scathing, acidic tone? Or, would she, perhaps, have laughed it off as of little meaning? Or, would she, much less likely, have allowed her palm to meet his cheek with resounding force?

Who are you trying to kid? she asked herself wearily. After three weeks of wondering, hoping, longing, you know exactly how you would have responded: You would have wrapped yourself around him like a wet bath towel!

The thought conjured the image and an anticipatory shiver feathered her skin, raising tiny goose bumps on her arms and thighs. Her physical response to the mere idea of being crushed to Brett's hard, lean body no longer had the power to shock her, although it certainly had the first time it had occurred.

Performing the routine before-bed ritual of cleansing her skin and brushing her teeth, Jo's thoughts backtracked to the first time she'd felt that hot-cold reaction to him.

It had certainly not happened that first morning, when he'd presented himself to her. She'd been much too flustered and embarrassed then to notice much of anything other than the fact that the Renninger brothers bore very little resemblance, physically or in personality.

Actually, he'd been in her office a very short time, during which he'd fired questions at her in a taut, angry tone that she'd later attributed to anxiety over Wolf's accident.

Somewhat proud of herself for the appearance of composure she'd maintained, she had answered his questions clearly and concisely. It was when it became obvious that he was about to make an abrupt departure that Jo, voicing a query of her own, received the impression of his dislike of her. Confused, wondering why he should dislike her when he didn't even know her, she had nevertheless repeated her question when he hesitated over answering.

"How *is* Wolf doing?"

"He is still on the critical list," he'd finally, begrudgingly answered, confusing her all the more by his apparent unwillingness to discuss his brother's condition. "I'm leaving now to fly back to Boston," he'd gone on coldly, long fingers curling around the doorknob, giving the impression he couldn't get out fast enough. "If there are any questions"—he'd paused, tone hardening—"pertaining to business, call the hotel and leave a message. I'll get back to you."

Stunned by both his tone and his attitude, frowning in perplexity, Jo had mutely watched as he opened the door then closed it again before turning to pin her with an icy, narrow-eyed stare.

"By the way," he'd almost purred, "I've tapped Bob Harley for the executive slot opening soon." The silky satisfaction in his voice went through her like the sound of a nail being scraped the length of a blackboard. "Sorry about that."

With a twist of his lips that was more a sneer than a smile, he strode from her office, leaving her staring after him in total bewilderment.

Four days later he was back.

Those four days had been rather trying for Jo—what with holding down the fort, so to speak, and worrying about Wolf, she'd been getting a teensy bit short-tempered.

In truth, Jo almost adored Wolfgang Renninger. In her admittedly prejudiced opinion he was kind, considerate, oftimes droll, and a dynamic businessman. Her liking for him had been spontaneous, her respect endless. Strangely, she had never felt even the mildest tug of physical attraction toward him. Wolf was employer, friend, and, during a few weak moments Jo had experienced, confidant.

Brett was a whole new ball game.

Added to the business responsibilities she'd shouldered—she'd be damned if she'd call and leave *messages* for *him*—and her concern for Wolf, Jo had further strained her nerves by repeatedly reviewing that scene in the office.

Why had Brett been so very tense, so very hostile?

Why had he seemed so smugly satisfied about informing her of Bob Harley's promotion? In Jo's opinion Bob was the logical choice for the job!

Why did he dislike her?

It was the last of the constantly revolving trio of questions that bothered her most of all, simply because, she assured herself, she had done nothing to warrant his disdain.

She had had no prior warning of his imminent return. Arriving at the office before her assistant that Tuesday morning, she had no sooner pulled her chair to her desk when the phone rang. Her response had been as it always was.

"Jo Lawrence."

"I want to see you, now, in Wolf's . . . my . . . office."

That was it. No time wasted on mundane pleasantries such as good morning, merely, in effect, get in here.

Staring at the receiver in her hand, Jo had rationalized the sudden burst of adrenaline rushing through her as her body gearing for a verbal confrontation, *not* in expectancy of the sight of him.

HA!

With all her assumed coolness intact, she had walked

briskly into Wolf's . . . Brett's . . . office, taken one look at him, and, metaphorically at least, begun melting.

It simply was not fair for one man to look that damn good! The image this man projected did not sneak up on one; to the contrary, his persona immediately ensnared, jolting emotions, tangling thoughts, luring the unwary to further investigate his seeming quintessence.

After four days of grappling with the fact of his apparent disdain, Jo was nothing if not wary. Lashes lowered over hazel eyes too bright with feminine interest, she viewed the splendor of his male form.

He stood so very straight, his bearing almost military, and so very tall, taller even than Wolf's six feet. His thick, silky-looking, fair hair was cut short at the sides and back. The hint of a wave in the sweep in front was an invitation to eager, feminine fingers. The shortness of his hair revealed the perfect sculpting of his head, his wide brow, straight nose, high cheekbones, and firm jawline lending an overall effect of a master sculptor's finest work of art. The very spare but sinewy flesh that covered his long frame enhanced the illusion of an elite warrior of a bygone era.

That magnificient human form should never be adorned in anything more than the merest wisp of draping over the hips.

The thought conjured the image. Her composure threatened by her own reflective imaginings, Jo had blurted the first unrelated subject her scrambled mind was successful in latching onto.

"Wolf?"

Jo was much too busy being amazed at the picture of aloof composure her cool tone had drawn for him to notice the glittery sheen that came into his eyes.

"He'll live."

Her amazement did not extend to missing the frost that rimmed his voice, but she ignored it in the relief that

swept through her entire being; not until that moment
had she allowed herself to face the very real possibility that
Wolf might actually die. Her sigh was more eloquent of
her feelings than any amount of words could have been.

The glitter in the gray eyes intensified, embuing a
molten steel quality. If his expression of cold hauteur was
assumed to intimidate, it worked admirably.

"But," he finally continued with icy deliberation, "if
you are eagerly looking forward to seeing me dispatched
back to Atlanta before long, forget it. Wolf will be a long
time in mending."

"His injuries were extensive?" With an unconsciously
beguiling sweep of her incredibly thick long lashes, Jo
forced herself to meet his direct stare, praying he could
not hear the *ba-bump* kick her heart telegraphed.

"Yes." Brett's clipped reply indicated he would not elaborate, thus it surprised Jo when he did. "The point of
impact was at the door on the left." At Jo's horror-widened
eyes, he nodded once, sharply. "Quite." His lips twisted
briefly, as if in memory of a painful sight. "There is hardly
an inch on Wolf's left side that is not contused, lacerated,
or fractured; not to mention concussed. When I left him
this morning he resembled a mummy more than a man."
The cloudy haze that had momentarily dulled his eyes dissipated. Once again he staked her with that glittering
stare. "As stated, the mending will take a long time." His
lids narrowed menacingly, causing a twist of alarm in Jo's
midsection. "Had that drunken bastard who ran into
Wolf's car not have died in his self-created hell, I'd have
sent him there with my own hands."

Jo did not doubt his word for a second. In that instant,
Brett looked frighteningly capable of perpetrating a
man's demise without weaponry. Appalled by the quiet
fierceness of him, feeling herself pale under the steely
rapier points flashing from his eyes, Jo slowly collapsed
onto the chair to the side of his desk.

Pray God I never incite this man's wrath! Holding her breath, fighting to control the series of shudders quaking through her, Jo gripped the slender arms of the chair, unmindful of her whitening knuckles.

"Okay. Business as usual."

Smothering a gasp, Jo started at his abrupt change in tone and facial expression. Oh, he still looked haughty, but the mien of murderous intent had vanished. Taking command of Wolf's high-backed chair, Brett drew it to the large pine desk, then, settling back comfortably, he arched one pale, aristocratic brow at her.

"Any more questions?"

Jo ground her teeth at his patronizing tone, cautioning herself against incurring his wrath before their interview was over. She truly did not care to leave his office the victim of his displeasure. The very idea of the scene injected steel into her backbone—very cool steel that manifested itself in her voice.

"Yes. Several."

Undaunted by a slight tightening at the edges of his lips, Jo led off with query one.

"Does the prognosis call for complete recovery?"

"At this point, yes."

"How long will he be confined to the hospital?"

"The word this morning was at least three, possibly four, weeks."

Four weeks! Jo swallowed her dismay at the thought of having to work side by side with this man for the better part of a month.

"May I see him?" She was further dismayed by the pleading note threading her voice.

"No."

Jo's eyes widened at his icily emphatic denial. What possible reason could he have for refusing her visitation rights to her boss? Or did he believe himself above the need for reasons? Her loss of control was evidenced by the angry outcry.

"But why?"

"The idea, *Ms.* Lawrence, is recuperation. You represent something altogether different."

Anger drowned in a flood of confusion. Had Brett really sneered that last assertion? Could he consider her role of assistant so unimportant as to be sneered at? Jo figuratively shook the consideration away. She knew he employed several assistants himself; he could not help but be aware of the responsibilities entailed. But then, damn it, why *had* he sneered at her?

Jetting her mind free of the quagmire of her own thoughts, Jo faced him boldly.

"You will be . . . filling in . . . for him the entire three or four weeks?"

"In every way required."

For some unfathomable reason, Jo was grateful for the ignorance she felt at not understanding the cause of his sardonic tone and matching smile. Thankfully, she was given no time to ponder either.

"Actually, I will very probably be in residence in this office a great deal longer than three or four weeks."

"But you just said—"

"I *said,*" Brett interrupted smoothly, "Wolf will be hospitalized for that length of time. Plans have already been made for him to complete his recuperation at our mother's horse farm in Florida."

Jo opened her mouth to ask the obvious. Brett anticipated her.

"Anywhere from four to six months."

Uh-huh. You bet. Why not?

Rapid fire, the seemingly unrelated terms sprang pell-mell into Jo's thoroughly rattled brain. I am not really hearing what I think I'm hearing, she assured herself a trifle wildly. He did not actually raise the possibility of six months—did he? I'll kill myself!

Had she been, at that moment, presented with a mirror, Jo would have been shocked. Inside, she felt somewhat like a quivering mass of mush. Outwardly she appeared unruffled and unaffected by the news she'd received.

Transmitting an order to her hands to release their death grip on the innocent chair arms, she laced her tension-numbed fingers together demurely in her lap. Between evenly spaced breaths, she managed to calmly ask the question whose answer would see her retained or deposed.

"You will be bringing Richard Colby to New York?"

Over the previous three years, Jo had heard much, all of it good, of Richard Colby, redoubtable right arm to the head of the mid-Atlantic Coast region. Her assumption that Brett would want his right arm with him now was natural, if unsettling.

"Not likely." Brett's disclaimer startled Jo; had she really detected a hint of amusement in his tone? His dry smile answered her silent question. "Richard hates New York." Brett's voice was every bit as dry as his smile and held a very deliberate drawl. "He hates the pace. He hates the weather. And, more than the preceding, he hates the hard, Yank-ee twang."

Staring at him in bemusement, Jo felt the melting process begin all over again. His soft, drawling tone turned her rigidly stiff spine to the consistency of soft wax. *Heavens, but he is beautiful! His face is beautiful. His body is beautiful. His voice is beautiful. He is probably magnificently beautiful in bed as well.*

Lost in her own suddenly erotic imaginings, Jo was sublimely unaware of the seconds sliding into minutes. What she *was* suddenly aware of was a longing to experience the magnificence of his beautiful body.

"Ms. Lawrence?"

Jo blinked herself back to reality. Though Brett's voice had lost the long drawl, its softness enticed a shivering response through the entire length of her body.

"Have I wakened you?" Brett's taunt was a mild reprimand for her inattentiveness.

Yes, damn you! Jo silently acknowledged the taunt for a much more earthy reason. *You've awakened me inside, where I live, and I don't particularly like it, especially since it's so very obvious* you *don't particularly like* me.

"No, sir." Jo's independent spirit cringed at the self-satisfied smile he flaunted in reaction to her unhesitating use of the respectful term.

"I'm relieved." His tone was a blatant denial of his assertion. "I'm certain that having a woman as lovely as you fall asleep while I'm speaking would do irreparable damage to my ego."

How very droll. How very sophisticated. How very deceitful. Positive her eyes were flashing her mental accusations at him, Jo lowered her lashes in concealment.

"Is your ego so very delicate?" she ventured softly, hating the surge of excitement that pulsed through her veins. What would it be like, she asked herself, to possess the power to damage this man's ego? You'll never know, her self answered with discouraging swiftness.

"No." Brett's reply was equally swift, equally discouraging, and amused in the bargain. "I'd say my ego is about as delicate as an enraged Brahma bull."

Well, now that I've been firmly put in my place, where do we go from here? Jo wondered bleakly. Apparently Brett's train of thought was running along the same track, only he knew the name of the next station was: Business first, always.

"Now." He sat forward in his chair and placed his palms flat on the desk. "If there are no further questions?"

Feeling anything but the highly efficient assistant she knew herself to be, Jo shook her head mutely.

* * *

Sliding between the cold sheets on the unfamiliar motel room bed, Jo sighed with the realization of the number of times she'd shaken her head mutely over the previous three weeks.

God! Had it really only been three weeks? It seemed like years, decades, a millennium! And every second of it filled to bursting with *him.*

Jo had no idea why it had happened. She had no idea how it *had* happened. She only knew most assuredly that it had happened. Against all reason or sense of self-protection, she was stupidly, hopelessly, mushily in love with Brett Renninger.

Balling the covers into a comforting bunch under her chin, Jo rolled onto her side, drawing her knees up almost to her chest. Then she did something she would have been mortified to have Brett witness: She cried long into the night.

Habits formed, good or bad, are not easily set aside. With less than four hours sleep, and that not very restful, Jo woke at her usual early hour. Filled with periodic spells of weeping and tossing, the long night had produced little comfort. As Jo lay staring through the large, square window at a brilliant blue Indian summer sky, her tired mind held on to the two concretes it had formed while blackness painted the window.

For good or ill, and very probably forever, she loved Brett Renninger—that was concrete number one. Concrete number two was wrapped around the fact that, at all costs, she had to diligently work at preventing Brett from discovering concrete number one.

How this feat was to be accomplished when the mere thought of Brett's existence on the earth was enough to activate the inner melting process, had been the major cause of Jo's sleeplessness. The thought had occurred of secrecy through distance. All she had to do to remove herself from temptation was resign her position as his assistant; she'd have as soon resigned her soul to purgatory.

As daylight seemed to have little effect in diverting her endlessly circling thoughts, Jo pushed back the covers, deciding she might as well face the morning—and her own haggard reflection in the mirror.

Thirty-five minutes later, securely hidden behind the magic of expertly applied cosmetics and a neatly tailored, pearl-gray suit with a complementing heather-blue blouse, Jo walked briskly into the apartment-cum-office and came to a disbelieving halt, incredulous at the sight her sweeping gaze encountered.

Attired for the work day in navy suit pants, crisp white shirt, and a blue-on-gray diagonally striped tie, Brett presented to her widened eyes the picture of domesticity as he turned to greet her from his position at the stove in the compact kitchen.

"Good morning, JoAnne. Pull a stool up to the counter, breakfast is almost ready."

The counter was atop a room divider that separated the living-room area from the kitchen. Shelves lined with books, both hardcover and paper, faced the living room. On the kitchen side, three stools, fashioned of cane, with padded seats, filled the space under the marble counter.

"Breakfast?"

Jo heard the blank confusion her voice conveyed to him and, hearing it, strove to correct the impression of early-morning dullness.

"You're cooking breakfast? For me?"

She had to repress a wince at the expression of boredom that flirted with his features. True, the voice now held alertness; it was the question that, being obvious, was therefore stupid.

"I could hardly fix breakfast for myself alone"—Brett

assumed the exaggerated drawl—"and still call myself a Southern gentleman, now could I?"

I could hardly smack your too-superior-looking face, Jo retorted bitterly, if silently, and still call myself any kind of rational woman, could I? The temptation to put thought into action was so strong Jo curled her slender fingers into her palms and held them rigidly at her sides, her body tightening with her determination not to respond to his taunt.

Brett's expression of boredom gave way to amusement as his sharp-eyed gaze swept over Jo's stiffening form. For some reason she could not begin to understand, he seemed to derive great satisfaction from knowing he had the power to rattle her composure.

A derisive half smile curving his far too attractive mouth, Brett swung back to the compact stove to dish up bacon and eggs.

"As is obvious"—a jerk of his head indicated the two place settings, complete with small glasses of orange juice and tall glasses of iced water, on the countertop—"everything is ready." Two steaming plates in hand, he turned to her. "If you will seat yourself, Ms. Lawrence, I will serve." His smile grew openly mocking. "You will then be among a small, select group of women who have the right to claim they have been waited upon by Brett Renninger."

What is he trying to do? Holding his glittering gray stare with assumed carelessness, Jo walked slowly into the small kitchen. *And why is he trying to do it?* The questions teased her mind repeatedly as she slid her trim, rounded bottom onto the thickly padded seat. Had she lost all perceptiveness entirely, or was his mockery self-directed?

The Brett Renninger? Mocking himself? Sure—with the first frost to paint the nether reaches of hell! Why mock himself when he had a much more likely target in the form of his unwanted, unwelcome, uncared-for assistant?

"My meager efforts do not appeal?"

The vocal nudge came from beside her, one stool re-moved. Blinking, Jo focused first on the bit of gray visible through narrowed lids, then, shifting her glance, to the golden toast, creamy scrambled eggs, and perfectly crisped bacon on her plate. When had he poured the coffee? This as her gaze was caught by the aromatic, dark brew in a cup near her right hand.

"No . . . I mean, yes, of course . . . I'm sorry, I . . ." Why wouldn't her mouth work this morning?

"How fascinating." The drawl was more pronounced now. "Are you always this articulate first thing in the morning?" Brett arched one beautifully shaped blond brow.

Why did I have to fall for this stiletto-tongued, twenty-first-century Adonis? Jo wondered, staring helplessly into a pair of gray eyes that danced with amusement at her expense. She had amused Gary at the beginning too. Perhaps it's true—the psychological thesis claiming women keep seeking out the same type of man. A vision of another Adonis, one with tanned skin, blue eyes, and dark hair, formed in her mind.

"Ah ha! I've solved the mystery!" Jo blinked at the sharp click of Brett's snapping fingers. "You're a som-nambulist and not really aware of being here at all."

"How fascinating." Jo managed a fair imitation of his drawl. "Are you always this brilliant first thing in the morning?"

"I'm always this brilliant, period," Brett retorted dryly.

"Modest too!" Jo simpered, oversweetly. Turning away with slow deliberation, she picked up her fork and stabbed at her eggs—prudently denying the urge to sink the long prongs elsewhere. Much too aware of his sudden stillness, she conveyed the utensil to her mouth, chewing consid-eringly before offering, sincerely, "Very good; creamy. Mine always come out too dry." She sampled the bacon.

"Perfectly cooked." The coffee came under her serious consideration. "Nectar," she concluded after one delicious sip. "You could very easily spoil a working woman with a passion for breakfast."

"And you have such a passion?"

His quiet tone and steady regard should have warned her. It didn't. She walked right into it.

"Yes," she admitted, "I'm a so-so cook who's a breakfast freak."

"I always fix my own breakfast when I'm at home." Brett ran a cool gaze over her before returning to her face to pin her with gray eyes that suddenly flared to glittering brilliance. "I would gladly perform the service *for* you"—a tiny pause—"in exchange for an even more basic service *from* you."

Jo's forkful of eggs hung suspended in midair. Was she pushed? Or had she jumped? Jo was uncertain of what method had brought it about, but she felt sure she had finally gone over the edge. She must have, it was the only reasonable explanation for this sensation of free-falling through space. As if it could anchor her to the stool, Jo gripped the handle of the fork and scoured her mind for a suitably scathing put-down. She couldn't find any— which was just as well, for she felt positive she'd misinterpreted his remark.

"I beg your pardon?" She certainly hadn't had to force the note of confusion into her tone; Jo was thoroughly confused.

"Is that a no?"

Jo blinked herself free of his impaling stare. He was serious! Incredible as it seemed, Brett Renninger, in his own peculiar fashion, had actually invited her—*her!*— into his bed!

Too damned much!

The temptation to thankfully, humbly, submissively accept his oddly offered proposition was so strong Jo's teeth ached—understandably, as they were locked together. Her answer required every ounce of willpower she possessed.

"Yes."

"Yes, that is a no?" Brett drawled mockingly. "Or, yes, you'll buy the first meal of the day"—a smile flirted with his lips—"with the last act of the evening?"

Cancel all doubt.

She had not slipped over reason's edge.

She had not misinterpreted him.

She had not passed go.

She had not collected two hundred dollars.

She *had* been propositioned.

The only doubt remaining had to do with her ability to refuse him.

"Yes, that is a no." Had she actually replied in that oh-so-cool, touch-me-not tone? Had she actually declined, when she was on fire and he was the only extinguisher? Was she, in fact, completely out of her mind? Hadn't she wept and writhed through most of the previous night in an agony of need for his touch, his possession?

The questions trembled, rapid fire, through Jo's mind while she strove to maintain a modicum of composure. She wanted him—yes, but not like this! Not at the casually proposed offer of breakfast. Breakfast, for heaven's sake!

The rotten bastard! Jo shocked herself with the silent accusation. But she loved him, she excused herself. *While he, he has the unmitigated gall to suggest he share my bed—for the paltry sum of filling my stomach!*

Jo was forced to lower her fork to the table as a shudder shook her slender frame. Brett obviously saw and misinterpreted her movement.

"Have I shocked your sensitive little soul?" he taunted softly. With a minimum of expanded energy, he slid from his stool to the one beside her. As he leaned still closer Jo felt his warm breath caress her ear. "I can guarantee satisfaction with both performances—in the kitchen and the bedroom."

Jo, teetering on the edge of capitulation, and desperate because of it, steeled herself against the entreaty in his soft tone. When the much yearned-for male lips brushed her ear, she jerked away frantically.

"Stop it!" Jo did not have to fabricate the angry tone; she was angry! All of a sudden she was explosively angry. The only explanation for his behavior that made any kind of sense was that she'd betrayed herself, her true feelings, to him. Positive he was merely tormenting her for having the temerity to fall in love with a Renninger, Jo lashed out at him defensively. "No, you have not shocked my sensitive little soul. I've been propositioned before." With cold deliberation, she injected a sneer onto her lips, venom into her tone. "And one does not take note of an amateur when one has been approached by an expert."

Jo hadn't the vaguest idea what she was saying, yet, whatever it was, it worked. Brett, his expression suddenly blank, went stiff all over. Moving slowly, he straightened, then stood up and carried his barely touched meal to the sink. The sound of the food being scraped into the disposal was loud and abrasive.

"An expert!" Brett's soft, considering statement was not aimed at her. Still, made fearful by his stillness as he stood beside the sink, she raised challenging eyes to his.

"An expert," he repeated even more softly. "Of course."

The challenge in Jo's eyes was replaced by bafflement. Something in his tone conveyed acceptance—of some truth or other. But what? *She* had no idea what she was even talking about; how could he?

"Brett?" Jo didn't have an inkling of what to say to him. All she knew was she had to break through his strange stillness.

"Never mind." Moving abruptly, Brett strode from the

kitchen. "Let's get this work cleaned up so we can get out of here."

Following his example, Jo scraped her own plate, then stacked their dishes in the dishwasher. As she absently performed the light kitchen duty, Jo told herself she absolutely had to get more sleep. She was beginning to talk off the top of her head, which, in itself, was bad enough. But, it would appear, she was also beginning to believe Brett fully understood her gibberish, and that was scary.

THREE

You are without doubt the most blundering of blundering fools on the entire East Coast.

Brett was, again, taking up space in front of the wide window. It was now some two hours since he'd stormed—childishly, he admitted to himself ruefully—out of the kitchen.

What devil had possessed him, prompting him to issue such an idiotic proposition? He didn't even like the woman, let alone desire her!

So your mind says, now convince your body!

Like or dislike, the cold fact was that he desired her with an intensity the like of which he'd never experienced before, and he'd known some raging passions.

I probably should simply fire her and have done with it.

The tip of Brett's tongue slid along the edge of his bottom teeth, and his unseeing eyes stared at the sun-sparkled Atlantic whitecaps.

If not firing then, at the very least, making her life pure misery was in order.

Damn!

Moving restlessly, Brett shoved his itching hands deep into the pockets in his pants, a wry, self-derisive smile curving his lips. He knew the itch in his palms was not caused by the need to inflict violence; the itch came from the need to caress her soft, pale skin.

God, he wanted her, wanted her as he'd never wanted another woman.

This is sick!

Brett's shoulders moved, as if trying to dislodge an unwelcome rider on his back. His purpose had been so clearcut at the beginning. What the hell had happened to confuse the issue? Not to mention him?

Even though it *had* been ridiculously easy to reassure his sister-in-law concerning his brother's fidelity, Brett's own newly aroused suspicions were not mollified.

In relating to Micki Jo's reasons for being in Boston on the day of Wolf's accident, Brett had injected a businesslike briskness into his tone. Couched in that manner, Jo's explanation sounded plausible. Micki had, gratefully, swallowed it whole. But, then, Micki had not been there to witness the face of fear Jo had worn regarding the accident. Nor had Micki been in the New York office several days later to see, firsthand, Jo's face whiten on hearing the full extent of Wolf's injuries.

Brett had been there. He had kept a sharp eye out for her slightest reaction to his news, only to find a sharp eye had not been necessary; Jo's dismay had been obvious.

Now, three weeks later, Brett realized it had been at the moment she'd displayed the most pain that he'd decided Micki's fears were based on fact and Jo was, indeed, Wolf's mistress.

Again Brett's tongue snaked across his teeth. It was also at that exact moment, he finally acknowledged, that he'd felt the first lick of physical desire for her.

That moment had occurred after his detailed account of Wolf's injuries. Jo had gone deathly pale, then had nearly fallen into the chair by Wolf's desk, hand groping at the chair arm for support. It was when she'd lowered her lashes in pain that he'd allowed his gaze to leave her face to roam freely over her slender body. It was then he'd suffered the first stirring of need for her.

The question of whether he wanted Jo because she *was,* or had been, Wolf's reared its nasty little head. Instantly, Brett assured himself that their past relationship had nothing to do with his present yearnings. Hard on the heels of that self-assurance came the fervent hope that he was not lying to himself.

Brett was well aware of the depth of feeling he held for his older brother. He had idolized Wolf for as long as he could remember, had always tried to emulate him. But to carry his hero worship to the point of wanting to possess Wolf's mistress was not only ludicrous, it was downright unhealthy.

The fact remained that Jo had belonged to Wolf; in his own mind Brett was now certain of that. He had uncovered just too damned many incriminating signs during the previous three weeks for their liaison to be strictly business. One of those signs now lay snugly in a long envelope inside his breast pocket, crackling faintly every time he moved. Brett had even had the fanciful idea that the blasted envelope was laughing at him every time it crackled.

You are sick!

The self-admonition was silently issued in an attempt to quell the strong urge gripping him to turn and feast his eyes on Jo's tall, delicately formed body.

Feast his eyes, hell! He wanted, longed, ached to feast his mouth, tongue, hands, and body on top of hers.

Again his tongue flicked at his teeth, barely withdrawing in time to prevent being lacerated by his descending hard upper teeth. Will you knock it off? She belongs to him! His hard white molars clamped together in frustration and self-disgust.

She belongs to him.

Without conscious thought, Brett's spine straightened and his shoulders squared. Face it, chum, he advised himself reluctantly. When Wolf comes back, should he so choose, it will be to take over Jo as well as the region.

Hot rebellion, more fierce than he'd felt throughout his rebellious teenage years, seared Brett's emotions. In an effort at maintaining control, he breathed in, slowly, deeply repeating the same phrase over and over in his mind: *You're out of line here, she is his.*

His ploy at self-chastisement was a total failure, for the rebel in his mind chanted back: *He can no longer have her, I will make her mine.*

Back and forth, the battle raged between control and rebellion, rendering him temporarily motionless while both vied for supremacy. The deciding factor came not from within but from without.

"Brett, I'm sorry to bother you." Jo's voice was entirely free of facetiousness. She genuinely sounded sorry about having to intrude on his thoughts; she also sounded genuinely confused. "There's something here I don't quite understand."

His given name, coming voluntarily from her soft lips, whipped Brett around as if he were attached to a string she held tightly in her slim fingers. Brett breathed a sigh of relief on realizing Jo had not witnessed his humiliatingly swift snap to obedience. Gleaming head bent, Jo scowled in consternation at the folder in her hands.

"Concerning what?" Strolling slowly—to make up for his earlier quickness?—to the desk, Brett held out one hand for the source of her confusion.

"The Vermont project." Unaware of his outstretched hand, Jo pursed her lips at the printed words under her perusal. "I thought Wolf had decided to scrap the idea of yet another condominium complex aimed at the skiing set, but, from the info here, he must have continued the preliminary investigation on his own."

Halting at the side of the desk, Brett leaned toward her. For a fleeting half instant he hesitated, fighting the impulse to slide his hand under her chin, tilt her head up, and taste her pursing lips with his own. The effort required to bypass her head and pluck the folder from her hands was evidenced by the barely discernable tremor in his fingers.

Jo had the good sense to remain quiet while he studied the folder's contents. Gradually, the tension eased out of Brett as his eyes skimmed the printed lines on each successive sheet of paper contained within the folder's cream-colored covers.

Yes. Yes. A tiny smile played over Brett's lips in appreciation of the thorough investigative job Wolf had done on the proposed project. Before he came to the final sheet, Brett fully agreed with his brother's conclusions. The location was good. Wolf's figures, if accurate—and Brett knew they would be—were well within reason for a complex of this size. The time for action was now if the groundwork was to be completed and excavation begun by late spring.

Behind the printed sheets were several handwritten pages. Brett's smile grew on recognition of Wolf's slashing, straight-line penmanship. In a bold hand, Wolf had outlined a comprehensive, detailed directive on exactly how the official prospectus should be blocked out.

Impressive bit of work, old son, Brett silently congratulated his elder sibling, then he mentally telegraphed a promise: *You very obviously wanted this. I'm going to get it for you. It may not be much in exchange for your oh-so-exquisite plaything here, but thems the breaks, bro.*

Raising his head, Brett focused his attention on the hazel-eyed plaything sitting very quietly, very patiently at Wolf's desk. Gazing into the amber-flecked depths, Brett reiterated what he'd known for a very long time. One could never fault Wolf's taste in women. It seemed his taste in assistants was faultless as well, for Jo Lawrence was every bit as efficient at her work as his own paragon,

Richard Colby. And that was a compliment Brett had bestowed on no other.

"You're staring, Brett."

Jo's tone conveyed enlightenment, not censure. Smiling wryly, Brett brought the cream covers together with a businesslike snap before handing the folder to her.

"Slide this into your briefcase," he ordered as he started to turn away from the desk.

"We're going to pursue it?"

"We're going to pursue it," he repeated, tilting his head back to her. "Can we wrap it up here soon?" he went on, deliberately stifling any attempt she might have made at questioning him further. "I'd like to be on the road by lunchtime, and I want to stop by the house on our way out."

"This apparently not-to-be-discussed report was the last of it." Jo held up the folder. "Are you positive you feel safe leaving it in my care?" Her tone betrayed her slightly out-of-joint, but adorable, nose.

"Simmer down, Ms. Assistant." Brett sighed. "We will discuss the thing, probably to your screaming point, after we're back in the city." Stepping back, he indicated she was free to leave the desk without fear of having to get too close to him. "Are you packed?"

"Yes."

"Good." Brett ran a quick glance over her and took another step back, advising himself not to tempt fate or his own swiftly dissolving control. "So am I. Let's get this place in order and get out of here."

Working together, the apartment was quickly restored to the neat condition they had found it to be in on their arrival two days previously. It was when Brett strode into the hall toward the bedroom to collect his suitcase that he felt the now-familiar tightening in his stomach muscles. The juices inside that particular organ began to roil much like the gray-green waves pounding against the shoreline.

Brett didn't see the waves, or the shoreline; he didn't even see the long wide window that took up most of one of the bedroom's walls. A grimace twisting his lips reflected his inner image. His eyes, a moody dark gray, were fastened on the oversized bed. The figures his actively churning imagination projected onto that bed were the cause of sudden nausea.

Within the luxury of that rich man's couch, Wolf had consummated his marriage to Micki. Brett knew that. What he didn't know and what had tormented him throughout most of last night was whether Wolf had also consummated his liaison with Jo Lawrence there as well.

God damn!

Standing perfectly still, his long body rigid with tension, Brett was not even aware of the fingers of his right hand curling into his palm; was not conscious of the urge that sent that hand hurtling out to make painful contact with the solid wood that framed the doorway. Consciousness came with the tongue of fire that shot from his knuckles to the base of his skull.

Eyes mirroring disbelief, Brett stared at the abraded skin covering his fingers. Although the door frame had been the recipient of his lashing blow, Wolf's face had been his mental target.

Wolf?

As he stared at his still-balled hand Brett's expression changed from disbelief to incredulity. Good God! Was he cracking up completely? He had never ever felt anything but near adulation for Wolf. Now, because of a woman . . . a shudder rippled through him. With a concentrated effort Brett uncurled his fingers.

Brett felt the sickness roil again as against his will his gaze drifted back to the opulent bed. Did he want Jo because of who she was, or because of *what* she was to Wolf?

Moving with an unusual jerky swiftness, Brett clutched the handles of his supple leather case and swung out of the room. There were connotations here he didn't want to examine at the moment. Later, when he was back in New York, and alone, he'd pick his mental and emotional feelings to pieces.

Jo stood patiently waiting for him in the hall, her tall, sleek body an invitation, her cool, aloof expression a denial of same.

Nodding curtly for her to precede him, he scooped up her travel bag, thankful for the necessity of bending over and thereby concealing the evidence of the need growing even greater within.

Following her smoothly swaying, ultra-slim hips along the corridor and down the open stairs to the first level, Brett wondered what had happened to his hard-won, tightly reined control. He had not touched his wife, Sondra, once during the last six months of the farce they'd called their marriage. And his celibacy had been by choice, not by Sondra's rejection.

His eyes caressing the enticing symmetry of Jo's tush, Brett's lip lifted in a sneer in memory of Sondra's professed willingness to, in her own words, share her wealth.

"Brett?"

The voice was not the soft, languid drawl that had captivated him five years ago but the businesslike clip of a motivated woman who had worked her way up from assistant hotel manager to assistant everything. With a mental shake, Brett banished the memory of his former wife—at least temporarily.

A frown on her more-than-merely-beautiful face, Jo held the heavy glass door for his passage.

"You have the look of a man who has forgotten something," Jo murmured as he strode by her. "Have you?"

I wish to hell I could forget everything, Brett thought

savagely. *Most particularly you!* He let a sharp movement of his head answer in the negative.

After a last-minute check on Wolf's house, during which Jo remained in the car—because of an aversion to entering the home Wolf shared with Micki? Brett wondered—he headed the sports car toward New York.

To Brett the drive seemed exceptionally long and rife with tension. Being confined in such a small area with a woman as purely enticing as Jo was not exactly conducive to tranquil travel. The fact that said woman smelled intoxicating, not of perfume but of pure, sweet female tormented him to the brink of squirming in the bucket seat.

I've got to have her, and it's got to be soon. The stark realization followed the silent sigh that slipped the barrier of his lips as Brett joined his car in jockeying for position in the melee laughingly referred to as New York traffic.

Jo's apartment, located in a fashionable if not exclusive section of the city, was relatively easy to find. Drawing the car to a halt in front of the high-rise, Brett stepped out of the low car and smiled sardonically at the doorman who moved with alacrity to assist Jo in alighting.

With a word to the obsequious man to stand by the Porsche, Brett again suffered the discomfort of trailing the delicate figure he lusted after. Confinement in the elevator proved almost as unnerving as confinement in the Porsche. Finally, after a long trek along the hall on the ninth floor, Jo came to a halt before an unmarked door. She had her key in hand. A long, oddly shaped key, the sight of which glued Brett's teeth together. He recognized that key. Was he not in possession of one exactly like it? Was it not, at that very moment, inside his pocket, nestled among the other keys on Wolf's gold ring?

He did.

It was.

God damn.

The emotions that welled to congregate in Brett's throat burned with a bitter sting. Fury, disappointment, disgust merged into a choking mass. Yet, overall, frustration reigned, prompting him to snatch the key from Jo impatiently when she hesitated at inserting it into the lock.

A quick, vicious turn of the key and the door swung open. Stepping back, Brett frowned a silent order for Jo to enter her apartment, knowing he had to get her inside as quickly as possible and get himself out of there.

Jo murmured, "Thank you."

Brett murmured, "You're welcome."

Then, being very careful not to look at her, he placed her bag next to the door and stepped back into the hall, one hand outstretched to her.

"I'll have the Vermont report," he clipped shortly. Jo's startled look made him add, more gently, "I want to study it tonight. Come to my office first thing tomorrow morning. We'll go over it together." Silently he urged: *Come to my bed tonight and we'll forget it together.*

The longing that swept through him shook Brett to the core. *Hurry, damn you,* he commanded silently, watching Jo fumble with the clasps on her briefcase. *Hurry, because if you don't I'm going to step back inside, throw you down, and take you right there on that expensive hand-loomed rug my prowling brother paid for.* The last thought brought with it a shaft of pain that blanketed Brett's mind with shocked disbelief.

Pain!

Automatically, Brett's fingers closed on the folder Jo extended to him.

Pain?

Automatically, Brett responded to Jo's baffled-sounding words of farewell. And automatically, Brett retraced his tracks to the elevator.

Why pain?

Examining the puzzling emotion, Brett absently

slipped a twenty-dollar bill into the doorman's hand before slipping behind the wheel of the Porsche. The key to the puzzle eluded him as he fought his way through the late-afternoon traffic to Wolf's apartment, which was located in a posh section of the city.

Inside the elegantly decorated duplex, Brett abandoned his case inside the door and drew a straight line to Wolf's well-stocked bar.

"There should be no pain involved here. Except of the physical discomfort type."

Measuring two fingers of amber liquid into a short, squat glass, Brett wasn't even aware of speaking the assertion aloud. After swallowing the aged single malt neat, he was fully aware of being vocal.

"Damn," he muttered as the whisky burned a path to his stomach. "The idea was to quench the desire, Renninger. Not burn a hole in your guts." He added ice cubes and water to the second drink.

Sipping at the diluted whisky, Brett retrieved his case and climbed the free-standing staircase to the apartment's second level and the largest of the two guest bedrooms.

Standing dead center in the room decorated in muted tones of blue, Brett relaxed his fingers and let the case drop carelessly to the carpet. He didn't even hear the muffled thud as the supple leather made contact with the wool fibers. His spine rigid, Brett fought against the urge tugging at him and lost.

Following the emotional dictate, Brett, cursing himself softly, spun around and strode from the room and along the short hallway to the master bedroom. Hinging the door open, he took one step inside then halted, his eyes riveted to the enormous bed—in which, Brett was sure, Wolf was undoubtably the master.

"Have you had her here, you bastard?"

The sound of his own voice was startling in its harshness. Still it persisted in erupting from his stiff lips.

"While that beautiful creature who bore your children went serenely, trustfully about the business of keeping your home for you in that classy pile of bricks beside the ocean, did you wantonly debase her, and yourself, on that damned island you call a bed, with *my* woman?"

The echo of his own words slamming back at his mind, Brett remained unmoving for a timeless moment, not seeing, not even breathing. Then, his eyes filling with something akin to horror, he slowly shook his head from side to side.

"No!" Brett's whispered denial came in cadence with his head motion. "No. I couldn't, I wouldn't do something as stupid as fall in love with her!"

Closing his eyes to blot out the offensive sight of Wolf's sensual playground, Brett's lips thinned in endurance of the shudder that rent the fabric of his soul. The body tremor caused a crackle in his breast pocket. In the silence of the room, the crackle had the muted ring of mocking laughter.

Raising his right hand, he slipped the long envelope from his pocket, then withdrew the legal document from it. A bitter smile twisting his lips, he opened his eyes and again focused on the huge bed.

"No, brother mine, soiling your own nest would definitely not be your style. You would ensconce her expensively, but apart."

The document Brett unfolded was the deed to the apartment he had so recently retreated from.

Retreat appeared to be Brett's order of the day, for now he backed away from his brother's sleeping quarters, quietly closing the door as he went.

If Brett had found it a struggle coming to grips with his unexpected, unwanted physical need for Wolf's partner in dalliance, that struggle was as nothing compared to facing the reality of a deeper emotional need.

Never a coward, Brett nevertheless decided that there

were times when facing reality was better done with a few stiff belts. Striding out purposely, he went back downstairs to the bar and the comfort of twelve-year-old Scotch.

It was while sipping on his third glass of barely diluted whisky, his elongated frame perched tiredly on a leather-covered, thickly padded bar stool, that Brett finally conceded defeat to the indefinable emotion commonly called love.

God, he hated it.

No doubt about it, chum, he taunted himself wryly. This time your engine has completely jumped its tracks. One might be forgiven for falling hard for the wrong woman once. But twice? Brett shook his head sadly. You, sir, seemed to have developed a penchant for loose-limbed, loose-moraled, shockingly beautiful females. But at least the first one had not been staked out by another man—and that man the silver-eyed Wolf, no less. Brett's soft, self-mocking laughter skipped the length of the short bar.

If she finds out, she will rip you apart.

So how do you go about keeping the very beautiful, very sexy, Jo Lawrence from finding out?

Propping his elbow on the polished wood bar, Brett held his glass aloft and frowned at the amber contents, a self-derisive smile curving his lips.

You are not going to find an answer at the bottom of a bottle of Scotch, he advised himself judiciously. Finish your drink and go rustle up some food to soak up the booze.

The refrigerator, kept well stocked by Wolf's part-time housekeeper, yielded the makings of a Reuben sandwich, which Brett prepared with the same ease as he had breakfast earlier that morning.

Deciding coffee would be the prudent drink to have with his meal, Brett brewed a full pot and polished off the sandwich in between deep bracing swallows, all the while resisting the surge of memories of his first disastrous foray into the baffling emotion called love.

As a rule Brett was successful at keeping all recollection of his time with Sondra at bay, but this evening, taut with anger, actually aching with physical frustration, and saturated with whisky, the self-imposed mental barrier refused to stay in place.

Sighing in defeat, his beautiful male lips curling in a sneer of self-mockery, Brett refilled his cup, stretched his long legs out under the table, and let the memories rip.

Sondra Malone had taken Brett's breath away from the first moment he saw her, greeting passengers as they entered the jet bound from Chicago to Atlanta. His first thought had been that she was overall gorgeous. Of average height, Sondra had a neat, trim body with delectable curves, a fantastic mane of fiery red hair, and a face that could, and often did, stop men in their tracks. Of course, there was no outward indication betraying the fact that she also possessed the morals of a back-alley feline. Completely bowled over by her, it was a long time later that Brett learned, the hard way, that Sondra would sleep with anything that wore pants—if the pockets in those pants were heavily lined with gold.

Sipping at the strong black brew, Brett allowed his mind freedom to wander down the pathway to yesterday, allowed his senses to experience the trauma of the time he'd spent with Sondra.

Now, from a five-year distance, Brett realized he'd been a prime target for any Sondra who happened along. He'd been more than tired. After six weeks of flying from Atlanta to Dallas to Honolulu to San Diego to Chicago, on orders from Madam President to "pull the outer reaches of the company together," he'd been bone weary. As he'd also been without female companionship the entire length of those six weeks, he'd been horny as hell.

Enter the gorgeous redhead!

With a snort of disdain, Brett jackknifed to his feet and began clearing the table. When the kitchen was again restored to its usual neatness, he walked slowly to his temporary bedroom, extinguishing lights as he went. After a quick visit to the connecting bathroom for a brief ablution, the plying of a toothbrush, and the natural draining off of some of the liquid he'd consumed, Brett stripped to the buff and crawled between crisp percale sheets, only then allowing his memory free run once more. This time, their time together replayed in his mind in detail.

Anger tightened his frame, simmered in his eyes as Brett strode along the boarding ramp to the plane.

Damned incompetents! If I performed my duties with the laxity of some of these airline baggage handlers, I'd be tossed out on my ear, Madam President's son or not.

The recipients of Brett's ire were the faceless airline employees who had somehow managed to mislay his bags between San Diego and Chicago. The mishandling in itself was bad enough but, on his second day in the windy city, he had been informed that his bags had been sent on to Atlanta and were awaiting him there. Thus Brett had been forced into an unscheduled shopping expedition. Brett detested shopping in general and clothes shopping in particular; he had remained furious over the incident throughout his entire five-day stay in the city. Nothing, not the fact that his exhausting back-to-back twelve-hour-day meetings had gone so smoothly or the congratulatory phone call from his mother, had soothed his abraded temper. That is, not until he'd caught a flash of flaming red hair as he approached the entrance to the plane.

God, she's fantastic!

Anger forgotten, Brett increased his gait, plunging ahead for a closer inspection of the passenger-greeting flight attendant.

"Good afternoon," Sondra flashed perfect white teeth. "Your seat is lo—"

"Do you have a layover in Atlanta?" Brett interrupted softly, insinuatingly, his thumb and forefinger dipping into his breast pocket.

"Yes, but . . ."

"If you feel the need of companionship." He again cut her off, pressing his embossed business card into her hand. "Give me a call." Giving her no time to respond or attempt to hand his card back, Brett strode into the plane.

Later, while delivering a drink to him, Sondra slid his card into his breast pocket with a whispered, "If you care to wait, I'll meet you in the departure lounge after we land."

If he cared to? Brett was grateful for the briefcase resting on his thighs, concealing the evidence of how very much he cared to wait. For the previous two weeks his body had been sending him signals of its need for release of sexual tension. Suddenly his need was centered on the tantalizing redhead.

Upon landing in Atlanta, Brett positioned himself at the long window in the departure lounge, his impatience camouflaged with cool composure, prepared to endure hours of waiting if necessary. The necessity did not arise as within a relatively short amount of time Sondra joined him at his sentry post.

"You're free to leave already?" Brett made no attempt to hide his pleasure at the sight of her.

"Free for three full days." Sondra smiled back at him.

"Three days!" Brett repeated, unabashedly delighted at the prospect. "Is that the norm for a layover?"

"No," Sondra admitted blithely.

"Then how did you manage it?" Brett grinned in anticipation.

"Wheedling, coaxing, and practically promising my firstborn to the girl who was due this layover."

Securing her elbow with his long-fingered hand, Brett steered her from the lounge. "Then let's get out of here before she changes her mind."

Smiling conspiratorially at each other, they hurried out of the terminal and into a cab.

Before the end of their first twenty-four hours together, Brett was thoroughly besotted with Sondra. She was not only gorgeous; she was bright, vivacious, and witty.

By the end of their second twenty-four hours, Brett decided Sondra was everything he'd ever wanted in a woman. He was so besotted he was beyond realizing that Sondra made a career out of being everything *every* man ever wanted in a woman.

Sondra's vacation never did end. The flight from Chicago to Atlanta was her last. After one particularly satisfying bedroom romp during their third twenty-four hours, Brett, positive he'd at last found a soulmate, proposed to her. They were married one week later at his mother's horse farm in Florida.

Brett, though not a confirmed workaholic, ran a close second in the energy and diligence he afforded the company. Sondra was a lotus eater to the marrow of her bones. The moment his diamond-encrusted wedding ring firmly encircled her finger, she prevailed upon him to come and play with her.

In truth, Brett needed very little coaxing to abandon duty for the intoxicating delights to be explored on the playground of her luscious body. For almost two years he was little more than a figurehead in his Atlanta office. It was only later that Brett would give thanks for whatever guidance had prompted him to hire Richard Colby as his assistant. For Richard not only held down the fort competently, he covered Brett's tracks completely.

The good life began to pall as their second anniversary crept over the horizon. Unnaturally tired, jaded, bored with it all, Brett announced his intention of going back to work one hungover midmorning.

At first, Sondra pouted prettily and coaxed beguilingly. When those tactics had no effect on Brett's determination, she turned on the waterworks. It was when the tears failed to dissuade him that she revealed the first glimpse of her true colors.

"God damn you," Sondra screamed at him. "What the hell do you expect me to do while you play at being the big corporate executive? Join a club of silly damned women who talk of nothing but their brats and redecorating the houses their husbands keep them chained to?"

Startled speechless, Brett had stared at her, unwilling to believe what he was hearing. Shock followed amazement as the tirade Sondra flung at him came straight from the gutter.

Though wealthy from birth, Brett had not led a sheltered existence. He had been all over the world. It would have been polite to say some of the places he'd been in were a mite unsavory. Yet he'd never encountered a female with Sondra's command of filthy language.

His head pounding from the effects of months of too much Scotch, too many late nights, and total abandonment to the physical senses, Brett, calmly walking away from her in mid-spate, strode from the room.

From that point the marriage that never really was deteriorated rapidly. The twelve months that followed were sheer hell for Brett. Sondra, no longer concerned about his opinion of her, flaunted her true personality. She was still bright, if bitingly so. She was still vivacious, if frantically so. She was still witty, if sarcastically so. She continually turned Brett's stomach.

As one month dragged into another, Brett spent longer and yet longer hours in the office, more and more days on the road. He was fully cognizant of the audacious, unfettered life style Sondra was pursuing. At the dawn of their third anniversary he no longer cared; at least he thought he didn't.

His own personal breaking point came less than a week before their third anniversary. Brett had been in Philadelphia the previous week supervising the final details of a twin hotel-condominium complex the company was planning to build there. Although he was tired, he felt good, for he had successfully ironed out all the knots and twists that accompany a project the size and cost of the one in Philadelphia.

His mood soured slightly on entering the lavish condo Sondra had insisted on being installed in. Brett loathed everything about the place.

Ignoring his surroundings with single-minded concentration, Brett cut a direct path to the bedroom, his one desire being a hot shower and clean, cool, light-weight clothing. At the doorway to the bedroom he came to a jarring halt.

It was the middle of the afternoon and Sondra was in bed. She was not alone. The fact that she was in the act of defiling both him and his bed with another man was bad enough. That the other man had been a friend of Brett's since their college days was like receiving a kick in the teeth.

The other man was a very elite member of the old guard, old-money aristocracy, a prominent banker, and loaded—in more ways than one.

At sight of the writhing, moaning couple, Brett's feeling of well-being drowned in the anger that erupted at his core and surged hotly through him.

At sight of the nearly empty champagne bottle and forgotten glasses on the nightstand by the bed, his anger reached the boiling point.

But it was the sight of the small sugar bowl half full of

cocaine that ignited the furious explosion that propelled him into the room.

Though his blood was running hot, Brett's mind remained icy cold. Fully aware of his actions, Brett strode across the white carpet. Grasping his former friend by arm and thigh, Brett lifted the smaller man and tossed him to the floor.

"What the . . . !" The squeak slurred from the other man's throat an instant before he found himself flying through space.

"Brett! Stop this at—" Sondra's shrill command died on her bruised lips at the face of cold hauteur Brett turned to her.

"You made your bed. Now you can lie in it." Not bothering to glance at the man just regaining consciousness, Brett whipped around and strode to the door.

"It'll cost you a bundle to get rid of me," Sondra shrieked after him.

Pausing in the doorway, Brett slowly turned to face her, his expression amused, his smile relieved.

"And worth every dollar of it."

It had required six months, and every dollar of that bundle, but Brett had reclaimed his self-respect and his freedom.

Now, eighteen freedom months later, Brett derided himself for once again finding himself a slave to his own emotions. Though he would not have thought it possible, he felt a crushing need for another, if totally different, type of woman.

They are really sisters under the skin, Brett warned himself wryly.

What I'm going to do is get the hell out of her vicinity for a while and cool off. Vermont, here I come.

His lips curving in self-derision, Brett flung his arms over his head and went to sleep.

FOUR

For Jo, besieged by a barrage of questions and memories, escape into unconsciousness was not difficult to achieve; it was impossible.

Wandering restlessly, purposelessly through the large, roomy apartment, her distracted gaze skimmed sightlessly over the material rewards of her work effort.

The apartment itself was a reflection of Jo's success in her chosen career. The fact that she did not actually own it yet, or that the monthly payments were staggering, was immaterial. Jo was confident of her ability to meet those monthly payments. At least she had been before Wolf's horrible accident and the subsequent arrival of the disapproving Brett.

The furnishings, a reflection of Jo's personality, had been selected carefully, at her leisure, with little regard for cost. As yet the furnishings and bits and pieces of enhancing decor were sparse. It was less than six months since she'd taken possession of the apartment. Besides, Jo felt no driving compulsion to have the decorating chore finished. She had savored the purchase of each and every piece.

As Jo's chosen style of decor leaned from classic to ultra modern, her task was made doubly difficult simply because the selection was abundant and varied.

Except for the kitchen and the apartment's two bathrooms, all the walls were painted eggshell white. The living room was given life by the occasional splashes of brilliant color: the cerise cotton that draped the large window with its stunning view of the city's towers; the vibrant shades of an obscure Matisse print; the jewel tones of the chenille scatter cushions littering the long white cotton sofa and matching club chairs, and, underfoot, the rectangular rugs in unrelenting black and white.

No, not at all the more common homey warmth. Yet it worked, and beautifully; the room invited conversation and relaxation. On this night Jo found little relaxation. Though the cause of her confusion had departed some fifteen minutes ago, Jo was still trying to grasp what had transpired while he stood at her door.

Was she, she wondered, so very infatuated with Brett she was beginning to imagine things? The night before she had felt certain he was on the point of kissing her before he'd turned away abruptly. Just moments ago she had received the impression that he was fighting a similar urge. Yet in both instances he had left her flat, and not very pleasantly at that! Was she reading something into Brett's behavior that simply was not there?

Hazel eyes cloudy with introspection, Jo walked slowly to her bedroom, switching off lights automatically as she passed them. With a featherlike touch to the dimmer switch mounted on the wall of her bedroom, different but equally resplendent colors sprang into view. Here the draperies were in a shimmering Pacific blue. The rug picked up the theme, while the quilt on the bed was a calming pattern in various shades from periwinkle to cerulean. A colorful impressionistic original was the only relief on one white wall.

Kicking off her shoes, Jo padded to the closet and began to undress. Damn the man, she thought irritably, what was he thinking, feeling? Her distraction was evidenced by the fact that, although she was standing before the opened closet door, she dropped her clothes carelessly onto the floor. Seconds later Jo stood frowning under a hot shower. Usually the jet spray had a soothing effect. Tonight it simply was not working; in fact, nothing seemed to work for her anymore! Sighing tiredly, Jo stepped out of the tub, dripping unconcernedly onto the thick bathmat. Patting herself dry, she ignored her own reflection—no mean trick as the walls were tiled entirely in mirrors. There was not a hint of white in this room. Except for the mirror walls everything in the room was in the same soft rose shade as the mat she now dripped upon, including the roll of tissue set into the wall. The combination of mirrors and soft rose imbued the room with an innocent eroticism. The effect was not at all accidental; Jo had very carefully planned every room in the apartment.

Hanging her sodden towel neatly on the bar mounted on the wall, Jo glanced up and found her gaze caught by the unhappy expression in the hazel eyes gazing back at her. Had Brett been on the point of making a move on her? Devoid of enlightenment, hazel eyes stared at her. If he had wanted to kiss her, why hadn't he acted on the urge? He knew she was free. She knew he was divorced. And what did a kiss mean, anyway?

Long lashes fluttered in a quick blink. You may attempt to fool any other person in the world, Jo Lawrence, she chided herself, but never, never try to con yourself. From any other man a kiss would not only have no meaning, it would be forcefully rejected; from Brett Renninger, it might very well mean the end of existence as you know it and the beginning of a whole new, incredibly exciting world.

Wearing nothing but a dreamy expression on her lovely face, Jo drifted into the bedroom and slid between wickedly expensive satin sheets. The feel of satin against her naked skin ignited a fire deep inside the very core of her being. Closing her eyes, Jo moved sensuously, her body growing vibrantly alive from the caressing touch of the cool, smooth material, her mind imagining that touch belonging to Brett's long, slim hands. Heat radiated from her now fiery core to lick hungrily through her veins, and Jo's trembling thighs parted in silent invitation. The low whimper that whispered through her dry lips alerted Jo to the folly she was indulging in. Moaning in frustration, she rolled onto her stomach and forced herself to lie perfectly still.

"Oh, God, why Brett?" Jo's cry was muffled by the silky pillowcase. "Of all the men in the world, why inflict me with the one who feels nothing but disdain for me?"

Jo grew still at the sound of her own voice, the context of her outcry. Why did Brett hold her in contempt? There were few people who knew her personal history. Still, could it be possible Brett had heard her rather pathetic story from one of them? Had he heard of her miserable attempt at playing mistress and dismissed her as a failure as a woman? Because she had failed. Gary Devlin had made sure she'd been aware of exactly how badly she'd fared in the male-female stakes.

The heat was gone, replaced by the chill of memory. Jo definitely did not want to think about Gary. Jo never wanted to think about Gary again for as long as she lived. But, given a choice between burning in the hell of desire's fire and reliving the hell she'd endured with Gary, she thought it prudent to think about him. Thoughts of him should not only keep her cool, they would very likely freeze her soul.

Gary. Had she really considered the possibility of spending the rest of her life with him? Yes, Jo admitted. At the beginning she had actually wanted marriage. Thank heaven Gary had hedged, opting for a trial, live-together period. That trial period had lasted a very short time. Jo shivered with the memory. She had not been able to hold Gary's interest for one full year! And, if he was to be believed, she had practically emasculated him as well!

Did all women who had reached a measure of success in their careers have this trouble in their relationships with men? Were all men intimidated by even the most mildly successful women? Jo didn't know the answers, and she was too private a person to ask the opinion of other professional women she knew.

Cool now, in body and mind, Jo rolled onto her back and stared into the darkness of her room. If their time together had emasculated Gary, she couldn't define what it had done to her. But she knew she was now afraid of any deep involvement with a man, and the very thought of making a commitment gave her the shakes. It's unbelievable, she mused sadly, how much damage two people can inflict on each other in such a short span of time. And it had begun so sweetly too.

She had met Gary while shopping one bright, warm morning in April in, of all places, a stalled elevator. Everyone on the car had become nervous immediately, including Jo. Gary had not. His tall, muscular frame propped lazily against the car's wall, he had coolly advised them to relax.

"This is at least the third time this has happened to me in this very car." Gary, a dry smile curving his lips, had offered the information in an attempt to calm a rather hysterical older woman. "We'll be moving again shortly."

Within seconds of his promise the mechanism clanked into motion, then glided to a smooth stop at the next floor. Inside those seconds, his laughing eyes had captured Jo's and he'd winked conspiratorially. Acting completely out of character, Jo had winked back. As she stepped from the car he caught her arm in a gentle grasp.

"Now that our crisis is over," he'd whispered dramatically, "how about joining me in a celebratory cup of coffee?"

Jo couldn't help herself, she'd laughed aloud. "What, exactly, would we be celebrating?"

"Why, our very survival, what else?" He blinked owlishly at her, making her aware of the summer-sky blue of his eyes.

Completely charmed by his boyish smile, his dark, clean-cut attractiveness, and his engaging manner, Jo, flinging caution to the winds, went with him for coffee. Six months later she gave in to his plea to allow him to move in with her.

Less than a week after Gary had lugged his belongings up the three flights of stairs to her cramped, one-bedroom flat, Jo knew the arrangement had been a mistake. He was carelessly sloppy with his clothes, she soon discovered, leaving them lying in rumpled heaps all over the place. To someone as neat as Jo, the mere sight of the piles of soiled clothing induced a shudder. But even that irritating habit might have been bearable if it had not been combined with Gary's absolute refusal to help with the everyday household chores, claiming he wouldn't be caught dead doing "women's" work. But, by far, Jo's biggest disillusionment came on their very first night together.

Jo had been to bed with Gary before he'd moved in with her, of course, but always at his apartment, which he shared with a young accountant. Their sexual activity had therefore been less than satisfactory due, Gary had assured her, to the fact that his roommate might walk in on them at any given moment. Yet, for some reason Jo could not explain even to herself, she had held firm in her refusal to having him spend time in her bed. When her capitulation came Jo had been every bit as surprised as Gary was.

In the darkness of a much more luxurious bedroom, Jo groaned in sympathy for the inhibited woman she'd been a few years ago.

Growing up in a home where her parents never displayed affection for each other, in fact rarely even spoke to each other except when absolutely necessary, Jo, harboring a wariness for the male-female relationship, had single-mindedly pursued first her studies, then her career. An only child, she had received an abundance of love from her parents, but always in separate doses. Jo was not yet ten years old when she realized her parents silently hated each other. Why they hated each other remained a mystery to Jo to this day. They never told her, she never asked.

Being a witness to this silent hatred through her formative years had inflicted fears as well as scars on her psyche. For as long as Jo could remember, everyone told her she was her mother all over again. In one respect this pleased her, for her mother was very beautiful. But in another way it frightened her, for her mother very obviously could not relate to any man. As she grew older Jo realized intellectually that looking like her mother did not necessarily mean she was like her mother. Still, no matter how she tried to convince herself otherwise, the fear of her own inability to express love for a man, either verbally or physically, would not be banished.

During her college and hotel-management training years Jo had dated infrequently, and always disastrously. Positive she would make a shambles of the evening, she always did. In fact, she said no so often that by her third year in college she had acquired the nickname No No Jo. It was only after she'd been working for some months that she began a slow emergence from her shell of fear. In the hotel business Jo naturally came in contact with different and varied types of people. Quiet and observant by nature, she studied the hotel guests and her fellow employees closely, most particularly the interaction between men and women. Slowly, as she conducted her secret survey, she came to the conclusion that she was not all that different from anybody else.

When, to Jo's own delighted surprise, she was promoted to assistant to the assistant to the head of the East
Coast region of the Renninger Corporation and had to
move to New York City, she discovered a whole new
world to contemplate. Dedicated to her subject, and also
to fill the hours when she was not at work, Jo devoured
all the magazine articles devoted to relationships and
every article she came across that dealt with the current
mores on sexuality.

Gradually the tight bud of her self blossomed into mature young womanhood. Feeling free for the first time in
her life, Jo felt ready for an adult relationship with a
man. Then she met Gary Devlin. By the time their affair was over Gary had just about annihilated all of Jo's
hard-won confidence.

In personality they were complete opposites. Gary was
outgoing, gregarious, and made friends easily, with just
about anybody. Jo was as susceptible to his charm as most
other women were. He was also the walking prototype of
the clichéd "tall, dark, and handsome." It wasn't until
after he moved in with her that Jo realized he was also
vain, shallow, and extremely immature. That Gary was
unspectacular in bed as well did not immediately become apparent to her. Having had only one painful, and
abortive, sexual experience while in college, Jo really
had no previous knowledge upon which she could base
a comparison. Gary accused her of being, if not frigid,
coldly unresponsive. Jo believed him, at least for a time.

The telling blow came when Jo was chosen for the coveted position of Wolfgang Renninger's assistant. Euphoric,
soaring on a natural achievement high, Jo rushed home
after work, burst into the apartment, and, flinging her
arms around Gary, cried joyfully, "Guess what?"

As Jo had been rather withdrawn for several weeks,
Gary eyed her warily, his expression suspicious.

"What?" he responded after a brief hesitation.

"I've been picked to replace James Mattern!" Jo bubbled, forgetting that, as Gary never had shown the slightest interest in her job, he hadn't the vaguest idea who James Mattern was.

"And that's good?"

"Good!" Jo exclaimed, laughing as he'd never seen her laugh before. "That's incredible! At this moment, you see before you Wolfgang Renninger's new executive assistant!"

Gary was obviously unimpressed. His expression said "big deal" though he didn't voice the opinion. To her dismay Jo had learned over the eight months they had been together that, unless it was in some way connected with the world of sports, Gary's interest in business was nonexistent. But he was interested in money.

"Will it mean a raise in salary?"

"Of course, silly," Jo said teasingly. She named a figure, then waited expectantly for his whoop of delight. A chill washed all the joy out of her when he stepped back, his face stiff with outrage.

"But that's twice what I earn a year!" he exclaimed harshly. "Exactly what do you have to do for this Renninger?" Before she could shake herself out of her shock to answer, he added nastily, "Boy, is that poor jerk in for a surprise!"

Jo didn't need to ask what he meant. After weeks of his verbal digs about her ineptitude as a bed partner, she knew. Still she was hurt. She was also suddenly blazingly angry.

"Renninger's a married man!" she defended her employer.

"He's a man, isn't he?" Gary sneered. "And for the kind of money you just mentioned, he's going to expect one hell of a lot of assistance, and not only in the office either."

Jo wanted very badly to believe Gary was merely jealous of her boss, but she now knew better. Although it was painful and demeaning, she finally faced the truth. Gary did not love her. Gary loved Gary. Gary also loved the image he had of himself. That image could not bear the idea of a woman who was capable of earning twice his salary a year. Jo was not surprised when he spat a command at her.

"Tell him to shove his damn job."

"No," Jo said quietly but firmly.

Amazement gave his face a comical cast for an instant. Not in all the short time they'd been together had Jo so adamantly refused to do as he dictated. Then his expression turned ugly.

"Either you refuse this job or I move out of here." Gary flung the ultimatum at her in the tone of voice a child might use when threatening a parent with: If you won't let me have another piece of candy, I'll run away from home forever.

Jo answered in much the same way a weary parent might, "Shall I help you pack?" The difference between Jo's query and that of a parent was, Jo meant it. She had met his ultimatum with one of her own. And like the child he so obviously was, Gary resorted to verbal abuse.

"God! Am I glad I didn't let you talk me into marriage."

That was the mildest of the insults he snarled at her during the three days required for him to find another gullible woman to move in with. When, finally, he was gone for good, Jo went through a brief but stormy period of weeping. Anger had kept her tight-lipped and dry-eyed throughout Gary's invective while removing himself from her apartment. Unfortunately his final barb came via the telephone while she was at work, in Wolf Renninger's office.

"Is your boss there?" he'd asked innocently.

"Yes." Although she'd felt a warning prickle, she walked right into his nasty-little-kid trap. "Why?"

"You can tell the bastard I hope he gets his money's

worth from you, but that I really doubt that he will. Men expect a little heat and cooperation from their bed partners once in a while." His derisive laugh burned Jo's ears as he hung up his receiver.

When the call had come through for her Wolf had pushed his chair back from the desk and walked to the window overlooking the busy avenue twenty-six floors below, thoughtfully allowing her a measure of privacy. Replacing the receiver with trembling fingers, Jo raised her eyes to the tall man at the window. Even though her chest felt tight from the pain caused by Gary's parting insult, she had to smile. Her sight blurred by welling tears, she perused the height of him, the breadth of him, the muscularly athletic build that put Gary's to shame. A low, choking sound, part sob, part laugh, drew Wolf's attention. At the shattered look on her face his brows arched questioningly before coming together in a frown.

"What's wrong, Jo?"

It was not the question but the concern in his voice that released the flood of tears. Gulpingly, at times incoherently, Jo blurted out the whole miserable story to him, omitting only Gary's assertion that she was a cold, unresponsive woman. Sobbing out her unhappiness, she was hardly aware of Wolf crossing the room to take her into his arms, but she was grateful for the strong comfort of his embrace and the soothing strokes of his hand on her hair. There was nothing at all personal in his touch, and Jo was grateful for that as well. After the storm had passed he continued to hold her protectively for several minutes.

The sudden realization of her cheek resting on his tear-dampened shirt brought Jo to her senses. Embarrassed by her outburst and the position she found herself in, she stirred restlessly against his chest. Wolf immediately released her and stepped back.

"I-I'm sorry, I . . ." Jo, feeling her cheeks grow hot, bit her lip in consternation.

Wolf's incredible silver eyes were soft with sympathy. "You don't need to apologize, Jo," he said quietly. Glancing down at his damp shirt, he smiled gently. "It'll dry." Then his smile twisted into a grimace. "He's not worth one of your tears, you know."

It was then that Jo learned that Wolf was not only kind but forthright. "I like you, Jo. I have since the first interview I gave you. You are bright and alert and ambitious, and I like that. But, like my wife, you have retained your femininity, and I like that too. Friends?"

Soon after Jo had begun working in the New York office she had heard, via the office grapevine, of how Wolf's wife, Micki, adored him. At that moment she understood why.

Wolf's brother Brett was something else entirely.

Brett.

Rolling onto her side, Jo groaned aloud in protest against the intrusive image of the object of her unwilling affections. After that shaming debacle with Gary, she had felt positive it would be a very, very long time before she'd find anything attractive in another man. Yet, here she was, a little more than a year later, sleepless, achy, and longing for the sight and touch of a man who very obviously did not like her.

But there had been those moments when she'd sensed desire in him, desire for her. Or was she seeing emotions in him that simply were not there? Why did he dislike her so?

"Oh, hell!"

With the exclamation Jo turned onto her side, pounding the pillow in an attempt to vent her frustration. She was weary of the questions that buzzed incessantly inside her head, tired of searching for answers that were not there. Clutching the pillow close to her body, she shut her eyes tightly, certain she was in for another sleepless night.

Within seconds Jo was oblivious to the world. She slept long, and deeply, her rest unmarred by remembered dreams.

Feeling and looking better than she had in well over two weeks, Jo sailed into Brett's office the following morning mere moments after he'd issued a rough-voiced command for her to do so. His appearance betrayed his own restless night. Though he was dressed immaculately, as usual, his eyes had a flat, dull look, faint white lines of strain edged his compressed lips, and a pallor underlay the tan on his cheeks.

"I'm leaving for Vermont after lunch," he said bluntly the minute she'd closed the door behind her. "I have no idea how long I'll be gone. It may be days, it may be weeks. Can you handle things here in my absence?"

"I have before." Jo was sorry for the arrogant-sounding assertion the minute it was out of her mouth. Would he think her statement too confident? The way his lids narrowed convinced her that he did. But, damn it, Brett knew her capabilities by now, didn't he? Brett gave further proof of his tiredness by shrugging instead of snapping at her.

"I'm relieved," he muttered irritably, tossing the folder that contained Wolf's project across the desk to her. "Okay, let's get at this. There's a lot to cover and I'm pressed for time."

Several times during the following hour and a half Jo had to fight back the urge to scream at him. Brett fired questions at her with the rapidity of a machine gun, merely grunting when she knew an answer, grating "why not?" when she didn't. Finally, after about his tenth "why not?" Jo's tenuous hold on her temper snapped.

"I don't know because your brother chose to keep this project to himself!" Feeling as though her back was to the wall, Jo lashed out at him. "You *know* I believed this project had been scrapped. You know, and yet you persist in badgering me with questions I can't possibly be expected to know the answers to. Don't play games with me."

For an instant the flatness fled from his eyes and they glittered like sunlight on gun metal, then the light was gone and Brett lowered his eyes to the slim gold watch on his wrist. "I have a lunch appointment," he droned without inflection. "Take the folder back to your office and familiarize yourself with the contents. I'll stop by and pick it up before I leave for Vermont." Raising his head he stared at her, his expression remote, his eyes again dull gray with disinterest. "You may go now."

Dismissed! She had been dismissed like a bothersome child! Jo had to bite her lip to keep from crying out in protest. Both chilled and subdued by his manner, Jo withdrew into herself before rising to her feet, her composure her only shield against Brett's attitude. "I'll see you in a while." Jo was amazed at the degree of coolness her tone conveyed, for inside she was anything but cool. Actually, she wanted to run back to her office and weep with frustration. Moving with calculated slowness, she walked out of his office, closed the door carefully, then, her composure slipping, ran along the hall to her own office.

You must have masochistic tendencies. Jo made the silent observation while sitting slumped in her high-backed desk chair. It was over an hour since she'd beat a hasty retreat from Brett's office. In that time she had done nothing but stare at the walnut paneling that covered the wall facing her desk. She had not found a single solution to her emotional condition on the beautifully grained wood. Why was she putting herself through all this? Hadn't she had enough pain with Gary? Why couldn't she simply dismiss Brett from her mind as ruthlessly as he'd dismissed her from his sight? The questions repeated themselves with boring insistency. The answer was always the same: *I love him.*

Love. What the emotion did to a woman should be against the law of both God and man! What unadulterated fools it makes of us, Jo decided sadly. Who needs it, anyway? she railed at herself. You do, her self mocked smugly. *I'm losing my mind! Am I actually arguing . . . with myself?* Tearing her gaze from the wall, Jo jumped to her feet and stalked to the oversized window behind her desk. *Yes, I am actually arguing with myself. It seems that love does that to us too. It makes us irrational!* Who but an irrational being would invite pain into her heart?

Staring at the minuscule pedestrian and vehicular traffic on the avenue far below, Jo sighed in exasperation. How many, she wondered, out of the millions that jammed this greatest of all cities, how many people have indulged in a like self-analysis? And how many have reached any concrete conclusions? Probably none. A wry smile twisted Jo's soft lips. Don't feel like the Lone Ranger, girl, the odds are that you have plenty of company. *So why don't I feel reassured?* The smile growing into a grimace, Jo turned and walked slowly back to her desk. Forget it. Forget *him*, she advised herself. Sliding onto her chair, Jo picked up the now-hated folder. As she opened the cover Brett strode into her office.

"Hard at it, I see," he observed complacently.

Jo didn't know whether to laugh or cry. She did neither. Instead, she held his strangely intent gaze steadily, silently challenging him to do or say anything clever or smart. Fortunately, perhaps for both of them, he read her mood correctly. His expression wary, he arched an attractive eyebrow at her.

"Any questions?"

At least a hundred, Jo thought. "None," she answered.

"Good." Turning abruptly, he walked to the door, then

paused, his hand on the knob, in much the same way he had weeks before. "Oh, yes," he said softly, "I've made up a list of things to do while I'm gone." Sliding his left hand into his jacket pocket, he withdrew a sheet of paper. Even from across the room Jo could see the list was lengthy. Holding the paper between thumb and fore-finger, Brett waved it languidly in the air. "You'll take care of everything"—the brow inched higher—"won't you?"

"Yes, of course," she replied quietly, fully expecting him to backtrack and hand the paper to her. Brett didn't move.

"Of course," he repeated in a near whisper, his tone dry.

He's going to make me go to him! The realization struck as a taunting smile feathered Brett's lips. Standing stock still, Brett's eyes transmitted an order for her to get up. Resentment burning like acid in her throat, Jo pushed her chair back and stood up. Suddenly she knew what this little charade was all about. With cool deliberation Brett was making it clear exactly who was the boss and who was the employee. Her restraint nearly snapped when he smiled in self-satisfaction.

"I've written down the phone number where I'll be staying," he murmured silkily. "If you have any problems, call me. Don't, I repeat, do not even consider calling Wolf. He is in no condition to take calls from you." Slowly, as he was speaking, his tone went rock hard.

Thoroughly confused, Jo frowned. Why in the world would he think she'd call Wolf? Had he no confidence in her ability at all? Did he believe she'd run to his brother at the first little snag she encountered? More hurt than insulted, Jo snatched the paper out of his hand, her gaze skimming the list swiftly.

"I think I can handle it," she assured him. *And anything else you can dream up,* she tacked on silently.

"Do you think so?" His tone sent a chill rippling down

her spine. Could the man read her mind? Releasing his grasp on the doorknob, Brett took the single step necessary to close the distance between them. "Do you really think so?" Slowly, his eyes holding hers, he lowered his head.

Jo did not have to fight to keep from stepping back; quite the contrary, she had to fight a sudden need to step into him. Holding herself tautly still, she watched his descending face, positive he'd turn away at the final moment. She was wrong. When his lips brushed hers her eyes widened in astonishment, then her long lashes fluttered and lowered. That whisper touch brushed her lips a second, then a third time. A ripple of pure delicious sensation shivered through her. Why, why was he teasing her with these almost kisses? And why didn't he touch her, embrace her, crush her to him?

Fully conscious of what she was doing, Jo parted her lips in silent invitation. Although he still made no move to bring his body into contact with hers, Brett accepted her invitation at once. Open hard male lips fused with Jo's, moving slowly to engulf and encompass. A soft half sigh, half moan rose in Jo's throat, only to be muffled by the intrusion of Brett's stiffened, searching tongue. Electrified, Jo stood, trembling violently, longing to feel her softness molded to his hard length, aching for the feel of his hands on her overheated skin. Still he did not touch her.

Jo felt rather than heard the groan that passed from Brett's throat to hers an instant before he deepened the kiss. Revealing raw hunger, his lips consumed while his tongue made a masculine demand for active participation from hers. Jo responded to his demand without hesitation, parrying each thrust, riposting in turn, savoring the sweet male taste of him. Now the murmur that issued from his throat had more the sound of growl than moan, a feral sound that spoke to something wild deep within Jo.

And wildly sweet was the sensation of her blood rushing through her veins, converging in her head, making her legs weak and her need strong, pounding out one cry in her mind: Touch me, touch me, touch me. Still Brett did not touch her.

Brett's plunging, scouring tongue was everywhere, learning everything about the moist interior of her mouth. Her mind spinning, her senses going crazy, desperately afraid she'd collapse at his feet any second, Jo's lips clung to his. Growing deeper, more possessive, more demanding by each instant, his kiss went on and on, reducing Jo to a receiver of the erotic messages Brett was transmitting through the medium of his mouth. Then, suddenly, he ended it. Drawing away with obvious reluctance, he lifted his head.

There was no power on earth, certainly not her shattered will, that could have prevented Jo from swaying when his anchoring lips were removed. Bereft, disoriented, she waited long seconds for the floor to stop shifting under her shaky three-inch heels before raising leaden eyelids. The gaze that met hers came very close to undoing her completely. Smokey gray with passion, Brett's eyes bored into hers, underlining the messages his lips had sent to her. He wanted her, very badly, but for some unfathomable reason of his own, he had exerted every ounce of control he possessed to keep from laying even one finger on her body. As if his eyes were an open book, it was all there for her to read. The only pages missing were the ones explaining why. Refusing her the opportunity to ask questions, Brett straightened to his full height and stepped back, his hand grasping the doorknob.

"You look very beautiful today," he said softly, throwing Jo into deeper confusion with the first compliment he'd ever given her. "That color is great on you. You should wear it more often."

Then he was gone and Jo stood staring at the door he'd

closed so very gently. Pulling herself together, if loosely, Jo backed up until the back of her thighs bumped her desk. Sinking onto the solid wood support, she released a long, heartfelt sigh. Well, if nothing else, one question had been erased from her mind. Gary had repeatedly accused her of being unable to physically respond to a male advance. Moments ago she had responded with every quivering particle of her being. Unashamedly she admitted to herself that, had Brett asked it of her, she'd have sunk to the floor for him without hesitation. In amazement, Jo realized that for the first time in her life she wanted, really wanted to experience a man's physical lovemaking. A tiny, sad smile feathered her lips fleetingly. How grand! Here she was, at age twenty-eight, prepared to offer everything of herself for the first time in her life and the donee of her largess flaunts his iron control in her face.

The thought was chilling, but had to be examined. Brett's involvement in their mouth embrace had been as total as her own, Jo was as sure of that as she was of leaves falling in autumn. But he had not touched her, had not taken advantage of the opportunity to assuage the hunger he'd revealed through his kiss. Why hadn't he? The answer was obvious, at least to Jo. She had spent most of the last three weeks with him. She had seen the expression of disdain and often contempt on his face when in her company; Brett hadn't made the slightest attempt to hide his feelings. For reasons known only to himself, Brett simply did not like her. So then, did a man . . . a man like Brett Renninger . . . make a lover of a woman he could not like personally? Jo asked herself. Not very likely, she concluded unhappily. *And where does that leave me?* She wondered. *Absolutely nowhere.*

But he does think I'm beautiful! Grasping at the thought for all she was worth, Jo glanced down at the dress she'd hastily chosen that morning. She had not known until she'd walked out of her apartment that the garment had been the perfect choice for a crisp fall day. The wool-blend material was in a vibrant russet that rivaled nature's brilliant autumnal display. The dress was cut in simple, classic lines that did full justice to Jo's slim yet curvaceous figure. Jo's lips twitched wryly as she remembered the enormous price that had been discreetly printed on the little dress's tiny price tag. At the time of purchase Jo had gasped at the cost. Now she was glad she had given in to temptation and whipped out her credit card before she'd had time to change her mind!

The buzzer on the intercom on Jo's desk peeled the information that her secretary, Reni, was back from lunch and back to work. And, apparently, Jo decided as the number-one button on her phone began to blink, so am I.

Leaning to the end of her desk, Jo lifted the receiver and asked with a briskness she was light-years away from feeling, "Yes, Reni?"

"Mr. Renninger's on line one, Jo," Reni reported calmly.

For one second Jo was certain she could not manage a normal tone. Fourteen questions jumbled together into a solid mass in her head. One stood out in glaring clarity: Is he going to ask me to go with him?

"Yes, Mr. Renninger?" How in sweet heaven had she contrived that coolly professional note?

"Ms. Lawrence, I hope you can help me. I need some information and Brett's secretary tells me he's out of the office."

Eric Renninger! Why hadn't Reni told her the caller was Eric Renninger? Closing her eyes against a sudden, ridiculous sting, Jo drew in a deep breath before answering softly, "Yes, your brother left less than an hour ago, Mr. Renninger. I'll be happy to help you, if I can. Exactly what do you need?"

While she was being her most businesslike self, a vision rose to play havoc with Jo's concentration. The vision had

slate-gray contemptuous eyes, a harshly unyielding coun-
tenance, and a mouth designed to make thinking women
weep.

Her eyes foraging over the desk in an effort to escape
the taunting image, Jo's glance settled on the cream-
colored folder. Perhaps he hadn't found it all that easy to
control himself. The austere Brett Renninger had forgotten what he'd originally come into her office for!

FIVE

Purring like a sleek, well-fed cat, the Porsche hugged the highway that unwound like a ribbon into the magnificent mountains of New England. Though now past the peak of brilliance, the world-famous foliage blazed in the waning afternoon sunlight, a spectacular free show for anyone with the eyes to see. Brett's awareness of fall's breathtaking display of colors was at a shallow surface level. His glance noted the panorama, his mind didn't register the glory of it at all. The tiny, picturesque villages tucked into the folds of Vermont's sun-kissed mountains went virtually unnoticed by gray eyes bleak with introspection. Grappling with his own conflicting emotions, he was immune to summer's fiery exit.

Why, Brett berated himself scathingly, in the name of peace of body if not mind, why didn't you take her right there in her office? She was willing. Hell, she was more than willing, she was eager! And you were damned near incinerated! The memory of the blast furnace created by the simple method of placing his lips to Jo's ignited a fresh burst of fire inside Brett's already overheated body. Lord! How many females had he kissed since he'd discovered how exciting the fusing of two mouths could be somewhere around his fifteenth birthday? A lot more then he cared to remember. Yet never before had he experienced the instantaneous, electrified arousal Jo's sweet lips had sent crashing through him. Even now, hours later, every living cell in his body cried more, more, more.

You are very definitely losing your grip, buddy!

Slicing a glance to the rearview mirror, Brett grimaced at the unnaturally pale visage momentarily reflected in the small rectangular of silvered glass. Without even trying, you win the "big stupe" award! There's a blotch on your psychological makeup. Only a true glutton for punishment would go panting after the wrong type of woman twice!

Yet, against all the rationale he could muster, Brett wanted to possess Jo Lawrence with an intensity that shook his so recently well-ordered existence. The emotional hold she was beginning to have on him had been the very element that had induced his exertion on his control. The knowledge of how perilously close he'd come to losing restraint still had his hands trembling as they gripped the steering wheel. With sardonic humor directed at himself, Brett relived his hasty departure from Jo's office.

His arms aching with the need to hold her against his hardened body, his *body* screaming with the need to invade hers, Brett had literally run after he'd closed the office door between them. Never before in his life had he been so sorely tempted to throw all caution, propriety, and plain common sense to the wind! The battle that had raged inside his most sexual of organs, the one he formally called his rational mind, had been of mammoth proportions. The fact that reason had won imbued an intellectual satisfaction that in no way appeased the physical hunger. Against all the arguments he could manufacture, he wanted her, all of her, last night, this afternoon, tonight, and, the most sobering, frightening thought of all, for every one of the forever days and nights to come.

Brett's fingers worked spasmodically on the wheel.

Frowning at his reflexive response to the mere thought of touching Jo, he advised himself to stop the lustful window wishing and concentrate on the job of work that was growing closer with each passing mile. He had things to do, and people to see, and he needed a clear mind and steady hand to accomplish the task he'd set for himself. Now, more than ever, he was determined to at least get the ball rolling on this project Wolf wanted.

One of the people he had to see was a Casey Delheny, the architect Wolf had chosen for the multi-unit. That Brett had never heard of Delheny before was not at all unusual. He was kept doubly busy looking after his own bailiwick. He rarely ever poked his nose into either of his brother's domains. Besides, were he inclined in that direction, Wolf would probably tell him to butt out. Brett smiled at the realization that their mother would very likely back Wolf. Violet Renninger had worked diligently at raising strong, independent sons!

That morning Brett had had his secretary call the architect to arrange a conference meeting. She had reported back to him that Delheny had a full schedule for the next day but would be happy to join Brett for dinner at the restaurant in the motel where he'd reserved a room.

If the man was that busy he was probably an excellent architect, Brett decided as he neared his destination less than fifty miles from the New Hampshire state line. Not at all disgruntled at having to wait on Delheny's convenience, Brett planned on spending the day checking out the building site and surrounding terrain. Wolf had delineated the proposed project with his usual painstaking care. Though Brett fully expected to find everything exactly as Wolf had described, still, he had to see for himself.

The motel was one of a large chain, fairly new, and decorated to blend in with the locale in an elegant early American motif. Thinking the early Americans never had it so good, Brett found his own way to the large, comfortable room assigned to him. He was tired but, having eaten nothing since lunch, he was also hungry. After depositing his case on the luggage rack, he washed his hands, splashed cold water on his face, then strode out of the room again in search of sustenance, preferably in the form of a two-inch thick steak with a side order of Scotch.

On entering the motel lobby, Brett had noticed a sign advertising a restaurant lounge. Back in the lobby, he followed the direction marker on the sign to a dimly lit room. As he neared the lounge entrance the melodic sound of an expertly played piano assailed his ears, along with the slightly off-key blending of several voices. Over half the tables in the large room were occupied with quietly conversing patrons. Every one of the high stools around the piano held a would-be soloist. The combined strains of an old Billy Joel hit was not at all unpleasant.

Settling his elongated frame into a well-padded chair at a table in a far corner of the room, Brett smiled when a discordant note rose above the harmonizing voices. His smile broadened as, undaunted, the man who had hit the sour note continued, still slightly out of tune, till the end. And he joined in with his fellow patrons when they offered a round of applause for the impromptu rendition.

The atmosphere in the lounge encouraged relaxation and conviviality, and Brett felt the tensions of the day ease out of his taut body. With conscious determination he relegated the disturbing thoughts that had traveled north with him to the farthest corner of his mind. The ambiance of the lounge imbued a feeling of well-being. Brett convinced himself good food would fill the emptiness inside.

The menu presented to him by a soft-spoken waiter was limited but included an open steak sandwich that Brett promptly ordered, medium rare, with French fries and a

small salad. He also ordered Scotch but, remembering his
foolishness of the night before, requested both ice and
water in it. He had consumed the steak and salad and was
putting the finishing touches to his fries when a young
woman entered the lounge, glanced around, then,
straightening her shoulders, walked directly to his table.

"Mr. Renninger?" she asked with just the tiniest bit of
hesitation.

"Yes." Brett eyed her interestedly but discreetly. Small,
well rounded without being at all heavy, the woman was
not actually pretty. Her looks were too strong to be de-
fined as anything but striking. Her features were almost
sharp. Her eyes were almost slanted. Her mouth was almost too full. Yet the combination was appealing. Hair as
fair as Brett's own was styled into a shining cap that framed
her face to advantage. His perusal completed in seconds,
Brett smiled in welcome of the diversion she presented.
"What can I do for you?"

"May I sit down?" Interpreting his smile correctly, the
hesitation disappeared from her voice.

Was she trying to pick him up? The idea intrigued
Brett. Besides, he was curious as to how she'd known
his name. "Please do," he invited softly, rising to pull a
chair away from the table for her. Brett didn't get the
chance to question her identity for she launched into an
explanation as he reseated himself.

"My name is Marsha Wenger," she said quietly. "Casey
Delheny told me you were booked into this motel."
When this statement drew one pale brow into an arch,
she clarified. "I asked for you at the desk. The clerk told
me you were in here."

"I see." Of course, he didn't, but, what the hell. He
shrugged mentally. He wasn't going anywhere, and she
was attractive. "May I order you a drink?"

"Yes, please." She paused, eyeing his empty glass.
"That is, if you're having another."

Brett's smile was unknowingly sardonic. "Oh, I was planning to have several others."

"All right then, I'll have white wine." Although her smooth tone had not altered, it was obvious his smile had confused her, for a tiny frown appeared momentarily between her perfectly arched blond eyebrows.

Satisfied with having thrown her slightly off balance, Brett's smile grew into a grin as he motioned to the waiter for a refill. He remained quiet, scrutinizing her with what he knew was unnerving intentness until their drinks had been placed before them and the waiter had departed. Then, lifting his glass in a silent salute, he sipped appreciatively, lowered his glass, and queried softly, "I can't help but wonder why Delheny would tell you where I'd registered." His smile turned suggestive. "Unless Casey decided I'd appreciate a little entertainment and diversion."

Although Marsha seemed startled at Brett's use of the architect's last name, her surprise was forgotten with his final conclusion.

"Casey decided no such thing!" she declared heatedly. "I am *not* a pros— call girl, Mr. Renninger!" Drawing a calming breath, she went on more quietly. "Casey mentioned your name quite casually and I—"

"Casually, Ms. Wenger?" Brett interrupted silkily, then added thoughtfully, "I beg your pardon. Is it *Ms.* Wenger?"

"Yes, it is." Marsha sipped distractedly at her wine. "And I said casually because . . . oh Lord, I'm screwing this up, and I wanted so badly to make a good impression!"

Now that he had her thoroughly rattled, Brett relaxed completely. You are a chauvinist bastard, he accused himself unrepentently. Somewhere on the very fringes of his consciousness Brett knew he was, in a very convoluted way, trying to get at Jo through this stranger. Yet, unwilling to face the power his vulnerability placed in Jo's hands, he refused to give a second thought to his own lack of logic. At this moment he simply enjoyed that fact that he had unnerved *any* woman.

"Don't despair, Ms. . . . may I call you Marsha?" he inquired respectfully—much too respectfully.

"Yes, please do. I-I—" Marsha had obviously not missed the nuance of a drawl in his overly polite request. Her expression revealing that she was indeed despairing, she grasped her glass and drank thirstily.

Suddenly Brett tired of the roasting game. Relenting, a little, he prompted, "You were saying my name was mentioned casually?"

"Yes, well, not really casually." Marsha took a final gulp from her wine, then dove head first into an explanation. "We had lunch together yesterday, Casey and I. When I mentioned"—she winced over the word—"that I'd just mailed a résumé off to you, Casey told me you were due to arrive in Vermont sometime today." She wet her lips before continuing. "The name of this motel was not offered. I asked Casey point blank where you would be staying."

"Résumé?" Brett pounced on the one word.

Marsha winced again but answered at once. "Yes. Through a friend in New York I learned about the managerial position open in your offices. As I'd been considering relocating to New York City for some time now, I decided to apply for the job."

"Go on," Brett prodded.

"That's all!" She smiled apologetically. "At least it was until yesterday. When Casey said you were coming here I decided to seek a personal interview with you."

"Here? Now?" Brett's expression and tone wiped away the image his casual pants and polo shirt projected, revealing the hard businessman that was never very far from the surface. "A bit unorthodox, wouldn't you say?"

Marsha had the grace to blush with embarrassment. But she espoused her cause just the same. "I know," she admitted boldly. "But I have always believed that the only way to get something is to go for it fearlessly. Up until now my method has always worked."

Brett laughed. He had to. The woman's honesty genuinely amused him. Settling more comfortably in his chair, he fixed on her with eyes sharp with interest. "Okay, Marsha Wenger, fire at will. Give me a verbal account of what is contained in your résumé."

Leaning forward tensely, Marsha began speaking in a tone devoid of inflection. Her recitation went on nonstop for a full twenty minutes. When she was finished she sat back and matched Brett stare for stare, her expression composed with the knowledge that her credentials were impressive.

In actual fact, Brett *was* impressed. He was also relieved. The open managerial position Marsha had referred to was the New England area manager's job, which had not been filled since he'd figuratively kicked Bob Harley upstairs, the day he'd gone to the New York offices at his sister-in-law's request. Brett had lost count of the exact number of people he had interviewed for the job during the last three weeks. Most of the applicants had been unqualified, some had been overqualified. Now, incongruous as it seemed, in a motel in Vermont, at a very late hour, Brett had found his new manager!

"You got it."

"I-I beg your pardon?" Marsha blinked in surprise. After his long silence, it was clear his sudden pronouncement had startled her.

"The job." Brett smiled. "It's yours. When can you start?"

Marsha straightened abruptly, as if she'd been pinched in a very delicate spot. "At once!" she squeaked, then hedged. "Or, that is, as soon as I can relocate to the city."

"All right." Brett nodded his acceptance. "If you'll drop all the pertinent information off here at the desk tomorrow, I'll fax it in to the office and have personnel fill out the necessary forms."

Marsha opened her mouth to agree but before she could speak Brett added, "Are you employed now?"

"Yes."

"You'll want to work out notice." It was not a question. Brett's tone indicated she had better want to work out a decent notice.

"I gave my firm a month's notice three weeks ago." Marsha was not quite successful in hiding her annoyance.

It would seem quite a bit happened three weeks ago, Brett thought wryly. The thought reminded him of Wolf and his own temporary tenancy as head man in the New York office. The thought also reminded him of Jo, and that coated his voice with irritation.

"You do realize, I assume, that I'm only filling in for my brother, and the status quo might change when he's back in command?" At the harsh sound of his voice Brett modified his question-statement. "Understand, he will take my recommendations under consideration, but the final decision is his."

"Yes, Casey outlined the current situation." Marsha smiled. "I was also led to understand that *if* you hired me, your brother would very likely retain me." Her smile widened, revealing small, straight white teeth. "Casey seems to know your brother quite well."

"Indeed?" Brett murmured coolly, wondering at both her smile and her opinion. How buddy-buddy had Wolf and this Delheny become? he mused. He did not voice the question to Marsha, preferring to judge the extent of the men's friendship for himself.

Marsha appeared to take Brett's coolness and preoccupation as a hint for her to leave for, after swallowing the last of her wine, she picked up her purse and pushed her chair away from the table. Her actions drew an alert, questioning glance from him.

"I've taken up enough of your time," she explained. "I'll leave you to enjoy the rest of the evening."

"Alone?" Brett's smile held sheer enticement. "Stay and join me for another drink," he invited softly. "We'll discuss your problem of relocation."

Brett found Marsha as easy to charm as most of the other women he'd come in contact with . . . excluding Jo Lawrence, that was. Again the flashing memory of Jo sent a spasm of annoyance through him. Damned woman! He'd wipe all consideration of her out of his mind, or kill himself in the effort! Giving Marsha his warmest smile, he underlined his desire to keep her company. "You will stay, won't you?"

"Well, yes." She laughed, a soft, melodic sound that was easy on Brett's ears. "If you like."

"I do," he assured her firmly, consigning all thoughts of a tall, willowy body, a breathtakingly beautiful face, and a pair of maddeningly arousing lips to the farthest reaches of hell. Brett was content to smile at Marsha encouragingly until their fresh drinks were served, *then* he encouraged her to talk. "Tell me exactly what has to be done to accomplish this move to the big city."

"First"—she held up a long, slim forefinger—"I must finish out my month's notice which, in actual days, amounts to seven. Then I'll have to face the distasteful task of going through my things to decide what I want to take with me and what I will store temporarily. My friend has offered me the use of her sofa until I can find a place of my own, so I can't take too much of my own stuff along." She paused to gaze contemplatively into her wine. When she again raised her eyes to him, they were cloudy with consternation. "I understand finding a decent apartment in the city is the next thing to impossible."

"But not completely impossible," Brett assured her bracingly. While she'd been speaking a germ of an idea had stirred to life in his mind. Now, playing for time to allow the germ quiet in which to sprout, he took a long moment to taste his drink, savoring its bite on his tongue. In his foolishness over one kiss, Brett felt sure he'd revealed far too much of his feelings to Jo. Here, sitting next to him, was a way to disabuse her of any notions she might have conceived about his emotional state. The consideration that he'd be using Marsha didn't bother him in the least. He would be helping her as well and he'd be careful she was in no way involved afterward. The decision made to proceed, Brett put his hastily formed plan into action.

"As a matter of fact, when I fax the vitals into personnel tomorrow, I'll have my assistant scout out a place for you." His smile could only be described as intriguingly wicked. "Jo is highly competent. I'm sure she'll have no trouble at all in finding the perfect place for you."

"Oh, but I can't infringe on your assistant's time like that!" Marsha protested, if not too convincingly.

Now Brett's smiled came very close to nasty. "She'll love it," he promised. "Apartments are her 'thing.'"

Though she looked suddenly skeptical, Marsha grasped at the offer. "Well, if you're positive she won't mind?"

She won't be given a choice, Brett thought with relish. Aloud, he merely reassured her. "She'll enjoy the search," he murmured facetiously. Controlling a prod from the devil to laugh out loud, Brett spun out another strand to his deception web. "I will be in Vermont for at least two weeks. If you can clear up everything here by then, you can drive back to New York with me." His smile was now sugar coated. "You could add the saved air fare to the rent money." His grimace was sincere. "The cost of renting decent living quarters is astronomical."

"So I've heard, and so I'd be a fool to argue over your offer." She grinned. "Thank you."

With a twinge of guilt he didn't wish to recognize, Brett

waved her thanks aside. They talked of other things then, the beauty of Vermont, the many and varied attractions it had to offer, not the least being the skiing, and Brett's purpose in being in the state in the first place.

"Casey did tell me about the project some time ago," Marsha said when Brett finished his very brief account. "But I guess I assumed the project would be dropped, at least until your brother was fully recovered from his injuries."

Sipping his drink, Brett reached the conclusion that this Casey Delheny talked too damn much for the Renningers' own good. Where in hell had Wolf found this blabbermouth? Carefully concealing his thoughts from Marsha, he watched her polish off her wine.

"Would you like another?"

"No, thank you." One well-manicured hand, complete with raspberry-colored polish, covered his when he went to signal for the waiter. "I must be going. My alarm clock rings at the same early hour every working day, no matter what time I stumble into bed."

"I'll be in touch with you as to exactly when I'll be leaving for New York," Brett promised.

"Oh, you'll probably be running into me all over the place while you're here." She grinned. "In a town this size, people have to work at not tripping over each other every other day or so." With a final grin and a wave of her hand, she strode lightly from the room.

Having risen when Marsha stood up to leave, Brett watched her retreating back in appreciation of her shapely form. Even in the soft light from the small lamp that had flickered away steadily during their conversation, Brett had reevaluated his initial judgment of her age. When she'd entered the lounge, he had guessed her age at mid to late twenties. Now he felt sure she was within striking distance of his own thirty-five years.

Twenty-five or thirty-five, he mused, Marsha Wenger is one very attractive woman; smart too.

Brett moved to sit down again, then, changing his mind, decided to call it a night. He paid the check the waiter promptly presented to him, added a tip that from the man's grin insured Brett would be remembered the next time he entered the lounge, and, fighting a yawn, sauntered from the room. Traversing the motel corridors from lounge to elevator, then from elevator to his room, he gave up fighting the tiredness pulling at him and yawned widely. It had been a long, tension-filled day. The hours Brett had escaped consciousness the night before had not counted more than three. He was beat, and he slipped into sleep mere minutes after slipping, buck naked, between the cool sheets.

Ten hours of uninterrupted sleep did wonders for Brett's mental condition. Waking with the bright October sun on his face around mid-morning, Brett stretched hugely before springing off the bed. He felt good, raring to go, but he also felt empty. By the time room service delivered the large breakfast he ordered, Brett was shaved, showered, and dressed to go roaming the project's site in jeans, a soft cotton shirt, a finely knit cashmere sweater, and tan suede boots.

In no particular hurry whatever, Brett savored every sip of the tart, chilled grapefruit juice, every forkful of creamy scrambled eggs, every crunching bite of golden-toasted English muffin, and every satisfying swallow of rich, dark coffee. Replete with good food and ready to face the day, Brett pushed the tray aside and reached for the telephone. The digits he heard register numbered eleven. The voice that answered at the other end of the line had already been familiar to him at age ten. The voice belonged to his mother's housekeeper at the horse farm in Florida. Even now it seemed to Brett that Elania Calaveri had been in residence at the farm forever.

When he responded to her hello, Brett's tone was warm with affection.

"Good morning, Elania. How are you today?"

"Still kicking." The reply was a stock one, reserved for the offspring of her employer. Brett's retort was also stock.

"Anyone I know?"

Elania's chuckle was as hearty at seventy-odd as it had been at forty-five. "Your brother if he don't start behaving himself. I swear, that man is the worst patient I've ever cared for."

Brett was fully aware of the fact that Elania Calaveri was the main reason Wolf had been transferred to the farm instead of his own home to recuperate. Having grown up in the streets of Sicily, Elania was one tough cookie. Nobody, not Wolf or even the hard-nosed businesswoman they all called Mother, gave Elania an argument. If Elania decided Wolf was going to recover completely, Wolf had damn well better do it, and without complaint! Smiling at the thought of the fire Wolf was under, Brett politely inquired if his brother was up to speaking on the phone.

"I wouldn't know why not." Elania gave a long-suffering sigh. "He's been up to driving me to distraction since before six this morning. Hold on till I prop the prowler up."

Brett's appreciative smile still lingered on his voice when he responded to Wolf's growled, "What's up, Brett?"

"Mind your own sex life," Brett shot back, laughing at Wolf's groaning response to his feeble attempt at humor.

"You have a sex-oriented mind, baby brother," Wolf accused grittily.

"Merely following in your size fourteen shoes, big brother," Brett chided laughingly. "May I inquire how you are today?"

"In comparison to what? The wreck of the *Andrea Doria?*" Wolf drawled dryly before, relenting, he allowed affection to color his tone. "How's it going, Brett?"

"Hey, big prowler! You're the one in the sight of Elania's formidable gun, not me!" Brett laughed. "Compared to the heavy weather you've got to ride out, my job's a piece of cake!" Brett's opaque terminology in reference to Wolf's injuries had been deliberate, simply because he knew an openly solicitous query would not be welcomed warmly.

"Yeah, I know, but don't tell the boss." Wolf's dry tone didn't quite succeed in masking his weariness. "If she finds out how easy I usually have it up there, she'll probably create a new region just to keep me out of trouble."

The tired huskiness in Wolf's voice shot instant concern through Brett yet, knowing his brother would not welcome a display of that concern, he decided to claim an appointment and end the conversation. "Look, lazy-bones, I'm going to have to hang up in a minute. I have to see a man about a house," he paraphrased an old saw. "But first, tell me how Micki and the kids are making out in Florida."

"Basking in the sunshine." Wolf's voice held a smile. "I'd let you talk to Mick but she's having her riding lesson at the moment." His soft chuckle hummed through the wire to draw a smile from Brett. "She's doing pretty good at it," Wolf added. "She's only tumbled twice."

Brett's smile disappeared. "Was she hurt?" he asked sharply.

"Micki! Hell no!" Wolf actually chortled. "That hoyden's got more bounce than half a dozen tennis balls. At the rate she's going, she'll put all the rest of us in the shade in no time."

Mingled with the relief Brett was feeling was a growing urgency to cease and desist, for Wolf's voice was now definitely reedy. Before he could ease into saying good-bye,

Wolf asked a question that jolted him upright in his chair.

"How is my best girl working out as your assistant?"

"JoAnne Lawrence?" Brett asked tightly, stupidly.

"Well, of course, Jo," Wolf chided. "Isn't she something?"

Oh, she's something, all right, Brett mentally sneered. "Yes, she's very efficient."

"Jo is more than merely efficient!" Wolf defended strongly, much *too* strongly, to Brett's way of thinking. "I'd say she could give your Richard Colby a run for his money any day of the week!"

Richard Colby's not wealthy enough to even gain Jo's notice, Brett retorted silently. "Perhaps so," he hedged. Then, simmering with renewed anger, and hating it, Brett rushed on, "Look, I really do have to get going. If I don't get the chance to call you again, I'll see all of you sometime over the holidays. Give my love to Micki and the kids."

After he'd cradled the receiver, Brett reached for the large manila envelope that had been delivered to him with his breakfast tray. Gone was the feeling of well-being he'd wakened with. He felt tense, and angry, and all because Wolf had asked about an employee. Had the query been about any other employee, Brett would have considered it the natural interest of an excellent employer, which Wolf was. But the question had not been about any other employee, it had been about Jo, and that annoyed Brett unreasonably.

A quick perusal of the envelope's contents was all that Brett required to assure himself of Marsha Wenger's qualifications. Everything she'd claimed the night before was true. She seemed perfect for the vacant manager's position.

Holding the pertinent papers in one hand, Brett lifted the receiver and made another long-distance call, this time to the New York offices. He spoke first to the personnel manager, setting the gears of Marsha's employment in motion. Then he asked to have the call switched to Jo's office. While waiting for the interoffice connection to be made, a slightly cruel smile of satisfaction curled his lips. Brett's anger intensified with the frisson of warmth the sound of Jo's voice sent rippling through him.

"Jo Lawrence," she answered, as she always did.

"I have a job for you," Brett said without preamble.

"Yes?" she clipped alertly.

Against his will Brett thought about the previous day and how the soft lips that had just moved in answer felt molded to his own. He could see her, he could taste her, and it hurt like hell. Groaning silently, he pushed the memory aside. When he spoke, the roughness of his voice reflected the effort he was exerting to contain his anger.

"I have found someone to fill the New England manager's job. It's a woman. Her name is Marsha Wenger. She'll be needing an apartment. I want you to find her one." Ignoring her muffled gasp, Brett went on ruthlessly, "You have two weeks. I'll be bringing her back to the city when I return." He paused long seconds, then added silkily, "Are there any questions?"

Even long distance Brett could hear the slow, deep breath Jo quietly drew into her lungs. After releasing it just as slowly she said calmly, "Yes, one. What if I'm unable to find an apartment by then?"

Brett knew Jo was holding on to her temper with every fiber of her being. The knowledge pleased him greatly. *Keep a lid on it, beautiful,* he advised silently. *You can't afford to blow your stack now. Your lover's in no condition to protect you. And if you explode at me, I'll teach you how to behave!* The method of how he'd accomplish this teaching process tantalized Brett's senses a moment. Then he came to his senses.

"In the event you're unable to find a *suitable* place for Marsha," he said smoothly, "I suppose she'll have to bunk with you until one *is* found."

This time Jo didn't gasp. This time she choked. "Stay with me!"

"You heard it. So you'd better get to work." Very gently, Brett replaced the receiver. *Now let's see how efficient the assistant-mistress really is,* he thought savagely.

Contrarily, as he strode from the room, Brett found himself hoping Jo would prove her capabilities to him. Shaken by his vacillation, he brought himself up short. You fool, he raged, you're so hot for her you don't know what the hell you do want! Scratch that, he jeered, storming out of the motel. You know exactly what you want . . . her! Her mouth, her body, everything that *is* her!

Brett worked the worst of his agitation off striding to, around, and from the huge land area Wolf had purchased for the multi-unit condo complex. The site was close to the base of the overlapping mountains and near existing ski trails. Off to the left, appearing to hang on the side of the tallest mountain, an attractive lodge sat in regal solitude. From studying Wolf's report, Brett knew exactly how many people the lodge could cater to. The motels located farther down in the valley accommodated some of the overflow but, when the skiing season was at its peak, quite a few hopeful schussers had to be turned down when seeking rooms. Wolf had estimated that with the growing popularity in the winter sport, the number of disappointed skiers would double, if not triple. Wolf's plan was for a Renninger complex to take up the slack, and make a great deal of money in the bargain.

Being a true Renninger, Brett fully approved of his brother's plan. As he walked back to the motel, his mind raced with ideas. Gone was the constraining anger of the morning. He had work to do. A great deal of work. And the first thing on his agenda was an in-depth discussion with the architect, Casey Delheny.

It wasn't until he'd finished a late lunch and had returned to his room to get Wolf's report from his briefcase that Brett discovered he'd come away without it. As a general rule, forgetting things was not at all his style . . . no matter what the provocation! And Jo's sweet mouth had been some provocation! Disgusted with his unusual lack of thoroughness, Brett snatched up the receiver and made yet another long-distance call. Jo's voice hadn't changed in the four hours since he'd heard it; it still had the power to fire his blood.

"Jo Lawrence."

"Fancy that!" Brett exclaimed in his most drawling tone.

"Yes?" The patience of a saint weighted her tone.

"I forgot the report," he said flatly. *I forgot to make love to you,* he thought longingly. "I want you to shoot it up—"

"I shot it up to you yesterday afternoon," Jo interrupted very gently, very sweetly. "You should be receiving it soon." There was a telling pause, then she asked nicely, "Is there anything else?"

Fresh-mouthed woman! The thought had no sooner entered his mind when Brett had to concede the truth of it. Jo's mouth had been delightfully fresh. Suddenly needing to jar her with a zinger, Brett purred, "Have you found Marsha an apartment yet?"

"Well, I'm considering one," she zinged back. "But there are a few details I want to check out before committing 'Marsha' to it."

"I'm glad to hear it," Brett growled in an effort to conceal the smile in his voice. "Maybe you just might be worth the enormous salary Wolf is paying you."

"Please believe me, I am worth every penny of it." Apparently Jo considered it her turn to hang up on him, for she did so, quite as gently as he had that morning.

Her parting assertion ate at Brett for the remainder of the afternoon. At one point, pacing the room in frustration, he caught himself thinking: She's nothing but a damned high-priced . . . At that moment, shocked at the direction his thoughts were taking, Brett forced his attention back to the folder that had been delivered to his room less than half an hour after she'd hung up on him. Brett played at being the dedicated businessman for several hours before giving up the farce.

A brisk shower and clean clothes did little for his disposition. Deciding what he needed was a stiff drink, Brett went to the motel's elegant dinning room some twenty minutes early for his appointment. After lining the maitre d's palm with a respectable inducement, he was ushered to a table with a flourish. He was three quarters into his second whisky when he glanced up to observe the maitre d' escorting a breathtakingly lovely redhead across the room. Wondering who the knockout was, Brett ran his eyes over her tall, well-proportioned body appreciatively. When the smirking maitre d' came to a stop at his table, Brett rose to his feet, one brow arched in query.

"How do you do, Mr. Renninger?" the knockout said, extending a long, slim hand. "I'm Casey Delheny."

Not another one! The protest jumped unbidden into Brett's suddenly alert mind. *Wolf has been busy since I visited him last!*

Within fifteen minutes of accepting Brett's hand during their cordial greeting, Casey simply and neatly disabused him of his initial opinion. Oh, Brett was quick to realize that Casey was indeed in love! But not with Wolf Renninger. The man she talked about in glowing terms of admiration and respect was a Sean Delheny, her husband of eleven months.

Gradually, as they savored their expertly prepared brook trout and steamed fresh vegetables, Brett learned that

Casey not only truly liked Wolf but that he would forever hold a place of affection in her heart. Wolf had introduced Casey to Sean. Over dessert, still smiling faintly at the idea of Wolf in the role of matchmaker, he acquired the additional information that Sean was the contractor Wolf had chosen to build the multicomplex and that he would be joining them for drinks after dinner.

"But why didn't he join us for dinner as well?" Brett wondered aloud.

"Because the appointment had been made with me," Casey explained. "Sean didn't want to, in his words"— she smiled—"butt in."

"He felt left out?" Brett asked sharply, responding to the hint of censure in her tone. Casey's shrug was eloquent. "Believe me, had I known of Wolf's intention to contract Mr. Delheny, I would have included him in on our meeting, whether he was your husband or not. I didn't know."

"But I don't understand." Her slight head movement caused a rippling in her hair that made Brett think of undulating waves on fire. "Didn't Wolf mention Sean at all?"

Before Brett could answer, a tall, brawny man with hair the exact same shade of red as Casey's came to a stop at their table. Brett immediately knew who the man was by the way her eyes lit up. After the introductions were made and fresh drinks ordered, Brett gave Sean a thumbnail account of the conversation prior to his arrival, then he answered Casey's last question.

"I didn't speak to Wolf about my decision to go ahead with this project." This time Brett's shrug was eloquent. "Wolf very obviously wanted this complex. I intend to give it to him. But, as his condition precludes any involvement with business matters, I am proceeding with the report he'd drawn up." He glanced at Sean and shrugged again. "Your name is not in the report."

"But surely Jo Lawrence knew of Wolf's intention to give the contract to Sean!" Casey exclaimed. "She's closer to Wolf than his own shadow."

Even as Brett assured Casey that Ms. Lawrence knew no more about the project than he did himself, his mind seethed with renewed anger. Exactly what, he fumed, had Casey inadvertently let slip with that last remark? Was she aware of the liaison between Wolf and Jo? For that matter, had everybody been aware of the affair but him?

The questions teased Brett's mind throughout the rest of the evening, hovering on the edge of his consciousness while he officially hired Sean as project contractor, discussed the pros and cons of the job ahead, and made plans to meet with the couple again the following day in Casey's office. After bidding the Delhenys' good night, Brett went to his room to spend most of the night tormenting himself with even more questions, questions that conjured visions, visions that drove his anger into fury. And, at regular intervals, he repeated one phrase as if in hopes of convincing himself of its truth.

Damn it to hell, I do not love her!

Surprisingly, after that one tension-filled night, Brett found little difficulty in sleeping. Perhaps it was due to the hours he spent poring over architectural drawings with Casey. Perhaps it was due to the hours he spent tramping over the building site with Sean. Then again, perhaps it was due to the evening hours spent in getting to know Marsha Wenger.

Brett called Marsha to invite her out to dinner the very next day. Squashing a ridiculous feeling of being in some strange way unfaithful, he shoved all thoughts and considerations of Jo from his mind. Marsha proved to be a delightful companion, easy to talk to and easy to laugh with. When she invited him in for a nightcap after he'd escorted her to the door of her apartment, Brett accepted, knowing full well he was going to at least attempt to make love to her. The scene that ensued would have been ludicrous, had it not been so sad.

Marsha made it clear that she was willing, so willing that the nightcaps were forgotten the moment they closed the apartment door. She came into his arms before the sound of the door closing faded in the room. Her softly welcoming lips moved with hungry abandon in time with his, sapping his strength as they sipped his taste. Their move from just inside the door to the bedroom was made smoothly, effortlessly, as were their movements as they undressed each other. It was after they embraced on the bed that they grew awkward. It simply did not work, and the harder they tried, each convinced the failure was their own, the less it worked. Brett finally ended the farce.

"I'm sorry," he muttered, appalled at his lack of a potency he had always reveled in. Rolling onto his back, he stared at the ceiling fighting a clawing fear that didn't bear thinking about.

"It's not your fault," Marsha whispered wretchedly. "I thought, after all this time . . ."

The misery in her tone caught his sympathy, the context of her words caught his attention. "All this time? I don't understand."

"I very foolishly divorced my husband last year when I found out he had been with another woman." Turning her head, she faced him unashamedly with tears trickling down her face. "I say foolishly because I've since learned it was the first and only time he had ever strayed." She smiled sadly. "He did have reason to seek solace elsewhere. At the time I was so wrapped up in getting my career off the ground, I neglected to remember we had a partnership."

Brett frowned, not in the least enlightened or re-assured. "But I still don't—"

"You are the first man I've been able to relax with since I left my husband over a year ago." Marsha sighed. "I thought that . . . maybe this time I could"—she actually blushed—"you know? I couldn't stop thinking of him, all the time you were . . . I love him." She blinked against a fresh onslaught of tears. "I really am sorry, Brett."

"Yes, so am I." Reaching out his hand, Brett brushed the tears from her cheeks. "Not only for you, but for my-self as well." His smile was as sad as hers. "It was not entirely your fault." Brett had never confided his most personal thoughts to anybody, not even Sondra. Draw-ing a deep breath, he decided that now, perhaps more than ever, he needed a confidant. "You weren't the only one unable to stop thinking of another. She has never belonged to me. Maybe she never will." A long sigh whis-pered through his lips. "But I love her. I shouldn't. I don't want to. But I do."

They spent the night together. Brett asked no ques-tions, Marsha didn't either. They did not make love. Giving and receiving comfort simply by holding each other close, they finally slept, secure in a friendship forged during the sharing of despair.

Two weeks later, after spending nearly all his evenings with Marsha, Brett left Vermont for New York. Marsha went with him.

SIX

The cab jarred to a splashing halt at the curb. Irritated, frustrated, and soaking wet into the bargain, Jo thrust a bill at the driver. Not bothering to ask for a receipt this time, she pushed open the door and stepped out of the cab, being careful of the miniriver rushing along the gutter. The cabbie pulled away from the curb as Jo was trying to hang onto her handbag and open her umbrella at the same time. The resultant spray of cold water against the back of her legs elicited a muttered, very unladylike curse from her anger-tautened lips. The umbrella slipped from her chilled fingers, exposing her bare head to the cold late October downpour. Straightening her arm with a jerk, Jo dashed for the entrance doors of the tall office building.

Inside the warmth of the building, she paused to catch her breath. *I must be totally out of my mind,* Jo thought waspishly. *No marginally intelligent person would run around like some kind of a nut looking at apartments in this weather! I wish Brett Renninger would go to . . . Atlanta!* Sighing with the realization that she really wished no such thing, Jo sloshed her way to the bank of elevators that would whisk her to the twenty-sixth floor and the comfort of her office, a place she'd seen very little of during the previous two weeks, most of which had been cold and rainy.

"Good grief, Jo, you look like you've just been pulled

from the river!" Reni greeted her with wide-eyed exclamation. "You also look half frozen!"

Slumping back against the door for a moment's respite,
Jo attempted a reassuring smile. "I think it's safe to con-
clude that Indian summer is truly over," she offered dryly.
"That rain feels like it could turn into sleet without halfway
trying." A shiver shook her slender body. "Why didn't I
simply go home and call it a day?" she wondered aloud.

"Because you're dedicated?" Reni asked teasingly.

"Or not too bright," Jo retorted, pushing away from
the supporting panel. "Well, since I'm here, I may as well
stay. I might even surprise everyone and actually get
some work accomplished." Stiff fingers fumbling with
the large buttons on her raincoat, Jo planted wet foot-
prints on the beige carpeting as she walked to her own
office. "But"—she paused to level an arched glance at
Reni—"all has not been in vain."

"You've found a place for her!" Reni piped hopefully.

"Yes, I've found a place for 'her.'" Jo smiled in satisfaction. "I've paid the first month's rent, the last month's
rent, and a security deposit." Her deepening smile softened the forbidding line of her lips. "Someone, either
'her' or our exalted leader, owes me a lot of money."
God! I hope it's her and not him! Ever since Brett had
literally ordered Jo to find an apartment for Marsha
Wenger, she had been torturing herself with the possibility of a relationship between him and the woman he'd
so quickly hired for the vacant manager's position. The
very idea of Brett sleeping with the unknown woman
during the last two weeks didn't bear thinking about. Yet
Jo had thought of little else but that! She had read the
data on the woman that Brett had faxed to personnel;
the woman was indeed qualified! Jo prayed that Marsha
Wenger's qualifications extended only to the position of
area manager and not to the much higher position of
Brett's current bed partner.

"Are you all right?"

Reni's worry-ridden voice brought Jo out of her disheartening speculation. Shivering again, Jo shook her head. "No, as a matter of fact, I'm not," she answered candidly. "I'm cold, and wet, and, as I missed lunch, starving." Shrugging out of the limp raincoat, Jo opened the door to her office. "Call the executive dining room and tell that ego-inflated chef I'd like an omelet and a gallon of hot tea."

Reni's giggle drew a grin from Jo. At one time or another, every person in the building had felt the lash of the sarcastic tongue of Hans Vogel, self-proclaimed chef extraordinary. Everyone, that is, except Wolf and Brett, the brothers Renninger. They'd have either fired him or decked him—possibly both!

Jo walked into her office, then walked out again moments later, a gray suit and a pale-gray blouse that had just been delivered at the office from the dry cleaners draped over one arm. As she sailed by Reni she smiled devilishly. "Don't tell anybody but, while I'm waiting for my lunch, I'm going to make use of the mahout's private bathroom. Maybe a hot shower will chase the shivers."

Jo returned to her office warm of body and dry of clothes, to find her tea and food covered and waiting for her. Ah! She sighed silently, sipping the hot brew. Being the assistant to the big man *did* have its compensations at times. But not always, she quickly reminded herself. There were other attendant duties that were downright onerous! Like running around in inclement weather finding the impossible find! This gal had better be good, she thought grimly, then cringed in contemplation of exactly what Marsha Wenger might be exceptionally good at.

Glancing unnecessarily at her desk calendar, Jo chewed a bite of the egg mixture thoughtfully. It was sixteen days since Brett had whirled into her office and then out again, leaving her shattered from one touchless kiss! During those two weeks she had swung from longing for the sight of him, to hoping she never saw him again.

After the lunch tray had been removed Jo got to work—or, at least, she tried to work in between glances at her digital desk clock. Where was Brett, anyway? He'd said two weeks, it had been sixteen days. When was he coming back? The questions skipped in and out of Jo's mind at regular intervals as the clock pulsed its way toward five, the last one always being: *Why should I care?* After the way he'd treated her before he left, then spoken to her on the phone, she really should not care if she never laid eyes on him again! But she did care, so deeply it scared her senseless. How very Cinderellaish; falling in love with the boss! Jo scowled at the contract she was holding in one hand. And Brett was certainly no Prince Charming! Focusing on the legal jargon, she reread the words that had little more meaning this time than they had the previous three times she'd read them.

"How impressively industrious she is!" The loved, hated, dreaded, longed-for drawl crept to her from the office doorway. "Perhaps I should reward her with a raise." He paused, deliberately Jo felt sure. "Or could I devise a more ingenious form of compensation?"

Was this man trying to drive her mad? At the sound of Brett's husky drawl, Jo's entire system had hummed with joy. Quickly glancing up, the hum had switched to a screech of fury. Brett was not even looking in her direction, but was instead gazing down at a small blonde who could be no other than the new manager, Marsha Wenger. Jo had to fight an urge to fling the contract at his damnably handsome face. Controlling herself with difficulty, Jo smiled prettily through her gritted teeth.

"Welcome back," she said overly politely. Rising gracefully, Jo nodded her head with queenly condescension at the petite blonde. "And this must be Marsha?" She arched one dark brow elegantly at Brett, receiving a frown that might have been fear-inspiring if she'd been in a frame of mind to be intimidated. As Jo wasn't in such a frame of mind, she countered his frown with a brightly inquiring expression.

"Yes." The way Brett bit off the word was a clear warning to Jo that she was skating on very thin ice. "Marsha Wenger, my brother's . . . ah . . . assistant, JoAnne Lawrence." Brett's smile drew a chilling line down Jo's spine. "Have you found an apartment for Marsha, Jo?"

Jo felt the double insult as sharply as if he'd slapped her face! Not only had he hesitated derogatorily over the title of assistant, but he'd refused her the courtesy of introducing Marsha to her in turn!

"As a matter of fact, I have," she answered in an extremely soft voice. "I think Marsha will find it eminently *suitable.*" Jo figuratively flung the last word at him.

"I knew you could do it." Brett's smile was positively feral. "I told Marsha you have a . . . thing . . . for apartments."

Jo was thoroughly confused, and not only by Brett's odd tone and equally odd phrasing. Marsha's expression of bemused compassion as she glanced from Jo to Brett and then back to Jo again had Jo wondering what the devil the woman could possibly be thinking. Had she missed something along Brett's hurtful conversation route? Or, Jo cringed inwardly, had she been the target of Brett's barbed tongue prior to their arrival at the office? The very thought coated Jo's response with acid.

"Well, my 'thing' worked." Picking up a long white envelope from the desk, Jo held it out to Brett, forcing him to cross the room to her. "You will find all the information in there." Carefully avoiding his touch, she placed it in his hand. "As you will see, there's a detailed account of money owed to me."

"Just give me a total and I'll write out a check for you,"

Brett snapped, thereby practically admitting his intention of "keeping" Marsha.

The pain that stabbed through Jo was unbelievable in its intensity. Though Marsha opened her crimson-tinted lips, Jo beat her into speech.

"There is no hurry. I'm in no danger of either starvation or eviction." Fleetingly, Jo wondered at the strange look of fury her assurance sent flashing over Brett's face, but she was too upset to probe for reasons. "Now, if there's nothing else pressing"—she glanced at the clock's digits as they moved to five fourteen—"I've got a blasting headache, and I'd like to go home." It was not a lie or an excuse. Within the last few minutes Jo's temples had begun to beat like a demented drummer! Along with the pain in her head was the sickening feeling that the omelet she had consumed earlier was not going to stay down!

Her discomfort must have been visible, for Brett's cold expression changed to instant concern. "Of course!" he agreed to her leaving at once. Then, confusing her even more, his tone softened into what sounded very like tenderness—although Jo felt sure she was mistaken, probably due to her headache. "Look," he urged, "sit down for a moment while I call for a car." When she would have protested, he added adamantly, "I won't have you running for a bus in this weather."

Jo had to choke back a peel of hysterical laughter. After running for days in rotten weather, Sir Fairhaired Knight belatedly blunders to the rescue! Her stomach lurched and Jo sat down with a plop. *Oh, fantastic!* she thought sickly. *He finally comes home, and I feel decidedly ill!* At that moment the room began rocking.

"Brett!" Jo heard Marsha's warning cry through a fog of dizziness. "I think Jo is really ill!"

* * *

When Jo woke, she was in her own nightgown, in her own bed, with only a cloudy recollection of how she had gotten into either one of them. Lying still, she probed her memory for enlightenment. As the clouds dissipated, bits and pieces of the puzzle began falling into place. With sudden clarity, Jo remembered the expression of alarm on Brett's face when he'd turned from the phone at Marsha's cry of concern. Never could she recall seeing anyone move quite so quickly as he did when he whipped around the desk to where she was slumped in her chair.

"God! She looks terrible!" he'd exclaimed in an oddly hoarse tone. Then, even more oddly, he'd gently pressed his palm to her forehead. "God, Jo, you're burning up!" He'd turned aside then to Marsha, saying harshly, "I've got to get her home."

Jo squirmed uncomfortably at the memory of what had happened next. Brett, his face set in lines of determination, gently slid one arm beneath her legs and the other arm around her back, to lift her.

Clutching her tightly to his chest, he had issued clipped orders to Jo's assistant. "I'm taking her home." He strode to the door, tossing over his shoulder, "Get a doctor . . . the best." He rattled off Jo's home address as he crossed the outer office.

Now Jo had total recall of the dizzying ride down on the elevator and of Brett's arms tightening reassuringly as he strode across the lobby. She could feel again the sting of sleet mingled with cold rain on her flushed cheeks, could clearly hear Brett's muttered curse as he dashed for the protection of the limo. Now Jo's face burned with embarrassment instead of fever as her awakened memory replayed the scene enacted in this very room after their rather over-the-speed-limit run from the office building to her apartment. Although she had been barely conscious by the time Brett carried her into the bedroom, Jo had struggled with him when he'd started to undress her. Concentrating fiercely, she attempted to reconstruct his exact wording of admonition.

"Damn it, Jo. Stop fighting me! You're ill, and you must rest, and you can't very well do it fully clothed." At this point her recall was not quite as total for he'd gritted his teeth, or something. At any rate, only snatches of what he'd muttered remained clear. "Obstinate woman . . . you'd think I was Jack the Ripper or . . . will you be still . . . Jo, please, I'm not so desperate for you I'd—"

Whoa! Hold it! Jo brought her thoughts to a jarring stop. Had Brett said "I'm not so desperate for you" or "I'm not so desperate for a woman"? Jo wanted to believe it was the former, though she was certain it was the latter. In any case, he had finally managed to remove all her clothes and slip a nightgown over her head, all the while displaying a patience Jo would not have believed him capable of.

Then came the doctor, very distinguished looking and extremely irritated at having been called out in such weather. Brett toppled him off his high horse with one scathingly, unrepeatable pronouncement. Now, hours removed from the incident, Jo could smile at it all, but at the time she'd been appalled at his arrogant crudeness.

Thoroughly cowed, the good doctor had examined Jo expertly, then, in an affronted tone, told Brett that she had contracted a virus.

Gazing down at her, he'd frowned. "Her pulse is a little rapid. Has she been under strain?"

To give the devil his due, Jo now admitted to herself that Brett had had the conscience to flush, if lightly.

"Perhaps," he'd answered tersely. "I'd have no way of knowing for certain, as I've just returned from a two-week business trip."

Both men jerked to attention when Jo choked. *A business trip indeed! Funny business! Monkey business! Physical business!* Jo's spasm of choking subsided as she ran out of

old accusations. Her reaction to Brett's pious excuse
gained her a calming hypodermic needle in the poste-
rior. Jo had fallen asleep within minutes of receiving the
injection.

How long had she slept? Twisting her head around to
the small alarm clock on her nightstand, Jo discovered
two things: the first that she had slept approximately
four hours as it was now nearing eleven P.M., the second
that her headache and queasiness were gone. She felt extremely tired but no longer sick. Sighing in relief, she
snuggled down again then groaned when she rubbed a
tender spot on her derriere. Within seconds the door to
her room was quietly pushed open and Brett's tall frame
was outlined in the doorway by a light in the hall behind
him. When he saw she was awake, and alert, he smiled.

"You groaned, madame?" His smile widening, he sauntered into the room. "You must be feeling somewhat
better," he opined, studying her closely. "You've lost all
that gorgeous green color." Bending down, he touched
her forehead lightly. "The fever's gone too. What you
need now is rest." His fingers lingered, then slowly
trailed down her temple and over her cheek.

Her breathing suddenly shallow, Jo had to grit her
teeth against the urge to turn her head to seek his palm
with her lips. She felt lightheaded again, only this time
she knew her loss of equilibrium was not caused by a
virus. Still his fingers lingered, stroking her cheek, her
jawline. When one long forefinger sought the delicate
line of her lip, Jo knew she had to say something to
break the tension twisting through her. Raking her
mind, she blurted the first thought that entered.

"How . . . how did you know I was awake?" she babbled
breathlessly, then nearly fell apart altogether with the
gentle smile that curved his lips. But her purpose was
achieved, for he straightened slightly and lifted his hand
to indicate a small, dimly lit box on the dresser.

"The intercom," Brett replied blandly. "I have the volume turned up as high as it will go. I could hear the slightest rustle every time you moved."

"But where did it come from?" Jo frowned. "I've never seen it before."

"I had Doug pick it up when I sent him to my apartment for some clothes." Straightening fully, he reached out to switch on the small lamp on the night table. Doug Jensen was Brett's driver, the same one who had helped her into the car that afternoon.

"I'm sorry," she whispered contritely.

"Forget it." His hand sliced the air dismissively. "The only thing I want you to concentrate on is getting well." Now his hand moved to his head, fingers raking through the blond strands distractedly. "Though you obviously did have at least a touch of a virus, the doctor seemed inclined to think your problem was more exhaustion than anything else." Gray eyes captured hers. "What have you been up to these last two weeks?"

What had *she* been up to? What had she been up to! He dared ask that? When *he* was the one who had assigned her the duty of finding *suitable* living quarters for Marsha Wenger? Jo was still feeling very tired, and very weak. Now she was beginning to feel very, very edgy.

"What have I been up to?" she grated. "I've been sitting in my office with my feet propped up on my desk, manicuring my nails, talking on the phone to all my friends, and generally goofing off. Isn't that what one is supposed to do when the boss is away?" Jo paused to draw breath, then demanded heatedly, "What the hell do you think I've been up to? I've been up to the end of my patience with running around in all kinds of weather, trying to scare up a decent apartment for your latest . . . manager."

"Jo!" Brett cautioned softly, "calm down. The doctor said you are not to—"

"Calm down! Ha!" Really agitated now, Jo jerked to a

sitting position, unmindful of the skimpiness of her nightgown. "I'll calm down when you and your stupid questions get out of here! I'm tired and, now that I think about it, I haven't felt quite right for days. Still, with your demands in mind, I've chased all over this damned city examining some very unsuitable dwellings." She grimaced. "I'm so weary of the very word *apartments* I could scream. And I do wish you'd get out of mine." The angry spate had consumed all of her breath and most of her energy. Feeling shaky, Jo eased back against the pillow with a soft sigh, her heavy eyelids drooping.

It was quiet for long minutes, much too quiet. Jo knew that Brett had not moved from beside the bed. She couldn't hear him breathing, but she knew he was there. Lifting her eyelids to mere slits, she stared at him balefully.

"Are you still here?"

"Do you always ask the obvious?" he retorted. "I'm here and I'm going to stay here . . . through the night."

Brett's flat statement sent a spurt of renewed energy zinging through Jo and, still unaware of her nearly naked state, she shot upright. "You are not!" she denied wildly. "I don't want you here. I'll be perfectly fine. All I need is a good night's rest and I'll—"

"You will stay in that bed for at least three days," Brett's adamant voice cut through her protest sharply. "Maybe longer if you don't behave."

"You . . . you can't . . ." she began sputteringly, only to be cut off again.

"I not only can, I will," Brett promised. "So be a good girl and stop arguing." A tiny smile quirking the corner of his lips, he ran an encompassing glance over her from hair to waist. "You know what?" he mused rhetorically. "Even in a state of . . . ah . . . dishevelment, you look very delectable." The quirk spread to a devilish grin. "If you're feeling so feisty, how about a quick wrestling match?"

Jo knew Brett expected her to clutch the covers to her chin with a maidenly blush. She was furious, yet she could not control the bubble of laughter that vibrated her vocal chords. "How many falls?" she gasped. "Two or three?" Placing her balled hands on her waist, she deliberately expanded her chest by drawing in a deep breath. "The mood I'm in at this minute, I'll probably pin you in seconds!"

Brett's grin disappeared and his eyes narrowed. "The mood I'm suddenly in, I'd let you pin me," he said seriously. "In fact, I'd enjoy it immensely." He took one step closer to the bed, then halted, as if catching himself. "I think you had better go back to sleep now," he warned softly. "You need R and R, not A S A." Turning abruptly, he started for the door.

A S A? Blinking, Jo racked her mind, finally giving up as he reached for the door knob. "What *is* A S A?"

"Abundant sexual activity, of course." The devilish grin flashed again as he stepped through the doorway and quietly closed the door.

Jo slowly slid into a prone position. Would he always have the last word in a confrontation with her? She knew he'd merely been amusing himself with her, yet . . . yet, Jo sighed. Stop dreaming, she chided herself. So he kissed you once, so what? So he's been very kind through this sickness thing, so what? You mean nothing to him. You are an employee. And, of course, now there's Marsha the manager! *Oh, damn!*

When she woke the second time, the angle of the sunrays in her room told her it was mid-morning. While stretching herself into full wakefulness, Jo discovered two things. First, she realized that she was very hungry. Second, she found that she ached all over. What you need, my girl, is a long, hot shower, she told herself firmly. Her firmness wavered a bit when she slid out of bed and stood up. Jo wavered too. Brett entered the room as she was inching her way to the bathroom.

"What in hell do you think you're doing!" he roared. "Get back in bed!"

Afraid she'd fall on her face if she so much as paused, Jo continued groping along the wall to the bathroom. "I feel grubby," she panted. "I'm going to have a shower."

"Forget it."

As shaky as she was feeling, Jo probably would have docilely, happily gone back to bed had he said anything else. "Forget it" definitely did not make it as a convincer, except to convince her to keep going—if it killed her! Jo kept moving with dogged determination. "I said I'm going to take a shower, and I meant it. Go away."

"Be sensible, Jo. You can't even stand up straight. Go back to bed." Jo hadn't heard him move away from the doorway, but now he was right behind her. His hands on her shoulders were warm, and reassuring, and, thankfully, supporting. "Let me help you."

"Do what? Take a shower or get back into bed?" Jo could have bitten her tongue for the smart, too-fast retort. She felt his fingers flex spasmodically into her shoulders, then she felt his warm breath feather her cheek.

"Both," he whispered. "If you like. In fact, I'll even join you—in both—if you like."

The idea was appealing, too appealing. Jo shrugged to dislodge his hands and found herself sitting on the floor. She didn't know whether to laugh hysterically or cry hysterically. She did neither, she simply sat there, listening to Brett swear as he bent to help her up.

"You have got to be the most obstinate woman I have ever met!" Though his voice was harsh, his hands were extremely gentle. "How the devil you ever got around Wolf—" He broke off to stare at the tears welling up in her eyes. "What's the matter?" he demanded, his face a study in concern. "Did you hurt yourself?"

"No." Jo shook her head, then sniffed. "Only my pride. What a dumb thing to do."

"Surprise, surprise!" Brett grinned. "We finally agree on something."

"But I really must have a shower," Jo murmured in a very conciliatory tone. "I feel so yucky. Please, Brett." The art of practicing cajolery was new to Jo. Not knowing quite how to go about it, she unconsciously did the right thing. Lowering her incredibly long lashes slowly, she repeated, "Please."

Brett was not at all a novice to the art, nor was he immune. A slow smile gathering along his lips, he knelt beside her. "Yucky, humm?" he murmured close to her ear. "Sounds uncomfortable." Raising his hand, he combed his fingers through her long, tangled mass of dark hair. "Okay, Delila." His quiet voice held a hint of teasing laughter. "You've chained me to the pillar. You may have, not a shower, but a bath. On one condition."

Victory within her grasp, Jo decided to push her luck. "Why not a shower? It's so much faster," she coaxed. "And on what condition?" she added quickly, hoping to put him off stride. Jo suspected her ploy wouldn't work. She was right; it didn't. Brett merely laughed aloud at her.

"First things first, my greenhorn temptress." A thread of tenderness wove through his chiding tone. "Consider your present position." Brett's gaze swept her crumpled form. "You could not remain erect with a wall to lean on. How were you planning to manage a curtained shower stall?" One silky blond brow arched exaggeratedly. "Have I made my point?"

"Point taken," Jo mumbled ungraciously. "But—"

"You simply do not quit." Brett shook his head in mock despair. "On to point two. My condition is, while

pleasant, at least for me"—here his tone hardened—
"absolutely necessary. I will supervise your bath."

The silence that descended on Jo, and the room, was
eardrum-cracking. To maintain that one could hear a pin
drop would be to understate the case; one could possibly
have heard a feather flutter to the floor. Unfortunately,
for Brett, the silence was short-lived and shattered by a
female screech.

"You will what!"

"There is certainly no lack of strength in the lungs
here," Brett observed to the room in general. "You
heard me, sweetie. No supervision, no bath . . . and no
arguments. Got that?"

Jo did not require an interpreter of facial expressions
to tell her Brett was not talking to hear the melodious
sound of his own voice. He was dead serious and equally
determined. As wishing he'd drop dead, period, was no
solution to her immediate problem, Jo declined from
voicing the observation. She was quiet a long time—a
very long time—wrestling with the pros and cons of her
boxed-in situation. Brett simply remained still, metaphorically playing out enough rope. She either bathed with an
audience of one, or she crawled back into bed without
even as much as cleaning her teeth. Yuck! Of course,
being a product of an age with a fetish for cleanliness, Jo
hanged herself.

"Oh, all right!" But she couldn't quite let it go at that.
"If you're so dammed desperate to play voyeur while a
woman bathes, let's get it over with."

Brett did not become angry at her nasty barb. He
cracked up with laughter. Flinging himself onto the carpet, he roared at the ceiling. "Oh, goody," he gasped
between barks of laughter. "I've been waiting thirty years
to leer at a woman in her bath. Now, that erratic, erotic
pleasure is to be mine." As Jo glared at him, Brett
whooped with delight. "And not only is this woman

beautifully pale of skin from a recent illness"—he paused to compose himself then went on—"she is also a trifle sick in the head."

Her back ramrod straight, Jo stared down at Brett in solemn consideration. Set into lines of superior austerity, Brett's face was breathtaking in its classical perfection. His visage softened by warmth and genuine amusement, he stole Jo's heart along with her breath. Suddenly, for reasons Jo didn't want to examine too closely, she was eager to undress for this perfect example of the magnificent male in his prime. Still, wary of his motives concerning much more than a silly bath, Jo was determined not to reveal her eagerness.

"You do have a rather strange sense of humor, Mr. Renninger." Jo offered her opinion with a solemnity that mirrored her expression. "Still, I would guess the undraped female form holds no mystery for you . . . humm?"

Brett literally fell apart again. The seizure of mirth lasted for several minutes, during which Jo fought valiantly against the onslaught of reciprocal laughter. When, at last, Brett brought himself under control, he sat up facing her and grasped her face in his hands.

"You know what?" he asked seriously. "*You* have a rather strange talent for tapping a deep emotional response from me, be it anger, or amusement, or . . . whatever." Jo would have liked to question the whatever part, but he added, frowning in thought, "I don't think I've laughed that spontaneously in at least twenty years." The corners of his mouth twitched with that funny quirk Jo was beginning to realize was all his own. "You may be a little weird"—he allowed the quirk to grow into a smile—"but you're a kinda nice weird." With that, he lowered his smiling lips to hers.

Turning her head, Jo robbed him of his target. "Brett, no!" She fought the insistent tug of his hands. "I haven't brushed my teeth!"

Brett's hands sprang away from her face as another paroxysm of laughter shuddered through him. "Okay, I give up!" Springing to his feet, he stared down at her, his chest actually rumbling with the effects of his amusement. "I'll run your bath for you. I'll even prop you up while you do your thing with a toothbrush. Then I'll wait right here, outside the door, while you perform your ablution ritual." He started for the bathroom, then paused to slice a sharp-eyed glance at her. "You know, I think you may damn well be worth every penny Wolf is paying you."

There was an underlying note in his voice that caused a chill in Jo's bones. Up until Brett's last statement, sexual tension had been drawing her nerves to a vibrating tautness. And riding the back of that tension was the faint spark of hope that Brett had revised his original opinion of her. With his sudden withdrawal the tension snapped and the tiny spark of hope was doused. What was it about her that turned him off? Jo asked herself as she sat, miserable and uncaring of her disheveled appearance. Listening to the rush of water into the bathtub, she stared into nothingness and scoured her mind for answers.

The physical attraction was not one-sided, Jo knew that. Brett felt the tug of sexual awareness every bit as strongly as she did. That single kiss they'd shared had revealed the depths of the physical desire Brett felt for her. Would he, she wondered tormentedly, have given in to his need a moment ago if she had not stopped him? As usual, when Jo began searching for answers to questions about the element of constraint between Brett and her, all she found were more questions. Circles, circles, circles. Whenever she contemplated Brett Renninger, her mind took on the characteristics of a carrousel.

"Have you passed out with your eyes open?" Brett's drawling query fragmented Jo's bemusement.

Oh, why couldn't she hate him? Or, at the very least, dislike him as he so obviously disliked her? Shaking her head more at herself than in a silent reply to him, Jo was unaware of the appealing picture she made with her mass of hair a riot around her head and shoulders and her slim, long-limbed body covered with the sheerest of nightgowns. All she was aware of was the suddenness of Brett's impatience with her.

"Well?" he snapped. "Are you going to sit there for the rest of the morning? Your water's getting cool."

As if she were a child, or a total incompetent, Brett assisted Jo into the bathroom. His hands impersonal of touch, but firm of grip, clasped her about the waist while she brushed her teeth and cleansed her face. Then he left her, his dubious expression a silent question of her ability to get into, then out of the tub without doing injury to herself. Quelling the urge to scream in frustration, Jo stepped into the warm water, a soft "oh" of delight whispering through her lips.

Brett had not only filled the tub to less than an inch from the rim, he had sprinkled her scented bath crystals into the water. Sighing with pleasure, Jo slid down into the fragrant silkiness. The soothing warmth lapping her chin, she closed her eyes in contentment and promptly dozed off.

"What am I going to do with you?" Jo's eyes flew wide at the sound of exasperation in Brett's voice. He was standing beside the tub, hands on his hips, actually scowling at her. "The idea was to become clean, not dead." Snatching a fluffy bath sheet from a towel bar, he held it out in invitation. "Let's go, water baby, bath time's over."

"You promised to wait outside!" Jo exclaimed accusingly.

"I waited outside," he grated. "Twenty minutes, to be exact. That water has got to be cold by now." He shook the towel lightly, impatiently. "Out." It was not a request but a definite order.

It was at that moment that Jo realized she was covered by nothing more than clear liquid. The fact that Brett had seen everything there was to see of her the afternoon before had little impact on her now. Feeling herself flush, and hating it, Jo launched a verbal attack.

"*You* get out!" she snapped. "I am perfectly capable of getting out of the tub all by myself." With deliberate insolence she swept his lean length with hazel eyes sparkling with anger. "If you don't move quickly," she threatened softly, "I swear I'll splash water all over your suit." Brett's response to her threat not only startled Jo, it shocked her.

"Screw the suit! I have dozens of suits. I have only one of you." His eyes narrowed in warning. "If you do not stand up and step out of that damned tub in five seconds," he enunciated clearly through gritted teeth, "I swear *I* will haul you out of there bodily. And I won't concern myself about what I touch, or how roughly I touch it."

Her head lifted in defiance, her eyes challenging him, daring him, Jo rose from the water slowly and stepped delicately onto the bath mat. Then, her head back, her bearing regal, she stood before him in nature's covering of blushing ivory-toned skin.

Except for his eyes, Brett didn't move. For several seconds he didn't even breathe. Starting with Jo's now-sodden, tangled hair, his glinting gray gaze inched the length of her body to the tips of her water-wrinkled toes. When his eyes slowly returned to hers, he stared into their depths as if he were trying to search out the deepest secrets of her soul. The intensity of his gaze stopped the breath in Jo's throat and liquefied all the strength in her body.

"God! You are beautiful!" Brett's hushed, reverent tone drained all defiance, all resistance from her. "Your hair is beautiful." Slowly, holding the towel aloft, he moved to her. "Your skin is beautiful." Flipping the huge terry sheet behind her, he wrapped her in its voluminous folds. "Your eyes are beautiful." Sliding his arms around her, he drew her to him. "And your mouth." His arms tightened to crush her to him. His voice lowered to a murmured groan. "God, your mouth!"

The mouth that Brett groaned over trembled in reaction to a sudden, searing need racing wildly through Jo's body. She was afraid, afraid of her own ineptitude, her own inadequacy, but she was also powerless against the force that urged her to arch her neck and raise her lips to him in silent offering. Brett pounced on her offering with the vengeance of an angry deity. With a guttural growl her lips were taken inside his mouth to be devoured, nibbled on, and then gently laved by his searching tongue.

Giving in completely to the rioting sensations storming her body, Jo worked her arms free of the confining towel and coiled them around his neck, driving her fingers into the silken strands of his hair. The heat rising inside her found a measure of release as she obeyed his silent command to part her lips, wider and yet wider. All rational thought suspended, Jo's mouth consumed while being consumed. When Brett's stiffened tongue pierced into the moist warmth, Jo drew a moan from him by curling her own tongue around his. This time Brett placed no restraint upon his hands. His impatient mutter filled her mouth, and then the towel was torn from her body and tossed aside.

His hands moving restlessly over her back, Brett slid his lips from hers. Biting little kisses sensitized her skin from the corner of her mouth to the delicately curved edge of her ear. With a maddeningly slow, erotic rhythm the tip of his tongue dipped in and out of her ear. When his evocative play forced a groan from Jo's dry throat, Brett's hands moved down to cup her rounded bottom to pull her up and into the burgeoning hardness of his body.

"Will you part your thighs for me as quickly as you parted your lips, water baby?" he coaxed softly into her ear. Lost to everything but the need to have him fill every particle of her being, Jo complied to his coaxing with a whimper of surrender. The whimper turned to a gasp as Brett thrust his body against hers. Even fully clothed, Brett's arousal imprinted itself on her forcefully. Releasing his grasp on her, he brought his hands up to cradle her face. His eyes glinting like new steel in bright sunlight, he stared down at her.

"I must have you," he said clearly, fiercely. "Against all reason . . . and my better judgment, I *will* have you. In all probability we will both regret it afterward but, while the fire rages, I will feed my appetite for you on it."

A cold finger of unease poked warningly through the fog of passion clouding Jo's mind. There was something wrong here, something in the harsh tone of Brett's voice, and the rigid set of his features, something that looked frighteningly like disgust, both for her and himself. Not understanding this new element of fear he'd injected into their intimacy, Jo attempted a protest.

"Brett, no . . ."

"No?" he snarled, obviously misinterpreting her protest as a refusal. Grasping her by the shoulders, Brett spun her around, roughly pulling her back to his chest, imprisoning her easily by clamping his hands over her breasts. "Look at yourself," he ordered tersely. In a room of mirrors, there was no possible way to avoid looking at herself. Jo recognized the incongruity of the picture reflected back at her, she stark naked, Brett fully clothed. But that incongruity was not the point Brett was trying to make, as he very quickly proved.

"How dare you tell *me* no?" he demanded. "Just look at yourself. Your lips are wet and parted in anticipation, your eyes are dark with desire, and your entire body is quivering with sexual hunger." Watching her examine

herself, Brett spread his fingers with cool deliberation.
Immediately her hardened nipples thrust through the
opening. Moving his hands slowly, he stroked the tips of
Jo's breasts with his index fingers. When Jo could not
deny the aching moan that whispered through her lips,
Brett lowered his head to place his lips to her ear. "Now
tell me no." As if to reinforce his point, he rotated his
hips enticingly against her derriere. "If you still dare."

Jo's rational thinking process dissolved as Brett continued to stroke and manipulate her tingling nipples.
Following the dictates of a passion flaring out of control,
she arched her spine to press her aching breasts into his
hands and twisted her head around, seeking his mouth
with her avid lips. Grunting in satisfaction, Brett released
his hold on her breasts to sweep her up into his arms. His
mouth clinging to hers, he carried her into the bedroom.
As he came to a stop beside her bed, Brett lifted his head,
then froze when his glance brushed the night table. Cursing softly, vehemently, he set her reluctantly on her feet.
Thoroughly confused, Jo stared at him in disbelief.

"Brett, what . . ."

"Gertrude will be here in approximately fifteen minutes," he cut her off harshly, still staring at the table and
the small alarm on it.

"Gertrude?" Jo repeated blankly, then, because she
only knew one Gertrude: "Gertrude Jorgeson? Wolf's
housekeeper?"

"Yes. *Wolf's* housekeeper."

The sudden, inexplicable anger in his tone and stiffened body as he turned away from her created an empty,
bereft feeling inside Jo. What had she done to anger
him? Surely her response had been evidence enough of
how badly she wanted him? Fighting a creeping sense of
failure, Jo bit down hard on her lower lip as she watched
him stride to the double dresser against one wall, pull
open a drawer, then, without bothering about being se-

lective, plunge a hand in. Grasping the first garment he touched, Brett withdrew it and flung it at her with a tersely snapped "Cover yourself."

Jo could not have been more shocked had Brett slapped her, hard, across the face. Blinking furiously against the sudden sting of tears, she pulled the filmy mid-thigh-length nightie over her head. By the time she'd tugged the short gown into place, Jo's hurt had given way to anger.

"What is Gertrude Jorgeson coming here for?" The cold, grating sound of her voice surprised Jo, and spun Brett around to face her.

"She's going to look after you for a few days." Brett's voice was as cold and grating as hers had been. What, Jo cried inside, had happened to all the passion of moments ago?

"I don't need anyone to look after me!" she exclaimed hotly. "I'm perfectly all right."

Cool eyes swept her from head to toe. "You are *not* all right. People who are all right do not faint. Nor do they fall to the floor the way you did a little while ago." Now Brett's eyes hardened in determination. "You will not return to the office until Monday."

"But this is only Tuesday, Brett!"

"Not before Monday," he repeated firmly. "And that is a direct order."

"But—"

"I said that's an order," he roared. "Now, get into that damn bed and stay there. Gertrude will be here shortly." Shooting his wrist from his cuff, he glanced at his watch. "It's just as well I remembered Gertrude's imminent arrival before undressing," he drawled—insultingly, Jo thought. "It's almost noon and I have an appointment at one." Shrugging his shoulders as if their abortive love-making was of little importance, Brett turned and walked from the room.

Still standing beside the bed, her eyes wide from the impact of his parting observation, Jo crossed her arms around her middle and hugged herself tightly in an effort to contain the pam clawing at her insides.

SEVEN

Monday morning Brett sat in his office, his gaze riveted to the digital clock on his desk. When the numbers read nine oh five, he thought, *I'll give it five more minutes, then I'll call and order her to come to me.* The small rectangle that contained the digits blurred as the phrase "come to me" echoed in his mind. Brett had not seen Jo since he'd walked out of her bedroom the previous Tuesday noontime. Now what he wanted, what he really wanted more than anything else in the world, was for Jo to come to him without the order to do so ever being issued. Brett knew, deep down in his bones, that what he wanted and what he'd get were two entirely different things. After the way he'd left her, he knew there was no way Jo would come anywhere near him without being summarily ordered.

Slicing a glance at the clock, Brett reached for his telephone. This morning Jo did not answer as usual.

"Yes?" Her voice came crisply to him over the wire.

"You have to be told?" Brett drawled slowly.

"You want me in your office?"

In my office. In my apartment. In my bed. Anywhere and everywhere, Brett tormented himself with the tantalizing thought an instant before replying to her leading question.

"If you can find the time."

"Now?"

"If you will." Brett sighed loudly, exaggeratedly, then gently replaced the receiver.

The moment Jo walked into his office Brett felt the presence of the invisible wall she'd erected between them. The presence was as cold and forbidding as her expression. If he was any judge of women, and Brett had cultivated a discernment since Sondra, he was in for a very chilly period. His nerves tightening with tension, Brett waved her to a chair, then wondered what in hell he'd say to her. Perhaps, he mused, clearing the air would melt the ice.

"Jo, about last week . . ."

"I don't want to talk about it!" she interrupted sharply. "Do you have work for me to do?"

"We're going to talk about it whether you want to or—"

"No!" Jumping out of the chair, she stood trembling and poised for flight. "If you have nothing for me to do—"

"SIT DOWN!" Brett barked the command. "I'll tell you when you may leave this office."

Her eyes shooting sparks at him, her delicate nostrils flaring with rebellious agitation, Jo defied his authority. "You can't make me . . ."

"Who the hell's going to stop me?" Partly amused, partly angry, Brett flung the question at her arrogantly. Jo did the one and only thing that could stop him cold. Calmly lifting the telephone receiver, she stared at him coolly as she punched the button for his secretary.

"Mrs. Jenkins, get me Wolf Renninger in Florida, please," she instructed the woman quietly.

"Damn you, Jo! Hang that phone up." Brett was so furious he had to push the order through his gritted teeth. You should have known better, you fool, he lashed himself scathingly. You really should have known better. Why did you assume, even for one wild moment, that she'd

let you order her around? She's got the ear of the big
prowler, his ear and every other vital part of him. You,
big mouth, are only his baby brother! Berating himself,
Brett watched as she spoke into the receiver.

"Cancel that Florida call Mrs. Jenkins. We've resolved
the problem." Cradling the receiver gently, Jo looked at
him impassively. " We have resolved the problem, haven't
we?"

Leaning back in his chair, Brett studied her through
narrowed lids. "You really would have called him, wouldn't
you?"

"Yes," Jo replied simply. "I really would have called him."

"Because I raised my voice to you, you'd have taken
the risk of disturbing him," Brett persisted coldly. "Regardless of his condition, or what a whining call from
you might do to him, you would have called him?"

Even though Jo's features tightened, she answered
coldly, "That's right, I would have." She paused to draw
a deep breath, then coldly reinforced her position.
"Let's have one thing clear here and now, *Mr.* Renninger.
I am your *brother's* assistant, not yours. At least, fortunately, not on a permanent basis. I am not a lackey. I
am not a go-for. I am not the resident whipping boy. And
I will not be spoken to like any of the above. If you are in
a foul mood, find someone else to snap at." A derisive
smile curled her lips. "You can always call Richard
Colby," she suggested sweetly. "And chew him out." Her
smile hardened.

Taut with anger, Brett curled his fingers around the
chair arms to keep himself from springing from the seat
and sprinting around the desk to her. He wanted to shake
the living hell out of her. But, more than anything else, he
wanted to kiss her insolent mouth. You are in big trouble,
boy, Brett advised himself, running a calculating glance
over her. This one's got you tied in knots that would make
a sailor blanch.

"Sit down, please," he said in a carefully controlled monotone.

"Why?" Jo didn't move.

Somehow Brett contained the curse that danced on the tip of his tongue. Forcing himself to relax, he sat up straight and folded his hands on his desk. "This is a business office, and . . ."

"Oh! You noticed, finally," Jo taunted coolly.

Of course, one could always *un*fold one's hands. Brett didn't. Instead, he drew a deep, cautioning breath. "You're right," he admitted, swallowing the taste of gall. "I stepped out of line . . ." He paused, then added firmly, "Here." He paused again, but her only reaction was a tightening of her lips. "It won't happen again." Once more he paused briefly. "Here."

"Why do I feel less than reassured?" Jo murmured tersely.

Brett could feel his facial muscles tightening with the insult. "I said I'll keep all our discussions on an impersonal basis here in the office. If I give you my word on it, will you sit down?"

Jo stared directly into Brett's eyes for several seconds, then slowly, stiffly sank to the very edge of the chair. Brett knew the elation he felt at her compliance was out of proportion to the situation, yet he savored the acknowledgment of her acceptance of his word. Staring into the hazel depths of her eyes, he nodded his head slightly. "Thank you." His husky tone caused a ripple in her mask of withdrawal, and that sent his elation up a notch. God! he mused, visually crawling into a hazel ensnarement. With very little effort, this gal could slip a ring through my nose and keep me grinning throughout the entire process! Time to pull your head together, Renninger, before you find yourself down for the count. Think of something, anything, but get your concentration back on the business of buildings.

"The Vermont project is underway." The suddenness of his stark statement shattered the tension Brett could feel sneaking along his nerve ends. It shattered a great deal of Jo's assumed composure as well. Two hazel traps blinked in momentary confusion, releasing their captive. "It would have been less awkward for me up there if you had seen fit to inform me of Wolf's decision to contract Sean Delheny for the job."

"But I didn't know he had!" Jo protested. "How many times do we have to go over this argument?" she added impatiently. "Brett, I will tell you once more that I had thought Wolf had scrapped the whole idea."

"Well, at least I'm Brett again." Brett was barely aware of murmuring the thought aloud. Jo hastened to assure him the status quo could revert at an instant's notice.

"For as long as you behave by maintaining a professional attitude."

The "behave" got to him. "I'm not a little boy, Jo," he purred with deliberate silkiness. "Be very careful of how you speak to me. You cannot remain in the building forever." He smiled gently, very gently. "Are you receiving my message?"

The expression that flashed across Jo's face activated a curl of excitement in Brett's lower region. She had obviously received his message loud and clear, and, although she now had her expression in rigid control, for a fleeting instant he had read blatant eagerness on her face. Oh, yes, my sweet, the time for A S A draws closer and closer for both of us, he promised silently.

"Brett, I did not know about Wolf contracting Sean Delheny." Jo's quiet but forceful disclaimer snapped the erotic thread Brett was weaving. Consigning his designing plans for their future of sensuality to the edge of his mind, he brought his concentration back to the cold world of business.

"Okay, but I felt like a fool. First of all, I didn't even know Casey was a woman! Then I find out Sean had his nose out of joint because he hadn't been included in our first meeting." Brett shook his head in memory. "As I said, I felt pretty foolish when Casey introduced me to Sean."

"I'm sorry. I could have saved you that embarrassment. I just never thought to tell you the architect was a woman. Of course, I knew that Casey and Sean were married, and that Sean was a building contractor, but . . ." She let her voice trail off as she shrugged lightly.

Brett's shrug reflected hers. "It's over and done with. Sean is now officially under contract. I suggested a few minor changes in design, which Casey is working on now, but, for all intents and purposes, the project is underway. Before I left Vermont I tossed the ball into your court. I instructed both the Delhenys to send their reports to you." Pushing his chair back abruptly, he stood up and strolled to the wide window behind his desk to stare up at the overcast sky. When Jo didn't respond for several seconds, Brett turned back to her. "Can you handle it?"

"Yes."

A tiny smile quirked the corners of Brett's lips as he silently applauded the simplicity of her affirmation. In effect, what Jo was telling him with her quiet assertion was "I'm good at my job, and I know it." In that respect Brett could empathize with her; he felt exactly the same way about himself. Brett went momentarily still with the realization of sharing yet another character trait with Jo. In his mind, he slowly ticked off the things they had in common. They were both good at their chosen work and knew it. They both had a somewhat offbeat sense of humor. They both enjoyed good food, especially of the breakfast variety. During the hours Brett had spent in Jo's apartment while she'd been sleeping, he had made a tour of the rooms. On completion of his inspection he'd decided her taste was excellent—very likely because it reflected his own. And, last but definitely not least, they shared a mutual physical hunger. The parallels were enlightening . . . and a little scary. Brett was positive he did not want to feel this affinity with *any* woman, let alone another man's woman!

"You don't believe me?" Jo's strained tone fragmented Brett's conjecturing.

"What?" Brett shook his head to clear his mind. "Oh, yes, of course I believe you. I . . . ah . . . was thinking of something else." Something I wish I'd never considered, he added mutely. "Understand, if there are any snags, or major problems, we'll work them out together but, well, I'd like the freedom to get on with an idea of my own."

Jo's immediate interest was evidenced by her alert expression and the eagerness of her blurted, "What idea?"

"I'm considering a complex, a very large complex, in the Pocono Mountains in Pennsylvania." His gaze steady on her taut form, Brett waited to see if she'd react at all. He didn't have long to wait. Jo was still for a moment, then, an appreciative smile baring her white teeth, she nodded her head once.

"Can you get the property?" She shot the question at him hopefully.

"There's a realtor negotiating the deal now, but I want to be there." He lifted his shoulders. "The man is completely qualified yet"—he smiled deprecatingly—"I want to be there."

"Of course you do." Jo's return smile said tomes more than her simple words.

A gentle quiet settled between them. An understanding quiet Brett had never before experienced with a woman. It was good. They both felt it and reacted to it. Neither one of them moved, nor did they break that fragile quiet with speech. But they spoke to each other with mirroring smiles and glances that touched and locked. Jo, a wondering look widening her eyes, finally snapped the both of them back to the here and now.

"When are you leaving?"

There was an odd, almost frightened edge to her carefully controlled voice that Brett was in complete communion with. He felt it himself, the accord, or *simpatico*, or whatever it was that shimmered between them—it kind of frightened him too. He also was careful of betraying no nuances in his tone.

"I can clear my desk by Wednesday," Brett said hopefully.

"Then go," she chided softly. "I'll mind the store."

Brett grinned, unknowingly revealing his relief at her willingness to assume command in his absence. When he'd gone to Vermont three weeks previously he'd had everything under control. Now things were beginning to hum a bit—the way things usually did when the youngest of the Renningers got into gear—and it was a definite relief to know he had a second in command in New York who was the equal to Richard Colby in Atlanta. Still grinning, he walked back to his desk. Propping a hip on the edge of the cluttered surface, Brett picked up a thick manila envelope and handed it to Jo.

"The Vermont project thus far. Skim over it. If you have any questions, jot them down. We'll confer tomorrow afternoon." Brett arched a pale eyebrow at her. "Okay?"

"Yes."

Again that simple matter-of-factness. Damned if she isn't something else, Brett mused, watching her rise and move to the door. As Jo reached for the knob, another consideration struck him.

"By the way—" He halted her action. "I've fully briefed Marsha on the project. As the New England manager. she will be at your disposal."

Five minutes later, Brett still stared at the door Jo had closed so very carefully behind her. What the hell had happened to all that understanding that had been flowing back and forth between them? Suddenly Jo had turned into the queen of ice! Surely it could not have been because he'd suggested she utilize the talents of another employee? But then, what the hell had chased all the warmth from her eyes and voice? All he'd done was mention the New England area manager and Jo had turned on the frost. Women! Shaking his head, Brett circled his desk and sat down.

As arranged, Brett met with Jo on Tuesday afternoon. The minute she entered his office Brett sighed with the realization that she had apparently applied her makeup with Jack Frost's paintbrush; he was still getting the ice treatment. Their meeting was terse, brief, and to the point. She claimed to have no questions whatever. Brett took her word for it. The minute she left his office, Brett called Marsha front and center.

"Has Jo been in touch with you about the Vermont deal?" Brett shot the question at Marsha before she'd even seated herself.

"No." Marsha made no attempt to conceal her surprise, or her curiosity. "Why?"

"No special reason," Brett hedged. "I was merely wondering."

"She's the one, isn't she?" Marsha murmured sympathetically.

"What one?" Brett's tone leveled a definite warning.

"Oh, Brett." Marsha chose to ignore the danger. "You know 'what one.' The one whose memory kept you from performing at"—she paused at the sudden stiffness

about him, but went on fearlessly—"full capacity, shall
we say?"

Brett's reaction was immediate and startling. "Damn
it, Marsha!" he snarled, jumping to his feet to stalk to the
window, then back again. "Do I taunt you by reminding
you of your failure that night?"

"I'm not taunting you, Brett."

"Then what the hell—"

"Brett," she cut in gently. "You're laying a smoke
screen, and you know it. Jo is the one, isn't she?"

"Yes," he grated harshly. "Christ! Am I that transparent?"

"Of course not." Marsha smiled. "And you know it. But
I was with you when you came back last week, remember.
I could actually feel the tension between the two of you.
And I saw your face when it became obvious that she was
ill. Poor Brett, you've got it pretty bad, haven't you?"

"Sometimes bad." Brett smiled whimsically. "And
sometimes good. But at all times frustrating."

"As to that, I have a million questions." She held up
her hand at the frown that drew his brows together.
"None of which I'd dare ask. But isn't there any way you
can resolve the situation?"

"Marsha, I fully intend to resolve the situation," Brett
assured her softly. "In my own time, and in my own way."

"There are times"—Marsha grinned—"my dear Brett,
when you actually give me the shivers."

"Oh, sure," Brett said dismissively. Moving restlessly, he
strolled to the window. "By the way, are you all settled
in?" he asked idly.

"To what? The job or the apartment?"

"Both," he grinned. "But primarily the job."

"Fairly well." She grinned back."Why do I have this
sensation you have a particular reason for asking?"

"Maybe because I have a particular reason for asking,"
he retorted dryly. "I'm going to hit the road again on

Wednesday," he explained seriously. "I was wondering if you had any questions before I leave."

"Where are you off to this time?" Not for a minute did Marsha think the query impertinent, which said much for the closeness that had developed between them in the brief time they'd known each other.

"The Pocono Mountains in Pennsylvania. I'm considering a condo complex there," Brett explained sketchily.

"For the skiers?"

Brett smiled. Marsha was sharp, but she was not quite as sharp as Jo. Jo had immediately picked up on his motivation. Oddly, knowing Jo was half a step ahead of most pleased him immensely.

"Partly." He nodded. "But I suspect that, before too long, that area will be booming the way the Jersey coast is now."

"Legalized gambling?" Marsha's eyes widened.

"The possibility is there." Brett shrugged. "What the hell, Columbus took a chance."

"And he's dead," Marsha drawled, straight-faced.

"Yes, well, nobody gets out of this life alive," Brett outdrawled her. "Well, do you have any questions?"

"None that I can think of offhand," she assured him.

"In that case, I have an assignment for you." Choosing his words carefully, Brett continued, "While I'm away I'd like you to use your connection with Casey Delheny to keep abreast of what's going on up there." Restless again, he measured the carpet in strides. "Jo has been put in complete charge but—"

"You don't trust her?" Marsha asked softly.

"I trust her implicitly!" His tone suddenly harsh, Brett stopped pacing to glare at her. *"But,* should she require assistance, I want you armed with the necessary data."

"Oh, boy," Marsha breathed softly. "You do have it bad." Before he could bite her head off, which he appeared ready to do, she asked, just as softly, "Are we friends, Brett?"

"You know we are," Brett snapped. "But that does not give you the right to—"

"Brett." Marsha silenced him with a wave of her hand. "Let me give you a bit of"—she shook her head at his scowling look—"not advice, but information. You know, the grapevine in this building is very alive and very active. I've picked up a few interesting bits and pieces since I've been here."

Positive she was going to say Wolf's name, and equally positive he did not want to hear it, Brett tried to shut her up. "I'm not interested in company gossip, Marsha."

"Then you should be," Marsha insisted, determined to have her say. "I'm told she's frigid."

"What!" With the memory of Jo's eager mouth, the way she melted against him, and her eyes, smokey with desire, teasing his mind, Brett was hard put not to laugh.

"Or afraid of men, or something. At any rate, she appears to have little or nothing to do with them. And they have tried, boy, have they tried! Apparently every eligible, and not so eligible, man in this building has approached her at one time or another. The rebuff is made gently, and very politely, but it is definitely a rebuff." Marsha shrugged. "I just thought you should know."

"And now I do," Brett replied roughly. "And now the subject is closed." No sane person argued when Brett used that roughly threatening tone of voice. Marsha knew better than to set a precedent.

Brett was away from the office for ten days. Ten days during which he was very busy, and strangely lonely, and tormented by thoughts of Jo. Only once did he give thought to his last conversation with Marsha, and then only fleetingly. Incredible as it seemed, apparently no one at the office had an inkling of the affair between Wolf and his assistant. That fact confirmed Brett's opinion of the two of them: Wolf and Jo were intelligent individuals.

One consideration did occur at regular intervals during those ten days, and that was his stated trust in Jo. Did he trust her? Brett asked himself repeatedly. Always, he answered his question with a question: How could he trust a woman who was involved with a married man? Yet, after days of self-questioning, Brett finally answered his conscience with the truth: He would trust her with his life.

It didn't make much sense, at least not Brett's kind of sense, but there it was, like it or not. He trusted her. He loved her.

On the flight back to New York, Brett told himself he was as dead as Columbus!

It was raining when Brett landed at Newark. It was raining when he dashed from the taxi to the doors of the Renninger Building. The cabbie had told Brett the radio newscaster had said there was a possibility of the rain turning to snow. The front desk receptionist informed him the TV newscaster had said there was a chance of snow. Not one of them told him what he wanted to know. After ten days of longing for her, missing her, the only subject of interest to Brett was Jo Lawrence.

On entering his office, Brett's first act was to ask his secretary to call Jo and request she join him. "And phrase it to her exactly that way," he instructed.

Beginning to feel a trifle foolish staring fixedly at the woodgrained door, he swung his gaze to the window, then wished he hadn't. The direction of the wind was driving the rain against the pane and, intermingling with the drops striking the glass, Brett could discern the occasional splat of a snowflake.

"Whoever heard of snow a week and a half before Thanksgiving?" he muttered in disgust.

"I beg your pardon?"

"There's snow mixed with that rain!" Brett growled, swinging around to confront the tormenter of his nights. Then Jo smiled at his disgruntlement, making him feel more a fool than before. *God! She's all I think about for over a week and, when I finally get back, I complain about snow!* You had better nail this woman down pretty soon, Brett advised himself. If you don't, they're going to come and cart you away!

"Well, don't blame me." Jo actually laughed at him. "I didn't order it."

Lost in his own thoughts, Brett stared at her in confusion a moment. Then the dawn broke in his mind. The snow! "Oh, well, I'm not used to the stuff. The South doesn't get a great deal of it."

"Do tell!" Jo gave a fair imitation of a Southern drawl.

Brett was immediately suspicious. Why was she so downright chipper this afternoon? One word sprang into his mind. A name. A name he didn't even want to think, let alone say aloud. Nonetheless, there it was. Wolf! Had she been in contact with her lover?

"You appear to be in fine spirits today," he probed carefully.

"And why not?" Jo grinned. "I received the e-mail you sent me three days ago." Her grin widened into a full, breathtaking smile. "You closed the deal on the property you wanted. I think that's plenty of reason for high spirits. Don't you?"

Brett nodded, grinned, and just sat staring at her. She is so damn beautiful, he thought achingly. Her smile alone brightens the dismal day. In concession to the weather, Jo was dressed in a full, dove-gray wool skirt and a pullover sweater in fuchsia that clung to her figure to the point of making Brett's hands itch. Her long, slim legs were encased to the knee in black boots of soft, pliant leather. Considering the overall picture she presented,

Brett decided she looked terrific. He also decided he'd love to undress her, very, very slowly. The beginnings of a frown marring her face drew him, reluctantly, out of the promise of a delightfully erotic daydream.

"Now the work begins on it," he said abruptly

"Have you decided on an architect?"

"I was considering Casey Delheny," Brett said thoughtfully. "I was really impressed with her designs for Vermont. What do you think?" Brett's question was not rhetorical. He really wanted her opinion, and he let it show in his tone.

"I think Casey's an excellent choice. Wolf thought so too. He'd inspected several of the buildings she'd designed and was very impressed. He also approved of the work of her interior designers."

Although Brett was not pleased with her use of Wolf as a reference, he let it slide. "Yes, I've seen some of her buildings myself, and I like the work of her interior designers as well. Okay, we'll go with Casey and let her use her own people."

"Do you always make decisions this quickly?" Jo laughed in a tone slightly tinged with awe.

"Usually." Brett shrugged nonchalantly.

"But don't you have to consult with headquarters?"

"Are you kidding?" Brett grinned. "I consulted with headquarters until I was afraid the phone lines would melt between Pennsylvania and Florida." His grin widened. "And do you want to know what the final word from the head honcho was?" Of course Jo nodded. "Mama told me, and these are her exact words, 'You picked up the ball, now run with it.'" Brett laughed out loud.

"Incredible!"

"I suppose." Brett shrugged. "But then, Renninger's is not run like most companies. In the first place it is entirely family owned and managed. Madam President *gives* orders, she does not take them." A gentle smile curved his lips. "In the second place, Mother gave each one of her sons the opportunity to do one complete job on his own. It was my turn. The Pocono project will be my baby."

"But what if you fail?" Jo blurted.

"No problem," Brett drawled. "She'll kill me."

Jo stared at him aghast for an instant, then joined him in laughter. "I think I'd like your mother," she said, when she could finally speak.

"I know Mother would like you," he assured her. "In fact, she wants to meet you."

"Me?" Jo blinked in astonishment. "Why would she want to meet me?" She eyed him warily. "And how would you know?"

"She told me." Brett met her wary glance with a smile. "While we were burning up the phone lines, she asked me how I was muddling along without the redoubtable Richard Colby. I told her I was indeed not muddling, but skimming, as I had Richard's double in drag in the New York office." Jo's gasp produced a slashing grin from Brett. "Again I quote my revered mother: 'I have got to meet the woman *you* admit is as competent as Richard!' she said quite seriously."

"Yes, well, the next time your mother is in New York, perhaps she'll peek into my office." Everything about Jo's attitude told Brett she didn't believe a word he said. "Now, back to the business at hand. Are you going to have the preliminary specs for the building drawn up by our people, or are you going with a general contractor?"

"What I said to my mother was incorrect." Brett groaned. "You are not like Richard. You are much, much more of a slave driver." Jo frowned. Brett got back to the business at hand. "I've decided to use Sean Delheny as general contractor. As with Casey, I've seen some of his work. I've also discussed it with the people he's worked for. The decision was unanimous: Sean is one damned good ramrod. He's done some fast-tracking."

Jo was well aware that the term fast-tracking applied to bonuses earned for a construction job completed ahead of schedule. Jo was also well aware of Sean's track record. He was very careful. He was very good. He got a job done right, usually ahead of time. Brett knew she made it her business to be aware of such things.

"Does Sean know he's been appointed for yet another Renninger project?" Jo asked dryly.

"Of course." Brett acted shocked, as if she should have known better than to even ask. "He's in the mountains now, checking out the local talent for subcontracting. I plan to confer with him again after Thanksgiving."

"Which reminds me," Jo sat up straighter in her chair. "I'm going to be out of the office most of Thanksgiving week. I'm going home for the holiday. I still have some vacation time due me."

"No problem." Brett shrugged. "Clear it with personnel."

Long after Jo had gone back to her own office, Brett sat, again contemplating the grain in the wood door. All his hopes of the previous ten days metaphorically laughing at him as they floated out the window. There were four days left to this week, four days in which he had one hell of a lot of work to catch up on. Next week she'd be gone. Come to that, so would he, as he had to fly to Atlanta to brief and be briefed by Richard. Then he was off again to Florida for Thanksgiving. A schedule, Brett decided glumly, that allowed little time for seduction.

Pushing his chair back, Brett shoved his suddenly tired body erect and stalked to the window to glare out at the rain that was rapidly changing to snow. At first he had envisioned taking Jo to his own bed. Then, growing desperate, he'd decided *her* bed would do just as well. Now, in a state of constant frustration, he'd happily make use of any damned bed or reasonably flat surface!

During the remainder of that week, Brett saw more of

Marsha than he did of Jo. A minor crisis had cropped up at a Renninger motel nearing completion in Massachusetts, and Marsha had come to Brett, mad as hell, because the ramrod of the project flatly refused to deal with a woman. When reason and diplomacy failed to budge the jerk, Brett had resolved the problem by telling the man to "Eat what you're served, or get the hell away from the table." If the injection of instant education didn't exactly cure the man's ailment, it did treat the existing symptoms; the fool decided he could work with Marsha.

In Atlanta, to Brett's immense relief, he found that Richard had everything under control, as usual.

"Are you attempting to ingratiate yourself into my office?" Their conference concluded, Brett and Richard were relaxing over a drink in one of Brett's favorite bars.

"Of course." Richard nodded. "The way I figure it, at the pace you've been working at since you and Sondra separated, you'll begin to burn out any day now." His grin was pure Machiavellian. "I intend to be prepared when Madam Pres finds herself in need of a new head man in Atlanta."

Free of tension for the first time in over a month, Brett leaned back in his chair and raised his glass in salute. "Good luck," he drawled, a grin lightening the new lines of strain on his handsome face.

Brett could afford the salute and the encouragement, very simply because he knew his assistant had no designs on his position. Richard Colby, small, dapper, urbane to his fingertips, was quite satisfied in his position as first assistant, and Brett knew it. Of course, Richard knew Brett knew it. Richard's mild threat was as close as he'd come to asking Brett to slow down. Brett, though appreciating Richard's concern, had no intention of paying heed to it.

Brett was in Florida barely long enough to sit down at the overloaded dinner table with the Renninger clan.

Within the eighteen hours he was at the farm Brett
learned that: Wolf was mending, if slowly; Micki was
well, and pleased with the way Wolf was mending; their
offspring were full of sun and the devil; Eric and his
family were happily increasing, as Eric's wife was pregnant with their third child; his sister Di was smugly
displaying her son's ability to perform back flips, and
his mother was, as always, the indestructible head of
Renninger Corporation—and all the assorted younger
Renningers.

Then Brett was off again, this time to Pennsylvania
and his prearranged meeting with Sean Delheny. Not
once during Brett's quick visit to the farm had JoAnne
Lawrence's name been mentioned. Not once had the
image of JoAnne Lawrence been far from Brett's mind.
In fact, by the time Brett returned to the New York office
in early December, his thoughts of Jo had become so ob-
sessive he was afraid that if he didn't see her soon he'd
begin snarling at everyone around him like a dog with
distemper.

Brett began snarling upon arrival at his office the following morning. He had wakened early feeling good with
anticipation and had even caught himself whistling while
standing under the shower. Walking to the office briskly in
the cold December air, he had counted the blocks and
then the pavement squares to his building. Entering the
outer office, Brett had politely asked Ms. Jenkins to buzz
Jo and request her to join him. Ms. Jenkins reply stopped
him cold two paces from his office door.

"Jo isn't in. She flew to Vermont yesterday."

Later, through Marsha and his second assistant, a
young eager beaver named Bob Kempten, Brett learned
that Casey Delheny had called about some technical
problem and Jo had decided to investigate personally. By
the time Jo returned, two days later, most of Brett's staff
were circling him from a distance, as if he were a rabid

dog. Determined he'd see her the minute she was back in
her office, Brett left a terse note for her on her desk. The
message consisted of three words: Get in here.

"You wanted to see me?" Jo asked as she gently closed
the door to Brett's office.

Brett was standing at the window, trying to stare holes
through the low-hanging, dirty-gray clouds. At the sound
of his door being opened every muscle and nerve in his
body tensed, but when he turned to face her he presented a picture of total relaxation. At the sight of her,
her cheeks pink from the cold, her dark hair tousled
from the brisk wind, and her lips slick with freshly applied gloss, Brett had to clamp his back teeth together to
control the urge to go to her and pull her into his arms.

"What was Casey's problem?" Brett tossed the question
at Jo as he strolled to his desk.

"Nothing really earth shattering, and nothing I
couldn't handle."

Every one of Brett's senses screamed an alert. There
was something wrong here, something in Jo's tone. Eyelids narrowing, Brett studied her more closely, his
sharpened glance probing past the glow imbued by
being out of doors. Her eyes were opaque, refusing an
observer access to her thoughts. Her features were carefully controlled, devoid of expression. Her attitude was
of polite, cool detachment. All the questions he'd
planned to ask her about Vermont fled before the confusion that fogged Brett's mind.

Before he'd left New York for Atlanta they had been
on friendly, almost warm terms. Now Jo looked at him as
if he were a stranger, and a not too appealing one at that.
What could have possibly happened to change her?
Brett wondered. And in such a short amount of time?

"Are you . . . all right?" Brett inquired gently, carefully feeling his way.

"Actually, no." Jo's lips tightened.

Brett's chest tightened too. "Is it something to do with that trouble in Vermont?" Even as Brett asked the question Jo was shaking her head in the negative. "What then?" he demanded, if softly.

Jo drew a deep breath, which nearly drew a groan past his compressed lips; Jo did fill a sweater to advantage.

"I'm not feeling right." She hesitated, then rushed on, too quickly. "I don't feel exactly ill, but I don't feel exactly well either. I'm . . . I'm tired all the time. Perhaps it's a holdover from the virus I contracted a few weeks ago."

Garbage. Brett knew Jo was lying, he *knew* it . . . yet, why? "Have you consulted a doctor about your symptoms?" Brett knew the answer to that too. He was right.

"No." Not a muscle in her face moved, only her lips. "I-I think all I need is some rest." Now she hesitated again, as if girding herself for battle. "I've used up all my vacation but, with your permission"—she grimaced, as if the last word was distasteful to her—"I'd like to take a leave of absence the last two weeks of this month."

"Jo—" Brett began, only to be cut off at once.

"That's not all."

"Go on. What else do you want?" Brett muttered.

"Permission to stay at the motel in Ocean City." Jo stared at him coolly.

"You want to go to the beach in December!" Brett exclaimed in an amazed shout.

"I want to rest!" Jo shouted back, revealing tension for the first time since entering his office. "It will be quiet there. And I love the sea. May I stay in one of the rooms there?" she insisted, her tone again without inflection.

"Aren't you going home for Christmas?"

"No!" The denial shot out of her.

Brett now had part of the answer, but only part of it. He was sure something had happened while she'd been home at Thanksgiving, and apparently that something had been

unpleasant. Brett was equally sure that was not the complete answer. Her attitude toward *him* had changed
drastically, so it was also something to do with him that had
caused this cold front she was presenting. But what had he
done? Brett raked his mind and came up blank. If she'd
only talk to him, or scream at him . . . but, from her attitude, it was obvious she was not going to budge from
behind her icy mask. Damn it, he raged inwardly, what can
I do but let her have what she wants? Nothing.

"If you're going to stay there the entire two weeks, one
room won't do," he said flatly. "You'll get cabin fever
before the first week is out. Stay in the apartment."

"But . . ."

"Don't argue!" Brett was skating very close to the edge
of his patience, and it showed. Jo subsided at once. "I'll
call Wolf's housekeeper, Mrs. Jorgeson, and ask her to
have the utilities turned on and to clean the place for
you." Standing abruptly, he slid his hand into his pocket
and withdrew a gold keyring. After working two of the
keys off the ring, he leaned across the desk and handed
them to her. "I'll also let security know you're coming."
A sardonic smile twitched at his lips. "I don't think you'd
enjoy spending Christmas in the slammer for breaking
and entering."

Jo's expression didn't change, in as much as she still
showed no expression at all. "Thank you." Her voice had
a cool, withdrawn quality that sent a shiver through Brett.

Brett mentally gnawed at the problem of Jo's attitude
long after she'd left his office. In fact, he was still rack-
ing his brain for an answer after her leave of absence
had officially begun. He saw little of her during the two-
week interval, and what he did see of her alarmed him.
She was pale, she looked liked she was not getting
enough sleep, and she was much too subdued. The Jo
Lawrence he had come to love had been anything but
subdued.

As Christmas grew nearer, and the office employees grew merrier, Brett's worry and frustration jelled into determination. Four days before Christmas he reached the end of his patience. Whether Jo liked it or not, she was going to get company. Damn it! He owned the place, didn't he?

Late that afternoon Brett signed the release for the employees' Christmas bonuses, locked his desk, and pushed his chair back. As he was shrugging into his coat the phone rang. Snatching up the receiver impatiently, Brett growled, "Ms. Jenkins, I told you I was leaving. I'm taking no calls."

"I'm sorry, Mr. Renninger, but I was sure you'd want to speak to this party."

Brett immediately thought of Jo. "Who is it?"

"The boss."

Brett smiled at her dry tone. Hell, he didn't know she was capable of dry humor! "You're right, Ms. Jenkins. I'll take the call." The moment Brett heard the switch click in, he drawled with his usual insolence, "Yes, sir?"

"I should have beaten you as a child," his mother said decisively, then added maternally, "You are coming to the farm for Christmas, aren't you?"

"Yes, of course," Brett assured her. "I should get there late in the afternoon on Christmas Eve."

"Good, we'll see you then," Violet said briskly. "By the way, if Jo Lawrence has no other plans, bring her with you," she tacked on as an afterthought.

Brett mulled over his mother's invitation all the way to Ocean City. Even though she had expressed a desire to meet Jo, it seemed odd to Brett that his mother had chosen this particular time to do it. Christmas was always a family time at the Renninger manse, wherever that happened to be when the holiday rolled around. There was, of course, one unavoidable consideration, and that was that Wolf had made a special request of Violet to include

Jo. Merely speculating on that possibility torched a blaze of anger inside Brett.

By the time he drove onto the motel parking lot, Brett had mulled himself into a fury. Deep inside his conscience, Brett knew he had no right to demand anything from Jo. At the same time, consciously Brett knew he was about to demand everything from her.

The small car, parked near the entrance doors, looked slightly forlorn on the large lot. As he pulled the Porsche up beside it, the term run-about slithered into Brett's mind. Had Wolf signed his name to a check for the toy? Brett tormented himself with the query as he strode to the wide glass doors. After making sure the doors were securely locked again behind him, Brett took the stairs two at a time, then loped along the hallway to the apartment. Key at the ready, he hesitated a moment, then unlocked the door and stepped inside.

Jo was standing with her back to the oversized window, having obviously spun around at the sound of his entrance. She did not look frightened, or even surprised. In fact, Brett had the strange sensation that she'd been expecting him. His anger changing to an even more basic emotion, Brett stood still for a moment, eating her with his eyes. Even though it was still early evening, Jo was dressed for bed in a lilac-and-orchid striped silk robe over a paler orchid nightgown. Her face was free of makeup and her hair was slightly mussed. Brett decided to muss it even more.

Without as much as a word, watching her eyes, Brett walked to her, shedding his leather jacket and dropping it to the floor as he went. With cool deliberation he walked right into her, a primitive thrill leaping in his loins at the shock of their colliding bodies. Then the aching emptiness of his arms was filled with the softness of her and his restlessly moving hands delighted in the

silk material covering her back. Still staring into her eyes,
Brett read surrender in the soft hazel depths.

The clean scent of her filling his senses, the feel of her
soft breasts crushed to his chest, and his own now-raging
desire snapped the thread of communication between
Brett and his conscience. Damn Wolf! Damn the whole
damned world! He must have this woman.

Giving Jo time to protest, or turn her head aside if she
wanted to, Brett lowered his head slowly. The fact that Jo
did neither, but parted her lips instead, set Brett's heart
racing. Gently, gently, he cautioned himself as he touched
his lips to hers. But then, at Jo's instant response, all
thoughts of caution dissolved in the blood that went rushing through his veins. Suddenly filled with the need to
conquer, Brett pressed his mouth against hers, unmindful
of the low growl that swelled his vocal chords. Jo reacted
by clasping his head to pull him deeper into her mouth.

Sliding his hands down her back, Brett grasped her
rounded bottom and lifted her up to meet the urgent
thrust of his body. At the same time he inserted his tongue
into the sweet moistness of her mouth. Jo rewarded Brett's
efforts with a low groan. Sweeping her into his arms, Brett
strode to the bedroom, his lips locked on hers. Coming to
a stop beside the bed, he allowed himself the pleasure of
sliding her body down his as he settled her on her feet.

Every one of Brett's senses urged him to rip the robe
and nightgown from Jo's body then tear his own clothes
off. Clamping hard on his back teeth, Brett brought
every ounce of control he possessed into play. He had
waited too long for her to rush the moment. No, there'd
be no ripping or tearing here. No hurried, frantic coupling. Brett fully intended to enjoy every minute of the
love play. He fully intended Jo to enjoy it as well.

Slowly, tenderly, Brett removed the robe and nightgown, then stepped back to feast his eyes on her. Beautiful,
God, she's beautiful, he thought, inching his gaze over Jo's

nakedness. Her breasts were not large, but firm and high. Her waist curved in neatly before flaring out again to rounded hips. Her legs were long, shapely as a dancer's, tapering to slim ankles and feet. And her thighs! Brett's gaze lingered on Jo's smooth thighs a moment, then slowly rose to meet her eyes.

"Brett . . ." It was the first word spoken, and her only word. The plea drew his eyes to her face.

"It will be good, Jo. I promise," Brett said in a hoarse voice he hardly recognized as his own. "Do you believe me?"

Jo swallowed, then wet her lips, making Brett long for the feel of her pink tongue in his mouth. "I—I want to believe you, but you don't understand. . . ."

"I don't need to understand," Brett cut her off urgently, positive she was going to attempt to tell him about Wolf. "It *will* be good. I swear to you."

Tugging the comforter free, Brett tossed it to the bottom of the bed, then, lifting Jo again, he laid her in the middle of the mattress. Straightening, Brett swiftly shed his clothes, his gaze locked on hers. When, finally, he stood before her as God had made him, he searched her face for signs of approval—or disapproval. Brett was not unaware of his attractiveness to women. Many of the women he'd dated, and slept with, had been articulate in their praise of his masculine good looks. Now, stripped of all the expensive trappings, Brett trembled as he watched Jo's eyes examine him. His trembling increased with excitement when he saw her eyes widen on sight of his arousal. Brett's excitement building, he watched her gaze shy away from, then return to his manhood before climbing up his body to his face.

"I—I'm not sure I can . . ."

That's as far as Jo got before, sliding on to the bed beside her, Brett closed her mouth with his own. Yet Jo's attempt at protest had shaken him. The prospect of rejection goading him, Brett set out to seduce her.

His lips teased hers. His teeth nibbled on the tender flesh inside. His tongue made gentle forays into the recess of her mouth, then thrust deeply over and over until she moaned and clung to him, silently begging for more. At the tiny sound Brett deserted Jo's lips to plant stinging kisses down her neck to the hollow at the base of her throat. The flutter of Jo's pulse against the tip of Brett's tongue set fire to his blood. Enjoying the sensation of liquid flames racing through his body, Brett ventured farther south. His lips adored the satiny smoothness of her breasts, his tongue worshiped the hardening nipples. Driven now by a passion running rampant, Brett closed his lips over one rigid nipple and drew gently, shivering with the resultant tightening in his loins.

His hands stroking Jo's softness, learning all the places that caused a movement or murmur of response from her, Brett imprinted his lips onto the skin of her body. His own ardor rising, he dipped his tongue into her navel, then slid his moistened tongue the length of her abdomen and around the perimeter of her dark triangle. Loving his work, Brett tongue-kissed Jo's legs to her insteps, then backtracked up the inside of her thigh. When his lips reached their desired destination, Jo stiffened.

"Brett, no! I . . ."

It was too late. Determined not to be denied, Brett tasted the honied sweetness of her. His hands clasped to her hips, he kissed and caressed her silky warmth. Jo remained stiff for a moment, then a smile touched Brett's lips as he felt her begin to move slowly, then with increasing frenzy, her breath rasping through her moaning throat.

"Brett, Brett, please . . . oh, please . . ."

In all of his fantasies about Jo, never had he hoped to hear her plead for him to love her. Sliding his body up between her thighs, Brett placed his lips lightly to hers.

"Did I promise you it would be good?" he whispered into her mouth.

"Yes!" she gasped, sending a shudder through his body.

"And have I pleased you so far?" he murmured, nipping at her lower lip.

"Yes," she moaned, sending a shaft of near pain into the lower part of his body.

"Shall I continue?" he teased, sliding his tongue along her teeth.

"Oh, yes," she sobbed, sending his control into retreat.

Brett talked to himself to keep from rushing and ruining it all: Take your time. There's no hurry now. You've waited and waited what seems like forever for this. Wrest every ounce of sweetness from it.

All the while he was advising himself, Brett was moving over Jo. Gently he settled himself between her enticingly soft thighs, pausing a moment to stroke her heated core with one hand while caressing a breast with the other. The movement of Jo's hips encouraged entrance and, sliding his hands beneath her, Brett lifted her to meet him. Then, slowly, savoring every incremental movement, Brett penetrated into the satiny sheath that felt like it was fashioned for him alone. Deep within her warmth, Brett felt himself savoring every sensation as he and Jo moved in slow rhythm as one.

The slow savoring could not last. For the first time in his adult life Brett's control shattered completely. Never had he experienced the fullness of the love act—a joining of mind and soul as well as flesh—and only now with this most magnificent of women. Increasing the tempo, Brett moved faster, and still faster, thrusting his body against and into hers, thrilling to the feel of her legs embracing him tightly, exulting to the strength with which she thrust her body against his.

Brett's body was bathed in sweat and his hands felt the slippery wetness of Jo's, and still he prolonged the final moment, waiting for her. When that moment happened for her, he stilled, holding her close, absorbing the shudders into his own body. When her shock waves had subsided, Brett began moving again, stroking deeper, and yet deeper, desperate to possess, equally desperate to be possessed. The explosion came within seconds of her own, and now Jo clutched him to her to cushion the reverberations.

When total sanity returned, Brett carefully moved from Jo's body to the bed. Without a word he drew her into his arms, close to his side. Then, his lips at her forehead, he murmured, "Thank you, water baby. Now, go to sleep."

Long after Jo's even breathing indicated to Brett that she was sleeping deeply, he lay awake, holding her soft body tightly to his own. Staring into the darkness, Brett attempted to sort out the tangle of conflicting emotions vying for supremacy in his mind. First and foremost was the indisputable fact that what he'd just been through had been *the* most shattering sexual experience he'd ever had. Even thinking it seemed strange, yet Jo had somehow enveloped him totally, not merely physically but spiritually as well! Stranger still was the stark realization that, not only did he not mind the . . . ensnarement, for want of a better word . . . he was actually rejoicing in it. He loved it! Hell, now, to himself, holding Jo close in a pitch-dark room, Brett felt free to revel in the truth that he loved her!

Pushing all other considerations aside, Brett whispered the words aloud.

"I love you, JoAnne Lawrence, completely, unconditionally, and, very likely, forever."

The vow at last spoken, even to one who could not hear, Brett sighed contentedly and went to sleep.

EIGHT

The sound of the wind, moaning like a soul in torment, woke Jo. Lying still, she listened to the shiver-inducing noise as gusts beat against the wide bedroom window in ineffectual fury. It was no longer dark beyond the pane, yet still not fully light, the time of morning when the lowest temperature reading is usually registered. In her mind, Jo pictured the ocean and breakers whipped to white-capped frenzy by the gale. All that potentially destructive elemental force, she mused sleepily. So very near.

A smile of contentment curved her kiss-swollen lips. She was warm and safe. The warmth came, Jo acknowledged, not so much from the covers tucked around her shoulders but from the heat radiating from the body beside hers. The feeling of safety came not from being inside a roof and four walls but from being enclosed within two strong, masculine arms. Dismissing the weather as not worth consideration, Jo snuggled closer to Brett's body, luxuriating in the delicious sensation of his nakedness against her own.

God, he was wonderful! A grin tugged at Jo's lips. *She* was wonderful too! She was a woman! Not merely a female, but a living, breathing, sexually responsive woman! Brett had proved it to her. Proved it in the most primitive way possible. He had made her his, figuratively as well as literally. Brett did not know it, and Jo prayed he never would, but with his possession of her he had earned himself a slave. Jo had been in love with him last night. This morning, what she felt for him came so close to adoration, it scared the wits out of her. Still, perhaps enslavement was worth the price for enlightment. All her fears and insecurities concerning her ability to respond physically to a man had been swept from her mind by the pulsating rush of sexual fulfillment.

Go to hell, Gary Devlin!

Jo gulped back a gurgle of laughter and snuggled still closer to Brett. She felt terrific! She felt fantastic! She felt . . . Jo compressed her lips to contain a fresh surge of laughter. She *felt* Brett's hand stroking slowly up the inside of her thigh!

"Are you trying to tell me something with all your wiggling around?" Brett's breath whispered over Jo's temple an instant before his tongue outlined the edge of her ear.

"I—I was just thinking how cold the wind sounds, and how warm it is in here," Jo explained, her breath catching as his hand found the apex of her thighs. The entrapped breath vibrated in her throat producing a tiny gasp when his long fingers began combing through the dark thicket.

"I have a feeling it's going to go from warm to red hot very quickly if you continue wiggling your fanny like that." Brett punctuated his assertion by stabbing the tip of his tongue into her ear.

Jo's tiny gasp matured into a deep-throated moan as Brett's fingers slid lower to explore the moist heat of her core. And it was heated! The realization was both a shock and a delight to her. She, JoAnne Lawrence, the woman who had believed herself incapable of responding physically to any man, had become meltingly hot by the simple process of snuggling closer to Brett's warm, naked body. She was ready for him! To a sexually experienced woman that sudden arousal would not have come as a surprise. To Jo it seemed a miracle.

Go with the flow. The buzz phrase drifted through Jo's mind and, reacting to it, she moved her hips sensuously. Brett reacted to her movement by exploring the region in depth. Soft, inarticulate sounds she was barely aware of making tickling the back of her throat, Jo arched her body, instinctively inviting deeper penetration. ·

"You like that, do you?" Brett murmured into her ear.

"Yes!" Jo admitted between shallow gasps. "Oh, yes!"

"Then you might return the favor," he chided softly.

Return the favor? For an instant Jo's passion-clouded mind grappled with his request. What . . . Oh! Did Brett mean for her to . . . ? But, of course, what else could he mean? she thought fuzzily. Were men also turned on by having their bodies stroked and caressed? Brett answered the question for her in a low groan.

"Touch me, Jo! Please. You can't imagine how long I've ached for you to touch me."

Shyly, hesitantly, Jo lifted her hand and placed her palm against his chest. Then, slowly, she stroked, a growing sense of wonder widening her eyes at the smoothness of his skin. When her fingers brushed lightly over the flat male nipples she paused, a question rising to tantalize her mind. All too vividly Jo remembered the piercing pleasure she had experienced from the touch of Brett's lips to her breasts. Would Brett experience a similar reaction? Intrigued by the idea, Jo shifted her body around until she was positioned almost on top of him. With a soft sign, Brett obligingly made a half turn onto his back. Lowering her head, Jo dropped a string of delicate kisses across his chest. When her lips reached the tight nipple she hesitated and a shiver rippled through Brett's body.

"Jo, please, don't stop now!"

His hoarse, excitement-tinged groan encouraging her on, Jo closed her lips around the taut bud and laved it gently with her tongue. Amazingly, Brett gasped and actually writhed beneath her. His response had the strangest effect on Jo. She was suddenly filled with a heady sense of power. She could make him writhe in pleasure! At the same time, Jo recognized that her own sexual tension was increasing. She'd had no idea of how exciting making love to a man could be!

All timidity forgotten, Jo continued to explore Brett's body with her lips. By the time she dipped her tongue into his navel, Brett's breathing had a raspy, uneven sound and his hands moved restlessly over her upper arms and shoulders. All the while her lips dropped tiny kisses, her palms were absorbing the feel of his skin. At his navel she again hesitated briefly, then bravely skimmed her lips down the concave of his abdomen to a hair-rough thigh. Now Brett's hands were in her hair, stroking, tugging gently in a silent plea for her to bestow the ultimate caress.

Understanding immediately, Jo stilled for an instant. During that instant a mini-battle raged. Could she? Did she want to? No! Yes! Damn it! Was she not a woman after all? Brett's hips thrust provocatively. The feeling of power washed over her again. Swiftly, before she could change her mind, Jo bent her head, sank her fingertips into his hard buttocks, and granted his mute request. Brett's low groan of intense pleasure urging her on, Jo caressed him gently, finding to her amazement that the more pleasure she gave him, the more she received herself.

Brett withstood Jo's ministrations for several moments, then he grasped her shoulders and growled softly, "Come up here and kiss my mouth, water baby, I want to feel your body covering mine."

Slowly, tormentingly, pausing at strategic spots to kiss teasingly, Jo sinuously slid up his body, unashamedly reveling in Brett's raspingly uttered words of praise.

"You're fantastic, do you know that? You've made me want you so badly I'm trembling all over." Then, when her mouth lightly touched his: "God! The scent of you! The feel of you! The taste of you!"

Digging his fingers into her hair, he pulled her head to his, his mouth taking hers hungrily, his tongue a hot spear branding her mouth as his own. Brett's lips locked onto hers, he grasped her by the hips and lifted her up, then settled her onto his body, branding her again with another spear.

Gasping aloud at the depth of his penetration, Jo let her head drop back and began to move her body in a slow, undulating motion.

"Yes, Yes," Brett crooned unevenly. "Perfect. God! You're perfect."

The lazy tempo was maintained for several minutes during which Jo felt the tension twisting into a wildness inside. She moaned as Brett's hands stroked lovingly over her tautly arched neck to her shoulders and then to her aching breasts before settling firmly on her hips. Slowly, directing her with his hands, Brett increased the tempo, his own body arching to meet hers. His action fed the wildness growing in her, and, grasping his wrists with her hands, Jo accelerated the tempo to a frenzied crescendo. Brett exploded under her. There was no holding back for him this time. Jo sensed his loss of control and gloried in the realization of having been the instrument of his loss. Reality' receding, Jo had the uncanny sensation of soaring through space, and then simultaneously they went crashing through the time barrier. For sweet, pulsating seconds time stood still while their entire beings experienced the highest of the highs. Then, slowly, gently, they drifted back to earth together.

Jo opened her eyes to the awareness of her head resting on Brett's shoulder, her face pressed to the curve of his neck. In gratitude and unspoken love she placed a kiss on his moist skin. Brett's arms tightened around her momentarily, then relaxed.

"Are you uncomfortable, sweetheart?"

Wanting to lock the sound of it in her mind and heart, Jo closed her eyes at the endearment. Uncomfortable? How could she possibly tell him that, at this moment, she desired nothing more than to remain coupled to him forever? Dreamily, she murmured something unintelligible and allowed him to disengage her body from his.

"Are you going to sleep again?" Brett teased, lightly caressing her thighs with one hand.

"I hope so," Jo murmured drowzily, lifting a lazy hand to cover a yawn.

"Self-indulgent wench," Brett chided. "I was hoping you'd come with me."

"With you?" Jo forced her heavy eyelids up. "Where are you going?"

"I thought I'd run on the beach." That quirky smile twitched his lips. "That is, after I've rested a bit. You do take it out of a guy."

"Run on the beach!" Jo exclaimed, choosing to ignore the double meaning attached to his assertion. "Are you mad? It's cold out there! And windy! Don't you hear it screaming around the building?"

"I'd have to be stone deaf not to." He laughed. "I'm not afraid of the wind."

"I'm not either," Jo assured him around another yawn. "But that doesn't mean I want to run in it. Good night, Brett."

Brett's laughter grew stronger. "But it's morning, honey. See? It's broad daylight."

Casting a narrowed glance at the window, Jo obligingly observed the broad daylight, then she pulled the covers up to her chin and closed her eyes. "So it is," she agreed. "Good night, Brett." Inside her mind, Jo was savoring the taste of his "honey."

"It *is* cold out there." The statement was made through lips that moved against Jo's ear. "And you *are* so nice and warm." His hand wove an erotic pattern up her thigh to cup the tightly curled thicket. "Wonderfully warm." With his other hand Brett drew her head back into the curve of his neck. "Maybe I'll sleep awhile with you. *Then* I'll run on the beach."

The second time Jo woke that morning she noticed three things at once. The wind had died down; the sun was shining brightly; and she was alone in the bed. Apparently Brett had decided to run on the beach. In Jo's opinion, anybody who would even consider running on the beach, or anywhere else, on a cold December morning was slightly nuts, but, she thought shrugging, each to his own brand of self-torture. For Jo, the torture would come in the form of the first meal of the day. Jo was a lousy cook. Turn her loose in the kitchen and within minutes it was a disaster area.

After a warm, revitalizing shower, Jo tugged skin-tight jeans over her slender hips and pulled a thigh-length, baggy sweatshirt over her head, then winced as she stroked a brush through her mass of tangled hair. When the dark mop had been beaten into submission, Jo tossed the brush aside and padded barefoot out of the bedroom. She was standing at the kitchen sink, filling the coffeemaker with cold water, when Brett swung into the apartment, out of breath, sweaty, and looking sexy as hell in a windbreaker and sweatpants.

"Hi!" he panted, flashing her an ice-melting grin. "If you give me ten minutes to jump in and out of the shower, I'll prepare brunch." Not waiting for a response, he loped across the living room and disappeared down the short hall to the bedroom.

Brunch yet! Jo smiled as she scooped coffee into the small basket. All the while she'd been showering, one worry had nagged at her mind: What would Brett's attitude toward her be now? The morning after! His spontaneous greeting and easy grin had laid that particular worry to rest.

Oh, there were other worries and considerations Jo realized she'd eventually have to deal with, but they could wait
until after she had fortified herself with food.

As if he'd timed it, Brett strode into the kitchen as the
coffeepot gurgled its last perk. Running a swift, encompassing glance over his lean frame, Jo decided he looked
even sexier in jeans and a black sweater than he had in
sweats. Without hesitation, Brett drew her into his arms.

"Now I can wish you a proper good morning," he said,
lowering his head to hers.

Brett's lips touched hers gently, almost tentatively,
until he felt her part her lips in response, then his kiss
deepened, although not in demand, but more like a
learning process. Wanting to learn more herself, Jo put
every ounce of herself into the meeting of mouths.
When Brett drew back to gaze down at her, his eyes
shimmering like silver, Jo promptly decided she'd adore
being wished a proper good morning in that fashion
every morning for the rest of her life. Smothering a sigh
of regret for the impossibility of foolish dreams, she
smiled tremulously back at him.

"How are you feeling?" The smile changed into a
frown as Brett examined Jo's upturned face minutely.
"When you left the office last week, you looked about
ready to unravel. Are you feeling any better . . . now?"

Jo did not miss Brett's deliberate hesitation before the
word now, and she knew he meant right now, since the
night they'd spent together. Should she take a chance
and tell him how deeply his lovemaking had affected
her? Could she bare her soul to this man? Don't be a
complete fool, the voice of cool logic warned scathingly.
Remember what happened the last time you spoke of
your feelings to a man. Staring up at Brett, Jo could actually hear the echo of Gary's taunting gibes. Gary's
ridicule had been hard enough to take; somehow Jo
knew she would not be able to bear it from Brett. No, Jo

cautioned herself, play it cagy, play it down, but for God's sake, play it safe!

"I'm feeling much better." Jo avoided the word now. "I simply needed some rest . . . as I told you last week."

Brett's sigh revealed to Jo how disappointing her reply had been. Like all men, she thought in sudden irritation, he wanted his ego stroked! Well, damn it, women had egos too! And she sure hadn't heard any soul baring from him!

"If you're feeling so much better," Brett chided gently, "why are you scowling at me in exactly the same way you were last week?"

"I'm hungry." Jo blurted the first excuse that came to mind. "I thought you said you were going to make brunch?"

From his expression, it was obvious that Brett didn't buy her disclaimer. But, fortunately, it immediately became obvious he was not going to push the issue. His grin back in place, if a trifle strained, he released her and stepped back.

"Okay, we'll leave it for now." A definite warning underlined his light tone. "Have you got anything interesting in the fridge?" Without waiting for a reply, he strode to the appliance.

"I have the usual breakfast foods, eggs, bacon, juice," Jo enumerated, following him.

"Then I guess that will have to do." Brett sighed dramatically. "How about a bacon omelet? You wouldn't happen to have a green pepper and an onion, would you?"

Jo did, and the resultant meal was delicious. As she polished off the last bite of toast, Jo pondered on the hows and whys of Brett's culinary skill. He had whipped the meal together with the panache of a professional chef—making as many dishes dirty in the bargain. How had he learned to cook like that? And, more important, why? Brett had grown up in the proverbial lap of luxury. Why would anyone born to a family of wealth learn to cook? Especially a male? And this particular male didn't merely cook, he created!

All of a sudden Jo felt very uncomfortable. Musing on the circumstances of Brett's culinary expertise brought home the realization of how very little she knew about him. Brett was still virtually a stranger to her, and she had shared his bed! What must he think of her? Had she been merely a convenient, easy lay? A cold shudder rippled along Jo's spine. Unable to look at him, she lifted her cup and stared into her coffee. Oh, God! Jo thought bleakly. What had she let herself in for here? Loving Brett as she now did, Jo felt sick at the idea of him using her simply to assuage a physical need.

"Were you planning to do anything today?" Brett's quiet voice shattered Jo's introspection.

"No." Jo forced herself to look at him. "There really isn't much to do in a resort town in December." Now she forced herself to smile. "I didn't come here to *do* anything. Remember? I came here to rest."

Jo's smile disintegrated at the memory of why she had needed to get away from everything. First there had been that disheartening visit home for Thanksgiving. Then, already feeling depressed, she had gone to Vermont, only to have Casey confirm what she had suspected about Brett and Marsha. And still, knowing they had been lovers before they came back to New York, she had not only not repulsed him, she had welcomed him into her bed, and herself. In the cold light of a winter morning, Jo told herself that loving Brett was no excuse for her self-indulgence. If she suffered later she had only herself to blame. But she could not think of it now, not with him sitting opposite her, frowning at her lengthy silence. Shaking herself out of her reverie, Jo rose and began clearing the table, deciding she'd have to think it all through later.

"What's wrong?" Brett's fingers closed around Jo's wrist as she reached for his plate. "Why are you so quiet?"

"I'm always quiet." Jo made a feeble attempt at a smile. "Didn't you know? I have always been quiet. It comes from being an only child and being alone so much." She was babbling, she *knew* she was babbling, but Jo hoped that by expanding on his second question, she could avoid answering the first one.

"You're not alone now." Brett's tone implied a lot more than his flat statement. Jo sensed that he was telling her something that, in her emotionally confused mind, she simply wasn't hearing. Brett didn't give her time to ponder on his meaning. "You do realize I'm going to stay here with you, don't you? That is, at least through the twenty-third." The twenty-third was two days away. Two very short days, Jo thought, sighing and lowering her eyes to the long fingers lightly clasping her wrist. Two days in which to soak up the sight of him, the feel of him, and then he'd be gone until the next time he decided to add spice to his sexual life by changing bed partners. The thought hurt so badly Jo closed her eyes, blocking out the vision of implied imprisonment. An instant later Jo's eyes flew wide at Brett's soft pronouncement. "When I leave I'm taking you with me."

"Taking me with you?" Jo blurted, rather stupidly, she was sure. "Where?"

"To the farm." Brett's lips tightened, as if in anger. "In Florida."

"But I can't go . . ." Jo began in protest.

"Yes, you can. And you will." Brett's tone indicated there'd be no arguing over the matter. "I was instructed to, and this is an exact quote, 'Bring her with you.'"

"By whom?" Although she was positive the answer would be Wolf, Jo asked anyway. Wolf was the only person who knew her family situation. Thus Brett's answer came as a complete surprise.

"By Madam President, herself."

"Your mother!"

"The one and only," Brett concurred softly.

"But why?" Oh, God, had Wolf discussed her with his mother? And, in turn, had his mother taken pity on her? Jo felt sick. And more than a little angry. Damn it, she didn't want or need pity!

"Who knows what motivates the great minds?" Brett replied in a careless tone that was belied by the glitter of speculation in his eyes. It was patently obvious to Jo that something about his mother's invitation had angered Brett too. The realization reinforced her decision not to go, and, shaking her head sharply, she told him so.

"I won't go with you."

Jo was totally unprepared for the swiftness of Brett's reaction to her refusal to accompany him south. Rising abruptly to his feet, he gave a sharp tug on her wrist that impelled her against his hard chest. Releasing her wrist, he imprisoned her within his arms, crushing her soft breasts to the rock hardness of him.

"You will go with me," Brett contradicted with soft menace. "When I leave here on the twenty-third, and when I fly south on the twenty-fourth." Releasing her as abruptly as he'd caught her to him, he said briskly, "Now, let's get this mess cleaned up." His lips curved into a wickedly alluring smile. "I want to go back to bed."

"You can go straight to hell!" Really angry now, Jo planted her balled fists onto her slim hips. Who the hell did he think he was talking to . . . the upstairs maid? Was there an upstairs maid? Jo shrugged the irrelevant thought aside. Damn him! One night in bed and he acted as if he owned her! Well, Madam President's fair-haired boy was about to learn that Jo Lawrence would not be owned . . . by anyone! She might love him but she'd be damned if she'd pander to him! She had learned the folly of pandering to a man the hard way. Never, never again, she vowed. "If you're feeling the need to work off the enormous breakfast you consumed," Jo said scathingly, "go beat your feet on the beach again." Her nastily voiced advice was followed by aloud gasp as she was immediately hauled into his arms.

"Oh, but I'd much prefer working off my 'enormous' meal by beating my body against yours," Brett purred with deliberate crudity. "Are you going to fight me?" One pale eyebrow arched elegantly. "Make me subdue you?" His lips twitched into a devilish smile. "How very intriguing."

"Let me go, Brett," Jo gritted warningly. "You'll get nothing from me by force." Jo groaned silently. If he didn't release her at once she'd be a goner! Already the melting process had begun, and she could feel the effects in the lower part of her body. Oh, God! Maybe the transition from female to woman had not been so wonderful after all. She was vulnerable to him now, much too vulnerable.

"Force!" Brett exclaimed on a soft burst of laughter. "Oh, honey, there'll be no need for me to use force." His liquid silver gaze seared her face. "Whether you realize it or not, your eyes are soft with desire. Your lips are parted, ready for mine. And"—his hands slid down her back to cup her derriere—"your hips are moving against mine very invitingly." Slowly, inexorably, he drew her against the hardness of his thighs and aroused manhood. "I accept your invitation," he murmured lowering his head. "Just as you are going to accept my mother's."

Jo wanted to scream a denial, and she would have if Brett's mouth had not taken hers so sweetly. Damn him, she sighed, mingling her breath with his. Damn him for being the only man able to ignite her physical fire! Fully cognizant of what she was doing, hating and loving it at

one and the same time, Jo coiled her arms around
Brett's strong neck and gave herself up to the moment.

The moment stretched into most of the afternoon! By
the time Brett allowed Jo to drift into sleep, she was completely fulfilled and thoroughly exhausted. This man, she
thought groggily, swiftly losing her hold on consciousness,
has more than enough stamina to accommodate two
women! Jo should have been upset by the observation,
and she would have been if she had not drifted so far
along the path to slumber.

The third time Jo woke it was to an oddly familiar stillness that was in no way connected to the fact that she was
alone in the bed. Frowning as her mind groped for an
explanation, Jo stared at the darkened bedroom window.
A faint splat against the pane brought instant recognition. It was snowing!

Snow. Jo's pulses leaped with a ray of hope. If it were
to snow long enough, and hard enough, maybe she
and Brett would be stranded through Christmas! Savoring the possibility for more reasons than she cared
to examine too closely, Jo snuggled deeper under the
covers. She really should get up, she supposed vaguely.
But then, she yawned, why should she? She was here
to rest, wasn't she? And she certainly hadn't had a great
amount of rest since Brett's arrival. The man was a sexual dynamo!

Groaning aloud, Jo rolled onto her side. Oh, damn! Jo
was reminded of the last observation she'd made about
him before falling asleep. Damn! Damn! Damn! Why
had she gone to Vermont? Why had she gone home for
Thanksgiving? Why had she ever been born? She didn't
want to think about Vermont. She didn't want to think
about Thanksgiving. She didn't want to think, period.
The room was too quiet. Quiet was conducive to contemplation. Sighing in defeat, Jo flopped onto her back
and let memory have its way.

* * *

On arriving in Brookhaven, the small southeastern Pennsylvania town Jo had grown up in, she had been greeted warmly, if separately, by her parents. The evening before Thanksgiving had gone rather smoothly, Jo thought. But then, of course, there were church services to attend and a united false front to maintain for the benefit of her parents' fellow church members. Thanksgiving morning had not been too bad either, as her father had gone fishing, which put her mother into a good mood. That is, except for the note Jo's father had left on the kitchen table for her.

Her eyes beginning to sting, Jo lowered her lids and bit on her lip. If she lived forever she would never forget that note! How very like her father it had been, and all over an early phone call from Marybeth, a friend of Jo's from their high school days.

He'd written:

My dear successful and independent daughter,

Marybeth will call you about nine thirty. She called earlier (would you believe seven thirty?) but I told her that, like most normal people on a holiday, you were still in bed. As you were still asleep, you could not answer the phone. Inasmuch as you could not answer the phone, Marybeth could not talk to you. I told her to call again somewhere in the neighborhood of nine thirty, because I doubted you'd be up much before then. If you were to sleep till ten, and Marybeth calls at nine thirty, she still would not be able to speak to you. Anyway, if the phone rings at nine thirty, and you are awake to hear it, it will probably be Marybeth. Happy Thanksgiving, darling,

Daddy

At first Jo had laughed at the note, another in a long line of similar, whimsical missives. And then she had cried, because he was so dear and trying so hard to appear lighthearted in the face of his unhappiness. As fate would have it, her mother had entered the kitchen as Jo was wiping the tears from her cheeks. In response to her mother's concern over her tears, Jo had silently handed her the note. After skimming the lines, her mother had smiled bitterly.

"All men can be charming when it suits their purposes," Ellen Lawrence said dryly.

"Oh, Mom." Jo sighed, beginning to feel the familiar tightness in her stomach that usually appeared on her visits home. "Why do you always use that tone of voice when talking about Daddy?"

"Because he's a man," Ellen retorted. "I would have thought your experience with Gary Devlin would have taught you that they're all the same. They want one thing from a woman, then, once they get what they want, they no longer want her."

Jo remained perfectly still in hopes that her mother would expound on her subject. To date, this outburst was the closest Ellen had come to explaining the problem between herself and her husband, Mark.

"You'd do better to concentrate on your career," Ellen went on. "And forget the myth about finding happiness with a man. That kind of happiness exists only in fairy tales."

Jo knew from her mother's flat tone that the subject was now closed, and she had learned nothing of why she had always felt that she was hovering in the demarcation zone between opposing forces.

As usual, when Jo returned to New York the day after Thanksgiving, she felt depressed and vaguely responsible for the failure of her parents' marriage. Intellectually Jo knew she was in no way at fault, just as she knew, intellectually, she was not a cold, unresponsive woman like her mother. Lord, hadn't she lain awake night after night aching for the touch of one particular man? Somehow knowing something intellectually did not erase the scars carried over from childhood.

Jo sniffed in the silence of the bedroom. Then, as if her visit home hadn't been depressing enough, she had received that call from Casey Delheny! Why the hell hadn't she followed her first impulse and sent *her* assistant up to Vermont? Because she'd been hoping for a mental diversion, Jo derided herself. What she had found had had more the effect of a blow to the solar plexus. Oh, the technical problem regarding the application of one of Casey's designer's ideas to the existing plumbing plans had been relatively easy to unwrinkle. Relating to what Casey had confided to her over one too many drinks the night before Jo was due to return to New York was infinitely more difficult to handle.

"Are Brett and Marsha still together?" Casey had asked Jo morosely, swallowing almost half of her third martini.

"Together?" Jo had prompted softly, telling herself Casey, unhappy because of her lengthy separation from Sean, who was still in the Poconos, was talking through a gin-and-vermouth haze.

"Yes, you know, like in bed. That kind of together." Raising her glass, Casey gulped down the remainder of her drink. "The kind of together Sean and I have been doing damn little of lately." Waving her glass in the air, Casey indicated to their waiter that she wanted another drink. Tilting her head, she ran an assessing glance over Jo. "You know, I do believe Brett's even more of a live wire than Wolf is." She laughed insinuatingly. "Business-wise *and* otherwise. I swear, he and Marsha spent every night together locked inside his room. Yet he was hard at work bright and early every morning."

Jo had returned to New York more depressed than

before, even though she had suspected an affair between Brett and Marsha since he'd called her and as much as ordered her to find an apartment for Marsha. Walking into her office the morning she returned to find that insultingly terse note ordering her to "get in here" had been the absolute last straw for Jo. Suddenly bone weary, she had gone to Brett's office in a cold rage, prepared to resign if he refused her request for a leave of absence. She had to get away, to think and to rest.

Circles, circles, circles. Would this mental merry-go-round never end? Jo sighed. Lord, she was tired of her own thoughts! How many times must she plow over the same row before she found ground fertile enough to sprout some answers? Were there any answers? Jo moved restlessly between the tangled sheets, enjoying the sensuous feel of the fine percale against her naked skin. A smile of physical contentment softened the taut line of her mouth. Brett had given her the answer to one question, perhaps the most important one. Her initial response to him had been an outright revelation! Always before, with Gary, she had gone positively rigid the moment he began to enter. But then the moment of penetration had always come mere minutes after he had drawn her to him. Now, after experiencing Brett's lovemaking and the infinite care he took to arouse her body to the point of readiness that equaled his own, Jo realized that Gary had only been interested in self-gratification, not mutual satisfaction. In the expertise stakes, one might say that Brett crossed the wire before Gary ever left the gate.

The rather silly analogy amused Jo. Pushing back the covers with one hand, Jo lifted her other hand to smother a giggle. Jumping off the bed, she shook her head in amazement; she never giggled! Giggling was strictly for teenage girls, usually in connection with teenage boys! Telling herself her gray matter was beginning to flake, Jo grabbed up her robe and strolled to the bathroom.

Standing under the stinging-hot shower spray, Jo came to terms with what she had already decided subconsciously. She would accept whatever Brett offered her of himself for as long as he offered it.

Turning around, she dropped her head to allow the hot spray to massage the tension out of the muscles in the back of her neck. Her decision was probably not a very intelligent one, Jo mused, sighing blissfully as the jet fingers reduced her muscles to rubber. I want him, she argued in her own defense, even if I have to share him. An image of Marsha Wenger rose to torment Jo's mind, and she gritted her teeth in determination. Bump Marsha Wenger! Brett's here now, with me, and I'll hang on to him for all I'm worth, even if it means going to Florida with him. And while I'm there, I just might have a word with that blabbermouth Wolfgang Renninger!

Applying the same sharp intellect that had earned her the position of assistant to Wolf, Jo ruthlessly refused to use the old feminine cop-out of not being able to live without Brett. She could survive very well, if not too comfortably, without him and she knew it. Then again, why should she? At this moment in her life she\was deeply in love, and she was Brett's, mind, body, and soul. When her time with him was over, she would accept the hand dealt to her without a wince. What the hell! Jo shrugged, oddly cold within the cascading hot water. She didn't want commitment either. Did she? Of course not, she assured herself bracingly. Jo was so consumed with her own rationalizing, she didn't hear the door being opened or feel a draft when the shower curtain was inched aside.

"Have you taken to sleeping in the shower now too, water baby?"

With a gasp that grew into a gurgle, due to water in the mouth, Jo flung her head back to glare at Brett. "Are you trying to drown me?" she sputtered indignantly.

"I don't have to," Brett drawled dryly, unmindful of his shirt as he reached in to turn the water off. "You're doing a pretty good job of it yourself." Curling a now soaking wet arm around Jo's waist, he lifted her off her feet. "Out, water baby, before you wash yourself down the drain."

"Brett!" Jo protested his handling of her, although she didn't struggle. Only a complete idiot would take the chance of slipping out of one arm to land in a painful heap on the hard floor of a bathtub! "I was not falling asleep! I was letting the hot water work the ache out of my muscles!" Jo was so annoyed she was unaware of exactly what she was admitting to. As Brett set her carefully onto the fluffy bath mat, Jo shrugged off his arm. "And I wish you'd stop calling me that ridiculous name!"

"But I like that ridiculous name." Brett grinned. "I also like to look at you when you're all wet and slippery." The grin grew up to be a leer. "You are one sexy baby when you're wet." Bending to her, he licked a drop of water from the tip of her breast. "Hmmm . . . nectar," he murmured throatily, curling his tongue around the swiftly hardening bud before, very gently, closing his teeth on it. "And ambrosia." He passed judgment on the taste of her.

"You're positively crazy!" Jo gasped, unconsciously arching her back to give him better access to his point of interest. "Oh, Brett . . . what are you doing?" Jo knew full well what he was doing; she could feel the results of his suckling lips through the nerve endings in her loins.

"You don't know?" Brett teased, skimming his tongue across her body from one breast tip to the other. "Maybe I'm not doing it right." Before her startled eyes, he dropped to his knees. "I guess I need a lot more practice. But first, I think I'll get rid of this sopping sweater." Straightening, he whipped the garment up his body and over his head, tossing it aside carelessly. It landed in the bathtub with a soft plop that neither he nor Jo heard. Then, his hands clasping her lightly around her rib cage, his eyes watching hers, Brett enclosed one nipple inside his mouth.

It was the most incredibly erotic action Jo could imagine, Brett watching her, while she watched him make love to her body! Lightheaded, feeling her knees begin to buckle, Jo grasped Brett's shoulders to keep from falling, a purring moan tickling the back of her throat.

"Ah . . . perhaps I am doing it right." He laughed softly. Slowly, tantalizingly, he lavished attention on her midsection, stringing moist kisses down to her navel. When he dipped the tip of his tongue into the indentation, Jo shuddered and gasped his name aloud. "You're trembling," he breathed against the damp skin stretched tautly over her abdomen. "From the cold outside, I wonder, or the heat inside?"

Quickly losing touch with reality, Jo sagged against him and, at the feel of his tongue dancing around the edge of her delta triangle, she lost all control of her legs and sank to the floor before him. It was a short, fast trip from her knees to her back. The soft fibers of the bath mat caressed Jo's spine while the prickly hair on Brett's chest caressed her breasts.

With her feet flat on the floor, and her knees bent and angled out, Jo should have been uncomfortable. She wasn't. Even the chafing sensation of Brett's jean-clad thighs against the inside of her own was more exciting than abrading. The realization of his arousal as he arched his body into hers was more exciting still. Brett's hands captured Jo's breasts as his mouth captured her lips. The assault on her senses was total. Spearing her tongue into his mouth, Jo dug her nails into his shoulders, glorying in the grunt of pleasure that exploded from his throat as he thrust his hips in reaction.

"I've got to get out of these damn jeans." He groaned,

heaving himself up and away from her with obvious reluctance. "Stay warm for me, babe," he pleaded hoarsely, his hands fumbling with the belt buckle.

In fact, he didn't get completely out of the jeans. As Brett was about to lever himself to his feet, Jo called his name softly, beguilingly. The jeans, along with the cotton boxers he wore underneath them, were forgotten the moment they pooled around his knees. Whispering her name in a voice made rough with urgency, Brett filled Jo's body with his own.

The tension building inside Jo coiled tightly, and still more tightly, until, Brett's name filling her mind in an endless scream and reverberating in the tiled room like an arching whimper, it snapped, springing her into near oblivion where she was conscious only of the ecstasy shuddering through her and the sound of her own hoarsely cried name beating against her eardrums.

Jo surfaced from the mind-blanketing fog of sensuality to the awareness of the crushing weight of Brett's collapsed body on hers and the soothing sensation of his hand stroking her hip. She was still wet, only now the moisture that sheened her body was the natural result of strenuous physical activity. Raising a lazily limp hand, she smoothed her palm down his equally slick back, her sensitized skin monitoring the responsive shiver that followed the path from shoulder to waist.

"God! You are one exciting woman," Brett rasped through uneven breaths, the tip of his tongue testing the saltiness of her skin. "I feel as though I've been pulled through the wringer and hung out to dry."

"Is that good?" Jo murmured, gliding her hand up his back to tangle her fingers in his sweat-dampened hair.

"Extremely good. In fact, it's what all the noise has been about all these many centuries." Brett laughed softly. "What do the French call it? The little death, or some such?"

"Some such." Jo sighed contentedly. "It must be true because I feel a little dead right now."

Brett's bark of delighted laughter pried her heavy eye-lids up, and Jo stared, bemused, into his laughing face. He was handsome when he laughed like that, but then, he was handsome when he didn't laugh like that too. At that moment, Jo knew she could refuse him nothing. Apparently, possibly because of the dreamy expression on her face, Brett knew it too.

"You'll stay here with me through the twenty-third?" Brett was all seriousness now.

"Yes." Jo smiled as she felt his chest expand, then depress on a sigh of relief.

"And you'll go with me when I fly south on the twenty-fourth?" His chest expanded again, then became still as he held his breath.

"Yes." Jo's smile deepened as his sharply released breath feathered her cheek. Why ruin the effect by telling him she had decided to go with him before his exhausting inducement?

"Hmmm . . . have I told you you're beautiful?" Brett nibbled gently along Jo's jawline.

"Not nearly enough." Jo laughed as he nipped on her chin in tender punishment.

"And did I thank you for wringing me out so deliciously?" He teased her lips apart with his tongue.

"I think your wringing was more than enough thanks." Jo admitted to her own intense pleasure in his body.

"Do you suppose we could manage to drag our two wrung-out bodies into the shower?" Brett's eyes were silver bright in appreciation of her candid reply.

"I suppose we had better," Jo mimicked his heavily laid on drawl. "Because if I don't get up very soon, the fibers of this bath mat are going to be imbedded in my back, and your chest hair will be imbedded in my front."

Jo felt the expulsion of air into her mouth a millisecond

before she heard his shout of laughter. Displaying what she considered a disgusting amount of energy, Brett eased his body carefully from hers, then sprang agilely to his feet. His shoulders still quaking with laughter, he kicked his legs free of jeans and boxers before bending to help her up. When Jo winced at the twinge of pain the sudden exertion caused in her thighs, Brett grinned wickedly.

"All that standing under a hot shower to ease over-worked muscles for nothing," he commiserated falsely, making her aware now of what she had unconsciously admitted to him earlier. "But don't fret, darling. If the hot water doesn't work this time, just keep in mind what the physical fitness enthusiasts claim." Afraid to ask, Jo arched a delicately winged brow at him. "Why, that regular workouts will keep the muscles from tightening up." His grin telegraphed the punchline. "And I intend to work those muscles very regularly."

For two days Jo basked in the light of Brett's lovemaking and approval. And for two days she ate better than she had since leaving home at age nineteen. Brett did all the cooking. Jo did all the cleaning up. Personally, she thought she was getting the better of the bargain. In bed, Brett was demanding but gently so and, with his expert guidance, Jo emerged from behind her psychological wall of inhibitions. Never had she felt so free, so light, so at ease in the company of a man. Unselfconsciously, she teased him, sometimes dryly, other times wickedly. Brett, laughing often, responded in kind, leaving no doubt that he was enjoying himself every bit as much as she was.

Nervous apprehension began eating at Jo as the purring Porsche entered New York City. What would she find on arrival at the farm in Florida, besides a houseful of Renningers? Why had Brett's mother invited her there on a traditionally family-oriented holiday? Had

Wolf related to his mother Jo's less-than-happy family situation? And if Wolf had turned blabbermouth, why? He's probably getting bored from inactivity, Jo answered her own question. Intermingled with the whys revolving in her mind was one recurring assertion. She did not want to go to Florida.

She was going to Florida. Jo examined the thought as the plane soared into the bright winter sunlight the following afternoon. She had coaxed and wheedled and pleaded to no avail the night before. Brett had remained adamant. Oh, he had loved being coaxed, and wheedled, and pleaded with, and he laughingly admitted it, but he had remained adamant none the less.

Strangely, Brett had grown tense during the drive to the airport and had barely spoken to her since he'd buckled himself into his seat belt. Now, sitting stiffly in her seat, Jo studied his rigid profile wondering what emotional tick had burrowed into his craw. He looked, she finally decided, like a man set in his determination to do a particularly unpleasant duty.

Trying to relax, Jo closed her eyes to the sight of Brett's harshly set features and her mind to futile speculation. But one thought persisted. Was Brett tired of her already? It was not a thought conducive to in-flight relaxation.

Relaxation in the form of sleep snuck up on Jo while she wasn't looking. She woke to the mild jolt of the wheels touching down and the realization that her seat belt had been fastened for her. Brett was busy zipping his laptop into its case, and ignoring the fact that she sat beside him. The moment the plane came to a stop he stood up, only then deigning to notice her.

"I think you'll be warm enough if you drape this over your shoulders." Brett held up the camel wool coat Jo had worn onto the plane. "The pilot said the temperature is in the low fifties."

How wonderful, Jo thought wryly, turning her head to glance out the small window. He doesn't say one word from New York to Florida, then he gives me a weather report! As she could discern nothing in the darkness except the blue-tinged lights delineating the runway of the small, private landing field, Jo turned back to face him again. Brett's features still gave the impression of having been carved in granite. As she rose to her feet, hands smoothing the matching cashmere skirt she was wearing, Jo sighed tiredly. What the hell was bugging Brett, anyway? If he was bored with her company, why had he insisted she accompany him? For one mad second Jo was tempted to confront him with the question, then, mercifully, the madness subsided. In all honesty, Jo admitted to herself that she was afraid of what his answer would be. For all her self-assurances of a few days earlier that she would accept whatever Brett offered of himself for however long he offered it, she was beginning to live in fear of him walking away from her.

Standing mutely before Brett in the narrow aisle, Jo closed her eyes at the brief touch of his hands as he draped her coat over her shoulders. How had it happened so quickly? How could it be that within a period of four days she knew that losing Brett would be as painful to her as losing a vital part of herself? Her throat closing in panic at the mere thought of his rejection of her, Jo preceded Brett to the door on legs suddenly unsteady.

The mild early-evening air felt balmy after the biting cold of New York, yet Jo wished herself back along the coast of Ocean City. The snow she had hoped would continue for days had lasted less than an hour but the wind had been blowing steadily, nipping at exposed cheeks and noses right up until they had boarded the small, sleek private jet.

On the ground, Jo could see little more than she'd viewed from the plane's window. Other than the lights

positioned on the roof of the low building she assumed
was a hangar, the surrounding area was as black as the
inside of a leather glove. As Brett, his hand at her elbow,
escorted her over the uneven ground, Jo began to discern the outline of a long vehicle as their destination. As
they approached the car Jo saw a man standing beside it.
When they were within three feet of him, he swung the
back door open.

"Evenin', Mr. Brett," the man greeted laconically.

"Hello, Josh," Brett replied in the most civil tone Jo
had heard from him in hours. "The mild weather feels
good after the cold up north." Brett grinned, handing Jo
inside the roomy backseat of what she could now see was
a black Cadillac limousine.

"Gunna rain," Josh replied with the implied wisdom of
a native.

"Perhaps you're right." Brett shrugged. "But it feels
good just the same," he tacked on, settling his long frame
beside Jo on the plush seat as their bags were loaded into
the trunk.

"Wouldn't know, never been up north," Josh grunted
before closing the door smartly.

As the car rolled smoothly onto a blacktop secondary
road, Brett sliced a glance at Jo. A glance Jo felt all the
way down to her toes.

"Are you comfortable?"

What would he say if I said no? Jo wondered. Brett's
behavior in combination with her nervousness was making her irritable.

"Yes." How could one not be comfortable ensconced
in the back of a luxurious car? she thought waspishly. "Is
it very far to the farm?"

"No. Not far," Brett replied slowly, then, in an oddly intense tone: "Are you getting anxious?"

"Anxious?" Jo frowned. Why did he sound so uptight?
He didn't have to walk into a houseful of strangers.

Thank heavens Wolf would be there! "A little," she admitted. "It will be wonderful to see Wolf again."

"Thanks."

Astounded at the bitter note in Brett's tone, Jo stared at his averted head for several minutes. What in the world? Why had he said "thanks"? And in that tone? Surely he hadn't taken her eagerness to see Wolf again as an insult to him in his capacity as replacement employer? Brett had simply never struck her as the type of man who'd need employee adoration—loyalty, yes, adoration, no. Brett was too confident of himself to feel petty jealousy over his brother's popularity. So then, why the bitter thanks? Shaking her head in utter confusion, Jo turned away to glance out the window. All she saw was total blackness. Actually feeling Brett withdraw into himself, Jo stared at the blackness, biting her lip to keep from demanding he tell the driver to turn around and take her back to the airfield.

By the time the car glided to a stop in front of the house, Jo's nervousness had drowned in the flood of her rising anger. How dare Brett insist she come south with him only to ignore her? Damn him! She'd enjoy this unexpected, unwanted holiday if it killed her!

Stepping out of the car, Jo stifled a groan. The horse farm, Brett had called it. So, naturally, she'd been expecting a farmhouse! Or perhaps a ranch house, maybe. What Jo was looking at was an elegant structure that would have looked right at home dead center on any antebellum plantation! The house was illuminated by spotlights on the outside and a blaze of indoor lights from every window on the ground floor.

As they mounted the three wide steps to the front door, it was flung open by a small, wiry woman who looked to be in her late sixties. Hands on her hips, the woman waited until Jo and Brett had stepped over the threshold, then she lambasted Brett in the tone of a field marshal.

"It's about time you got here." Dark, still-young eyes snapped a quick encompassing glance over Brett. "Much later and you would have missed Christmas Eve altogether." Now the dark eyes did their snapping dance over Jo. "And you must be Jo?"

"Yes, this is Jo Lawrence," Brett answered for Jo, who was busy staring at his smiling face in consternation. How could he leap the distance between bitterness and lightheartedness so effortlessly? Jo wondered. The sound of her name shattered her bemusement. "Jo, this is Elania Calaveri, housekeeper to my mother and friend to us all."

"How do you do?" Jo murmured, offering her hand.

"So so," Elania replied surprisingly. "My arthritis is acting up. It's going to rain."

Jo had to hold her breath to keep from laughing. Brett made no attempt at self-containment. Laughing aloud, he wrapped the small woman in his arms and hugged her tight. "Josh said the same thing, so I guess it must be true."

"Of course it's true," Elania scolded. "Josh is no fool." Disentangling herself from Brett's embrace, she held out her hand. "I'll take care of your coats and bags. The gang's in the living room." She frowned at Brett. "Your mother expected you before dark. Now get in there. Supper will be in an hour."

Throughout Elania's tirade, Jo had been glancing around the enormous hall, admiring the wide, curving staircase, aware of the murmur of voices issuing from behind two oversized doors to her left. Feeling somewhat as if she'd stepped back into history, Jo was barely aware of Brett slipping the coat from her shoulders to hand it to Elania.

"Do you like the house?" he asked softly, his gaze following hers as it touched a beautifully made parson's bench along one wall.

"Like it?" Jo breathed in awe. "It's absolutely beautiful." Dragging her enthralled gaze from the rich patina of the parquet floor, she looked at him in amazement. "You grew up in this house?"

"Off and on," Brett drawled. "When I wasn't in the house in Miami, or the original family homestead in Lancaster, Pennsylvania."

"Your family's from Pennsylvania?" Jo exclaimed.

"Yes," Brett frowned. "I assumed you knew that."

"But . . . how would I have . . ."

"Brett Renninger!" Elania interrupted impatiently. "Your mother is waiting. You can show Jo over the house after dinner."

"Yes, of course." As if he suddenly remembered he wasn't speaking to her, Brett's face closed up again. "Come along, Jo. Mother's waiting." An odd grimace fleetingly twisted his lips. "They are all waiting."

Shepherding Jo across the wide hall, Brett slid the two intricately carved doors apart and motioned for Jo to precede him into the living room. As she stepped through the portal Jo did not actually see the generously proportioned room, or the many exquisite pieces of furniture that adorned it, or even the people who reposed on the delicately crafted, probably priceless, chairs and settees, although she was aware of all of them. From the moment of entrance, Jo's gaze homed in on the man sitting in a wheelchair, his left leg encased in a hip-to-toe cast that stuck out straight as a board in front of him, his left arm nestled close to his chest inside a sling, and his right arm outstretched, palm up, to her. As Jo had noted months ago, there was very little facial resemblance between the man beckoning to her and the man standing behind her. As if drawn by a magnet, Jo unhesitatingly crossed the room to Wolf Renninger.

"Ah . . ." Wolf's masculinely attractive voice revealed satisfaction. "There you are." When Jo placed her hand in his, Wolf's fingers tightened in reassurance. "How are you, Jo?"

"I'm . . . I'm fine, Wolf," Jo finally managed to whisper around the thickness in her throat. Blinking her eyes against a surge of hot moisture, she smiled tremulously at the man she loved almost as much as her father and easily as much as she would have an older brother. Wolf's year-round golden tan had faded somewhat from confinement to the house, and he had lost weight but, in essence, he was the same ruggedly attractive man upon whose broad shoulder Jo had cried—not once but several times. This tough-tender man was the only living person Jo had ever confided in about her mixed-up emotional state. And now, the realization flashed through Jo's mind, that state had progressed from unsettled to near chaos. Pushing all thoughts of herself aside, Jo studied him intently. "How are *you?*"

"As you see"—Wolf laughed, indicating his immobilized left side—"out of commission." A grin lit his face, revealing even white teeth. "But only temporarily. We'll talk later, Jo, but now—" His right hand covered a slim one resting on the arm of the chair. "You remember my wife, Micki?"

"Yes, of course." Jo's glance shifted to the woman sitting on Wolf's right. Jo had met Micki on several occasions and each time her original opinion that Micki was the perfect mate for Wolf had been reinforced. After two months in the Florida sunshine, Micki was tan, and healthy looking, and more lovely than ever. Jo's smile was soft and genuine. "You're looking very well, Micki," Jo complimented quietly. "The climate? Or your husband's improvement?"

"A little of both, I'm sure." Micki smiled serenely. "But more the latter than the former," she hastened to add when Wolf's dark brows drew together in a mock frown. "You're looking as beautiful as ever yourself," Micki returned Jo's compliment. Before Jo could respond, Wolf made a motion with his hand for Jo to turn around.

"And now, my dear." Wolf grinned. "Gird yourself to

meet . . ." He paused for dramatic effect. "The Boss."
Wolf's eyes telegraphed the message that he was fully
aware of her nervousness. His smiled confided that he was
also fully aware that Jo would never betray her nervousness. Her composure intact, Jo turned to face the
president of Renninger Corporation, actually amused with
the realization of how very well Wolf knew her. "Mother,"
Wolf said gently as Jo crossed the room to the fair, still-
beautiful woman, "my assistant, JoAnne Lawrence."

"How do you do?" Jo murmured in a tone of complete
self-containment. "Thank you for inviting me."

"The pleasure is ours, JoAnne," Violet Renninger assured Jo. Waving her left hand, she said, "We'll take the
introductions as we sit." Turning to her left, she said,
"This is my second son, Eric."

Jo pivoted to face the man patiently standing next to
his mother and felt the breath catch in her throat. Eric
Renninger was the most incredibly handsome man Jo
had ever seen. Dark-haired like Wolf, Eric had sapphire-
blue eyes that sparkled with good humor and a
singularly endearing smile.

"I feel I know you, JoAnne," he said warmly. "I've
heard so much about you." Before Jo could ask the stock
question, Eric answered it. "All of it good. So good, in
fact, that, if ever either one of my brothers gives you as
much as an uncomfortable moment, you call me. I'll
have an office ready for you within twenty-four hours."

Feeling the tension being drawn out of her by these
warm welcoming people, Jo laughed easily. "Thank you,
Eric. I'll definitely keep your offer in mind."

Releasing the hand Jo had offered to him, Eric made a
half turn to his left. "And this very pregnant lady is my
wife, Doris. Honey, the much raved-about JoAnne
Lawrence."

Doris Renninger was Jo's second shock within minutes.
Compared to Eric's heart-stopping good looks, Doris was

actually plain—except for the most arrestingly lustrous eyes Jo had ever gazed into. Dark brown with gold highlights, Doris's eyes glowed with an inner beauty.

"How do you do, JoAnne?" Doris smiled. "I'm sure this must be an ordeal for you, so I'll simply keep the ball rolling. The woman sitting next to me is the baby of this clan. Diane, called Di by all."

Di, as fair as her mother and brother Brett, had the same attractive smile that Jo was beginning to think of as pure Renninger "Hello, JoAnne," Di chirped. "Besides yourself, I am the only woman in this room who is not a Renninger. And all because of this good-looking dude standing by me. JoAnne, I'd like you to meet my husband, Hank Carlton."

"The pleasure is mine, JoAnne," Hank assured in a rich baritone, taking Jo's hand in a warm, solid grip.

"And mine. Thank you, Hank," Jo replied, beginning to feel a trifle groggy. At that moment, Violet revealed how astute she was.

"You must be parched by now," she said crisply. "Will you have a cocktail? Or a glass of wine?"

"White wine would be lovely." Jo turned to smile at her hostess. "Thank you." Relieved as she was, Jo knew there was more to come. "But where are the children?"

"Having their supper in the kitchen, fortunately." Violet's softened eyes belied her last word."They'll be descending on us soon enough. Hank, would you get JoAnne a glass of wine? And you, Jo, take that chair beside Wolf. Maybe *you* can keep him in line."

"Fat chance." Wolf chuckled, echoing Jo's exact thoughts.

"Now," Violet went on in an aggrieved mother tone, "where *is* Brett?"

"Right here, sir." Brett's tone was deliberately insolent and drew every eye in the room to where he lounged lazily yet elegantly against the closed double doors. "I didn't

want to intrude on Jo's . . . ah . . . moment of excitement."
As he spoke, he pushed his slender frame away from the
doors and strolled into the room, a cynical smile playing
on his chiseled lips.

Watching him, Jo felt a thrill, both of apprehension
and appreciation. Why the sarcasm and cynicism? she
wondered in confusion. While, at the same time, she accepted the fact that, although Brett wasn't quite as
rugged looking as Wolf or as handsome as Eric, he was
the only male she really cared to gaze upon. Sighing for
her own seemingly hopeless love, Jo observed Brett's
greetings to his family from beneath lowered lashes. As
Brett made his way, hugging the women, shaking hands
with the men, around the room, Jo registered the increased rate of her heartbeats. When Brett came to a
stop in front of Micki, Jo felt a stab of pain in her chest
at the softness of his eyes and the tenderness in his smile.

"And how are you, Micki?" he murmured, bending to
kiss Micki's tan cheek.

"I'm fine . . . now, Brett," Micki murmured back. "Welcome home."

"Thank you." He held her hand a moment longer, then
he cocked his head at Wolf, his eyes sharply assessing.
"Well, big prowler, you look like you might just make it,"
he drawled in the same insolent tone he'd used earlier.

"You can bet your Porsche I'll make it, baby brother,"
Wolf retorted, every bit as insolently. "If only for the pleasure it will give me to boot your ass out of my office."

Everyone in the room, including Brett, laughed, except for Jo, as Violet gently chided her eldest. "Behave
yourself, Wolfgang!"

Jo's initial foray into the Renninger stronghold presaged the entire visit. The children were children.
Delightful in their excitement of the day to come. Christmas day dawned, not cold and bright as Jo was accustomed
to but mild and rainy, as Elania and Josh had predicted.

The day, as all happy days are wont to do, seemed to flash by in a continuous din of laughter and family camaraderie. Though Jo had been fearful of receiving gifts proffered by people she had just met, the Renningers displayed both breeding and tact by offering none.

By the time the small jet with Jo and Brett ensconced inside soared again into the blue sky, its nose pointed north, Jo's mind was a seething mass of emotions and impressions, some good, some bad. The good impressions derived from eight days spent in the company of a truly "together" family whom, in the security of their affections for one another, had unhesitatingly included Jo within their circle of bantering communion. Savoring the memories of each day, most of which were rainy or gray outside, all of which were sun-bright inside, Jo tucked them away in a safe corner of her mind, to be taken out and enjoyed whenever she felt down.

Every one of Jo's bad impressions had been instilled by Brett. Though he had appeared to be relaxed and every bit as holiday-spirited as the rest of his family, Jo had seen through his lighthearted facade, possibly because she had come to know him so intimately. Throughout their entire visit, Brett had treated Jo with unfailing politeness. In fact, so very polite had he been, Jo had been repeatedly tempted to smack his face!

Now, sitting beside him as stiffly as she had on the flight south, Jo tried, as she had continuously over the past eight days, to equate this silent, hostile man with the ardent, laughing lover she'd come to know in the apartment in Ocean City.

Failing miserably in her attempt to understand Brett, Jo spent every quiet mile of the flight preparing herself for his leave-taking. A mask of cool composure blanking her face, Jo writhed with pain inside, knowing the pain was only a tiny measure of the agony that would strike her with Brett's final good-bye.

NINE

His facial muscles beginning to ache from being kept under rigid control, Brett curled his long fingers inward and grasped the arms of the seat to keep himself from reaching out to pull Jo into a hard embrace. Smothering a sigh, Brett faced the ills tormenting him. His arms ached to hold Jo's softness close. His lips burned with the need to crush her mouth. His body screamed to lose itself in the velvety warmth of hers.

Damn. And damn. And double damn! Brett had been mentally swearing, sometimes mildly, other times violently, for the better part of nine days. There was a knot in his stomach that felt like a rock. His neck was stiff from tension. And, after eight days of celibacy, he felt mean with frustration. Exerting every ounce of control he possessed, Brett sat statue still, staring straight ahead, positive that if he moved he'd explode, his bitterness and incrimination destroying the woman he both loved and hated.

You need help!

Right.

A muscle twitched at the corner of Brett's jaw. What the hell *can* a man do when he finds himself involved with a woman who belongs to another man? Another man who just happens to be his own brother. Resting his head against the seat back, Brett closed his eyes.

There has to be some way, some answer.

Sure, there's an answer to everything. All you have to do is find it! The problem teased and tormented Brett as the jet streaked through the winter sky. One by one he rejected each solution that his mind presented for inspection.

The most obvious solution was, of course, to simply walk away from her. To do what? Brett wondered. Merely asking himself the question was enlightening. Always before, through any kind of personal upheaval, including the last months he'd been with Sondra, Brett had invariably found surcease in his work. The business of speculating on real estate had excited him from the first time he'd ventured into his mother's office at the advanced age of ten. Now the very thought of the work waiting for him in his office merely added to the weariness Brett was experiencing.

Weariness, and frustration, and anger. Three very debilitating emotions. Brett's nervous system had become ragged from those emotions, and others, during the last nine days. You had better get your head together, pal, Brett advised himself wryly. If you're not careful, your blood pressure is going to go up and your natural resistance is going to go down. God! What an unholy mess!

Wolf.

Brett exhaled a long, drawn-out sigh, no longer caring if the woman sitting beside him heard or not. Never, never would he forget the joyful expression that had momentarily set Jo's face aglow at her first sight of Wolf. Brett was positive none of the others in the room had seen that fleeting, betraying look of love on Jo's face—with the possible exception of Wolf himself. But then, Wolf's rugged features had worn a like expression.

Moving restlessly in his seat, Brett could see again Wolf's outstretched arm, could hear the emotion in his brother's voice as Wolf growled, "There you are." Brett's teeth clamped together in much the same way they had on

Christmas Eve. And that had only been the beginning of a week full of instances when Brett had not only wanted to snarl but to lash out both verbally and physically.

They had all fallen in love with her, every one of them. His mother; Eric, Doris, Di, Hank, all the kids, Elania, and even, before Jo had been there two full days, Micki. Brett sighed again. If nothing else, he could congratulate himself on a job well done in convincing Micki of Wolf's fidelity!

Jo was depressed now. Brett felt he could actually feel the vibrations of sadness that enveloped her. Yet, up until the moment he had handed her into the car to leave for the airfield, she had been lighthearted and carefree, seemingly content simply to be within the radius of Wolf, Micki or no Micki.

How many times during their visit had he conquered the urge to grab hold of her to shake some sense into her? Brett smiled in derision. About as many times as he'd conquered the need to go to her room during the night to restake her and his claim.

What the hell had they talked about? The question stabbed at Brett's mind at regular intervals. On the three separate occasions Wolf and Jo had been closeted together in Wolf's bedroom, of all places, what had they discussed? It sure as hell had not been one Brett Renninger, for Jo had emerged from those meetings flushed and laughing! She wasn't laughing now. In fact, Brett had the distinct impression Jo was within a hairsbreadth of breaking into sobs.

Brett shifted position, as if unable to find comfort in the confining seat. The discomfort was in his head, not his butt, and Brett knew it. He also knew that were she to lose a single tear, he would haul her into his arms, promising anything, anything in an effort to stem the flow.

Brett felt a rising flood of despair. What could he do?

Exactly what in hell could he do? Perhaps if they talked about it. But what would he say? *Could I stand to hear Jo say she loves Wolf and could never give him up, even if it meant ending her relationship with me?* Brett asked himself. *No, I could not stand it,* he replied honestly. Could not. As far as Brett could see he had two choices. He could accept the status quo, or he could take a walk.

Jo was too close. How could he think clearly with her sitting less than two feet away? It had been over a week since he'd held her in his arms. And, damn it, it had been the same length of time since she'd held him.

Brett was a proud man and he knew it. Now, although the taste was vile, he swallowed that pride. He *wanted* the feel of Jo's arms holding him close to her softness. He *yearned* for the touch of her fingers stroking through his hair. He *longed* for the sound of her voice whispering love words against his lips. Walking away would not erase the wanting, the yearning, the longing, and Brett knew it. He would just have to learn to live with the status quo.

"Brett."

Brett came slowly, reluctantly out of a half sleep in which he was reliving the days spent along the shore with Jo. Turning his head, he opened his eyes to stare into hazel depths darkened by disillusionment. God! He'd give his soul to be able to set those amber flecks glimmering like gold in happiness.

"It's time to fasten your seat belt for landing."

Brett nodded in answer and, straightening his cramped body, turned away. Even her voice has a dead, toneless sound, Brett thought tiredly, automatically engaging his belt. Taking Jo to the farm had been a mistake, just as he'd known it would be. What arrogance had led him to hope that three days and four nights with him would be enough to wipe the memory of Wolf out of her mind? For, in truth, that was what he had hoped for. But they had been such wonderfully contented days, and such satisfyingly ecstatic nights. Brett had convinced himself Jo had become as lost in him as he was in her. At any rate, he qualified mentally, he had tried to convince himself. Yet, even before they'd boarded the plane the tightness had begun in his insides, and it had continued unabated until now he had the sensation of carrying a rock around in his gut.

"Will there be a car waiting?"

"Yes, of course." Brett was immediately sorry for the impatience edging his tone. For God's sake, man, he berated himself, she asked a simple, quiet question! Was it really necessary to snap at her? It's either snap or beg, and I sure as hell cannot and will not do that!

Jo asked no further questions, nor did she make any remark whatever from the time they left the plane till the limousine drew up in front of her apartment. Brett broke the silence once, to inquire if Jo's car had been returned to New York from Ocean City.

"Yes," Doug replied promptly. "I drove it in myself. It's parked in the garage at Ms. Lawrence's apartment."

Telling Doug to wait for him, Brett followed Jo out of the car and into the building. Traversing the hall beside her, Brett felt his lips twist in a grimace when Jo dug the large oddly shaped key from her purse. At the door to her apartment, he frowned at her trembling fingers as she stabbed at the slot in the lock.

"You're tired." Brett was careful to keep his tone free of inflection as he set her case inside the door. "We'll talk later. After you've had some rest." Jo's reaction startled him in its swiftness.

"No!" Jo spun to face him. "We will *not* talk later." Her eyes were no longer sad. They actually seemed to shoot sparks at him. Her voice was no longer quiet. Her tone was razor sharp with anger. "I don't know what sort of game you think you are playing, Brett, but you can deal me out of it. I thought I could . . ." Jo paused, as if to steady herself. "But I can't . . ." Her breath caught, then she repeated, on a sigh, "I just can't." Very slowly, very quietly, Jo closed the door in his face.

His body rigid, Brett stood frozen for one full minute, then, swinging around, he strode back to the elevator. What prompted him to do it, Brett had no idea yet, as he approached the security guard's desk he paused, then stopped.

"Do you remember who I am?" Brett ask the guard arrogantly.

"Yes, Mr. Renninger. Ms. Lawrence gave you clearance to enter at will two days before Christmas."

"That's correct." Brett's lips smiled at the man. "I wanted that point quite clear. I may be back some time later this evening, and I did not want any hassle over admittance. I will not have Ms. Lawrence unnecessarily disturbed. Are we in accord?" Brett deliberately arched one brow imperiously.

"Yes, sir."

What a bastard you are, Brett accused himself wryly as he pushed through the entrance doors. But then, if you never take a step, you never get anywhere, in *any* direction, he exonerated his rather overbearing behavior.

In the car, Brett gnawed on the wisdom of returning to see Jo later that evening. He *knew* his attitude had been less than charming throughout their stay at the farm. On reflection, he admitted he'd acted out the part of the name he'd moments ago called himself to the letter. Why couldn't he just go to Jo and confess that he was so miserable, because he was so miserable?

On entering Wolf's apartment, Brett set his suitcase aside, tossed his jacket onto a chair, poured himself a double shot of Scotch then, telling himself he had to be hungry since he'd eaten nothing since early that morning, ambled into the kitchen. Opting for eggs, as he was certainly not in the mood to wax creative, he popped two slices of bread into the toaster while melting butter in a small frying pan. Breaking two eggs neatly in one hand, he dropped them, yolks intact, into the sizzling butter. A moment later he turned away from the stove to butter the toast, then, turning back, he grasped the handle of the pan to shift it gently back and forth a few times before, with a slight snap of his wrist, the eggs slid up and over, perfectly flipped. Brett waited another moment, then lifted the pan from the burner to slide the over light eggs onto a plate. He had taken three steps to the table when, spinning around, he walked to the sink to dump the combined eggs and toast into the disposal. Brett tossed back the last of his whisky as the mechanism ate his supper.

Brett returned to the living room for a second helping of his liquid meal. His second double shot tempered with ice and water, he climbed the stairs to his bedroom. Between long sips at his drink he undressed slowly. He strolled into the bathroom where he brushed his teeth, shaved his face, and showered his body. He pulled on pants, a soft sweater, and ankle boots, and scooped his jacket from the chair on his way toward the door.

His bootheels hitting the sidewalk with a muffled thud, Brett strode purposefully in the direction of Jo's apartment. Damned if he'd lie awake one more night, aching with the memory of how good their lovemaking had been! Damned if he'd give up on a relationship he *knew* would be satisfying to the both of them—if she'd give it a chance to get off the ground! And damned if he'd let her get away with closing the door in his face!

At his destination, Brett nodded curtly to the doorman, and a moment later he dipped his head again to the security guard. Neither man attempted to impede his progress.

At Jo's door, Brett stabbed the button to her doorbell with quick impatient motions of his forefinger. Nothing.

Grumbling an expletive, Brett slipped his hand into his pants pocket and withdrew his gold keyring. Detaching the large key from the others, he unlocked the door and stepped inside.

"Jo?"

Nothing.

"Jo?" Brett crossed the living room to the bedroom. "Where are you?" Brett's question was answered not by a voice but by the sound of the shower in the bathroom. As he entered the room, the sound came to an abrupt stop. Standing in the middle of the room, facing the bathroom door, Brett waited. Two minutes. Five minutes. He was pulling the sweater up over his shoulders when Jo came out of the bathroom tying the sash on the striped robe she'd worn in the apartment in Ocean City.

"Brett!" His name exploded from her lips with a gasp. "How did you get in here?"

"I'm a second-story man in my off hours," Brett muttered through the soft wool.

"And what do you think you're doing?" Jo demanded, charging across the room to stand before him, hands on hips.

"I'm getting undressed for bed." Staring her in the eyes, Brett tossed the sweater aside and began working on his belt buckle.

"Like hell you are!" Jo choked in fury.

"Like hell I'm not," Brett corrected softly. "It seems bed is the one place you and I can communicate. And, the way I feel right now, I just might communicate through most of the night." As he lowered the zipper on the pants, Brett watched Jo stiffen with outrage. Well, he shrugged mentally, at least when she's furious she talks to me.

"You know," she finally managed through gritted teeth, "for an educated man, you certainly have a flair for crudity."

"Nothing crude about it," Brett contradicted smoothly. "And you know it." Slowly, deliberately, he let his eyes caress her body, feeling a quickness in his loins at the realization that she was wearing nothing but satiny skin underneath the classy, sexy robe. "I said we'll talk later," he went on softly, unselfconsciously stepping out of both pants and boxers. "And we will talk . . . later." By now Jo's eyes were wide, her gorgeous lashes fluttering, her breath coming in short, angry puffs. God! Brett marveled. She is one beautiful woman.

Reaching out, Brett caught the tie belt of her robe and began loosening the knot.

"Brett!" Her throat worked spasmodically as she swallowed. "Brett, you can't do this! I won't let you."

Brett slid the loop free.

"Brett! Stop this!" Jo demanded in an unconvincing whisper.

The knot untied, Brett gently slid the silky material off Jo's trembling shoulders. Dropping his arms, he stood still, drinking in the longed-for sight of her. It had been nine nights since he'd held the slim loveliness of her close to his own hardness. It seemed more like nineteen years. Stifling a groan, Brett reached out again, this time to lightly grasp her shoulders. The feel of her under his hands set off a chain reaction Brett could not have controlled had his life depended on it. Sliding his hands urgently down her back, Brett drew the warmth and softness of Jo against him, a sigh of real pain escaping his tightly constricted throat.

"Jo . . . my Jo."

Brett, unaware he was saying it all, felt he needed to say so much, much more, yet all that came out was her name. The tips of her breasts touched his chest with the effect of electric probes, creating shock waves that spiraled wildly through his body. Brett's arms tightened convulsively, crushing her to him. His hands, hungry to touch her everywhere at once, moved with restless abandon from her shoulders to the base of her spine and back again.

"Oh, Brett! Oh, Brett."

There was a universe of mixed-up meanings contained in the husky, defeated sound that whispered into Brett's mind as well as his ears. His mind, totally absorbed with the overriding need to make her finally, irrevocably his, caught only the nuance of passion in her tone. Elation singing through him, Brett took her mouth with commanding force. Jo's capitulation was immediate and frenzied. Her hands skimmed the length of his body to grasp his buttocks, fingers clenching, urging the ultimate intimacy.

Brett literally went wild. Shuddering with the desire rocketing through his body, he began moving, backing her to the bed. Then he was on the bed, on Jo, in Jo, taking, taking, wanting more, and yet more, greedily demanding she give everything of herself, his body quivering in exultation of the primitive possession, his mind chanting: mine, mine, mine.

It was over very quickly. His head thrown back, Brett could feel the tug of strain on the taut tendons in his neck. Striving, driving, propelling himself to the very limit of endurance, Brett gasped harshly at the intensity of near pain at his moment of culmination, reveling in the echoing gasp that was torn from Jo's throat.

In a state of complete collapse, Brett lay with his head against Jo's breast, dragging great gulps of air. Brett lay still while his body went through the process of regeneration. His mind, emerging from the fog of sensuality, began clicking away like a well-made timepiece.

Never, never, not even that first time with Jo in Ocean City had Brett so completely lost contact with reality during the act of lovemaking. And never had he wished to remain so completely lost. Even in his exhausted condition a burst of adrenaline shot through his system at the memory of what he'd just experienced. Brett had always doubted the existence of the absolute sexual pinnacle. He doubted no longer.

Monitoring Jo's still-rapid heartbeat, a thrill snaked through Brett's insides. Jo had not surrendered! The thrill changed direction to skitter up his spine. Jo had *not* surrendered! If he had been impatient, rough, demanding, and he had, Jo had been equally so. He had witnessed the same tautness cording her slim white neck that had tightened his with tension. He had felt the sting of her oval nails in his buttocks as her fingers flexed and gripped in a frantic effort to draw him deeper and yet deeper into her body as if in craving to absorb him totally within her being. His lips now tasted the salty flavor of her sweat-sheened skin. Joyous delight followed the path of the thrill. In no way had she surrendered!

I love her! I love her. With my mind, with my body, with my soul! God! Why can't she love me too?

Brett felt an unfamiliar hot sting in his eyes and his brain went numb for an instant. He could not! He could not! He hadn't wept since his father's death during that stupid yacht race! Holy Mother of God! What *was* he going to do? The mere possibility of losing Jo now froze his heartbeats. *I can't let her go,* Brett's mind roared back to life. *I cannot let her go.*

The slight stirring of Jo's body beneath him alerted Brett to the realization that he was very likely crushing her slim frame with his weight. Easing himself from her, he stretched out beside her on the now-rumpled spread. Brett knew he should move, if only to get under the spread. Jo was so quiet. Was she sleeping? Shifting onto his side, Brett gazed down on her, a tender smile curving his lips at the sight of the dark swath of hair partially covering her face. Raising his hand to her face, he gently smoothed the swath away from her temple before trailing his fingers to her cheek. Several obstinate silky strands clung to Jo's eyelashes. Being careful not to startle her, Brett brushed her lashes with his fingertips, then became absolutely still.

Jo's lashes were wet! Her face was *wet!* Why was she crying? Had he hurt her! But she had not cried out, had not withdrawn in any way! Quite the opposite, she had attacked, consumed, devoured! As if, as if . . . A chill pervaded Brett's body. Jo had responded to him with all the fervor of a woman with the man she . . . No! Brett closed his eyes in an attempt to block out a face. He could not close his mind to the taunting whisper of a name.

Wolf.

Brett shook his head sharply once.

No. No. Please, no. He didn't want to hear it. Still, he had to know.

"Why are you crying?" His voice was soft, but tight with strain. "Did I hurt you?"

"No!" Jo's lids flew up and her head moved briefly on the pillow.

"Then why are you crying?" he insisted.

"It . . . it's nothing, really." The nothing started a fresh flow trickling down her cheeks. "I'm . . . being silly."

"Is it him?" To keep from shouting, Brett whispered. "Were you thinking of him?" Suddenly incensed, he leaned over her, his face close to hers. Teeth clenched, he rasped, "Was *he* in your mind . . . while *I* was in your body?"

"Brett!" Wide-eyed, Jo stared at him. "I don't . . ."

"Was he?" Brett's shout cut across her voice.

"NO!" Jo shouted back at him. "It's over, Brett. I swear it's over. It's been . . ."

"All right!" Brett again cut her off harshly. "I don't want a blow by blow of the ending." He leaned even closer to her. "As long as it is completely over. I want your word on that, Jo. I won't allow you to use my body to appease a hunger for another man."

"Use *you*?" Jo exclaimed on a shriek. "How—"

"Your word, Jo," Brett inserted quietly, ominously.

"You have it!" Jo actually snarled at him. "And don't you ever, ever again accuse *me* of using *you*. Do you understand?"

"Perfectly." Brett's teeth snapped together. Now what? Brett wondered, returning her glare fiercely. Well, when in doubt . . . kiss her! Closing the inches that separated them, Brett covered her mouth with his own.

At first Jo's lips remained stiff and tightly closed. Then they softened. Then they parted. Then they grew warm. The warmth quickly turned to heat. Heat burst into flames. Instant replay; another conflagration. Tongues pierced, hands searched, bodies melded, one into the other. Who owned whom?

Normal breathing restored, Brett drew Jo's sleep-heavy body close to his own. Already half asleep himself, the thought wafted through his mind again. Who owned whom? Beginning to drift, Brett lifted a hand to smother a yawn.

Who owned whom? *Who cares?*

The automatic alarm that jangled inside Brett's head every working morning at seven fifteen pried his eyes open the next morning. His eyes wide open, he frowned. When, he asked himself, had he and Jo made the move from on top of the comforter to beneath the covers? Memory stirred and Brett vaguely recalled waking in the night feeling chilled. Rousing Jo, he had coaxed her up enough to allow him to pull the covers down. She was back to sleep before he'd finished tucking the comforter around the two of them.

Throwing his arms over his head, Brett stretched his body awake. Lord, he was hungry. He needed some food. He needed a shower. But, first, he needed a kiss. Turning onto his side, he propped his head up on one hand. His expression soft, Brett studied the woman he loved. In sleep, Jo was even more beautiful, but in a different way. She looked younger than her twenty-eight years, defenseless, more vulnerable. Staring at Jo's sleep-flushed cheeks, her tender mouth, and her wildly disordered hair, Brett felt his throat constrict with emotion.

Frowning in concentration, Brett raked his mind for a single memory, a single instance when he'd ever felt so very strongly about another woman. His mind came up blank. Oh, he'd experienced the usual instinctive protectiveness for Sondra. Sondra had been his wife and as his wife she deserved his protection. Brett smiled. What he'd felt for Sondra paled to transparent in comparison to what he was feeling now for Jo. Brett's smile broadened in self-derision. Of course, he had faced the fact long ago that what he'd felt for Sondra had more to do with self-indulgence and infatuation than love. The woman he gazed upon now Brett loved with every fiber of his being. Brett's smile vanished.

On consideration, the whole concept was pretty damned scary!

Brett lowered his head, then caught himself up short less than an inch from her lips. Don't wake her, let her sleep, his conscience advised. She gave you infinite pleasure during the night, not once but several times. Let her sleep, she has earned it. His smile back in place, Brett eased his body away from Jo's and off the bed.

Twenty-odd minutes later Brett was tugging his crumpled sweater over his head when a slight movement on the bed caught his attention. Pulling the garment into place, he glanced up to find Jo watching him guardedly.

"Good morning." Brett offered the greeting in a neutral tone.

Jo continued to watch him unblinkingly, her expression wary. "Good morning," she responded in a sleep-husky murmur. "Have you eaten?"

"Not yet." Brett stood still, his hands at his sides, regarding her closely. What was she thinking? The alert, somewhat fearful expression in her eyes puzzled him. It was almost as if she was waiting for an inevitable blow to fall. Why? Unable to come up with an answer, Brett shrugged. "I thought I'd stop for something to eat on my way back to the apartment."

"I see," Jo replied tonelessly.

What does she see? Brett felt a stirring of anger. What the hell was going on in that beautiful head of hers? Jo ended his fruitless search for answers.

"You were going to leave without waking me?"

The mild reproach in her voice put a spur to his anger. "Of course not!" Brett was barely aware of his fingers curling into his palms. Cool it, he cautioned himself. Make haste slowly here. What had he expected from her this morning? The query was rhetorical, and Brett knew it. He'd expected Jo to be as she'd been on the mornings they'd wakened together in Ocean City . . . warm, responsive, smiling. The disappointment that lanced through Brett robbed him of a portion of the energy he'd felt on awakening. Choosing his words carefully, Brett went on, "I had every intention of waking you. I put the coffee on to brew. It should be ready in a few minutes." A small smile Brett didn't particularly like shadowed Jo's lips.

"The holidays are over," she said flatly.

"Jo, what . . ."

"You'd better go," she interrupted impatiently. "You'll be late. And so will I."

Now what in hell . . . ? Brett frowned. Was she throwing him out? After last night? Oh, no! No way! Brett's balled hands tightened into hard fists. "I was going to suggest you take an extra day off."

"Why?" Jo shot the word at him.

Why? Brett was hard put not to laugh. God! He'd have thought it was obvious. He had loved her to a standstill; she'd been exhausted when he'd finally allowed her to rest. Come to that, so had he . . . and he felt, or at least he *had* felt, like he could fight his weight in wildcats. An unknowing, sardonic smile played on his lips. Hell! He was having trouble fighting his weight in JoAnne Lawrences! Exasperation serrated the edge of Brett's tone.

"Why not?"

"I don't want to stay home!"

"Then don't!" Brett snapped. Immediately regretting his loss of patience, Brett drew a deep calming breath. Jo was still lying flat on the bed, the covers up to her chin. Very probably, Brett decided, because she was naked. He didn't like the connotations to that consideration. During their time together by the ocean, Jo had been completely unselfconscious with him. An uncomfortable sensation of defeat crawled along the floor of his stomach. Hanging on to his temper, Brett explained calmly, "You had requested a leave to rest. What with one thing and another"—he shrugged—"you've had very little of it. I thought you could take the day to just . . . catch up."

"I'm fine," she assured him quietly.

"Okay, then I'll see you in the office?" Brett lifted one eyebrow slightly.

"Yes."

Brett didn't move. Staring into her eyes, he waited to see if Jo would say anything else. She didn't. She stared back at him, her expression also one of waiting. Say it. Now. The command flashed from Brett's brain to his lips.

"I'll transfer my things tonight." Barely breathing, Brett watched Jo's eyes flicker and widen, observed the sudden rigidity of her body.

"W-what . . ." Jo stopped to clear her throat before continuing in a husky whisper, "What are you saying?"

"I'm moving in with you." Brett heard the steel underlining his soft statement. From her expression of shock, it was obvious Jo heard it too.

"Brett, is . . ." Jo paused to moisten her lips with the tip of her tongue. "Is that wise?" Grasping the covers in one hand, she sat up to stare at him in consternation. "I mean, word of it will zing through the office grapevine within a week!"

Brett had to put a clamp on the elation that was dancing wildly through his system. He had won! Hot damn! He had won! Jo had not denied him the right to share her world or her body! She was simply concerned about propriety! He swallowed a whoop of laughter.

"Need I tell you what the office gossips can do to, and with, themselves?" he drawled. The amusement swelled at Jo's expression of censure. How in hell, after being Wolf's mistress, had she retained her naivete? The query killed Brett's amusement. Why had he had to think of Wolf, and the role he'd played in Jo's life, now? A fresh spurt of anger threatened to swamp his elation. *Had* played, Brett repeated in an effort to contain his emotions. The operative word here is *had*. While calming himself, Brett let his eyes feast on Jo's invitingly disheveled appearance. Taking one step toward her, Brett caught himself up short. You've got to go to work, Renninger, he cautioned in an attempt to quell the sudden need to hold Jo in his arms. Get started on the day, he advised himself. The night will come more swiftly if you keep busy in the interim.

"Why are you staring at me like that?" The wariness was back in Jo's expression and her voice cracked with uncertainty.

"I'm thinking about having you for breakfast," Brett answered softly, his elation soaring again as her wariness and uncertainty were washed away by a look of surprised delight.

"I think you'd probably work a lot better on bacon and eggs," Jo replied, straight-faced.

This time Brett made no effort to contain his laughter. "I'd say you are probably right," he agreed, grinning. "Even though it won't be near as much fun." Brett held his breath. Was the tension gone for good? Was the easiness between them back to stay?

"Perhaps not," Jo murmured. Then, to Brett's delight, she fluttered her long lashes at him coyly. "You could always plan on having me for dessert. Anticipation sharpens the appetite, you know."

Brett took another step toward her. "If my appetite gets any sharper," he growled, "I'll slash myself on it and bleed to death." Brett had no qualms whatever about admitting to Jo how very much he desired her. Hadn't he admitted as much silently, with his body, throughout the long night?

Sheer enjoyment of her tempered Brett's arousal. Laughing softly, he strode to the bed. Bending to her, he brushed her mouth with his lips, afraid to allow himself a deeper taste of her. He *had* to get to work!

Brett spun away from the bed to stride across the room. Scooping his jacket off the chair he'd tossed it onto the night before, he slanted a devilish glance at Jo.

"Move it, water baby," he ordered gently. "I want to see you in my office at nine thirty." Still grinning, he sauntered out of the bedroom.

That evening, as promised, Brett transferred his clothing and few personal belongings to Jo's place, ignoring the taunting thought that he was moving out of Wolf's apartment into Wolf's apartment. As he stowed his shaving gear onto the medicine cabinet shelf Jo had cleared for him, Brett decided to contact a real estate agent about finding another place for them.

Surprisingly, they made the adjustment of living together very quickly and, within two weeks Brett wondered how he'd ever thought he was content living alone. They learned and accepted each others faults—in Jo's case, her habit of kicking her shoes off the moment she entered the apartment and forgetting to pick them up again; Brett did it for her. In Brett's case, his failure to snap the cap on the toothpaste tube; Jo did that for him. They worked together well. They played together joyously. They laughed together often.

Near the end of January Brett asked Jo if she'd like to go skiing. Jo's response was less than enthusiastic.

"I don't know how to ski, Brett. And, to be honest, I'm not all that eager to learn how."

"You could give it a try, honey," Brett coaxed, itching to get on the slopes again. "If you don't like it, you could always relax by the fire with a hot toddy while I attempt to break a leg."

Jo hesitated but Brett gave her such a woebegone expression she laughingly relented and agreed to go with him, exactly as he'd hoped she would.

"Terrific!" Brett exclaimed as eagerly as a kid might have. Jumping out of his chair, he walked restlessly around the living room, unaware of the gentle smile curving Jo's lips as she watched him. "Let's see now." He began making plans aloud. "Accommodations are no problem. I've retained the room at that motel up in Vermont for office space in case I needed it." Brett was equally unaware of the slight tightening of Jo's lips. "I have that meeting in Atlanta next week." Jo had absolutely refused to go to Atlanta with him. Brett was still not completely reconciled to her stand on Atlanta but, with this new victory, he decided to stop badgering her about it. "Suppose we say the week after next?" One brow lifted quizzically, he swung to face her. "Okay?"

"You love skiing that much?" Jo laughed.

"Yes," Brett answered simply. "And I haven't stepped into boots once this winter."

This time Brett was fully aware of Jo's gentle smile. "Okay," she agreed softly. "The week after next."

Brett thanked Jo, twice, after they'd turned out the light in the bedroom that night.

Atlanta was a drag for Brett, even though the meeting he'd set up with a local realtor proved satisfying to both of them. Brett missed Jo as much as he would have the loss of his right arm. His impatience to get all existing details cleared up did not go unnoticed by Richard Colby.

"Is she beautiful?" Richard asked out of the blue while they were discussing swamp drainage, of all things, the day before Brett's departure.

"Very," Brett responded immediately. Then, his tone dangerous, Brett retorted, "Why?"

"No reason." Richard, unperturbed by Brett's tone, smiled easily. "It's obvious you can't wait to get back to her. Why wait till tomorrow? We can clean this drainage thing up by dinnertime. I can handle all the nitpicking details myself. There's no reason you could not fly back to New York tonight." His smile broadened. "Unless, that is, you're enthralled with my company."

Brett's smile was as broad as Richard's. "Thanks, buddy. Remind me to give you a raise."

"Why do you think I made the suggestion?" Richard drawled dryly.

It was late by the time Brett let himself into the dark, silent apartment. Moving cautiously but unerringly, he made his way through the living room to the bedroom. Inside the bedroom he placed his case carefully out of the way, then stood still to allow his eyes to adjust to the unrelenting darkness. When he had his bearings, Brett walked softly to the side of the room's one large window to tug gently on the cord that worked the draperies. The heavy, lined drapes slid silently apart giving access to a pale shaft of moonlight. A low moaning sound froze Brett in his tracks as he turned from the window. Every sense alerted, he focused his gaze on the moonlight-washed figure lying on the bed.

Jo moaned again and, frowning with concern, Brett crossed to the bed in three long strides. The sight that met his eyes stole Brett's breath.

Jo was lying on her back in the center of the bed, her arms flung wide, her fingers grasping at the sheet, nails scratching the smooth surface. Her naked body was only partially covered, and even as Brett stared her legs thrashed about, dislodging the comforter completely. Gazing transfixed at her white skin gleaming in the moonlight, Brett felt a kick of desire in his loins. A sighing sound drew his eyes to her face. Her head moved restlessly as another sigh whispered through her slightly parted lips.

She's dreaming, Brett concluded in bemusement. Watching her legs, Brett's heartbeat accelerated. She's dreaming she's making love! Brett closed his eyes as another low moan sent a shiver of excitement careening through his body. Barely conscious of what he was doing, Brett opened his eyes, then, fastening his gaze on her writhing body, he began to undress. When the last piece of his constricting clothing had been discarded, Brett stepped up to the bed. Sliding onto the cool sheet beside Jo, he ran one palm lightly from her ankle to her hip. Immediately Jo's leg moved to press against his hand and a low groan of need murmured from deep in her throat. Brett was sliding his hand over her rib cage when a chilling thought stopped him cold.

Who is she dreaming she's making love with?

Watching her, wanting to know, not wanting to know, Brett closed his mind to the visage and name of one man. *She's mine,* he raged silently. *Awake or asleep, Jo is mine!* Blocking out the idea that what he was doing could very well be wrong, Brett deliberately took possession of her silky-skinned breast.

"Brett."

Not even a whisper, hardly more than a sigh, yet his name swelled to a joyous crescendo in Brett's mind. Jo was dreaming *he* was making love to her! Unhesitatingly, Brett carefully slid his body between her soft thighs, determined to make her dream a reality. Covering her gently, yet not joining their bodies, Brett touched Jo's parted lips with his own. Before entering her, Brett wanted her fully conscious of who was doing what to whom. The touch of his lips and hands feather light, Brett adored her body.

"Brett?" Jo's voice was fuzzy. She was not yet fully awake.

"Yes, love?" Brett murmured, kissing the corner of her mouth.

"Oh, Brett. Is it really you?" Jo was coming out of sleep, but falling into passion. Her hands forsaking the sheet, she grasped Brett instead.

"Yes, love," Brett assured softly. "It's really me." He gave her the feel of his tongue along her bottom lip for proof.

"I missed you so." Jo's arms tightened; her thighs relaxed. "Don't make me wait. Please." She arched her body to his with the plea and sighed when Brett granted it.

Moving slowly at first, savoring the velvety softness of her, Brett twined his fingers in Jo's hair and kissed her tenderly on her cheeks, her eyes, her chin. When his lips brushed hers she groaned.

"Kiss me. Love me. Oh, Brett, I need you." The moan deepened into a sob. "I need you." That's when the brainstorm hit him. Teasing her with his body's slow strokes, Brett brushed Jo's quivering lips again.

"Marry me, Jo." Brett's voice was low but firm with conviction.

"What!" Jo's heavy lashes fluttered, then lifted. She stared at him with passion-clouded eyes. "What did you say?"

"Marry me." Brett increased his stroke, restraining a smile at the immediate response she made with her body.

"But . . ."

"We're good together, love," He brushed her lips harder. "You know we're good together. Not just like this." Brett thrust against her, then slowed again. "We're good together in everything."

"Brett, we can't!" Jo's breathing was shallow now and getting more shallow with each passing instant. "We don't . . ."

Brett closed her mouth with his own, certain he didn't want to hear whatever she was going to say. He let his tongue match the motion of his body. When Jo was clinging to him, whimpering in need, Brett denied her his mouth.

"Will you marry me, Jo?" Brett stopped moving entirely.

Jo seemed unable to open her eyes. "Brett . . . please," she wailed.

"Will you marry me, Jo?" Brett kissed her very hard, and very fast.

"Yes."

The whisper trembled through Jo's lips. Relief trembled through Brett's body. Strength, power, followed on the heels of relief and, positive he could fly at that moment if he so wished, Brett gave in to the fire raging in his body.

Sated physically, satisfied emotionally, content in his mind, Brett lay cradling Jo's relaxed body close to his own. "Are you asleep?" Moving his head slowly, he brushed a few damp tendrils away from her temple with his lips.

"Yes." Jo's warm breath tingled the skin on his chest.

Lifting one hand to her chin, Brett turned her face up to his. "You won't back out. Will you, Jo?" he asked quietly, staring directly into her love-softened eyes.

"No, Brett, I won't back out."

Brett fought the urge to close his eyes in relief. Although he wasn't overjoyed at the underlying note of calm acceptance in Jo's tone, he consoled himself with the realization that her tone had also contained firm conviction. For now, Brett decided he could live with the knowledge that Jo would not attempt to repudiate her agreement to legalize their union on the grounds of duress. They could make it work, he *would* make it work, Brett vowed. He had to because he really had no other choice; Brett knew he could not let Jo go now. Brett knew also that he belonged to Jo every bit as much as he felt she belonged to him. It was somewhat scary but, Brett shrugged mentally, there it was. Bending to her, he kissed her tenderly.

"We can be married in Vermont next week." The suggestion made, Brett held his breath, waiting for her reaction. He didn't have to hold his breath long.

Jo's eyes, suddenly clear, alert, widened in shock. "Next week?" Her voice cracked and she cleared her throat. "Vermont? Brett, I can't be ready to get married in less than a week!"

Positive he detected a note of panic creeping into her tone, Brett tightened his grasp on Jo's chin. "You can be ready." To punctuate his assertion he kissed her deeply. "You *will* be ready." His mouth crushed hers again. "We will be married"—another brief kiss—"next week . . . in Vermont. I'm sure Casey and Sean will be delighted to stand witness." Brett's punishing kisses were beginning to backlash. Feeling his body harden with renewed passion, Brett conveyed his need to Jo with his mouth, and his tongue, and his groaning words.

"Say yes again, Jo, please."

"To which question?" Jo gasped as he trailed his fingers from her chin to her breast. "The one you're asking with your words? Or the one you're asking with your body?"

Laughing softly, Brett sucked gently on her lower lip. "Say yes to both."

"Yes to both," Jo parroted at once, then qualified, "On one condition."

As by now the fire racing through Brett had consumed his brain, he would have consented to almost anything. "Name it," he murmured into her mouth.

"This time"—Jo hesitated, then rushed on—"I want to make love to you."

This was a condition? Laughter shook Brett's body. Ringing his arms wide, Brett threw himself back away from her to lay stretched out on the bed. "Take me," he cried, grinning wickedly. "I'm yours."

Brett was to remember his words several times over the days that followed. And, every time he did, he felt again the thrill he'd experienced in being taken by Jo. When that exceptional woman decided she was going to make love to a man, she put her heart and soul into the effort. Days later Brett's body still tingled from the effective way she'd tormented him with her soft, caressing hands and her sweet, hungry mouth. Marriage to Jo, Brett decided, still lost in bemusement, should prove to be one interesting experiment.

Surprisingly, as the days until their departure for Vermont shortened, Brett found himself growing more and more nervous. Why the tension? Why the jumpiness? Why the crawly sensation in his stomach? Brett quizzed himself repeatedly. It was not as if he were being coerced into matrimony. Quite the contrary. If a charge of coercion were to be leveled, *he'd* be the guilty party. Strange, he thought, he had no recollection of any nervousness at all before he and Sondra were married. Brett's thinking process danced around the edges of the answer to his uptight feeling right up till he and Jo arrived in Vermont.

As Brett had predicted, Casey and Sean were both delighted and flattered to be asked to witness the nuptials.

Casey, bubbling over with the news that she was pregnant, threw herself into the wedding spirit and, by the time the legalities were taken care of, had made all the arrangements for the ceremony.

Brett and Jo were married in a picturesque New England church on a Thursday morning in early February. Immediately following the brief service, Casey and Sean whisked them off to an equally picturesque but decidedly elegant restaurant for a champagne wedding breakfast that lasted through four bottles of the expensive wine and most of the afternoon. From the restaurant, the Delhenys poured Brett and Jo into a cab with the advice to do everything they might do.

"Which should take you until sometime tomorrow afternoon," Casey confided laughingly.

It was then that Brett, not drunk by a long shot, but feeling little pain, faced the reason for his nervousness during the previous week. In a word, Brett identified his malady. That word was fear. The cause and symptoms had vanished when Jo signed her name to the marriage certificate.

The first thing Brett did after he'd locked the motel room door was kiss his new bride, satisfyingly and thoroughly. The second thing he did was lift the telephone receiver and dial his mother's private office number in Florida. When his mother answered in her endearingly brisk tone, Brett, wasting no time on formalities, went directly to the reason for his call.

"Jo and I were married this morning, Mother." Not being able to resist, Brett added insolently, "We'll accept a large check for a wedding present." From behind him, Brett heard Jo's shocked gasp and grinned. His grin widened at his mother's retort.

"You'll accept what I choose to give you, smart ass." There was a telling pause, then Violet said solemnly, "Congratulations, Brett. JoAnne is a lovely young woman."

Violet's tone changed to reveal confusion and a tinge of hurt feelings. "But why didn't you let us know? You could have been married at the farm."

"I've done that. Remember?" Brett's grin was gone, replaced by a grimace. Brett had coolly and deliberately chosen not to inform his family about his plans simply because he knew his mother would suggest the farm as a perfect site for the wedding. Brett's reason for not wanting to be married at the farm had absolutely nothing to do with memories of Sondra and everything to do with Wolf being in residence there. At his mother's sharply indrawn breath and murmured "Oh, Brett, how foolish of me. I'm sorry," Brett made an effort to soften his rough tone. "It's all right, sir, forget it. Besides, I wanted to go skiing on my honeymoon.

Following his mother's request, Brett handed the phone to Jo, then stood patiently while she responded to her new mother-in-law's well wishes. When the connection to Florida had been broken, Brett again handed the receiver to Jo.

"Your turn to face the firing squad," he teased. "But make it quick, love, your bridegroom is getting itchy."

Wondering at the odd expression on Jo's face, Brett studied her as she placed the call. There was something wrong with Jo's family situation, Brett knew. Something that had hurt her. And, although Brett knew Jo had informed her parents that she was getting married, it was obvious she was not happy about making this call. Brett listened intently to Jo's short, terse conversation, anger stirring when she winced at something that was said to her. The moment she'd replaced the receiver, Brett enfolded Jo in his arms.

"It's all right, water baby," Brett soothed as she began to weep. "Don't cry, love."

"You don't understand," Jo sniffed, burrowing into his chest. "Talking to my mother always makes me cry. You see, my mother and father hate each other. And it's so sad . . . They're both so very unhappy."

What could he say to comfort her? Coming from a happy family, Brett hadn't the vaguest idea. So, instead of words, he comforted her with caresses. Jo didn't cry very long.

TEN

Jo woke to the delicious sensation of her husband's lips exploring her face.

Her husband! A shiver of pleasure rippled through Jo's mind and body. Brett's arm, bent at the elbow, made a V on her chest; his fingers combed through the tangled mass of her hair. Circling his wrist with her hand, Jo lifted it to peer at the face of the slim gold watch, he'd forgotten to remove in the heat of the moment the night before. The digits pulsed to eleven fifteen. She had been Mrs. Brett Renninger for over twenty-four hours!

Eleven fifteen! Good heavens! Jo stared at the watch in disbelief. She never slept past nine in the morning, not even on her days off or on holidays! Of course, that was before one very handsome man breezed into her life, and her bed, keeping her awake until the darkness of night gave sway to the pearl gray of predawn. A memory thrill tiptoed down Jo's spine. Had any bride ever had a more ardent bridegroom? Had any bride ever experienced such consummate ecstasy? Jo very seriously doubted it. But, even so, it was time to get up! Even if she infinitely preferred to lay luxuriating in her marriage bed.

"Brett?"

"Hmmm?" Brett's warm breath caressed her ear.

"Do you know what time it is?" Gulping back a gasp, Jo managed a steady tone.

"Time to make love to you again?" Brett responded immediately, hopefully, gently nipping at her earlobe.

Jo tried, and failed, to suppress the laughter that bubbled into her throat. "What are you?" she demanded in a falsely stern voice. "Some kind of sex maniac?"

"No," Brett denied calmly, poking the tip of his tongue into her ear. "I'm every kind of sex maniac." Raising his head, Brett gazed at her with eyes so soft with tenderness, Jo's throat closed with emotion. "But," he qualified seriously, "I only suffer this libido madness when in the company of one particular woman. The rest of the female population is absolutely safe from me."

Even Marsha Wenger? Jo, cautioning herself against being stupid, ordered the question to remain silent. As far as she knew, Brett had not seen Marsha outside the office since he'd followed her to Ocean City. *Marsha's loss is my gain,* Jo decided with a feeling of ruthlessness she had never before experienced. *Brett is mine!*

"Have you been eating raw oysters and swallowing vitamin E capsules while I wasn't looking?" he teased, banishing all consideration of Marsha.

"Not necessary," Brett murmured, the quirk at the corners of his mouth telegraphing the coming grin. "Merely touching you here—" His wrist slipped out of her hand and his fingers blazed a fiery trail from her throat to the tip of one breast. "And here—" His fingers drew a straight, tantalizing line down her body. "And especially *here*—" His fingers slid into the moist warmth of her. "Is all the aphrodisiac I need." Brett moved his fingers enticingly and Jo, her breathing already erratic, arched her hips into his hand. All traces of Brett's grin disappeared as his eyes swept down over her body.

Jo felt the heat rising in her in reaction to his close scrutiny of her responsiveness. Watching her intently, Brett stroked a particularly sensitive spot, his eyes flaring silver with passion when her body writhed in pleasurable agony. Embarrassed by having him witness her abandoned response, Jo tensed her muscles in an attempt to withdraw from his maddening fingers.

"Brett . . . what are . . . you doing?" Jo pushed the protest out between short, rasping breaths.

"There are many ways of giving and receiving pleasure, love," Brett said softly, continuing his mind-divorcing slow stroke. "Together you and I are going to explore most of them. Relax, sweetheart," he husked, luring the tension out of Jo's muscles. "Enjoy. I am."

Jo was beyond protest. Closing her eyes, she surrendered to the moment and the clamoring demand of her body for release. Jo knew Brett was watching her every frantic move, hearing her every labored breath but, suddenly, inexplicably, she no longer cared. Instinct or unformed intelligent reason routed all shame. Brett was her husband, the man she loved more than her own life. How could she feel shame in loving his lovemaking? She couldn't. Sighing in relief, Jo reveled in the enjoyment Brett offered her, thinking, vaguely, his turn would come.

Jo's vague thoughts proved correct some fifteen or twenty minutes later. When the last of his shudders had subsided, and his weight was a sweet heaviness on her seemingly boneless body, Brett lifted his head to kiss her softly. "I love—" He paused—because he was still out of breath? Jo wondered, afraid to think or even hope—then, disappointingly, he went on, "being with you, being around you, being in you." As if, no matter how much he had, he couldn't get enough of her, Brett kissed her again. "You love it too, don't you?"

"Yes," Jo admitted, swallowing the tightness in her throat that presaged tears in her eyes. "I love it too." The sense of defeat, of disappointment, was crushing. She had known Brett was not in love with her, still Jo had dared to hope. Hope gone, Jo consoled herself with the thought that, although Brett was not in love with her, he was not in love with any other woman either.

The very idea of Brett loving another woman made Jo tremble in fear of losing him.

"Are you cold, love?" Brett asked at once, then answered for her. "Of course you are." Carefully lifting his weight from her, Brett rolled to the edge of the bed and sat up. "Come along, honey. A hot shower will warm you up." Tilting his perfectly sculpted head, Brett slanted a teasing look at her. "Then, after you're all nice and warm, I'll take you skiing, and you can get cold all over again."

Although Brett extended their stay in Vermont, the days disappeared like spring snow in warm sunshine. They spent most of their afternoons skiing, Brett on the high runs, Jo with the beginners. Their nights and mornings they spent alone, usually in bed. They were sitting in bed on their last morning, sipping coffee, when Brett asked casually . . . far too casually:

"What if you're pregnant?"

"I'm not," Jo answered calmly, ignoring the sudden wish that she was.

"How do you know?" Brett persisted. "We've certainly tried hard enough."

"I'm on the pill, Brett." Drawing a deep breath, Jo looked him straight in the eyes. What was he probing for? Jo speculated, searching his eyes for an answer. Was he hoping she was pregnant? Was he praying she wasn't? His eyes darkened with confusion and something else Jo could not identify.

"Since when?" Brett's quiet voice made Jo uneasy.

"Since the day you moved into my apartment," Jo replied in her self-enforced calm. "I already had the prescription. All I had to do was have it refilled." Jo grew chilled at Brett's sudden shuttered, withdrawn expression.

"Of course." He smiled wryly, increasing Jo's chill. "How stupid of me." Moving with a swiftness that startled Jo, he slid off the bed and stood up. "I guess we'd better pack. We have a long drive ahead of us."

Brett remained terse and withdrawn throughout the entire drive back to New York. Both confused and hurt by his quick change in attitude, Jo gave up her frustrating, fruitless attempts to draw him into conversation forty-five minutes into the trip.

Watching his hands control the powerful sports car with effortless ease, Jo sighed silently. This was not the first time Brett had coldly shut himself away from her without explanation. Was he opposed to her taking birth control pills? If so, why hadn't he simply told her he was? She'd like nothing better than to flush the things down the toilet. God! Jo shivered in the warmth of the car's heater. A good screaming match would be preferable to this freeze-out.

Sliding down into the supple leather of the bucket seat, Jo rested her head on the high seat back and closed her eyes. Would she ever understand this complex man she'd married? She knew his body intimately and his mind not at all. What motivates him? she mused. He works like a Trojan, yet doesn't need the money he accumulates. He laughs and teases like a carefree boy, then broods like an overburdened man. He amuses me. He confuses me. He scares me to death. Unaware of the sharp-eyed glances the object of her thoughts slanted at her periodically, Jo sighed in longing for the carefree boy who amuses.

Jo opened her eyes briefly when she heard a clicking sound, then closed them again as Brett finished sliding a CD into the player on the dashboard. The music that filled the small interior of the car surprised her. If she'd been asked to guess what kind of music Brett enjoyed, her last guess would have been Spanish guitar, yet that's what she was now listening to! Losing herself in the intricate beauty of the piece, Jo let her thoughts drift.

There was a danger in allowing one's thoughts to drift, Jo found to her chagrin. Unfettered, thoughts tended to drift in the wrong direction. Unwelcomed by Jo, the memory of her two phone calls to her mother sidled into her mind. Sighing again, she gave the memories free rein, hoping she'd then be able to put them out of her mind. Jo had made the first call to her mother the day after Brett's wildly unorthodox proposal of marriage. Quite like Brett had done when he'd phoned his mother after the fact, Jo had not beat around the bush.

"I'm getting married next week," Jo had said starkly, wincing at her mother's gasp of dismay.

"You're out of your mind!" Ellen had exclaimed angrily. Not "do you love him?" Or even "to whom?" Just "You're out of your mind."

Jo had dug her nails into her palm in reaction to the scorn in her mother's voice. Controlling her tone with sheer will, Jo had replied, "Perhaps so but, nevertheless, I'm getting married." Then, though unasked, she offered the name of the groom. "I'm going to marry Brett Renninger."

"Your boss?" Ellen asked with sudden interest.

"Yes." Jo had been totally unprepared for her mother's next words.

"Well, when the bubble bursts, at least you'll have money to fall back on."

"I'd never accept money from Brett like that, Mother," Jo had said with quiet determination.

"Now I'm convinced you're crazy," Ellen had retorted disgustedly. "Well, I won't waste my time wishing you happiness. The rich ones are even worse than the men without money. They can always buy their way out, and they know it. What I do wish is that you'll change your mind before it's too late. Live with him, if you must. But think twice before you commit yourself."

"Are you hungry?" Brett's voice was soft but the unexpected sound of it startled Jo into opening her eyes.

"No." Thinking the denial too uncompromising, Jo added quietly, "Are you?"

"No."

Closing her eyes again, Jo deliberately dredged up the memory of her second phone call to her mother. Knowing Brett was listening to her side of the conversation, Jo had chosen her words very carefully.

"It's Jo, Mother," she'd said with all the lightness she could muster. "I'm calling from Vermont to tell you Brett and I were married this morning."

"You have my deepest sympathy." Ellen sighed before adding, "Is he there with you now?"

"Yes, Mother." Jo had fought to keep her tone even.

"Tell him I said he's to take good care of you, even though I know he probably won't." There'd been a pause, then her mother had gone on in a muffled tone, "I love you, honey. I wish . . . I wish . . . well, it doesn't matter what I wish. I *do* hope you'll be happy, but . . ." Her voice trailed away.

Feeling the hot sting of tears behind her lashes, Jo opened her eyes and sat up abruptly, shaking her head sharply to dislodge the sound of her mother's sad voice.

"What the hell?" Brett sliced a frown at her. "What's the matter?"

"Nothing. It's nothing. I got a cramp in my neck from my awkward position," Jo improvised, lifting her hand to rub the side of her neck. "It's fine now."

Brett returned his attention to the highway but his frown remained in place. "Even so, I think it's time we stopped to stretch and, while we're doing it, we might as well eat something."

The restaurant Brett found was unpretentious but

clean and the food was superior. Jo ate less than half her dinner. When Brett motioned the waiter to indicate he'd like a second beer, Jo reached out impulsively to grasp his hand.

"Brett! You've got quite a distance to drive. If you expect me to get into the car with you, don't have another drink."

Brett Renninger was not at all used to being told what to do, and Jo knew it. She also knew there was no way she'd ride in a car with a driver who was not only in a foul mood, but three sheets to the wind as well. Her resolve rock hard, Jo stared defiantly into Brett's icy, narrow-lidded eyes. Amazingly, Brett relented first, albeit angrily.

"A wife of little more than a week," he sneered, waving the waiter away. "And already you're issuing ultimatums." Brett extracted several bills from his wallet and tossed them on top of the check the waiter slid discreetly onto the table. Glancing back at Jo, he pinned her to her seat with eyes the color of cold steel. "This is the second time I've backed down to an ultimatum from you." Brett's voice was as steely as his eyes. Jo, her spine tingling with apprehension, had a memory flash of their confrontation in his office the day she'd lifted the phone to call Wolf in Florida. Raising her chin, Jo managed, just, to meet his stare unflinchingly. "Three strikes and you're out, babe," Brett said grittily. "Don't push your luck . . . or me too damn far."

Jo's gasp burst into the tension hovering in the air between them. Was Brett threatening her? Well, of course he was! Jo swallowed the taste of panic. What, exactly, was he threatening her with? What form would his retaliation take? The answer that stole into Jo's mind was accompanied by a choking nausea in her throat. He'd said "three strikes and you're out." Out as in: out of a job? Out of his life? Out of his sight? Out of a husband? Jo was very much afraid Brett meant every one of the outs that marched through her rattled brain.

The nausea lasted only a moment, then fled before the onslaught of fury. If Brett Renninger thought he could frighten her into quivering submission, he was in for a very rude awakening! Gritting her teeth, Jo leaned across the table to enable him to hear the rage in her soft voice.

"Don't you ever threaten me again. *You* are the one who followed me to Ocean City. *You* are the one who moved into *my* apartment. *You* are the one who insisted on marriage." Jo paused to gulp air into her constricted lungs, then, forcing her teeth apart, made a threat of her own . . . or at least attempted to.

"If you ever threaten me again, I'll . . . I'll . . ."

"You'll what?" Brett inserted in a quiet tone that in no way concealed his own fury. "Call the big prowler?"

"I don't need Wolf to protect me from you," Jo retorted. "Now, if you are tired of me, or bored with this situation you forced the both of us into, take a hike!" Pushing her chair back, Jo jumped to her feet, grabbed her coat, and, still glaring at Brett, underlined her position. "I don't need you, Brett," she lied convincingly. "I don't need any of the Renningers." Sliding the coat around her shoulders, Jo strode out of the restaurant.

For the remainder of the drive to New York the sports car took on the qualities of an abandoned tomb. There were moments when Jo was certain the silence would shatter her ear-drums.

It was early evening when they arrived at the.apartment. Jo's fury had long since burned itself out. By the time she walked into her bedroom, Jo was combating an overwhelming feeling of loss. Disregarding Brett's warning, she had issued one final ultimatum. She had figuratively pointed out the direction of the door. Now Jo was terrified Brett would literally walk out of it. Throwing her coat at the chair she had spent weeks shopping for, Jo stood in the middle of the room, stiff as a board and scared witless

"Jo?" As soft as it was, Brett's voice jerked Jo around to face him.

"What?" Jo was amazed at the steadiness she'd managed to convey. In actuality, she was afraid to hear whatever he was about to say.

"I'm not at all tired of you." Brett walked to her slowly as he made the tension-relieving statement. As he drew near, Jo could see that all his anger was gone too.

"You're not?" Jo had to fight the urge to fling herself into his arms.

"No." Brett shook his head, a conciliatory smile tugging at his lips. "I'm also not bored with our situation."

"Then . . . why . . . ?" Jo gazed at him in confusion, her eyes begging for an explanation.

"It was the mention of a preexisting prescription for birth control pills." Brett shrugged, as if trying to rid himself of an unbearable weight. "No man likes to be reminded of his predecessor." Raising his hand, he touched her hair very gently. "I'm . . . sorry." Brett's hesitation was telling; he did not make apologies often. The relief that washed through Jo was shocking in its intensity.

"I'm sorry too," she whispered, blinking against a sudden rush of tears.

Jo gulped back a sob as she was hauled into Brett's arms. God! It was heaven, like being ushered into a warm room after standing naked in the freezing night. Burying her face in his chest, she slid her arms beneath his jacket and around his waist.

"Honey, are you crying?" The concern in Brett's voice was nearly Jo's undoing.

"No." Sniffing, Jo rubbed her face against his rough wool sweater.

Brett's long fingers caught her chin to lift her face to his scrutiny. "You are crying. And I'm a bastard for making you cry. Honey, don't! He brought his other hand up to brush at the tears. His tone solemn, he said quietly, "I'd prefer it if you didn't take the pill anymore."

"Not take it!" Caught off guard, Jo stared at him in consternation. If things were different between them, if he loved her instead of loving to be with her, around her—Jo shivered in memory—in her, she'd glory in conceiving, carrying, and bearing his child. But Brett did *not* love her. He did not yearn to have proof of that love expressed in the form of a child. Brett's sole reason for asking her to discontinue the pill had more to do with pride than any other emotion. In his own words, Brett did not like being reminded of his predecessor—Gary Devlin. Still, after basking in the warmth of his arms and recent concern, Jo shuddered with the fear of having him revert back to the cold stranger he'd been all day. Could she refuse his request?

"Tough decision, huh?" Brett's soft voice held a betraying thread of tension, tension that Jo now knew could quickly change to icy withdrawal.'

Jo's sigh was the harbinger of her approaching capitulation. She didn't like it. In fact, she resented his use of coercion, especially this type of coercion, yet she knew she would yield in the end. She really hadn't much of a choice. It was either give way or face the cold stranger. Damn! Her mother was right, Jo thought distractedly. Being in love hurt in more ways than Jo had ever thought there *were* ways! If Jo had once believed Gary was a manipulator, she now knew he was a piker in comparison to Brett Renninger; Brett was a master of the art!

"Jo?" Brett was losing patience. He was attempting concealment with his low tone and the tender way he brushed her forehead with his lips, but Jo could hear the warning knell of impatience loud and clear.

Jo's face sought comfort in his sweater again. "All right, Brett." Tightening her arms around his waist, Jo clung to his lean frame in silent, possessive desperation, facing the unpalatable truth that she would very likely do anything to keep him satisfied—and with her. "I'll stop taking them . . . if that's what you want."

"Yes. That *is* what I want."

Holding him tightly, Jo could feel the tension easing out of his body. Could feel that tension being replaced by an unmistakable quickening. Brett's long thigh muscles tightened to press against hers in an urgent, demanding way. Moving his body suggestively, Brett made Jo excitingly aware of his arousal.

"You won't be sorry, love." Brett's caressing words were every bit as enticing as his body language. "I promise, you won't be sorry."

Jo's capitulation was complete she was his, mind, body, and soul. Of course she knew it and, if his triumphant laughter as he urged her toward the bed could be used as an indicator, Brett knew it too.

The month of February seemed even shorter than usual for Jo. Except for a few minor irritants, Jo sailed through the cold, snowy month wrapped in a warm cocoon of marital bliss.

The one major irritant was the mere sight of Marsha Wenger. Fortunately Jo saw the New England area manager seldom, but every time she did see Marsha, Jo smiled coolly and cursed silently. That what she was experiencing was rampant jealousy, Jo readily admitted—to herself. It was a new emotion, one Jo was positive she could very well have done without. She hated it and the mean way it made her feel, but there it was, all blatant and green eyed. Strangely, Jo had never felt the slightest twinge of jealousy over Gary, and the females had fluttered all over him wherever they had gone. Reluctantly, Jo faced the fact that what she had felt for Gary had been infatuation . . . and a rather shallow infatuation at that. She hadn't been in love with Gary at all, merely in love with the idea of being in love! It was a home truth Jo accepted, then put from her mind. Perhaps everyone had to experience the trauma of near love to appreciate the real thing when it finally did come along.

Early in March, Brett was away for the longest five days Jo had ever lived through. Both Brett and Sean were in the Poconos, ironing out some labor union wrinkles, and while he was away Jo began to understand Casey's attitude of the previous December. At the time, Casey had been frustrated and cranky, and all because Sean had been away. During the five days, and what seemed like twice as many nights, that Brett was away, Jo was tormented by a like frustration and crabbiness.

On the fifth night when he returned, Brett looked tired, and windblown, and cold, and absolutely beautiful. He was outfitted in dark corduroy jeans, low boots, and a thigh-length, pile-lined suede jacket, and he looked like he'd just left the project site. Jo, both surprised and delighted by his early return, opened her mouth, but before the words of welcome and question could be formed, Brett explained in three terse words.

"I missed you."

Jo stopped breathing at the expression in Brett's eyes as he crossed the room to where she was sitting.

Staring into his eyes, as soft as the feathers on a gray dove, Jo felt all the tension and irritation drain out of her. It was always the same. All Brett had to do was lower his voice and look at her tenderly, and she was completely his. *It's not fair!* A small spark of defiance tried to make itself heard above the flutter of Jo's pulse. *It is simply not fair for him to have this much control over me, when I have no effect whatever on him.* Well, that wasn't quite true and Jo admitted it. She did have some effect. Jo could see the effect on Brett's body and in the tiny flame beginning to leap in his eyes. Jo knew she had the power to arouse Brett's body. There had been moments when she'd connected with his mind. Why couldn't she touch his heart?

Brett's lips twitched in the quirky smile that had become so very endearing to Jo. "I've slept alone for four nights." The quirk progressed at its usual rate into a grin. "Let me rephrase that statement. I tried to sleep alone for four nights. I did not succeed very well. I missed you like hell, Jo." By the time Brett had finished speaking the grin was gone.

Jo was long past deciphering Brett's intricately simplistic admission. Merely knowing he had missed her was enough, for now. "I—I missed you too, Brett. I didn't know what to do without you here." The murmured confession escaped through Jo's unguarded mental barriers while she was otherwise occupied by becoming lost inside the gray prison of Brett's eyes. Vaguely, Jo wondered why the flame in those gray depths suddenly leaped wildly. As it was where Jo had wanted to be since he'd walked into the room, she never entertained the thought of resistance when Brett drew her into his arms. Home. Jo sighed with relief. The scent of him, his aftershave, even the faint, woolly odor of his sweater, all were now the scents of home to Jo.

"I was going to suggest we go the usual route in our learning process of getting to know each other better." Brett's lips skimmed her forehead. "You know, open a bottle of wine, get comfortable on the sofa, and talk until we run out of words." As if drawn by a lure too enticing to resist, his lips made a direct path down her small nose to her mouth. "But, on consideration, four days without you is three and a half days too long. We'll still have a bottle of wine, but I think we'll drink it in bed." Brett's lips teased Jo's for mind-bending seconds. "After we've communicated in a more basic language," he whispered into her mouth.

Brett proceeded to converse very fluently without speaking a syllable. He began the dialogue with his lips, and his tongue, and his hands. Then, with his body, Brett presented a brilliant dissertation on communication. Distracted by sensations seemingly tripping over each other as they raced crazily through her body, Jo was ignorant of the fact that her own silent thesis was being presented with equal eloquence.

Brett eventually did get around to opening a bottle of wine, but only after they had both had a short, reviving nap and a long, revitalizing shower. Brett went to the kitchen while Jo remade the thoroughly disordered bed. Clad in the striped silk robe, she was reclining against the headboard when Brett strolled into the bedroom, a bottle of white wine and two glasses in one hand and a tray of sandwiches in the other.

"It's a good thing this is Friday night," he observed dryly. "As I'm planning to lay siege to your mind, and your body, through most of it."

"Actually, I was thinking of going into the office tomorrow," Jo lied unconvincingly. In truth, she had glumly looked forward to pacing the apartment till he came home. "There's a report I should finish to have ready for Monday."

Placing the tray of sandwiches on her legs, Brett slid onto the bed beside Jo and poured wine for the both of them.

"I don't know anyone else who can make me feel like you can." He leaned to her to kiss her gently. "It feels good to laugh with you." When Brett lifted his head he was smiling. "Come to that, practically everything we do together makes me feel good. How about you?" he probed blatantly.

Jo's smile was a reflection of Brett's. "Makes me feel good too," she offered softly. "For the most part, I've enjoyed our being together."

"For the most part," Brett repeated quietly. "Well, that's a start." Picking up a piece of sandwich, he examined the ham-and-cheese filling as if he'd never seen it before. "Time for the learning process to begin, I think." Taking a tentative bite, he chewed it thoroughly and washed it down with a healthy swallow of wine. "I already know you are terrific at your job and can't cook worth a damn," Brett finally continued. "What other talents, or lack thereof, are contained within the beautiful package you call yourself?"

"I'm great in bed." It was not a declaration but a question, if a teasing one. Although Brett obviously understood, he chose to treat Jo's query as a statement of fact.

"Granted." Brett's concurrence was made in all seriousness. "What else? And please feel free to elaborate."

Jo hesitated briefly, then, thinking—*what have I got to lose?*— opened her mind, if not her heart, to him. "I am, by nature, quiet. But I think I told you that before?" Jo arched a brow at him in question; Brett nodded. "I like almost all kinds of music, from classical to country western. I love movies, especially science fiction. I have a passion for clothes that by far exceed my budget."

"No longer," Brett inserted at this point of her litany. "I'll take care of your clothing bills."

Jo stiffened noticeably. She didn't want him paying her bills. Why having Brett assume financial responsibility for her should make her feel like a kept woman, Jo didn't know, unless it had something to do with Brett not loving her. Jo had conscious knowledge of being his wife; the emotional impact was missing. She would much prefer to pay her own bills. Now, for Jo, the problem was how to convey her feelings to him. Brett was way ahead of her.

"Don't say it, Jo," he warned softly. "We've got the beginnings of a good picnic going here." Jo was well aware

Brett was not referring to the impromptu supper he'd put together. "Don't rain on it."

"Brett . . . I—" Jo faltered. Was her independence really worth the price of this tenuous reaching out they had embarked on? She *was* Brett's wife, all legal and binding—or at least as binding as any marriage could be in this enlightened age. Leave it, her common sense advised. Meet him halfway, see what develops. You have nothing to lose and the world to gain. "I play a fair hand of poker."

Brett stared at her blandly for an instant, then a grin of mixed delight and relief instilled animation; he grinned like a summertime-happy boy. As if he were suddenly starving, Brett wolfed down another sandwich. Waving his hand at the depleted plate, he ordered her to follow suit. "Dig in, honey." Brett's grin removed the sting from the barb that trailed his invitation. "*I* do know how to put a sandwich together."

They ate and drank in silence until the plate and bottle were empty, then Brett made himself comfortable by stretching his long length out full and throwing his arms over his head.

"I'm going to toss another responsibility at you next week," he told her lazily.

Busy brushing bits of breadcrumbs off the sheet, Jo didn't even look up. "Really?" she replied idly. "What sort of responsibility?"

"I'm going to put you to interviewing applicants." He yawned. "The job bores the hell out of me."

"Applicants?" Jo glanced up to frown at him. The only applicants Brett ever personally interviewed were for managerial positions, and, to Jo's knowledge, there were no positions of that type open. "Applicants for what?"

"New England area manager." Brett exhaled in exasperation. "We've got less than a month to replace Marsha, Jo."

Marsha! Jo froze. Marsha was leaving the firm? At first the news thrilled Jo. Then the thrill was chased by apprehension. Why was Marsha leaving? And why hadn't Jo known about it? Had Brett deliberately kept the information from her for reasons of his own? Jo could think of only one reason Brett would have for keeping silent, and that reason did not bear thinking about. Pushing a sudden, explicit image of Brett and Marsha together in much the same way Jo and he were now, Jo made a production out of finding the last, tiniest crumb.

"Why is Marsha quitting?" Jo directed her question at the smooth sheet.

Brett hesitated for seconds that were pure agony for Jo. "Well," he began slowly, "I know all she'd say was her reason was personal but—" Again he hesitated, drawing Jo's nerves to quivering tautness. "What the hell, you are not only my assistant but my wife. Marsha's going to follow her husband."

Jo could not have been more stunned if Brett had told her Marsha was going to have a sex-change operation! Added to Jo's bafflement at Brett's seeming assumption that she'd known of Marsha's intention to leave the company, Brett's revelation of a heretofore unheard of husband left Jo totally speechless. Had she been beating her emotions to death since December for nothing? Had there ever been anything personal between Brett and Marsha? And does being in love make jackasses of everybody? This last consideration jolted Jo out of contemplation and into speech.

"Brett, let's clarify a few details here." Jo's voice contained a harsh undertone. She was fed up. She never had liked playing games, and this love game was starting to get to her. As Jo had never particularly liked mysteries either, she wasn't about to tolerate Marsha's. "Detail one," she said flatly. "I knew nothing about Marsha's resignation. Detail two: I knew nothing about a husband."

"Former husband," Brett inserted.

"Former or otherwise," Jo bit angrily. "Which brings about detail three: I was under the impression that you and she had indulged in a flaming affair last October in Vermont." Sitting up straight, Jo stared Brett directly in the eyes, defying him to deny, an alliance with Marsha. When Brett didn't respond immediately, Jo added, "And what the hell do you mean, former husband? If they are no longer married, why is she leaving an excellent job to follow him?"

"Are you finished?" Brett asked softly. "Or are there more details on your list?"

"I'm finished." And very likely in more ways than one, she added silently. But, good grief, how long could she go on living with this silliness? Jo demanded of herself. Sex, in itself, was not a panacea, the be-all and end-all of any relationship . . . let alone marriage! There had to be more or, if there was not, then her mother was right!

"Detail one." Brett's quietly controlled voice intruded on Jo's introspection and riveted her attention. "I honestly believed you did know of Marsha's resignation. She tendered it this past Monday." He regarded her steadily. "I thought I'd mentioned it before I left for the mountains. I'm sorry, but I was rushed. Okay?"

Jo let a nod suffice for reply. If he was on a roll, she certainly wasn't going to call a halt now.

"Detail number two is a little more involved. Marsha has been unhappily divorced for over a year. The marriage fell apart because Marsha, admittedly, neglected it in favor of her career." Brett shrugged. "Apparently, like most men, Marsha's husband labored under the illusion that he should come first. When he discovered he didn't, he sought comfort elsewhere."

"How delightful!" Jo exclaimed. "He sounds like a real charmer. And Marsha is going to repress her ambition to chase *him*?" Incensed at the very idea of what Marsha was doing, Jo momentarily forgot how relieved she'd felt on hearing of the woman's intentions mere moments ago.

She was angry, really angry, and yet she was trembling with excitement. She was actually loving every minute of this argument! Geared for mental battle, Jo missed the significance of her enjoyment, and that was that the lines of communication were wide open!

"Jo!" Brett shouted in exasperation. "Marsha loves the man. She has been miserable for over a year! But she has decided to meet him halfway . . . no more. Can you honestly sit there and insist she's wrong?"

"Brett, how can you insist she is only meeting him halfway?" Jo argued heatedly. "She's giving up her job. She's going to him. What, exactly, is *he* doing? No! Don't tell me, I know. *He* is waiting for her to come to her senses! Right?"

"I don't believe this! I positively do not believe this." Brett glanced around the room as if seeking guidance. "We are actually fighting over another couple's marital problems!"

"Yes," Jo responded impulsively. "Isn't it fun?"

Brett grinned, then sobered almost at once. "It would be, if we didn't have a few problems of our own." Brett met Jo's glance and held it. "There was no affair in October." He hesitated, then went on determinedly, "But not for lack of trying on my part."

Jo sat perfectly still, staring at him, while her conscience went to work on her. She longed to dissect his last statement, but did she have the right? No, she did not, her conscience advised. In actual fact, she'd had no right to ask him about October in the first place. Obviously Brett had assumed she'd pounce on his admission.

"No questions?" he probed, a strange note of disappointment edging his voice. "Aren't you curious . . . at all?"

Jo sighed. "Yes, I'm curious. But it really is none of my business. Is it?" After the effervescence of their argument, Jo felt flat. "What you did, and who you did it with, before we married, is, in fact, none of my business." Jo broke the hold his eyes attempted to maintain.

"And so, of course, I have no right to ask you about your previous affair." Brett's tone had a corresponding flatness, tinged with accusation.

So he did know about Gary! Jo raised her eyes to encounter a blank wall. Brett had withdrawn. The lines of communication had snapped. Following Brett's example, Jo mentally withdrew.

"Not in that manner." Jo was amazed at the distant sound of her own voice.

"It doesn't matter." Brett's shrug had the impact of a blow to Jo's heart.

He doesn't really want to know, because he really doesn't care! The thought froze Jo's mind. Moving carefully, as if afraid she'd shatter into a million shards of ice if she hurried, Jo slid off the bed and walked into the bathroom, thinking: The learning process is now over.

ELEVEN

Brett sat behind his brother's desk, staring fixedly at his computer screen. It had been a very long three weeks since he and Jo had reached dead end the night he'd returned from Pennsylvania.

Why hadn't they been able to break free of constraint since then? Brett was afraid he knew the answer and simply didn't want to face it. *Damn it, if she loved me* . . . The desk chair was shoved back roughly as Brett jerked to his feet.

Stalking to the window, Brett scowled down at the miniature people scurrying about their business twenty-six stories below.

If she loved me.

Brett was relieved at the intrusive noise of the buzzer on the telephone. Swinging back to the desk, he scooped up the receiver. "Mrs. Renninger on line two." Brett's distraction was evidenced by his subdued greeting to his mother. He forgot to call her sir.

"Yes, Mother?" he queried.

"Are you feeling all right?" Violet demanded in concern.

Brett frowned. "Yes, of course. Why?"

"If you have to ask, I must be working you too hard," Violet answered. Then, without warning, she sprang her news on him. "Wolf has been declared fit to go back to work. He has decided to remain at the farm until after

Easter. That gives you a week and a half to clear up whatever you're on at the moment and re-gear your mind for Atlanta. You can bring him up to date when you and JoAnne come down for the holiday. You *were* planning to come down for Easter, weren't you?"

Brett was in no mood for pretense. "I really hadn't thought about it," he admitted starkly.

"And now you don't have to," she shot back at him. "It's family conclave time, Brett. I'm considering another branch on the Renninger's company tree. Wolf needs to be brought up to date. And you sound like you need a rest. When will you and JoAnne arrive?"

Brett couldn't deny the smile that curved his tight lips. "What rank did you carry in the marines?" As the question was moot, he went on through her laughter, "We'll fly down sometime during holy week. I cannot be more definitive at this point. Okay?"

"I guess it will have to be." Violet sighed. "Sometimes I think I trained my sons too well. Give my love to JoAnne, Brett."

Give my love to JoAnne. The phrase revolved in Brett's head long after he'd replaced the receiver.

I want to give my love to JoAnne.
Does JoAnne still love my brother?
Did JoAnne ever love my brother?
Does JoAnne know how to love?

They had come so close that night, so very close to a breakthrough, to a meeting of the minds as well as of the flesh. Brett swallowed the bitter taste of defeat coated with self-destructive jealousy. Both emotions were unfamiliar and unacceptable to him. Brett knew he would have to do something to rectify the situation, and soon. The question was what?

I hate this!

The silent cry came from the soul. There was nothing new or unique about the protest. Brett had been living with it now for what seemed like most of his life. Stalemate. To Brett, the marriage was in a position of stalemate. So what do you do? he taxed himself. Write it off? Brett refused to as much as consider calling it quits without a fight.

What had gone wrong? Brett's lips curved wryly. What had ever been right about it . . . other than the purely physical? Then again, there had been some moments, times when he and Jo had been in smooth accord. Those times had been a lure, a teaser, promising a rich relationship if they could bridge the gap.

That was what had been so exciting for a little while the night he'd come home from the Poconos. Brett could still feel the tremor of expectation that had shivered through him that night. For a brief, breathless moment, he had allowed himself to believe Jo was beginning to care for him. Jo had talked more openly than ever before, she had even revealed signs of resentment for Marsha. For an instant, Brett had actually convinced himself Jo's resentment was caused by jealousy. Euphoric, Brett had felt the time right to mention Jo's affair with Wolf. Jo's sudden, chilly silence had said more than any lengthy explanation. Jo had stopped talking and, during these interminable three weeks, had conversed on a surface level. It was only after they were in bed that Jo displayed animation.

Brett felt his body harden in reaction to a flashing image of Jo, her breathing shallow, her lips parted, writhing and moaning beneath him. Their physical union was as close as Brett had ever hoped to get to perfect. The strange thing was, his desire appeared to be feeding itself. The more Brett had of Jo, the more he wanted her! Satiation was transient. Hunger was self-renewing. Need. Need. Need.

Turning abruptly, Brett strode back to his desk. He didn't have time to indulge in wishful thinking. His movements purposeful, Brett drew a pile of reports to the center of the desk. After reading the first sheet of paper contained in the first report for the second time, he closed the folder and pushed the pile away again. Resting his head against the chair's high back, Brett stared sightless at the large photograph of the first Renninger-built condominium on the wall opposite his desk.

His concentration was a thing of the past. Perhaps his mother was right and he did need a rest. Brett's smile was both bitter and derisive. He certainly didn't expect to get much rest at the farm! Not if he had to play the role of watchdog around Jo and Wolf. At the thought, Brett went rigid in the well-padded chair.

Is this what being in love had brought him to? Brett shuddered at the idea of himself sniffing at the heels of his wife and brother.

God damn it! No! He'd see them both in hell first! She was not worth it. No woman alive was worth it! *Damn Wolf! Damn Jo! And damn my own love for her! If, when Wolf is once again in residence behind this desk, they still want each other, I'll go back to Atlanta alone! I can live without her!*

But, oh God, I love her!

A short distance down a wide, plushly carpeted hall, Jo sat in a similar, if smaller office, at a similar, if smaller desk, coming to a similar, if softer decision. Jo had not damned Wolf. Jo had not damned Brett. Jo had not even damned herself. Jo had reached the same conclusion as Brett. She would remain in New York when Brett went back to Atlanta.

The relationship they had so very suddenly dived into was crumbling with equal swiftness. How long could she go on living with a stranger? Jo had grown weary with the repetition of the question. How long could she bear coexistence with a man who was always polite, most times even pleasant, a searing flame in bed, but a stranger nonetheless?

Was it worth it? Jo lowered long lashes over eyes stinging with hot moisture. Another failure. Was she to go
through life drifting in and out of affairs? Successful in her
chosen career, ineffectual in any personal relationship? Or
was her mother right after all? Was it all a hoax, a shimmering facade—this idea, or ideal, of a real, lasting love
between a man and a woman?

Rebellion stirred deep inside Jo. If the whole concept
of love was nothing more than a myth, then what was the
purpose of life? Without the humanizing presence of
love, romantic love, humans would be reduced to the
lowest level, and life itself would become a barren waste.
Every atom of intelligence Jo possessed rejected the cold
precept. Her mother was wrong! She *had* to be wrong! Jo
refused to view life as a grinding ordeal, or humans as
automatons, untouched or unsoftened by the gentle kiss
of love.

Why can't Brett love me?

Shivering, Jo opened her eyes to stare at the plain,
narrow gold band on her left ring finger. Jo wanted to
live to be a very old lady and still be wearing that gold
band when she closed her eyes for the last time. But
without Brett's love, the ring was valueless.

Reflective of her husband's actions, Jo pushed her
chair away from the desk and walked to the window. If
only Brett had not mentioned her affair with Gary in
quite that accusing tone! Or was she too sensitive about
that fiasco? Why couldn't they just sit down and talk like
two intelligent, mature adults? Maybe she ought to look
Brett straight in the eyes and say: I love you. Now what
are you going to do about it? Jo sighed. She knew full
well that it was the fear of Brett's answer that kept her
from speaking to him about her feelings. Still, Jo knew
that something would have to give, and soon. She simply
could not continue to live in this void.

Jo stood at the window a long time, her thoughts

revolving, always coming back to the same point. Something, or someone, would have to give. Jo had the very uncomfortable feeling that the someone would be JoAnne Lawrence Renninger.

Since their marriage, whenever Brett was in the office, he came for her when it was time to go home. It was after six before he strode into Jo's office that afternoon. As usual, the sight of him set Jo's pulses racing. Today Brett's grim expression increased the pulse rate to a gallop.

"Are you ready to leave?"

For all the work she'd accomplished, she might as well have stayed home in the first place! Jo refrained from offering the information. Come to that, there hadn't been all that much work to do! Had Brett been as idle as she these last weeks? Jo rejected the idea at once. From all reports, he had not allowed his first wife to interfere with his work, and he had been in love with her! Jo nodded in answer and began collecting her briefcase, handbag, gloves, and coat, suppressing the longing to have the power to interfere with his daily routine.

"Well, at least I'll soon be saying good-bye to this place." Brett made the thickly drawled observation as they entered the apartment.

Startled, and more than a little shocked, Jo's gaze trekked Brett's as he scanned the room. She would have sworn he liked the apartment! The full content of his statement hit her in a rush. Was Brett obliquely telling her he was leaving her? Jo's fear hid itself behind a calm tone.

"Are you going somewhere?" God! She sounded bored! And, from the sharp glance Brett sliced at her, he did not appreciate her enforced smoothness.

"*We* are going somewhere," Brett enunciated harshly. "I had a call from Mother today." Removing his coat, Brett held it in one hand and reached for Jo's with the other. "She is expecting us at the farm for Easter," he continued as he hung the garments in the closet. Jo felt pinned by his steely eyes when he turned to face her. "It's time to return to Atlanta." Brett walked to within a few inches of her before adding, "Wolf's ready to resume control of the New York office."

"But that's wonderful!" Jo momentarily forgot her own unhappiness on hearing about Wolf's recovery. Brett brought her back to earth with a crash.

"Are you going with me?" Brett's quiet tone conflicted with the muscle jumping in his jaw.

To where? Jo wondered in confusion. To Florida or Atlanta? And why was he suddenly so tense? And, damn it, why did he sound so relieved about leaving the apartment? Ask him, you fool! Jo opened her mouth, then closed it again, damning herself for the coward she'd become. Fortunately, Brett unwittingly gave her a reprieve.

"I told Mother we'd fly down the middle of next week," Brett went on when it became obvious she was not going to respond. "It seems there's a family conference awaiting us. Will Wednesday be convenient for you?"

"Yes, of course." Jo frowned. "What is the conference all about?"

"Who knows?" Brett shrugged. "But, knowing Mother, it will probably mean more work for all of us."

Brett breathed in deeply as the plane soared off the runway into the clear morning sky. After a week of figuratively holding his breath, it was a relief to breathe without constraint. At every minute of every hour of every day Brett had expected Jo to tell him she was not going with him. Now, with Jo strapped into the seat beside him, Brett allowed his taut body to relax. The ending would come soon enough. Until the final moment was upon him, Brett wanted her right where she was, by his side.

My beautiful, fragile-looking, tough-as-a-marine wife. Brett smiled sadly inside his mind. Since meeting Jo the previous October, Brett had revised every one of his opinions about her but one. At that time, he had concluded that Jo was a confection spun of pure steel. Now Brett knew his conclusion had been correct. Then again, perhaps Marsha's theory held merit. Maybe Jo simply did not like men! Not once in the two months they had been together had Jo looked at another man with even a hint of interest. As to that, Jo hadn't revealed a hell of a lot of interest in him, either, except in the bedroom!

Brett had to clench his teeth against the bitter laughter that rose in his throat. Now, there's a switch! Weren't men forever getting rapped for being unable to communicate outside of the bedroom?

Brett had never consciously thought about it before but, at that moment, he decided that most of what he'd heard and read about the differences between the sexes was simply nonsense. Once the obvious hurdle was cleared, the fact was there was very little difference between the male and the female.

The fact denoted equality.

The thought sprang into Brett's mind and refused to be dislodged. In all honesty, he had to admit, at least to himself, that Jo was indeed his equal.

They should make a brilliant combination, Brett mused. The ideal team. So, why didn't they?

Because she does not love you.

Square one. From a distance that seemed like light-years, but was in fact not yet two full years, Brett acknowledged that the love he'd thought he'd felt for Sondra was as water compared to wine in what he felt for Jo. What he felt for Jo was a totally different kind of loving. Other than in the physical sense, he'd really not needed Sondra. Brett knew he needed Jo, in every sense known to man. If he required proof, all Brett had to do was remember the desperation he'd felt while making love to Jo ever since he'd received the phone call from his mother. For Brett, the act had gone far beyond the physical coupling of a man and a woman. In effect, what he had been attempting to do was draw the essence of Jo into himself; in a sense, to store up on her for a rainy day. And yet Brett still felt empty.

Emptiness has to be filled with something: Brett filled his personal void with anger. His fury was unreasonable and he knew it. Yet there it was, eating through him like a hot tongue of fire. Anger at Wolf, the brother he idolized. Anger at Jo, the woman he adored. Anger at himself, for getting involved in the first place. Brett's anger fostered determination. He could not . . . would not give Jo up without a fight!

The same black Cadillac with the same taciturn driver was waiting for them at the small airstrip in Florida, only this time the sun was shining brightly and the temperature hovered in the mid-seventies. There was not a hint of rain, either in the air or on the horizon.

Jo, grateful for Brett's suggestion that she wear light clothing, looked around with interest as they walked to the car. The airstrip and the small office-hangar had the appearance of having been plunked down in the middle of nowhere, so isolated were they.

Josh's greeting was every bit as terse and laconic as it had been in December. Brett's reply was as tight-lipped. Dismissing both men from her mind, Jo sat close to the window, her gaze skimming over the lush green pasture land they were driving through.

"Those trees are beautiful!" Jo exclaimed, indicating the huge pines that dotted the pastures and the large, tree-shaped cones that decorated the grass beneath the widely spread branches.

"Yes."

Brett's short reply robbed Jo of her delight in seeing

Florida basking in the sunlight. Her first glimpse of sleek Thoroughbreds ambling serenely behind white rail fences restored her enthusiasm. Jo had never seen a Thoroughbred horse before, yet even she could recognize the fine lines and elegant appearance of the animals. It was not exactly love at first sight. Oh, the horses were very beautiful, but they were also very large. Jo decided she'd prefer to admire from a distance.

The drive seemed much shorter, and the house much larger, than before. As the car glided to a smooth stop in the curving driveway in front of the house, Jo was again struck by its likeness to pictures she'd seen of antebellum plantation homes. The word tranquility sprang to Jo's mind. As she stepped from the car, Jo fervently hoped she'd find a measure of that tranquility while she was within its walls. As Jo and Brett mounted the steps, the door was flung wide open.

Elania Calaveri was exactly as she had been in December. Jo smothered a bubble of laughter as the woman again took Brett to task.

"Well, what a surprise!" Elania exclaimed in mock amazement. "Only half of holy week gone and you're here already! Are you sick or something?" As they entered the imposing hall, the housekeeper directed her comments to Jo in a confiding manner. "Never could keep this hellion in one place for very long. He was always eager to be gone, even as a boy. He'd be up and out of the house so early, I had to teach the scamp to cook his own breakfast to make sure he'd get a decent meal inside him, as he seldom came home before dark."

Jo shot a gleaming glance at her scowling husband. One bursting sentence from Elania had cleared up the mystery of how and why Brett had learned to cook. Eager to be gone. The words reverberated in Jo's mind. Did that explain Brett's strained behavior of the past several weeks and his obvious relief about leaving the apartment soon?

Was the adult Brett still the same as the boy—eager to be gone? Caught up in speculation, Jo missed Brett's greeting to Elania, snapping to attention when she heard her name.

"I'm sorry, I was . . . admiring the house and didn't hear what you said," she lied unevenly when Brett repeated her name impatiently.

"I said," Brett reiterated, "Elania has just told me that none of the others know we've arrived as they are in the dining room having lunch. Would you like to freshen up before we join them?"

Annoyed by Brett's too-quiet tone, Jo answered sharply, "Yes. If you don't mind?"

"If I had minded," Brett bit back, "I wouldn't have asked in the first place." Ignoring the tiny gasp that burst through Elania's suddenly tight lips, Brett ushered Jo up the stairs.

On her first visit to the house, Jo had been delighted with the bedroom Elania had escorted her to. Now she followed Brett as he swung in the opposite direction at the top of the wide staircase. Apparently, Jo mused, this side of the house contained the family bedrooms. A twinge of pain twisted in her chest as she wondered how much longer she'd be a member of the Renninger family.

The room Jo trailed Brett into was large and square and definitely masculine in decor. Jo loved it immediately. The absence of unnecessary clutter appealed to the Spartan in Jo. Standing just inside the door, Jo inventoried the rich dark-brown carpet and matching drapes, and the stark white of unadorned walls. An overstuffed, comfortable-looking chair in copper silk shantung gave the room focus and color. Jo did not have to be told that Brett had selected the decor himself. In some strange way the room was Brett.

"I love it." Jo might as well have said "I love you."

Brett's face relaxed at her stamp of approval. "Somehow

I knew you would." He stared at her intently for a second, then indicated a door on the wall to her right with a wave of his hand. "The bathroom. You don't need to fuss, it's only family." A smile flickered over Brett's tautly drawn lips. "You always look perfect anyway."

Jo stared at him, unable to move for an instant. Would she ever get past the point of melting inside at the slightest suggestion of a smile from this man? *It's not fair,* Jo protested silently. *It's simply not . . .*

"If you don't move," Brett's sensuously warm voice drew her out of her thoughts, "I might be tempted to demonstrate the resiliency of the mattress on my bed." His lips curved invitingly. "Are you as hungry as I am?"

Incredibly Jo was suddenly starving, in exactly the manner Brett's slumberous eyes told her he was! How was it possible? Had they not skipped breakfast in favor of . . . Jo shivered in memory of the feast she and Brett had indulged in that morning. Fleetingly, Jo concluded that if they could remain in bed forever, they would have no marital problems. She wanted him, again, very badly, but, there was more to a marriage than that. There had to be. "Brett, I . . ." Jo's breath caught in her throat as he took a step toward her. "They are all down there," she finished lamely.

"And we are all up here." Brett took another slow step. "All two of us." His smile promised everything. "The perfect number for a luncheon party." One more step, and Jo felt like she was coming apart at the seams.

"But we haven't even seen Wolf yet!" Jo grabbed at the excuse in desperation. What if Elania had mentioned their arrival? What would they all think? The change in Brett was as confusing as it was sudden. His body stiffening with tension, Brett pivoted away from her.

"Yes, of course, Wolf." His back to her, Brett stood as still as if carved from rock, his voice as hard. "Will you go do whatever you have to do, so we can get out of this room?"

Jo wanted to scream. Jo wanted to throw things. She walked into the bathroom. How did one keep up with a man whose moods changed with mercurial swiftness? Jo stared at the pitifully wan face reflected in the mirror above the marbleized sink. With the eyes of a critic, she examined the makeup she'd applied so carefully that morning. Her pale cheeks were in need of a touch of the blusher brush. Her disordered hair needed taming. Jo pictured the needed articles inside the flight bag Brett had placed on the long double dresser as he'd entered the room. She could either go and get the bag, or ask Brett to hand it in to her. Jo's eyes avoided her face. Lifting her hands, she smoothed the mass of dark hair. She would not ask him for anything and, when she did walk out of the room, she would be ready to go downstairs. Brett was in a strange mood. He had been moody for weeks. The smell of showdown was in the air around them. Jo knew the slightest incident could trigger it. Raising her long lashes, Jo read the plea in her own dull hazel eyes; not now, not today, hold on to him as long as you can.

Jo's smoothing hands drifted down over the white linen suit jacket she wore over a crisp lilac shirt, then down over hips covered in a pencil-slim skirt that partnered the jacket.

"Jo!"

Jo's hands stilled at Brett's impatient call. Dismissing the sad-eyed woman in the mirror, Jo opened the door and walked out of the room, her spine straight, her shoulders back, her head high, and her expectations gone. The sight of Brett had the usual, melting effect on Jo's senses. In chinos and a charcoal gray turtleneck, Brett didn't project quite the forbidding appearance as when he was decked out in battle array of conservative business armor.

They descended the romantic staircase in an unromantic silence. As they neared the dining room the muted sound of genial conversation filtered through the closed double doors. Drawing a deep breath, Jo forced a smile to her stiff lips, prepared to follow Brett's lead in whatever image he created concerning their marriage.

Determined to play out the role of the happy bridegroom if it killed him, Brett pasted a parody of a smile on his face. His facial muscles ached in protest of the switch from down to up. Over the last weeks those muscles had grown used to the down position. As Brett followed Jo into the dining room, the ache was relieved by the scene that met his eyes. Brett frowned. Where were Eric and his family, and Di and her brood? The question spun out of his mind at the sound of his brother's voice.

Wolf's liquid-silver eyes swept Jo's willowy body. "What a delightful treat for dessert!"

Everyone laughed. Everyone but Brett. Cursing silently, Brett ordered a faint smile to his lips. Every muscle in his body tightened. He hated it, yet there it was. Brett knew without doubt that should Wolf presume to lay one hand on Jo, he would find himself on the floor, on his back, and hurting like hell. Without conscious command his fingers curled into his palms, readying for action that didn't come.

"Wolf! Will you never learn to behave?" Violet chastised, bestowing a welcoming smile on Jo. "Come sit by me, JoAnne. It's long past time you were welcomed into the family." She shot an arched look at Brett.

"It's been a busy winter, Mother." Brett offered the lame excuse for not bringing Jo to visit sooner, then strode to where Wolf had risen in place at the end of the table. "You're looking good, big brother." The truth of his compliment brought an equal mixture of joy and pain to Brett. He had prayed for Wolf's recovery, while at the same time dreading it. Brett knew Wolf's return to vigor might well mean his own loss. The emotions in conflict inside him were tearing him apart.

Wolf's silver eyes darkened with concern. "I'm sorry I can't say the same about you. You look very tired, Brett." Wolf's glance sliced to Jo. "Are there problems?"

"No! I . . ."

"No more than usual," Brett cut across Jo's too-hurried denial. "I'll be glad to get back to running one region." Terminating the subject, Brett turned to kiss Micki's cheek in greeting, then frowningly directed his gaze back to his mother. "Eric and Di not here yet?"

"No. And they won't be coming." Violet waited till Brett seated himself opposite Jo before explaining. "Dirk is covered with chicken pox." She smiled in sympathy for Di's youngest child. "And, as Doris has been having mild cramps for several days, her doctor has forbidden her to travel."

"But it's not Doris's time yet. Is it?" Brett truthfully couldn't remember: he had had other, more important things on his mind since Christmas.

"Close enough," Violet drawled. "We might have another new member in the family by Easter."

His mother's comment elicited speculation from the others at the table about whether the new arrival would be a boy or a girl. Brett, making a show of eating the salmon Elania set before him, let the conversation swirl around him as he studied his wife's animated face. A new baby. His baby. From Brett out of Jo. Now, at this moment, Brett knew he wanted a child. Jo's child. Brett was painfully aware of the fact that he would probably never see such a child.

"Brett!"

The exasperation that tinged his mother's tone was a clear indication that it was not the first time she'd said his name. Shifting his gaze to Violet's face, Brett smiled ruefully. "Yes, Mother?"

"Are you feeling all right?" Violet's exasperation was

overshadowed by concern. "You've barely touched your food."

"I'm fine," Brett assured her quietly. "I was just wondering if the family conclave has been postponed . . . due to chicken pox and confinement."

"Not at all." Very motherlike, Violet searched Brett's face for telltale signs of illness.

"Brett's a big boy now, Mother. I'm sure he knows how to take care of himself," Wolf inserted dryly. "Even if handling both Atlanta and New York are too much for him."

Brett chose to ignore Wolf's taunt, which caused his mother's frown to darken. "How do you propose to have a family conclave with only half the family here?" In an effort to ease his mother's worry, Brett arched one pale brow exaggeratedly. Before his eyes, mother changed into Madam President.

"Have you ever heard of teleconferencing?"

Out of the corner of his eye, Brett caught the gleam of the appreciative grin that revealed Jo's even white teeth. *Damn, she is beautiful!* Dragging his concentration back to his mother, Brett nodded. "Yes, sir." His own grin wouldn't be denied when Brett heard Micki's soft laughter whisper down the length of the long, highly glossed table.

"That's more like it." Violet's expression of concern faded at Brett's apparent return to more normal behavior. "I've slated the conference for three o'clock. That will give you and JoAnne a chance to change clothes, or whatever."

Brett's inclination was to opt for the whatever but, for the moment, he focused his attention on getting through lunch without making a complete ass of himself. He'd already aroused his mother's concern and Wolf's taunting speculation. The last thing he needed was to create a scene at the lunch table. Elania would never forgive him!

Fortunately, Wolf chose to be briefed over the dessert,

and the remainder of the meal was consumed along with dry business details. By the time Brett and Jo went back upstairs to his bedroom less than forty-five minutes were left till conclave time.

Their cases were placed neatly side by side on the storage chest that ran the width of the bed at its base. Maintaining the cool silence that had enveloped them since leaving the dining room, Jo set to work immediately unpacking her case. Watching her from behind half-closed eyes Brett knew revealed both longing and desire, Brett sprawled in the padded chair with deceptive laziness, as Jo moved gracefully back and forth between suitcase and closet.

When her case was empty Jo closed the lid and snapped the locks. Would she unpack his case? She would. Brett felt a thrill shiver through his body at the sight of Jo's slim hands on his clothes.

Brett sighed silently. You are positively besotted! When you can be turned on by observing a woman handling your faded Levis you have gone beyond the pale!

"Brett?" Jo's near whisper revealed the fact that she thought he was sleeping.

"Hmmm?" Brett raised his lids slightly, just enough to show her he was awake.

"Am I expected to attend this family conference?" Jo asked hesitantly.

"Are you a member of the family?" Brett laid the drawl on with a spade.

Jo responded indirectly. "I . . . I'm going to have a quick shower. I'll only be a moment."

"Take your time." Brett's smile mocked her. "We won't have to punch a time clock as we enter the boss's study." His smile disappeared as, with a toss of her head that betrayed her impatience with him, Jo strode into the bathroom.

Biting back a rather pungent, self-descriptive epithet,

Brett jerked to his feet, crossing to the double dresser in four long strides to retrieve the shaving kit Jo had placed there. Tugging the zipper midway around the case, Brett inserted his fingers and withdrew a small velvet box. Flipping the lid, Brett stared down at the flawless, pear-shaped, three-carat diamond beautifully displayed in a delicate, intricately fashioned setting. The lid closed with a tiny snap.

Sliding the top dresser drawer open, Brett dropped the box onto the neat pile of underwear inside, then slammed the drawer closed forcefully. Brett knew now that Jo could not be bought, either physically or emotionally. He had known it for some time. If Jo had been with Wolf, it had not been for the apartment, or the small car that was seldom moved out of the apartment parking area, or to advance herself in the company. If she had been with Wolf, it was because she had *wanted* to be with him.

Brett's body became absolutely still, while his mind pounced alertly on his last thought. Because she wanted to be with Wolf. Raising his head slowly, Brett stared into the wide, gray eyes reflected in the oversized mirror on the wall above the dresser. Because she *wanted* to be with Wolf!

She's with me now!

The gray eyes staring back at Brett suddenly glittered silver with hope. Could that mean . . . *does Jo want to be with me?* But Wolf's well now. A little thin, a little gaunt, but well! A shudder tore through Brett's slender frame.

I have got to get her away from here!

There were twelve minutes left to go before the appointed hour of three when Jo rushed out of the bathroom. Clamping down on the urge to grab hold of her and run, Brett strode into the bathroom to replace her under a cold shower. When Brett walked back into the bedroom Jo was gone, as were the minutes till the hour of three. Pulling open the top dresser drawer, Brett smiled at the small velvet box before removing a pair of boxers. Stepping into faded Levis, Brett imagined he could feel the warmth of Jo's recent touch, smell her scent on the soft denim. A pale-blue cotton shirt, a double stamp into supple leather ankle boots, and Brett went striding out of the room, eight minutes late and primed to fight.

Four pairs of eyes swiveled to observe Brett's entrance into the study. Sweeping a look over Brett that told him she was now "boss" not "Mother," Violet said crisply to Eric, who was on the computer screen, "And now your brother has condescended to join us." Brett met her drilling stare with calm detachment.

"Congratulations, Brett." Eric smiled. "You picked a winner this time."

Brett's eyes easily broke the hold of his mother's to stalk those of the "winner." "Thanks, Eric." Pride swelled inside Brett as Jo stared back at him serenely. It was as if she was saying, There's not a Renninger alive who can make me lose my composure. *She is magnificent!* The observation hardened Brett's determination to keep her. Refusing to release his visual hold on her, Brett added, "And how is your winner?"

"Doing fine," Eric assured. "You may be an uncle again before the night is out."

"Then what the hell are you doing talking to us?" Brett startled everyone, including himself, with his sudden harshness. "You should be with Doris, Eric." Brett felt the edge, of patience, of reason, of . . . whatever, looming closer. If he didn't do something soon to resolve this mess he'd created, Brett decided, he'd fall headfirst over that precarious edge.

A stunned silence held sway for an instant, then Di's soft voice broke it. "Brett's right, you know. Eric should be with Doris, and I should be with Dirk. Mother, can we wind this meeting up fairly quickly?" Before Violet could respond, Di added, "Brett, Jo, I hope you'll be very happy. I'm holding my gift to you until you have a permanent address."

At that point Jo stole the initiative from Brett. Maintaining his oddly intense stare, and wondering what the devil was going on in his head, Jo infused warmth into her voice. "Thank you, Di. And you too, Eric. I'm keeping my fingers crossed for a boy."

Eric's laughter was cut short by Violet's brisk voice. "Of course, Brett and Di are both right. We can have an in-depth meeting when everyone is well again. But there is one consideration I'd like you all to think about. Eric and I have discussed this and we are in complete accord. It's time for the company to expand again. I want to open another region—the northwest region, from Colorado west, including Oregon and Washington." She glanced at Brett. "I had considered giving Richard Colby the mid-Atlantic region and, as he was a bachelor, asking Brett to take over the new region." A soft smile curved her lips as she shifted her gaze to Jo. "But as Brett is now married . . ."

"We'll take it."

Jo blinked, for a second stunned by Brett's hard, decisive tone. Then swift anger rushed through her. How dare he presume to make decisions for her? Not that she would object to going to the Northwest or, for that matter, hell, as long as she was with him, but she would appreciate being consulted first! Breathing deeply, Jo managed to keep her tone neutral.

"Brett, I think we should discuss this in private." Jo's tone was belied by the flash of amber in her hazel eyes. "I don't know if I . . ."

Brett's eyes glinted a warning for her to be silent; his tone was thick with ice. "Mother, we will take it."

"Brett!"

A chorus of voices, in varying degrees of shock, cried his name. Jo's was not one of them. Without even being aware of having moved, Jo was on her feet, her body shaking with humiliation and fury. Wolf was on his feet also, a protective alertness in his stance.

"Brett." The big prowler's voice commanded attention. "What in hell do you think you're doing? Apologize to Jo at once."

"Mind your own god-damned business, Wolf." Taut with anger, Brett ignored the collective gasp his snarling voice elicited. "Jo is *my* wife. I don't need you, or anyone else, to instruct me on how to handle her."

Jo heard without hearing. Her eyes stinging with tears of shame, and hurt, and a jumbled mess of other emotions, she stared at the beauty of Brett's chiseled face until it blurred, then she ran, blocking out the angry voices that bounced off the paneled walls of Violet's study.

What had come over him? What had she done to turn Brett into a snarling dictator? Did he hate her so very much? The questions hammered in Jo's mind as she ran along the hall, through the spotless kitchen, and out the back door. Where could she go? Jo's tear-filled eyes swept the wide expanse of bricked courtyard behind the house, passing then slicing back to the two vehicles parked there. A jeep and a pickup truck, keys in the ignitions of each. If she could get to the airfield, or an airport . . .

No!

The protest was a rebellions scream inside Jo's mind. No, damn it! She would not run again! In effect, she had run from a bad situation—not of her making—when she'd left home at nineteen. If only in her mind, she had run from the pain and humiliation inflicted upon her by Gary. And, at least figuratively, she'd been running from a showdown with Brett since the first day she met him. How long could the mind employ evasive tactics? How many avenues of escape could her consciousness scurry along in avoidance of the truth? Besides, Jo had the uncomfortable feeling that if she ran now Brett would not follow her, and that would prove her mother's theory about love, and the relationships therein, correct. Sniffing, Jo shook her head in silent denial.

Ignoring the vehicles and the tears trickling down her face, Jo slid her fingers into the back pockets of her jeans and began pacing off the distance between the kitchen door and the four-car garage set to the right and rear of the house.

What the devil had come over Brett? Again. Jo came to an abrupt halt midway between house and garage, the single word repeating in her mind. Again? Yes, again. Even though there had been constraint between them since the night he'd returned from the Poconos, Brett had unfailingly treated her with polite consideration. What had caused his sudden harsh thoughtlessness? Jo raked her mind, examining every minute since their arrival at the house. A recent scene flashed into her memory, and, frowning, Jo relived it slowly.

"Are you as hungry as I am?"

The echo of Brett's sensuously warm voice tantalized her memory; he had certainly not been cold before lunch! But wait! Jo's frown deepened. Brett *had* turned cold before they'd gone down to join the family. What had she said to him? Something about the family waiting? No. That hadn't chilled his ardor. What then? Jo kicked at a tiny pebble in frustration; damn it, what else had she said? Memory clicked.

"But we haven't even seen Wolf yet!"

Wolf.

Wolf?

Jo went absolutely statue still. Brett had grown frigid at the mention of his brother's name . . . and not for the first time! It was almost as if Brett was jealous of Wolf, as if he believed . . . *Oh my God!* Could Brett really believe that she . . . and Wolf? Remembered images flashed through Jo's mind again, not entire scenes, but small, isolated fragments, beginning with Brett refusing to let her see Wolf after the accident.

Brett, warning her not to call Wolf while he was in Vermont. Brett, oddly backing down the time in his office when she'd lifted the phone to call Wolf. Brett, telling her they'd probably both regret it but that he had to have her. Brett, suddenly coldly remote when they'd come to the farm at Christmas time. Brett, withdrawing from her on learning about a preexisting prescription for birth control pills. Brett, mentioning her previous affair in that odd, intensely accusatory manner.

Could it be . . . could it possibly be . . . Jo spun around at the sound of the kitchen door closing, breath catching in her throat at the sight of Brett's face. His expression austere with grim determination, Brett walked to her with slow, measured strides. In the seconds required for him to reach her, Jo tried, and failed, to suppress the wild hope rioting through her. As he drew close, Brett's eyelids narrowed over eyes gleaming silvery with intent, increasing her hope tenfold. Could it be that the fire raging inside Brett was caused by love for her? Was Brett jealous over her? All this time? All this long wasted time?

Brett had reached the very edge; it was either fish or cut bait, and he sure as hell was not about to cut bait at this stage of the game! Stalking his wife, Brett conceded that he might have gone about it with more tact, but, tactless or not, Jo was going with him to Colorado! And, after the way his family had ganged up on him when Jo had run from his mother's study, Brett was perfectly primed for an argument.

She is mine, and I will not give her up.

The avowal revolved in his mind as Brett studied Jo's face through the slits of lids narrowed against the glare of late-afternoon sunlight. The evidence of tears on her cheeks gave him momentary pause. Brett felt a twist of pain in his chest. Damn fool! You've hurt her again! I'll make it up to her, he soothed his stinging conscience, but I cannot give her up!

Two steps from her, Brett hesitated; he could not talk, or argue, with Jo in the courtyard, not with his mother, Wolf, Micki, *and* Elania for an audience! One step from her Brett reached out, grasped her wrist firmly with his hand, then, pivoting, strode back to the house, a gasping Jo stumbling behind him.

"Brett!" Jo gave an ineffectual tug of her arm. "Have you gone mad?"

"Be quiet." Brett snapped the order without turning his head. "You'll have plenty of time to talk when we're alone in our room."

When he got to the kitchen door, Brett thrust it open and strode through, tugging firmly on a now angrily sputtering Jo to keep her following him.

His gait unchecked, Brett loped along the hall. He had made it to the bottom of the stairs when the door to his mother's study was flung open and Wolf, Violet and Micki at his heels, rushed into the hallway, only to come to a dead stop at the sight of Brett literally dragging Jo through the house.

"For Christ's sake, Brett!" Wolf's voice held a note of sheer disbelief. "What in hell are you doing? Let her go!" Snaking out a long arm, Wolf caught Jo's other, flailing wrist.

At the command "let her go" all the accumulated months of frustration exploded inside Brett's mind. When Wolf put his hand on Jo, anger exploded out through Brett's mouth.

"Don't touch her!"

For long seconds shocked silence smothered response, then bedlam took over as everyone protested at once.

Even Elania, coming from the living room to investigate the cause of all the noise, added her two cent's worth of condemnation. Brett's voice, coldly, frighteningly savage, cut through the babble.

"I want silence." Brett knew his objective was achieved through shock; he knew it and used it. His eyes dropped to rest deliberately on Wolf's fingers, curled around Jo's wrist. When he lifted his gaze, Brett's eyes had the look of opaque ice. "I told you not to touch her."

For whatever reason—curiosity, surprise, whatever—Wolf's hold on Jo's wrist relaxed, then fell away.

"Don't *ever* touch her again." Once again Brett spoke through an outburst of protest. "If you will all excuse us?" Tugging gently on Jo's arm, he started up the stairs. "Jo and I would like to have an argument in private."

Trailing Brett's anger-tightened body up the stairs and into their room, Jo felt excitement stir, then radiate through her system. Incredible, unbelievable as it seemed, Brett *was* jealous of Wolf. Why he was jealous of Wolf was the question Jo hoped soon to have the answer to. All these months! Why hadn't Brett simply asked her?

Hearing the door snap shut behind her, Jo spun to face her husband, trepidation closing her throat at the glittering glance he raked over her. Barely breathing, Jo watched his eyes until a flicker of movement caught her attention, drawing her gaze to his hands. The purposeful work of Brett's fingers as they unbuttoned his shirt opened Jo's throat enough to allow the passage of a startled squeak.

"What are you doing?"

His expression mocking her for asking the obvious, Brett yanked the shirt free of the jeans waistband and tossed it carelessly to the floor. His fingers found employment at his belt buckle as he began walking to her. Eyeing him warily, Jo edged toward the bathroom door.

"All right!" Jo felt rather proud of the steadiness of her

tone; inside she was a jumbled bundle of excitement-tied nerve ends. "I know *what* you're doing. I thought we were going to talk."

His mocking smile deepening, Brett sauntered past her to drop onto the edge of the chair. "I've changed my mind." His eyes laughed at her evasive edging toward the bathroom. Lifting one leg, he tugged at his boot; it landed on the floor with a soft thud. As he pulled at the other boot, Brett motioned at the bed with a brief nod of his head. "I've decided to give you a demonstration of the resiliency of the mattress after all."

"Brett . . ."

"You must admit," he went on, ignoring her attempt at protest, "the bed is the one place we communicate beautifully." The second boot plopped to the floor. "You had better get busy," he chided softly to the background sound of the descending zipper. "I'm way ahead of you."

Way ahead of you. Way ahead of you! A light clicked on in Jo's mind. Good grief! Had she left her reasoning power behind in the yard? Watching Brett's slim, muscularly corded length emerge from the jeans, Jo's adrenaline kicked all her senses into overtime. Brett may have been referring to her fully clothed state, but Jo interpreted his words in a different light. His cool detachment was nothing more than a facade! Introduce her to the bed's resiliency indeed! Brett was hell-bent on making a statement of ownership! He was not only jealous, he was running scared! Clamping her teeth together to contain a whoop of joy created by the wave of relief washing through her, Jo tore uncaringly at the buttons on her pure silk shirt. A raging fire? Jo's shirt landed unaimed on top of his. She'd show him an inferno!

Watching the play of emotions across her face, Brett knew the moment Jo reached a decision. When she began tearing at her clothes his already aroused manhood took on the quality of pure, painful iron. As her silky loveliness was exposed to his hungry stare an earlier thought reasserted itself.

She's with me now!

"Jo."

Brett wanted to say much more, so very much more, yet the only sound he could force through his constricted throat was the anguished whisper of her name. Consuming desire combined with a desperate need to claim erased all other consideration.

They both moved at the same instant.

There was no time for teasing kisses. There was no time for stroking caresses. There was no time for tiny erotic nuances. Mouths locked together in all-consuming need, they dropped to the bed, Brett thrusting into her on contact, Jo welcoming his invasion with a cry of exquisite pleasure. Never had their lovemaking been quite so fierce, or quite so savage, or quite so shatteringly satisfying.

The words that should have been said months before were purged from Brett's throat at the moment his life force erupted from his quivering body.

"I love you, Jo. Oh, God, how I love you!"

Sweet, sweet release. Release of tension. Release of fear. And, finally, unashamedly, release of long-pent-up tears . . . both hers and his.

A tender smile softening his chiseled lips, Brett lowered his head to dry the salty moisture on her cheeks with his mouth. "You haven't said the words." Raising his head again, he gazed compellingly into her eyes. "Say it, Jo. Please. I need to hear it."

"I love you."

Jo felt the tremor that ripped through Brett's body in her palms still gripping his hips, in her body still pressed to his, and in her soul, now, at last, at one with his. Though complete, Jo was not so lost in euphoria she missed the significance of Brett's declaration without question. The significance thrilled her. Brett still labored under the illusion of a previous affair between her and his brother. What, Jo wondered mistily, had it cost Brett to make that declaration? Very likely a lot more than she'd ever know.

"You'll go to Colorado with me?" The uncertainty underlying Brett's tone drew Jo from speculation.

"I'd go to the moon with you." Jo's firm response brought a teasing gleam to his eyes.

"We've just been there."

Floating in contentment richer than whipped cream, Jo sighed as, levering his body a few inches from hers, Brett caressed her skin with his right hand. Long fingers drew a gasp of pleasure when they outlined the contour of one breast, the murmured confession that followed drew a gasp of dismay.

"I'd hate to have to admit the times I tormented myself with the thought of Wolf's hand stroking you like this."

"Brett—" Jo choked on the protest.

"Or," Brett continued raspily, "his mouth drinking from yours."

"Brett . . . please, listen."

"Or," Brett went on, unable to stop, "his body resting in the cradle of your thighs."

"Brett, stop this!" Releasing her hold on his hips, Jo brought her hands up to grasp his face, forcing him to look into her eyes. "There has never been anything personal between us. Never. *Ever.* Wolf has been my employer and my friend, nothing more." Jo sighed. "You should know better than I how very much Wolf adores Micki. I can't imagine where you ever got the idea that Wolf and I . . ."

Oh, God! Levering himself out of and off her completely, Brett lay beside Jo on his back, staring at the stark white ceiling. To believe the worst all these months, to live with the agony, day in, day out, only to find . . .

"He owns the apartment you live in." Started now, Brett had to have it all out.

"He does not own it!" Jo corrected, her tone revealing a hint of anger. "Wolf is holding the mortgage on it. Without his help I never could have managed it."

Brett turned his head to find Jo's eyes glaring at him. She was telling the truth and he knew it. Still he kept on, needing to hear it all. "He has a key to the place."

"Yes," Jo admitted readily on a sigh of exasperation. "He has a key. I gave it to him, but not, I assure you, for any unsavory purpose." Jo smiled wryly. "I have a bad habit, you see. I lock myself out on occasion."

Brett smiled, then laughed aloud as he gathered her close to his side. "Oh, hell, honey. I feel like such a jerk!"

"You should." Jo wasn't about to let him off the hook easily, not after the trauma of the last months. "Not for having the doubt in the first place, but for not asking me straight out if your suspicions were correct."

"Forgive me?" Brett hid his seriousness behind a grin. He'd take the rap, for there was no way he'd bring Micki's name into the discussion.

"Yes, of course." Jo snuggled closer to his warmth, shaking her head in wonder at her own obtuseness. "And here all the time I believed you were resenting Gary," she admitted in a murmur that turned to a yelp as Brett sat bolt upright.

"Who in the hell is Gary? And why in the hell didn't I know about him before now?" Brett asked angrily.

"Brett, you had to have realized there was someone before you," Jo said carefully.

"Yeah, sure, but I thought it was—"

"And now you know it wasn't," Jo interrupted gently. "Gary was the first, the only one before you." Praying that he wouldn't spoil what they had just found together, Jo explained her one disastrous affair in minute detail.

His expression contemplative, Brett stared down at Jo for long seconds when her recital was finished. He didn't like the idea of Gary Devlin, and not only for the hell he'd put Jo through. "Were you in love with him?" The question was a mild form of self-torture. Contrarily, he wanted her to say yes and no at the same time. Yes, because he couldn't abide the idea that Jo would live with a man she didn't love. And no, because he hated the mere thought that she'd loved a man before him. It was irrational. Brett knew it was irrational. Hadn't he thought himself in love with Sondra?

"I thought I was," Jo finally replied, unknowingly voicing Brett's last consideration. "Of course I know now that I was merely infatuated with him. But it's too late to change things now, isn't it?"

"Yes." Bending to her, Brett brushed his lips over hers. "And it no longer matters." Surprisingly, it didn't, Brett realized in relief. Hell! Screw Devlin! "I don't mind not being first." His movement swift, Brett nipped gently at her lower lip. "As long as you make damned sure I'm the last."

"And what about you?" Jo arched a forbidding brow at him. "No more Marshas?"

"Jo, I told you . . ."

"What you told me, exactly, was 'Not for lack of trying on my part.'" Jo repeated his exact words. "I would like an explanation of that remark." The demand made, Jo held her breath. She knew she really had no right to an answer, but then, neither had he, and she'd been honest with him. Deep down, where she lived, Jo knew she was testing not only his love for her but his trust in her as well. When Brett smiled her personal world settled into place.

"The explanation is simple." Brett's hesitation was

hardly noticeable. Damn it, man, he scorned himself, she trusted you, it's your turn. "I meant exactly what I said. We were alone in Marsha's apartment in Vermont. We were undressed. We were in bed together." Brett paused as Jo's eyelids closed to conceal her pain. "Look at me, love." When her lashes lifted he stared into her eyes. "I was thinking about you, and I couldn't make it. Do you understand what I'm saying? I could not make it with another woman. I *wanted* you."

Jo blinked against a fresh swell of hot moisture and trembled with a fresh surge of hot response. Lord! Jo felt sure that if Brett touched her now he'd burn his hands! Lifting her hands, she grasped him around the waist to guide his body onto hers. "And now that you have me," she whispered, "what are you going to do with me?"

"I've been thinking about that," Brett answered solemnly, his eyes betraying his growing heat.

"And?" Jo prompted, moving against him sensuously to speed up his thinking process.

"I've decided to keep you." In retaliation, Brett angled his hips into hers, smiling at her gasp of pleasure. "And let the fire rage forever."

ABOUT THE AUTHOR

Joan Hohl lives with her family in Pennsylvania and is currently working on her next Zebra contemporary romance, which will be published in 2004. Joan loves to hear from readers and you may write to her c/o Zebra Books. Please include a self-addressed stamped envelope if you wish a response.

More by Best-selling Author
Fern Michaels